THE
BELLE
HOTEL

THE

BELL
JAR

THE
BELLE
HOTEL

CRAIG
MELVIN

Unbound

Unbound
6th Floor Mutual House, 70 Conduit Street, London W1S 2GF
www.unbound.com

© Craig Melvin, 2019

Cover design and illustration © David Shrigley, 2019

Text Design by PDQ

A CIP record for this book is available from the British Library

ISBN 978-1-78352-665-9 (trade pbk)
ISBN 978-1-78352-667-3 (ebook)
ISBN 978-1-78352-666-6 (limited edition)

Printed in Great Britain by CPI Group (UK)

Special thanks to Steve Kircher, David Melvin & Connie Gartner, Peter Nunn, Ben Stackhouse and Jane Stackhouse for their support of this book

To Mel, Max & Rosa

Belle Hotel

Krug '73   1500
Pickled Egg 1.50

HORS D'OEUVRVES

Chicken Liver Parfait 5.75	York Ham 6.20 *grilled brioche*	Charlie's Angels on Horseback 3.50	Chicken Satay 6.00 *Janet's Peanut Sauce*
Leek and Truffle Flan 7.50	Carpaccio of Beef 7.25	Franco's Foie Gras 14.50	Sevruga Caviar 30g/50g 30/50

SALADS

Caesar Salad 7.50/10.50	Salade Niçoise 8.75	Rocket and Parmesan 4.75 *balsamic reduction*	Tomato and Basil 4.50
Chef's Salad 9.75	Salad of Fried Egg, 8.75 Lardons and Watercress	Roquefort Salad 8.50	Carrot Beetroot Slaw 3.00

SOUPS

Vichyssoise Fanny Craddock 5.50	Fish Soup 7.50	Soupe à L'Oignon 7.50	Mulligatawny 6.75

SEAFOOD

Potted Shrimps 9.75	Lobster Belle Hotel 25.00	Bouillabaisse à L'Épuisette 12.75	Scallops Sheridan 12.75
Oysters 8.50	Prawn Cocktail 8.50	Savoy Dressed Crab 8.50	Moules Marinière 13.75

EGGS AND PASTA

Eggs Benedict 7.50/10.50	Omelette Arnold Bennett 12.50	Mac Cheese 7.50/12.00 *with bacon*	Herb Omelette 6.00
Spaghetti alle Vongole 7.50/11.50	Langoustine Ravioli 8.00	Asparagus Risotto 7.50/9.50 *with parmesan*	Spaghetti Menton 9.25 *with Belle pesto*

FISH

Flounder Noilly Prat 14.75	Fish and Chips 12.50	Sinkers Salmon Fishcake 12.75 *sorrel sauce and spinach*	Kippers Olivier 8.00
Coriander Turbot 18.50	Dover Sole 40.00 *for two*	Kedgeree 11.50 *made with smoked salmon*	Fish Pie 12.50

ROASTS AND GRILLS

The Belle Burger 11.50	Daube of Beef Provençal 18.50	Chicken Kiev 14.50	Rib Eye Steak 22.50
Brampton Pork Chops 15.75	Duck à l'Orange 19.50	Loin of Venison 15.7 *sweet peppercorn sauce*	Poulet des Landes 40.00 *truffle jus and dauphin potato (for two)*

ENTREES

Shepherd's Pie 9.25	Coq au Vin 14.7	Ham, Egg and Chips 9.25	Pondicherry Poulet Rouge 9.25 *with cardamom rice*

VEGETABLES AND POTATOES

Bubble and Squeak 4.50	Gratin Potatoes 4.50	Buttered Carrots 3.75	Mash 4.50
Rösti 5.00	Noodles 4.50	Truffled Green Beans 6.50	Sprouting Broccoli 4.40

DESSERTS, PUDDINGS AND SAVOURIES

Crêpes Suzette 6.75	Chocolate Torte 5.75	Tarte Tatin 15.00 Three Cheeses 7.50 Welsh Rarebit 4.50	
Trifle 5.50	Sticky Toffee Pudding 6.00 Lemon Meringue 5.50 Crumble 6.25 Cheese Soufflé 6.25		

COFFEES AND TEAS

Coffee: Ethiopian Full Roast Espresso *(dbl)* 2.50	Filter 2.50		Belle Breakfast Tea 2.50
Belle Hotel Chocolate Truffles *(2)* 4.0	Cappuccino *(am only)* 2.75		Lapsang Souchong 3.50

**THE MANAGEMENT ACCEPT NO RESPONSIBILITY
FOR ANY INJURIES SUSTAINED ON THE PREMISES**

DO NOT ENTER THE KITCHEN UNDER ANY CIRCUMSTANCES

A man can become a cook,
but he has to be born a chef.
                    Brillat-Savarin

Prologue

Credit Crunch

Legal Notice of Repossession

13 October 2008

Dear Charlie,
Unless you pay £10,000 by noon today, Belle Hotel will be repossessed under section 21 (4a) of the Property Act.
This is your final warning, Charlie.
Yours,
Paul Peters,
Banker

13 October 2008
9am: Charlie
Tick-tock, tock-tick, crunch.

13 October. One day that would not be going down in Charlie Sheridan's grandfather's book as a good one. Charlie had three hours to save the two loves of his life. Paul Peters, his exasperated banker, waited with the bailiffs to change Belle Hotel's locks on the stroke of noon. Charlie had already blown it with his other love, his long-suffering girlfriend Lulu. Lulu had chucked Charlie by text after her new suitor, Graeme, showed her the latest tabloid scandal involving 'My Night with Belle Hotel Celebrity Chef'.

Sweating into his chef's whites, Charlie thumbed a last-ditch attempt from the kitchen of Belle Hotel.

Give me another chance, Lu, I'll make it up 2

The phone company cut Charlie off on U. He slung the knackered Nokia into the sink, where it plunged through a sea of crushed Stella cans, and swung out of the kitchen door and into the alley leading to Ship Street. Charlie left a salty trail of disaster in his wake. Uncollected bins, disconnected water, gas and electric. Fridges bare, broken hearts and plates.

9am: Lulu

Lulu sat at her paper-free desk in the hushed surroundings of the Hotel Epicure management office. Time passed. No reply. Not for want of looking. Lulu stood, tucked the stray strands of her long bob behind her ears and let out a slow release of breath. Charlie bloody Sheridan, you've really blown it this time. Typical. Just as they were finally getting things right and Lulu was seriously considering going back to him and Belle Hotel. Home. The place they'd done their growing up. Belle Hotel yesterday, the location of the ghastly scene between the two of them when she'd delivered her news and, then, the magazine article. It blared up at her where Graeme had thoughtfully left it, just within view. Charlie had made her decision for her. Lulu looked at Graeme: clean-shaven, neat, reliable. Everything Charlie was not.

'He's had his last chance. Let's do this.'

Graeme clicked the spreadsheet shut. He stood, slipped off his starched 'Executive Head Chef' embroidered jacket and eased into the leather Hugo Boss trench coat he deemed more suitable for stealing another man's work and woman. Paul Peters had been more than receptive when they'd called the banker with the offer for Belle Hotel. Be there with the banker's draft by nine thirty and we'll whisk through the inventory together. Peters' faith in the word of a Sheridan had gone to the grave with Charlie's grandfather. The public's faith in Paul Peters' bank was dead and buried, too. Graeme had read out the headlines to Lulu from the live feed on his computer. Hookes Bank was now publicly owned and Paul Peters would be desperate to sell Belle Hotel to the two of them asap to cover his mismanagement of the account for over three decades.

Lulu watched the digital clock hit nine thirty, shook her head and stood to take Graeme's outstretched arm. The brand-new business partners walked arm in arm down the salty shaft of Ship Street to Belle Hotel.

9.30am: Charlie

Charlie pushed on along a wind-whipped Ship Street, moments before Graeme and Lulu appeared. Ten grand. That was a lot of lolly to haul in by lunch. Who'd help? Who was still on his side? The bloody bank had got him hook, line and sinker this time. Hook, line and sinker. Sinker, his fishmonger, yes! The old miser always kept cash at his seafront arch. Charlie whooped with delight, racing out across Kingsway to the prom, too drunk on debt to give a damn about traffic lights, pedestrian crossings, all usual warnings of the dangers that lay ahead. He flicked the bird at Hotel Epicure as he passed. Lulu, his love, the one he could not be with, was in there plotting against him with that chef-accountant, Graeme. Go to hell, Graeme. The bailiff's note, what was left of it, half burnt in Charlie's pocket. He'd rolled and used it to light his morning fag from the pilot light on the stove, sputtering along on what was left of the disconnected gas.

The one-man credit crunch slid to a halt on the slippery cobbles outside the flaking paint sign of 'N. Sinker, Fishmonger. Est 1788'. The heavy wooden door, faded Brighton blue, was firmly shut against the hostile elements. Right, get a grand off Sinker and buy some time. Charlie flicked the butt of his fag in an oily puddle and banged on the door. A radio playing in a nearby arch broke the news that Hookes, Belle Hotel's bank for four decades, had been bailed out by the government a day late to get Charlie off it. Hookes off the hook; Charlie not. Typical.

'Go away.'

'Sinker, it's me, Charlie.'

'Definitely go away, then.'

Charlie banged harder on the heavy door.

'Come on, Sinker, open up. You've gotta help me. Save Belle Hotel.'

Charlie could hear a shuffling behind the door and then the slow slinging of locks. A set of beady eyes glinted out through the gap in the door. The stench of fish assaulted Charlie's nostrils.

'Save Belle Hotel. What, lend you money? You're joking, aren't you. You owe me over nine hundred in unpaid bills. Why would I help you?'

'You've been supplying my hotel for thirty-five frigging years, Sinker. And now you're quibbling about a few hundred quid. Come on, mate. Give us a break, here. If not for me, then for Belle Hotel's sake.'

Charlie kicked the bottom of the door to make his point.

A warm quid coin shot through the narrow gap in the door, struck the cobbles and rolled under a pile of lobster pots.

'There's my contribution. What you're worth. Try your luck in the slots on the pier. Then try and live within your means, like your grandfather taught you.'

Live within yer means, that was Franco's maxim. But Franco was dead and Charlie was left to live by whatever means necessary without him.

9.30am: Lulu

Paul Peters waited at Belle Hotel's front door to meet them.

'I feel strange to be doing this, Paul, going behind Charlie's back.'

'Strange times indeed, my dear. I expect you've heard our news? Nationalised at noon. Bloody disgrace, Thomas Hooke will be turning in his grave. So, Belle Hotel. It's not as if you don't know your way around. Shall we?'

Graeme stepped back to let Lulu pass. Sort of thing that Charlie would never do. Charlie never did. Past tense. She shuddered at the reality of what she was about to do and then shook it off with the thought of the hundred K of her father's money Charlie had burned through in less than six months. It had to be done, there was no other way. For the sake of Belle Hotel. Her father was right.

'Lead on, Mr Peters. We aren't the legal owners yet. I'm guessing you've brought all the paperwork with you. Dad said you'd be keen to shore up the Hookes balance sheet today. With the chancellor breathing down your neck.'

Graeme reached out for her hand, but she was reluctant to take it. Not yet. He'd get his way later, Charlie had made sure of that. But take care of business first. Isn't that what her father always said? Graeme had impressed Roger Hardman when they'd met. Good head for figures, that lad. Polar opposite of that Charlie Sheridan. Looks like he knows how to run a tight ship. Happy to serve frozen cod, keep the margins fresh. Good lad.

10am: Charlie

Charlie set off towards the pier with the quid in his pocket. Well, it was a start. Nine thousand, nine hundred and ninety-nine more to go.

How many times, how many more times would he have to do this? Borrowing from Tom, Dick and Harry to pay Paul Peters. Fucking credit crunch. Fucking Hotel Epicure, Fucking Graeme. Judas. Charlie couldn't bring himself to curse Lulu. He loved her, but could not be with her. So much had happened to them both over the years. It had always seemed their destiny to be together, yet every time they got close something happened to snatch their happiness away. Recent nuclear bombshells and today's carnival of chaos were just the last in a long line of lamentable epic love and work fails that killed the chances of them ever being together.

Charlie needed that 10K badly. It was enough to clear the

emergency over-overdraft and buy himself another month's trading and some time to set things straight with Lulu. Although it may already be too late for that. Too many lies and betrayals. If he told her the whole truth, what little chance they had of getting back together would be gone.

Charlie glanced at the Roman numerals on the pier clock. Hurry up, Charlie, Belle Hotel becomes a pumpkin at noon. Get on with it. At this rate, Charlie'd never get back with enough cash in time.

Charlie pulled the quid from his pocket, yanking the repossession letter from the bank along with it. What was it with the bits of paper? Notice of repossession, court order, removal from the *Michelin Guide*. Bring back the old days, when Franco's book bulged with glowing reviews, drop-top Jag purchase notes and recipes that held the secrets of Belle Hotel's success.

Maybe he should take Sinker's advice and gamble the quid on the pier's pound waterfall? Charlie cut under the flashing sign and set off across the salty planks for the arcade. Off on yet another wild goose chase, hoping against hope that he could turn a pound into a pot of gold.

10am: Lulu

'And on this floor, sea-facing doubles, carpet, worn, er, very worn and one fire extinguisher. Last serviced in, er, December nineteen ninety-nine.'

Lulu looked at the time on her phone. Two hours to go and still no word from Charlie. All it'd take was one word. If his mobile was shot, he could always call her from a payphone. She'd pick up. And it wasn't as if he'd have any problem remembering the number. It was one digit off his. They'd been to the One-2-One shop together in Churchill Square. Got the phones so that he could call her from Le Gavroche while she was working at Belle Hotel and not have to speak to his mum or grandfather. Lulu shook her head and stuck her phone back in her handbag.

'I think we've seen enough of the bedrooms, Mr Peters. We know they need a major refurb. Let's go and see Belle Hotel Restaurant and do a stock-check.'

Graeme nodded in agreement and placed a guiding arm around Lulu's back as they descended the wide flight of stairs. Lulu sidestepped away from him and bent to pick up a plastic cigarette lighter that someone, Charlie probably, had dropped.

10.30am: Charlie

Half an hour later, Charlie was on a roll, his blue-and-white checked pockets bulging with golden coins. Then, as was Charlie all over, just when he was on a winning streak, his luck changed and he lost the lot. Quid after quid went back onto the waterfall and not one bastard coin came out.

Then Charlie had an idea. Time to use a skill he'd learned as a kid. The old arm inside the machine trick. Looking around, checking that none of the polo-shirted pier attendants were about, Charlie dropped to his knees and pulled up the sleeve of his chef's jacket to the elbow. He popped his last quid in the slot while holding down the refund button with his left hand. Right, Charlie had thirty seconds to shake as many coins out of the beast before the tilt-tamper alarm was re-activated. In a flash, his right arm was in the hole and into the guts of the machine.

Charlie felt the sweat bead on his brow as his body took the full weight of the thing, while fishing about with his bent right wrist. Christ, this thing was heavy. Then, just as a wave of coins spilled out onto the patterned carpet, Charlie felt the thing begin to tip.

11am: Lulu

'This'll have to be renewed. I want metric calibrated equipment, vac-pacs, water baths.'

Lulu looked at Graeme looking at Charlie's kitchen. Her heart hurt. She'd watched Charlie earn his star on those knackered copper pots. Seen Franco, his grandfather and mentor to the two of them, throw most of them at the back door in one decade or another.

'This door will have to be replaced. Looks like it has faced the firing squad. I'll need a bacteri-seal delivery door like we have at Hotel Epicure.'

Graeme was beginning to sound like he knew who was about to be boss, which he didn't. Whatever funds Lulu had scraped together to buy Belle Hotel back from the bank had come from her own years of hard graft in the catering business. Belle Hotel, Quaglino's, The Wolseley and Hotel Epicure. Sure, her father was wealthy, the self-made carpet king had made most of his loot outfitting Brighton's hotels. But what wealth Roger now had was sunk into his new Academy school and any surplus he had squirrelled away in an Icelandic bank, off the thin ice of Britain's credit crunch. Graeme, for all his fancy certificates, had little more in savings than she did. Lulu chided herself for not having the guts to go Belle Hotel alone. Shame that Janet, Charlie's mother, was a sozzled wreck. It would have been good to keep her on with the business. Paul Peters had popped in to see Janet at the Belle Hotel pub and exchanged a few salty tales for old times' sake before nipping back through the adjoining door and making sure he'd locked it from their side.

Lulu looked from Graeme to Paul Peters and gave them both her young-restaurant-manager-of-the-year award-winning smile.

'Righto, that's quite enough time in here. There'll be no new pans till we turn a profit, but I can promise you a deep clean, just to get rid of the smell of him, I mean, grease.'

11am: Charlie

Charlie eased his head from side to side and tried to lift the machine off himself. The pain in his right wrist, trapped and snapped inside the machine, was unbearable. But he had to bear it. Had to pick up the mound of pounds that he'd been covered in when the thing came over on him. Then, Charlie's thirty seconds of grace were gone, the tilt alarm sounded and four burly polo-shirted pier attendants exploded from the change booth. Charlie screamed blue murder from the scene of the crime and promptly passed out from the pain in his broken wrist.

11.15am: Lulu

'I think we can safely conclude that we'll not be seeing Charlie this side of noon. Mr Peters, can we proceed with the contracts? I've got the banker's draft, here. How about we get everything ready then sign at noon? He has to be back at Belle Hotel before noon with funds, right, or it's yours to repossess?'

Lulu felt sick inside.

11.15am: Charlie

Charlie came to on a bench outside the arcade, the sound of heavy seas singing in his shell-likes, and waited for whatever mess he was in to come clanging back to him. Belle Hotel. Lulu. Midday. Christ. What time was it? Charlie struggled to sit up. As his eyes began to focus, Charlie noticed two policemen walking towards the arcade.

The failed quid machine heist. His wrist, limp at his side, spiked pain when he tried to move it. The pier attendants must have called the cops. Explaining things to plod was not an option. Charlie had been too much of a regular down the cop shop of late for all that. There was only one thing for it.

11.30am: Lulu

'So we sign here and here, yes?'

Lulu's hand shook a little as she held the paperwork. This was painful. Damn Charlie for pushing her to it.

11.30am: Charlie

Charlie crawled up the shingle on the nudist beach. The swim had been horrific, trying to keep his head up above the churning water. Hoping like hell that the cops didn't spot him. Charlie shook his soaking head and looked up, trying to ascertain from the height of the watery sun above what time it was. He picked up the track that wove from the beach and up onto Whitehawk Hill. The pathways of his youth, walked in happier circumstances, pathways that led down to Charlie's home, Belle Hotel.

It'd be a good half-hour walk and his wrist was killing him, but he had to get the money. Charlie needed a friend right now. And preferably a friend with funds to lend. As he crossed onto Whitehawk Hill, Charlie looked back to take in Brighton, the city by the sea. Arcs of pastel-hued terraces ran down to the pier, blue light of the cop car still flashing, and, hidden behind the rock shops, the briny slit of Ship Street and Belle Hotel.

Charlie walked and the adrenalin ebbed away with the salty water. It was replaced by an overwhelming feeling that it was all his fault. If he'd not been so fucked, he'd never have had to go near the pier. If he'd not gone on such a bender after Franco's death, and if all those secrets hadn't come out, his right wrist would still be straight. What had Lulu shouted at him down the phone? Walking disaster. That was it. He'd better walk a bit quicker, or it really would be a disaster.

The pain in his wrist was excruciating, but two hours in A&E was not an option. He had to get back, needed an alibi that placed him away from the scene of the pier incident, something to keep him out of the cop shop. Last thing Charlie needed was another night in the cells.

The track snaked up past the electric thrum of the Whitehawk transmitter. His allotment was near. Dawn was near. The earth mother he hoped would show him some love. The allotment gave Charlie his alibi, too. Something to place him away from what happened at the pier. He'd needed some fresh air that morning, he'd say, turn up at Belle Hotel with some vegetables from his allotment, hide the wrist,

Napoleon-style in his chef's jacket; no one would be any the wiser. Slip Paul Peters the wedge. Give 'em the old Charlie Rock Star Chef smile. Cook up a spot of lunch. Back in business. Bingo.

The allotment was quiet, smoke belching from chimneys, but nobody up and about. It was, after all, barely lunchtime. Charlie weaved through the assortment of handmade shacks looking for something to take away. Near his own, long-neglected, Belle Hotel allotment, Charlie spied what he was looking for and grabbed a bunch of carrots, recently pulled kicking and screaming from the earth. The carrots had been neatly laid in a stack by the water butt and Charlie thanked the heavens that he didn't have to break the autumn soil with his one good hand.

He rapped on the door of Dawn's railway carriage.

'Charlie, what a surprise.'

Dawn was still in the day-glo T-shirt she used as a nightie. Her body felt warm and soft as she leaned in for a hello hug. A moment or two later and Dawn fully woke up.

'OK, Sheridan. What is it this time?'

She sighed. This wasn't the first time he'd come begging, but to be fair he had always paid it back with a chunk on top. Eventually.

'I'll go and get me spade.'

Dawn made Charlie wait blindfolded in the railway carriage as she dug up her treasure. She trusted him, but not that much.

'There you go, sunshine. Two grand. My life's savings. Be sure to pay it back. And Charlie… be good, eh. Try not to hurt anyone.'

Charlie took his favourite route back to Belle Hotel, due south down Whitehawk Hill along the track carved out by his grandfather, Franco.

'Straight to the sea. This way you cut out all that council estate concrete. Here we go, Charlie Farley, you want a hand over this stile?'

As Charlie made his way past the county hospital, cutting a swathe through the pub sided, seagull-shat alleyways of Kemp Town,

11

a wobbly theatre flat of seediness and sophistication, Charlie broke out with his bunch of carrots and limp wrist onto the seafront.

Larry's house was up for sale again. Number four Royal Crescent's black ceramic tiles glinted in the sharp October sun. The great man was long gone, heaven via Steyning, an alabaster plaque all that remained to remind us.

> *BARON OLIVIER of BRIGHTON OM*
> *ACTOR*
> *1907–1989*
> *Lived Here*
> *1961–1979*

Charlie raised the bunch of carrots, a greeting for his grandfather's most famous friend, and set off westward along the prom.

Charlie knew it must be nearly noon and he was nowhere near his target. Charlie had blown it once and for all. All he'd had to do was get back with enough cash and he'd already saved Belle Hotel, got it firing on gas, got on the track to getting his Michelin star back. How hard was it to stride into Belle Hotel, stick it to Paul Peters, pop his head into the pub and pat Janet, his mother, on the head, stuff what was left of the Hooke's repossession notice in the back of Franco's book, strap on his apron (kitchen hook where he left it), scrub, turn, blanche and serve the buttered carrots for three pounds seventy-five's worth of salvation. That was all that Charlie had to do. His one last chance. And he'd fucked it up.

Midday: Lulu

Lulu turned the cigarette lighter over and over in her hands. The Belle Hotel dining room was as old as she was. Peters pushed the papers towards her and Graeme. This was it.

'Do you have a pen?'

Of course Graeme did, he'd brought his space pen. The one that wrote upside down. Lulu took Paul Peters' proffered Bic.

Midday: Charlie

His timeworn key wouldn't fit in the lock. The shiny new face of the hole repelled Charlie's ham-fisted attempt at entry. Disgusted, he flung the only key left on his ring in the gutter and set off for the side twitten of Belle Hotel and the hotel's pub.

Janet, his mother, was propping up the bar. Or rather, the bar was propping her up. Twin tracks of mascara trailed down her face.

'Ma, they've locked me out. I'm back with the cash.'

'Too late, darling. Peters has already sold her.'

'Like fuck he has. Over my dead body.'

'No, sweetheart, over Franco's dead body.'

'Where are they?'

Janet jerked a thumb over her shoulder. Restaurant.

His restaurant. The bloody cheek of it. He ran at the door that separated the pub from the rest of the hotel and was surprised to bounce back off it rather than plough through. What a friggin' liberty. Peters had locked the brass, slid it shut from the other side. Charlie looked back at Janet and cracked out his lucky grin.

'How long's this thing been locked?'

12.04pm: Charlie & Lulu

Lulu heard the thud and knew it was him.

'It's not fair. We should at least let him in.'

She rose, left her co-conspirators, went into the lobby and shot back the bolt.

As Lulu walked back to the dining room, Charlie made his entrance with an almighty crash. Expecting to break the door down, he'd run at it like a bull in a china shop and flown through the lobby when the door yielded easily to his shoulder barge.

Charlie lay dazed on the wooden floor. He'd hit his head on the reception desk and was out cold for what felt like decades. When he came round, Charlie struggled to work out when he was. He knew exactly where he was, but he hadn't seen Belle Hotel from floor height since, when? Was he, two, crawling around on the floor with Lulu, getting under people's Cuban-heeled feet? Or maybe thirteen, back from the fishing trip and collapsed in a dirty heap before Franco scooped him up and brushed him out of sight. Or, wait, it's the morning glory after the night before, Oasis at the Brighton Centre and the after-party to end all after-parties, hadn't he crashed out with Noel in this same spot? But, look, what's this, Lulu looking down at him, and what's this, Paul Peters spoiling the view and then, from out of shot, the nasal twang of that excuse for a chef, Graeme.

'Is he all right? I mean, Lulu, shouldn't we call the police, or something?'

'He's fine, Graeme. Come on, Charlie, get up. We want to talk to you.'

Lulu helped him to his feet, took him by the shoulders and shook some sense into him. This was business now, not love.

Belle Hotel's grandfather clock struck noon. Set five minutes late, Brighton time, it had been at the hotel almost as long as Franco had owned it. Bought it from the pawnbroker's, Franco did. Cost a pretty penny, even back then.

Charlie clocked the clock chiming and an idea struck him.

'Lu, tell these vultures to wait. I'll be right back.'

Charlie braced the clock against the shoulder of his one good arm, tipped it back and lifted. He was gone, back out of the bar entrance before anybody had the time to do anything about it.

Graeme and Paul Peters went back into the restaurant and took their place on the brass-studded green leather banquette at table one, the family table. The table at which the Sheridans broke bread and

14

talked business. Loyalty, conflict, power. Franco, Charlie and Janet. Four decades of family business and now this. Outsiders staking their claim. It was too much for Janet to take, so she took it out on the beer pump in the pub, swilling her glass and swaying along like the drunken sailor. She watched Charlie heading past with Franco's clock and shook her head.

Ten minutes later, Charlie was back, grinning from ear to ear. Lulu was still waiting for him in the lobby. She'd passed the time looking at a Hockney-ish portrait of Franco, Janet and a cat that hung over the key rack. Charlie collapsed into Lulu and then rolled into the restaurant on his ex-girlfriend's arm, letting himself be led to face the firing squad. Peters spread the papers in front of him, covering the stain-spattered tablecloth with words, deeds and numbers. The restaurant that rang down the decades, percussion of cutlery on china, was deathly silent.

'I am sorry, Charlie, for Franco's sake. You missed the deadline. But for the future of your grandfather's legacy it is essential that you countersign these papers and let Graeme and Lulu open the hotel tonight as a going concern. They have bookings that they can overspill from Hotel Epicure and a healthy few pencilled in for dinner tonight. Come on, Charlie, be smart, take a leaf out of Franco's book. Who knows, play your cards right and Graeme may even offer you a role in the kitchen, you know, show him the ropes, make sure Belle's reputation stays intact.'

Quite a speech from Peters, though Charlie was barely taking things in. He could feel Lulu's grip on his good arm, the searing pain from the other, and as Peters came to the end of his words, Charlie's gaze settled on a nodding Graeme. Not so much on Graeme's bonce, but on what the thieving, talentless bastard had in his mitts.

Franco's book.

The leather book Larry gave Franco.

Franco's book, which held the story of Belle Hotel. Four decades of secret recipes and receipts. Every important document relating to the Sheridan family and Belle Hotel. Under Graeme's fist.

'Paul, I'm back. I was back before twelve, helping Mum out in the pub. Ask her if you like. I tried to enter my hotel, but you seemed to have locked the interconnecting door from your side. Is that legal? Locking me out of part of my own hotel? And Paul, I have the money you requested. Not… all of it, but enough.'

Charlie twisted out of Lulu's grip, reached around for the roll of Dawn's tatty tens and twenties and the pawnbroker's crisp fifty-pound notes. He yanked the roll from his back pocket and flung it onto the table where it bounced twice and plonked in Peters' lap.

'Put that in your pipe and smoke it.'

'Charlie, I, er, we've come too far to—'

'Five K. Enough for five more days. Come on, Peters, you owe me that. I'll give you the other five grand in five days' time. Don't you dare lecture me about financial prudence. You should hear what they're saying about your fucking lot on the radio.'

'Charlie, I—'

'Lulu, please, this isn't about us. This is between me and Peters. And you,' Charlie dead-eyed Graeme, 'don't even think of squeaking.' Charlie held out his good arm for Franco's book and left it there. 'Give me that book.'

'I'm waiting for Mr Peters to tell us all exactly who is the owner of Belle Hotel and all its assets before I hand over what, to the letter of the law, is now about to become my property.'

On 'property', Charlie leapt, the tines of the fork he'd grabbed from the waiters' station glinted in the sun that poured in through the coloured glass windows.

The fork only glanced across Graeme's neck, with just two of the four tines piercing the skin, a touch wide of the pronounced Adam's apple that Charlie had so mercilessly mocked in the past. It was his left hand, after all, and he'd had a knock to the head. Graeme was on his feet and in the karate stance in less than half a second. He broke the stance momentarily, touching the back of the book-clasping hand to his neck, checking for blood.

'You crazy mother. I'll have you for this. You'll get years. They'll be handing down more than anger management this time.'

Lulu screamed and dived at Charlie, grabbing his long greasy hair with both hands and pulling him away from Graeme with a force that shocked even her. The fork fell from Charlie's hand and skittered across the mosaic floor.

The table tipped and clattered to meet the fork as Peters rose to his feet. Charlie and Graeme grappled left-handed with Franco's book, Graeme still holding his stronger hand in the knife hand position. Charlie supported his broken wrist in his chef's whites, flexing his bicep against Lulu's violent tugs.

The moment that Peters yelled 'Enough!', Graeme dropped an extremely well- executed chop onto Charlie's nose, the force of which propelled Charlie backwards in an arc of blood and caused Franco's book to yank from Graeme's hand and follow Charlie onto the skull-shattering surface.

The four of them watched the book, its worn leather covers wings in flight as it released all four of its brass clasps and let forty years of memories out like a confetti bomb.

Charlie came to for the second time in as many minutes with the gentle caress of fusty paper fluttering across his face.

'Enough!' It was Peters, at full height and finally taking control of what had fast become a very out-of-control situation, 'Charlie, Graeme, Lulu. Enough. Stop it, the three of you.'

The last leaf fell from space, a birth certificate, Second World War paper. Light as a prisoner of war.

'Enough. Charlie, you've bought yourself five working days. Five days, you hear me. Got yourself off on a technicality and only come up with half of the money. I shouldn't be doing this. Count yourself lucky that things are in such disarray at the bank. I'm ashamed to say that the Hookes balance sheet is not reading well. We have too much bad debt, Belle Hotel's included, and Her Majesty's Government are going to have to bail us out. Lulu, Graeme, we should leave now. We'll be back in five days' time to do this again properly. You've no chance of turning this around, Charlie, I mean look at you. Your grandfather will be rolling in his grave. No need to get up, Sheridan, we'll let ourselves out. Oh, I expect you'll be needing these.'

The shiny new set of keys bounced off Charlie's chest and came to rest among the scattered papers. Charlie let his eyes close as he listened for the footfall to fade, ignoring the whispered 'Charlie' from the stilettoed step that hung back a little from the rest. He couldn't face Lulu now. It was just too complicated. More complicated and awful than even Lulu knew. What had gone on between them, what he now knew he'd done, must never, ever, come to light. He'd lost his childhood sweetheart, for sure. From where Charlie lay, the first thing he saw upon opening his eyes was the black-and-white photo of Charlie and Lulu as children peering over the lip of Franco's stockpot on the stove. The old man had taken it as a joke, the pot was clean and stove cold, and framed it for the customers' amusement. The kids in a stockpot picture sat at the centre of a gallery of over three decades of Belle Hotel family life. Snaps of Charlie and Lulu as teenagers wrestling in Christmas jumpers by the giant tree in Belle Hotel's lobby. Franco in his chef's whites showing Charlie how to serve a whole salmon at table, Lulu grinning at his side, waiting with the silver service spoon and fork. Caught on celluloid in memory of a shared past and sympathy for a separate future.

The sound of Belle Hotel's main doors banging shut brought Janet rolling in and she helped Charlie pick up their past, rise to room 20, and there begin re-binding the book of Belle Hotel.

1970s

The Kipper Wars

<u>Eggs Benedict</u>
Two Eggs
One Muffin
Ham
Hollandaise Sauce

Poach the eggs, split and toast the muffin, serve the eggs on the ham on the muffin, smother in hollandaise, flash under the grill. Voilà, happy as Larry!

Franco Sheridan fought in the Kipper Wars. They changed his fortunes for ever. For over half his life, Franco fried, roasted and poured his way up and down the London to Brighton line. Head steward on the *Brighton Belle* train. Brighton–Haywards Heath–Victoria. Victoria–Haywards Heath–Brighton. Clickety, click; clackety clack. Up there for breakfast, elevenses back. Things had been pretty much of the same until, one day, Lord Olivier looked up from his *Times*.

'Franco, old boy, you know we are under attack?'

The steward kept pouring, with the Balcombe bend fast approaching and Larry's teacup only half full. He grunted and staggered back to the steaming galley for some milk.

'Yes, under attack, our wretched government want to cancel breakfast on the *Brighton Belle*. Over my dead body.'

'Your kippers, Larry.'

'What, oh yes, thank you, Franco. Damn bureaucrats. Want to stop my bloody—'

The two men, so different in rank and standing, took in, in silent wonder, the view from the viaduct. Arched locomotion shadowed lush Sussex. For Franco this counted as worship.

Soon they were crossing the Thames. The great actor drained his teacup. Quick slap of Franco's starched jacket and *The Times* changed hands. At Victoria, Larry hailed a Hackney Cab to the Old Vic. Larry was nearing the end of both his tenure and his tether as Director of the National Theatre and ready for more time in his seaside home. The Eugene O'Neill play currently running, directed by and starring Larry, had been a long day's journey into night. Otherwise known as the last train back to Brighton. Larry was bone-tired and in no mood to have his morning comforts fucked up. The kippers kept repeating on him.

'Bloody Westminster. I'll win this one yet.'

In the end he won the battle, but lost the war. By sheer force of will (and a full-page advertisement in London's *Evening Standard*) Larry got breakfast reinstated on the *Brighton Belle*. Franco kept his job and Larry kept himself in kippers. Not that he was going to be ordering kippers again. The day that breakfast was back on the *Belle*, Larry boarded the train in Brighton, ordered a bacon sandwich and passed Franco the recipe for Eggs Benedict that he'd enjoyed on a film set in the States. Those Yanks knew how to break their fast and Larry decided that he wanted New York brunch as he passed over Balcombe Viaduct

But, by the end of 1972, the train had been taken out of service. Franco got a plaque on platform 4 and a not so handsome payoff from British Rail. Not enough to buy Belle Hotel. Folk wondered who'd bankrolled the rest, some noticing that Larry never paid for breakfast.

Franco had been passing her on his way to and from work for donkey's years. Seen her fade from her post-war grandeur into boarding-house dilapidation. Now he had his chance to bring her back to her former glory.

He stood at the three-way crossroads on Ship Street and squinted the better to see her, and because smoke was getting in his eyes. A handsome Belle Epoque building: wrought iron, sandstone and rose-tinted glass. Beautiful. Bloody awful name though. Franco'd have to think on that. He watched with satisfaction as the flat-capped workman banged the sold sign over the door of his hotel. His hotel. Franco's eyes watered and this time it wasn't from the sunshine or the smoke.

'Right, let's get to work.'

It was 1973 and the United Kingdom was under the decree of the Conservative government, conserving electricity to beat the striking miners, and working a three-day week. Franco knew who was doing the other four. Lazy sods. Work was in short supply, the dole queue got longer, rubbish piled up in the gutter and everybody blamed the government. Franco whistled a show tune, one of Larry's, as he sauntered home to wait for the small hours.

Four am on a three-day weekday. Franco's up with the larks. At Brighton railway station Franco slowly backed the Granada under the British Rail sign and backwards up the ramp. The 3.5 GL strained for a moment as the uneven automatic gearbox got used to the gradient.

'Now then, quietly, Franco,' he muttered to the no one he hoped was about, '*nemo nos impune lacessit*.'

A memento from Franco's war. No one fucks with Franco. They can capture him and half starve him to death for the duration of the war, but he'll bounce back stronger. The lumbering hulk of the Granada levelled out on the platform, brake lights flashing the silent carriages in a shock of red.

He cut the engine and felt his way along the bunch of keys for the longest one in the sudden darkness. The car was about as close to the locked galley door as was humanly possible. He'd done this a thousand times before, usually in broad daylight, then loading things on. This morning things were going the other way. Stealing. No, taking what was his by right. Bric-a-brac. No use to British Rail. Nationalised nonsense, he could hear Larry declaring over his kippers as they rushed through Haywards Heath. Nationalised nonsense that had put a stop to decades of decadent travel between Brighton and the Metrop.

Franco listened in silence. Nothing. An hour at least before the milk and papers went into Smiths. Another before the first bleary-eyed commuters pitched up for the six o'clock express.

He unlocked the galley door and felt hissing water drip onto his feet. Normally by now Franco would have been up and into his tool bag, adjusting the temperamental boiler, tinkering with the carriage's ancient plumbing. Not now. No point. The two beautiful Pullman carriages were off to the sidings this afternoon to be left to rot. Well, Franco was going to bloody well have what he was owed, and who else needed Belle-embossed cruet anyway?

Half an hour of steady, methodical work and the Granada's capacious boot was filled with crockery and silver. He fetched his Phillips screwdriver from the tool bag already waiting for him on the front seat, and went off to unscrew his favourite pictures.

The irony of this action was not lost on Franco. Once a week, on a Monday, he'd toured the two carriages giving each of the simple scenes, *Balcombe Viaduct in Spring* and *Brighton Station in the Snow*, a little tighten to the right. The undeniably ropey track shook each picture to its hinges until enough of a gap was opened to create an irritating rattle.

'Franco,' Larry would bellow from behind his *Times*. 'Rat-a-tat-tat.'

Out came Franco with his trusty turner and the weekly cross-carriage chat about the importance of the crosshead screw design and its self-centring properties.

'Phillip's major contribution was in driving the concept forwards to a point where it was adopted by screwmakers and car manufacturers.'

'Henry F. Phillips, 1889 to 1958, Portland, Oregon. I once received a film script based on the man's life. He lost his patent in 1949, you know, never came back from it. Fucking Yanks. I say, Franco, what about a screwdriver?'

The watercolours safely back against the carriage walls, Franco would return to the galley and prepare a gleaming tray of vodka, ice and freshly squeezed oranges for the whole carriage. A tidy sum went onto Larry's bill and straight into Franco's pocket. Well, the job had to have its perks, and where did they think the Granada came from, steward's wages?

Franco made a final trip back to the galley once he'd loaded the pictures onto the back seat. Trays, the trays… he piled the battered silver salvers onto the counter. That'd give his hotel a flying start. Hot food coming out on gleaming platters and no more swaying train. Oh, yes, Franco was looking forward to this hotel lark. About time he made his mark. Now then, time to beat a hasty retreat.

He jumped down from his former place of work, a nimble leap for a man in his sixties, swung the wooden door shut and slung the lock. He didn't want thieves getting in, now, did he?

Franco eased himself into the smooth polyurethane driver's seat, flicked out a John Player Special from the packet on the dash and took the time to light it from the flush-fitted cigar lighter mounted by his gearstick, electric red ignited Virginia leaf, and with that, Franco marked with a deep, satisfying drag his transition from steward to hotelier.

*

Hookes Bank

Franco Sheridan
Belle Hotel
Ship Street
Brighton

25 January 1973

Dear Franco,
Congratulations on the opening of Belle Hotel, that was quite a party! This letter confirms the following transactions on your newly opened account.

+£100,000 Funds transfer from L.O.

–£75,000 Purchase of twenty-bedroom Ship Street hotel property with pub and restaurant.

–£10,000 Bar stock, Rhône Wine, Krug Champagne, Talisker Whisky. Transfer from Tooley St Bonded Vintners

–£2,500 1000 Cohiba Robusta Cigars (kind permission Fidel Castro) 10,000 packs of Benson & Hedges cigarettes.

–£2,500 One Wurlitzer Jukebox, purchased from Bar Italia, Frith Street.

–£10,000 Habitat c/o Terence Conran design, soft and hard furnishings for the Belle Hotel bar

Hookes have proudly banked The Savoy for a century and now Belle Hotel. I look forward to assisting you now and into the future.
Yours,
Paul Peters

The twenty-bedroom property came with an internal garage that gave directly onto the cellar: handy when it came to offloading contraband. Franco had already taken a day trip to Dieppe and come back with a boot full of extra liquor to add to the stock of his padded bar.

Larry was the first to christen it, on the day of his retirement from the National, with a very good bottle of Krug. 'To Belle Hotel and freedom!'

They raised glasses and Larry gave Franco the most precious memento of his time on the South Bank, the framed review by Kenneth Tynan that he'd hung on the wall to make the bad ones more bearable.

Laurence Olivier at his best is what everyone has always meant by the phrase 'a great actor'. He holds all the cards; and in acting the court cards consist of (a) complete physical relaxation, (b) powerful physical magnetism, (c) commanding eyes that are visible at the back of the gallery, (d) superb timing, which includes the ability to make verse swing, (e) chutzpah – the untranslatable Jewish word that means cool nerve and outrageous effrontery combined, and (f) the ability to communicate a sense of danger.

These are all vital attributes, although you can list them in many orders of importance (Olivier himself regards his eyes as the ace of trumps); but the last is surely the rarest. Watching Olivier, you feel that at any moment he may do something utterly unpredictable; something explosive, possibly apocalyptic, anyway unnerving in its emotional nakedness. There is nothing bland in this man. He is complex, moody and turbulent; deep in his temperament there runs a vein of rage that his affable public mask cannot wholly conceal. I once asked Ralph Richardson how he differed, as an actor, from Olivier. He replied: 'I haven't got Laurence's splendid fury.'

Franco accepted the gift and put it up on the shelf next to *Brighton Station in Snow*. From the first day of its opening, Belle Hotel had a touch of glamour that the old hotels, The Grand and The Metropole, just couldn't touch – something about the spirit of the joint, its chutzpah, that made it the place you wanted to be when you were in Brighton.

The theatrical connection helped. Franco did a shrewd deal with the Theatre Royal within his first month of opening. He'd take the casts of all the touring productions at B&B rates, just for the glamour they brought into the building. Glamour, sex and money. Soon Belle Hotel was bursting at the seams with wine, women and song. Franco hummed along, *if I were a rich man*, and kerchinged the recently decimalised notes into his cash register. The place had a tantalising whiff of old and new money meeting for debauchery. George IV, Brighton's patron saint of fucking and eating, would have been proud.

The early days of January 1974, as *Cinderella* played its final few performances, saw Belle Hotel at its most divinely decadent: Larry at the piano, giving the room his best Archie Rice, an ugly sister on each arm.

Franco, the fabled poor man, had found the goose that laid the golden egg. All he had to do was keep every other fucker from killing it and depriving him of the gain he'd worked tooth and nail for. It was his name above the door: Franco Sheridan Licensed to Sell Intoxicating Liquor. His name, not British bloody Rail. Franco let it go to his head. Finally, Franco had a pot to piss in. In fact, he had about twenty of them, and he wasn't minded to go back to stewarding any time soon. No thank you. Let him mind his own business and other folk kindly mind theirs.

HMRC Tax Demand

5 April 1974
Franco Sheridan t/a Belle Hotel
£8,247

Then Franco was in for a bit of a shock. With the arrival of his first tax demand some of the partying had to stop. Same mood, but stricter controls, just when he'd had his eye on the new E-Type V12 Roadster, a drop-top Jag with a bodyline to die for. The Granada was getting a little battered, what with all those day trips to France. Franco was screwing every last farthing – sorry, ten pence – out of liquor. It was time to turn his attention to those other high-profit areas, rooms and food.

For rooms, he'd need to use to his son and daughter-in-law. Johnny, the son he'd largely ignored since the end of the war, apart from setting him up as a bellboy at The Grand once Johnny had flunked out of school at sixteen; and Janet, the chambermaid who'd caught Johnny's eye in The Grand staff canteen. They'd been married at Brighton Registry Office, Franco grumbling about having to take a day off from the trains to attend. Married but a handful of years, Johnny already had the pallor of a man twice his age and Janet, knocked up with Charlie on the night of Belle Hotel's opening party, had her hands full to say the least. In a purely selfish move, Franco poached them both from The Grand and set them hard at the task of making the bedrooms pay for their board and lodging, and his Jag.

Food, Franco knew about. A steward since the war, he knew all about buying food, doing it up and flogging it on a padded chair for profit. Sod it, he'd do the food himself. Let young Janet run the bar, after she finished cleaning the bedrooms. Franco was going to make his fortune out of food.

He knew all the best dishes by heart – British classics, either by conquest or by design. He needed to write those down somewhere, but then he still had to look elsewhere for inspiration when it came to new food. Franco found salvation in Fanny Craddock. Her cookbook, *Modest but Delicious*, had been a Christmas gift from Larry. The great man was getting hungry for somewhere to spend his evenings now that he was down by the sea most of the time and it looked like Fanny had the answer.

Franco had been a fan of her television programmes for many years, used to watch them of an evening with his dear, departed Vera. Little did he know at that point that Fanny was, in turn, inspired by Escoffier, the granddaddy of all good food. The first celebrity chef, Fanny had, with sheer brute force, raised the culinary bar for British housewives from the 1950s onwards. Her influence on their eating habits crept out of the home and into the commercial catering arena. If they were being introduced to canapés and prawn cocktails on the box, then they wanted them again when they went out for something posh.

If people wanted Fanny's food when they went out to eat, then Franco was going to damn well give it to them. He mastered crêpes Suzette, even cajoled Johnny into swiping one of those flaming trolleys from the dining room at The Grand.

'They won't miss it and, anyway, they owe us something, after working you two to the bone all that time,' said Franco, handing Johnny and Janet their list of the day's tasks.

Franco ordered himself three sets of chef's whites from the catalogue, thirty-inch waist from boy to man, and set about expanding his repertoire. Learning from Fanny about taste, flavours and presentation. Trusting himself for the right balance of sweet, sour, salty and bitter.

Fanny's lobster was a bit rich for Franco's tastes, so he took out some of the cream and added more fish stock. Franco knew his onions and noticed the tang of allium added a certain something to the dish. It certainly was easier cooking at the giant hob with a solid floor, swept by Janet, under his feet than in the swaying galley of his formative food years.

Modest but Delicious
French Trifle

This is served quite frequently in simple French bistros as a pudding, and is immensely popular with small fry too. You can make it in a small bowl for two persons with four slices of roll cut ½ inch thick, or a big family one with a quart syrup fruit jelly and a whole Swiss roll filled with either jam or jelly. You serve it from its glass container and it will be the talk of any dinner party or special occasion.

1¼ pints any sweetened fruit syrup from bottled fruits
1 oz powdered gelatine
4 tbsp cold water
6 slices of fresh or stale Swiss Jam roll

Franco looked up chocolate in the index. He needed a signature sweet to sit there alongside the apple crumble and crème brûlée. There, that was it. Chocolate torte. Johnny bustled about in the larder, gathering ingredients to Fanny and Franco's command.

'Three ounces of milk chocolate. Four ounces of caster sugar, quarter pint double cream. So much cream, Fanny, you're costing me a bleedin' fortune. One egg white. We'll keep the yolk for glazing. There. In that cup.'

Johnny watched in silence as Franco melted the chocolate in a *bain-marie*. The water bath was improvised from a Pyrex in a boiling pan of water, no money for fancy kitchen gadgets in those days. Franco poured the fluff into a tart tin, tutting at the brown specks that dotted his jacket – Janet would have to give that a scrub before service. Ten minutes later and the three of them were sitting in the dining room tasting the torte with a pot of tea.

'Yes,' said Franco, 'that's going on the menu. With a white chocolate sauce and raspberries. We can freeze the rasps and pull out a handful as we need them. Janet, love, I need raspberries.'

Franco joined the Hospitality Guild, the caterers' industry body, and before too long got himself made Grand Master. Larry had pulled strings, the rest of Brighton's hoteliers grumbled. Franco ignored them and made friends with Albert Roux, a fellow Grand Master and holder of the UK's first Michelin star.

'Michelin star,' muttered Franco to himself on the train on the way home, high on camaraderie and cognac, 'I'm having me one of those.' As Franco slept the Balcombe Viaduct flew by beneath him. Franco knew that a star was beyond his reach, Albert had told him as much. Need to be at the craft from apron height. But in his dream, Franco saw a Michelin star over Belle Hotel's door. He saw the star and he knew who'd be getting it for him.

One day Franco stripped back decades of boarding-over and crumbling plasterwork to reveal some mint condition, belle époque panelling across the ground floor. Curvilinear forms and nature-inspired motifs danced tantalisingly between the restaurant and bar.

'It may not be in vogue right now but it's better than that flocking wallpaper. Come on, Johnny, grab that hammer, we're going to see what's behind this wall.'

Jaguar Motor Car Company
Receipt
E-Type V12 Convertible
£3,343 paid in cash in full with thanks

Rummaging about in the cellar, Franco came across a dusty box of Masonic ornaments. He'd already thrown out the throne, didn't want any of that lot in Belle Hotel. Now he took the solid gold mumbo-jumbo straight round to the pawnbroker's, dusty cardboard grating along the narrow lane, and flogged the lot for the price of his Jag.

As he was leaving the pawnbroker's, a grandfather clock struck noon. Clock, Belle Hotel needed a clock for the lobby. Something to keep the place running like the trains. Franco bought the clock on the knock and carried it home on his shoulder. It was taller, by far, than the old man himself, though it weighed not a pennyweight more. Lumbering down Ship Street, Franco was back in El Alamein, fallen comrade a dead weight as he scrambled over the slippery sandbank to safety.

The clock was a stunner. Eighteenth-century Kieninger Triple. Chime, date and time. Perfect, even if it was a kraut clock.

22 June 1976
12.30pm
Tick-tock. Tock-tick.

Roar.

The sound of Franco's new Jag as he fired her up in Belle Hotel's garage. Janet could feel the rumble four floors up. Now that was a beautiful car. Made his Granada feel like a truck. He took his grandson Charlie out in it for a treat one Sunday between services, dashing along the Sussex lanes to Ditchling, the young fellow strapped in deep into the seat beside him. Charlie's podgy hands holding out an imaginary steering wheel as he aped the old man. Made the dry old desert rat weep.

By that blazing summer of 1976, Belle Hotel was firing on all cylinders. The bar bustled with seaside and conference trade, rooms full to bursting with dirty weekenders, and the restaurant had become the place to see and be seen. Franco's passion for food and doing things properly had travelled far and wide. He found himself sitting at the head table at Guild dinners next to Albert Roux and the head chefs of The Dorchester and The Savoy.

Success tasted rather sweet to Franco. He swung on the barstool next to Larry.

'I had my chance and I took it. Look at all this, Larry. Belle Hotel. Enough to make an old man die happy.'

Old men? They were only knocking seventy, decades in them both yet. Larry, high on the success of his *World at War* voiceovers was regaling Franco with tales from his latest Hollywood stint filming *Marathon Man*. Larry slapped Franco with his *Times* on the punchlines.

'So I said to him, Dustin, my good fellow, there really is no need to stay up for three nights. Why not try acting, dear, it's much easier? Eh, Franco, why not try acting? Talk about madness in the method. Well, old chap, how about a toast to Belle Hotel's continued success. More champagne?'

Janet tramped wearily down to the cellar. At thirty, she was already getting the gait of a middle-aged woman. What were most girls her age up to this time of night? At home with their feet up watching *Last of the Summer Wine*, not serving it to these two old farts. *Are You Being Served?* By Janet? *Some Mothers Do 'Ave Em*. Johnny, the once charming bellboy from The Grand, had become a miserable mute under Franco's dictatorship. More like being married to a ghost. At least she had Charlie to make it all worthwhile. The boy spent most of his time running around after Franco, while she lugged crates of Schweppes up from the cellar. What a carry on. How could she forget the year before when Franco had invited the entire cast of *Carry on London* down for the night after their sell-out theatre run in London? Janet saw things that night that made her eyes pop out of her head. She thought after a working life in the catering trade that nothing could shock her, but one night of capers with Sid James and Barbara Windsor put paid to that.

They belted out bawdy music hall numbers into the small hours and those guests that couldn't beat them came down to join them in their dressing gowns for a knees-up and a night cap. *Money makes the world go round*, sung to the sound of cash crossing the counter. Not that she or Johnny saw any of it. Franco paid them every Friday, the same wage as they had received at The Grand, with a kiss for Janet and slap on the back for his son.

Johnny's back was still smarting; he reversed the Granada into the last remaining space at the cash and carry, pulled on the handbrake and sat in silence as the engine wheezed itself to death.

He very slowly lowered his head to the steering wheel and let it rest there for a few moments before lifting it up and letting it fall with a crack. Fizal Moondi, the Ship Street newsagent, tapped on the Granada's window. Johnny tried to ignore him, then relented and wound the window down.

'You all right, mate? Don't let the bastards grind you down. Some bloke behind me in the queue just thumped me for being a slow Paki. Cheer up, it could be worse. You could be me.'

'It is worse. I am me. At least you're your own boss.'

'Hey, look out for the snack aisle special offers, I got me half a ton of pork scratchings for a tenner. Reckon they'd go down well in your bar.'

Johnny shook his head.

'Franco's given me a list. I deviate under pain of death.'

Fizal wobbled his head and winked, his own Ango-Indian trademark, and wheeled the packets of pigskin to his clapped-out Maxi. Johnny let out the longest sigh of defeat and made to wind the window back up. The handle came off in his hand.

Franco's food was getting him noticed. Belle Hotel Restaurant was now the must-eat place on the conference circuit and politicians of all stripes had dined off its stolen cutlery. Franco was storing his menus, just to make sure he didn't repeat himself on someone important. His recipes and receipts were scattered over the floor every time goods were delivered. There were only so many times he could yell, 'Door!' at the top of his voice then call for Janet to come pick up and chronologically sort the scraps of card and paper that contained the secrets of his success. Something would have to be done about it.

Charlie was growing up. Before long it would be time for him to start playgroup. Mondays had already become something of a family institution, sitting down for a late lunch after service and some quality time together. This Monday in July 1976 was hot. So hot the tarmac had turned to sauce outside the open windows of Belle Hotel Restaurant.

Franco was hot, bothered and feeling his full sixty-six years. He'd built Belle Hotel out of nothing but a boot full of national treasure and a recipe for chocolate torte.

'What do you think of the trifle? Better with Madeira, or do you prefer the sherry?'

Janet looked like she was thinking about it. Johnny, a snoozing Charlie balanced on his knee, sat staring into space.

Franco lifted up, then cracked down the ashtray on the hard edge of the table, the place he knew would hurt the most. Charlie stirred and began to cry. Johnny's pretty-vacant stare vacillated towards a what-the-fuck-d'you-do-that-for glare.

'Glad to have your attention.' Franco couldn't have made the speech looked more prepared if he'd read it. 'I've decided to take some time off from arduous kitchen duties and am in need of a replacement. Janet, love, your hands are more than full with the bar and your housekeeping duties. Johnny, you ponce about front of house as if you own the place, which you don't. I've decided it's time to teach you the craft. You are going to learn how to cook. Fanny taught me and now I will teach you. Make yourself useful. I can't go on for ever. I'm sixty-six, you know.'

Johnny held his son tight and looked at his father. Sixty-six, can't go on for ever... Don't make me laugh. You'll carry on for years, you bastard. Making my life a misery. So it's cooking, now, is it? Not good enough that I work out front, you've got to drag me back there and really turn the heat up. God help us both, you steely old sod.

Johnny completed his silent speech, nodded meekly and mumbled, 'Yes, Dad.'

Janet and Franco could barely hear that.

'We can barely hear you, lad. Speak up.'

'I said yes, Dad.'

One day a young man in a cheap suit came knocking at the kitchen door, fighting his way past three weeks' worth of uncollected rubbish. Roger Hardman had the gift of the gab and kept Franco chatting long enough to burn his meringues.

'Your boy, is he? Oh, your grandson. Lovely age. I've one of my own about the same age. Lulu. We lost her mum, my wife, in childbirth. Tragic. Still, life must go on. Do you want to take a look at the Axminsters?'

Franco, unsure what to do with this information, busied himself with shag piles and paisleys. Roger rabbited on.

'I'm just starting out on my own in carpets. Need all the help I can get. Tell you what,' Franco's eyes and finger-backs lingered over red Marrakesh, 'hundred per cent wool. I'll do the whole place for five grand.'

Franco sucked his teeth and narrowed his eyes.

'I tell you what, son. I'm about to be clobbered again by the tax man. You need some help starting out in life. What say we come to a little arrangement?'

Invoice
Hardman Carpets
Axminster Marrakesh carpet with underlay throughout Belle Hotel Stairs, Landings and Bedrooms £10,000

The invoice was punched and slipped into the leather binder that Larry had bought Franco to stop his life falling about his feet every time some bugger opened the back door. It sat behind the recipe for hollandaise sauce that Franco had hand-typed on his old Remington, hole-punched at the front desk and clasped through swing doors to the kitchen. Roger paid back the five-grand loan in fifty-quid instalments, slipping it behind the cash he spent at Belle Hotel bar with his prospective customers as they touched pile and stroked weft on Franco's stools while perusing the full Hardman Carpets selection.

Janet had solved two problems for Roger. They'd been friendly for a while, met when Roger fitted the carpets for her former employer, The Grand, and he'd chatted Janet up. They'd dated a couple of times before Janet married Johnny. Roger was one of the rent-a-crowd Janet and Johnny had invited to the Belle Hotel's opening night. The crowd that Franco slung out for being rat-arsed. It was Janet who'd suggested Roger tap up Franco for work and it was Janet who solved the problem of what to do with his daughter, Lulu, on those nights he did business at the Belle Hotel bar.

'Bring her over to play with Charlie. I can as easily neglect two children as one. They can be playmates.'

And play they did. Like brother and sister. Charlie stealing Lulu's dolls and throwing them down the laundry chute. Lulu screaming the place down and pulling Charlie into the bar by his hair. Most guests mistook them for siblings. As much as they argued, they were as often to be found sprawled out on the floor of the restaurant of a quiet afternoon colouring the backs of menus. Franco clamped one special picture they'd drawn into his book. It was the two of them at the door of a wonky Belle Hotel. Smiling sun and Charlie neatly drawn by Lulu; lashing rain and Lulu shoddily scrawled by Charlie. Their favourite place to hide was the cubbyhole behind reception. There was just enough space for the two of them to squeeze in and Franco took a snap of their faces peeking out from an oval hole in the wood.

'Come with me, you two. I want to take a snap of you in my big cooking pot. Look sharp, yer mum'll be back from the laundry in a bit. There's a Curly Wurly in it for you both.'

Franco had splashed out on a tri-fold brochure not long after he'd opened Belle Hotel. He'd had his British Rail colleagues hand out the brochure until all ten thousand copies were gone and every seaside visitor with the cash to travel first class was the proud owner of a full colour shot of Belle with her red-and-white rock-striped awnings out.

Franco got a quote for another load of brochures and binned it when he saw the greedy printers had doubled their prices. Sod it, he'd ditch the print and go for it big time.

Pearl & Dean Cinema Advertising
Invoice for Belle Hotel Advert
'Only a hundred yards from this cinema.'
£850

Franco made Johnny take Charlie and Lulu out to the Palace Pier for duration of the filming. Said they'd only get in the way. Made sure that Janet had her shortest dress on, he did. Treated himself to a nice white polo neck from John Smedley just for the occasion.

'And, cut. Mr Sheridan, can we just do that one more time and, er, try to act natural.'

'What do you mean natural? This is natural.'

The cameras rolled for the umpteenth time that morning and Franco's cronies, press-ganged into being extras with the promise of a free lunch, did their best to keep straight faces while the old man fluffed his lines.

By noon, the director had given up, muttering to the cameraman something about the floor not being the only wooden thing in shot and calling it a wrap before sitting down to a prawn cocktail on the house.

The Belle Hotel advert amused cinema-goers for years. The crackly film and jumpy editing perfectly suited Franco's stilted delivery. Franco's catch-phrase, 'Goes down well at the Belle', and his wink became something of a local legend. For Brightonians it was up there with national TV favourites like 'I'm a secret Lemonade drinker… R. Whites. R. Whites. R. Whites Lemonaaaaaade', much copied, much loved and much good it did Belle's takings, too. Larry, when pressed by Franco after he'd seen it before *The Spy Who Loved Me*, had to admit that it had been… very well lit.

Hollandaise Sauce
8 crushed peppercorns
20 large egg yolks
¼ pint lemon juice
¼ pint vinegar
40 oz butter

Place the peppercorns and vinegar in a small sauteuse and reduce to one-third. Add 3 tbsp cold water, allow to cool. Mix the yolks in with a whisk. Return to gentle heat and whisk continuously cook to a sabayon (like cream, sufficient to show the mark of the whisk). Remove from heat and cool slightly. Whisk in gradually the warm melted butter until thoroughly combines. Correct the seasoning. Pass through a fine chinoise. NOTE: Cause of hollandaise sauce curdling is either butter added too quickly, or because of excess heat which will cause the albumen in the eggs to harden, shrink and separate from the liquid. First attempt at hollandaise will almost certainly fail. Try again. Should sauce curdle, place a teaspoon of boiling water in a clean sauteuse and gradually whisk in the curdled sauce. If this fails to reconstitute the sauce then place an egg yolk in a clean sauteuse with a dessertspoon of water. Whisk lightly over a gentle heat until slightly thickened. Remove from heat and gradually add the curdled sauce whisking continuously. To stabilise during service, add béchamel before straining.

1 May 1979

The day Franco gave Johnny his first and last cookery lesson made a lasting impression on a watchful Charlie. At nearly six, Charlie could just see through the portholes of the kitchen door from the safe vantage point of the cubbyhole behind reception. Franco, having spent the morning up at his allotment, now had his book down from its place above the pass and was taking Johnny through the finer points of hollandaise sauce. He failed to mention the first attempt fail rate. It was not going well.

'Useless.'

Grandad shouting at Daddy. Charlie hearing, though not seeing, the thrown pan.

'Look at it, man. It is a sodding *sauce*, not a cunting *custard*. What is *wrong* with you?'

'What's wrong with me? I'll tell you what's wrong with me. You lied to me, kept me in the dark, and now—'

'Now what, young man, now *what*?'

'Dad, you lied to me to save face and you've been punishing me for finding out the truth ever since. And, for your information, I'm a father myself now, so you can cut the young man talk. Save it for your staff. Your staff, Franco, you bastard, and I, from this moment on, am not one of them. And I'll tell you another thing—'

Charlie could neither see nor hear Daddy. Franco's roar covered Johnny's parting shot. The back door of the kitchen doused the porthole with sunlight and suddenly Daddy was gone.

Franco took his time putting the recipe back in its rightful place. Chefs scuttled about him clearing up the mess, wiping down the walls, putting pan, spoon and gloop in the sink. Franco scrubbed his hands at the small sink by the door, using the nail brush to work out any remaining specks of dirt. He raised his wet hands and was given a clean hand towel that was then picked up from the floor once he'd made his way through the swing doors.

Franco placed a hand on Charlie's shoulder, spoke two words softly to the boy and then bellowed the rest up four flights of stairs.

'He's gone. Janet, love, can you come down. He's gone.'

Janet joined them at the reception desk, duster in hand and Franco initiated the family hug. Charlie, still dazzled by the sunlight, clung to his mother and grandfather. Soft drops of salty water plopped onto his unbrushed hair. Janet shuddered and pulled away from Franco, taking Charlie into her arms. Just the two of them. Franco was left standing slightly apart, slowly shaking his head.

'He's gone. Janet, do you want to go with him? No, I thought not. Charlie, he's gone. It's just the three of us now. Family. He's gone.'

Charlie looked at Franco and wanted to go to him, but he didn't want to leave his mum. And he didn't understand why Daddy had had to go. But he knew that he wasn't coming back. An ache settled in the middle of his ribs. Charlie pulled away from Mummy and looked towards the kitchen. He let himself have a small cry, then wiped his eyes and snotty nose on his sleeve. Belle Hotel was silent, but for the tick-tock of Franco's clock and the creak of the floorboard under the foot of Charlie's scuffed shoes. He liked the sound and rocked back and forth faster and harder until he could forget the fact that his daddy had just left. Then Franco gave him a clip round the ear to stop it and the world fell silent. The three of them looked at one another as if to say, now what?

Franco's clock struck noon and the old man tightened his apron strings and looked towards his kitchen. Lunch wasn't going to cook itself and there was still the hollandaise to be made.

Janet twisted the duster between her fists and stared for the longest tick-tock at Charlie. Shaking her head she set off up the stairs to get a Mogadon and carry on with her housekeeping duties, using the duster's dirty yellow softness to dab her eyes.

Franco patted Charlie on the head.

'Now then, that's enough of all that. We Sheridans don't cry for long now, do we? Work to be done. Work to be done.'

And with that, Franco turned and walked slowly back to the kitchen to start his ten-year shift, counting off the years that he'd need to man the stoves before he could foist it on to Charlie, with each step.

Charlie, blissfully unaware of his birth duty, soon bored of kicking his legs against the reception desk and set off upstairs to get under his mum's feet. The ache in his chest pulling with every step.

Lulu was invited over to stay that weekend to take Charlie's mind off things. Franco watched in wonder as the two of them played chef and restaurant manager, aping the grown-ups. It made the old bastard smile, seeing Charlie pass imaginary plates to Lulu and her taking them to the table with a hello and thank you and enjoy your meal. With Johnny gone, maybe the next generation would ensure his legacy, win him that Michelin star, do Larry proud, make him the talk of the Guild. Franco gave the two of them a ten-pence tip for their hard imaginary work and sent them off to the newsagent for a *Racing Post* for him and a tin of pop for the two of them.

Tock-tick. Tick-tock. Everyone's paying on the knock. Franco paid off his clock and vowed never to borrow or lend again. He let a shifty arty type stay a week without taking any cash upfront, then surprised himself when he let the fella off paying, skint he'd said, and accepted a portrait of himself, Janet and a cat in lieu of payment. Charlie and Lulu started off in the frame, but had to be painted out as they kept giggling and dashing out on a chase around the bar and back. Janet had to set them up with crayons and old menus. Listening to them talking while she was being painted gave Janet nothing to smile about and it showed.

'Who are you going to draw, Charlie? I'm doing my mummy. Daddy says she lives with the angels.'

'I'll draw my daddy. Mummy says he lives at The Savoy.'

Nobody bothered to ask the artist's name, too busy. David something, it was. Northern bloke with glasses. Franco found the picture rather flattering and hung it over the key rack behind reception where he could admire it when he gazed up from his Remington.

10 Downing Street

Franco Sheridan
Belle Hotel
Brighton

6 May 1979

My Dear Franco,
Denis and I would like to thank you sincerely for the discreet
hospitality you have shown us over these difficult past years
in opposition.

We understand that things are now going to get a lot more
difficult, as I said on entering Downing Street yesterday, 'Where
there is discord, may we bring harmony. Where there is error,
may we bring truth. Where there is doubt, may we bring faith.
And where there is despair, may we bring hope.'

Where there is trouble, may we be brought to Belle Hotel.
Yours,
Margaret
Hon Margaret Thatcher, Prime Minister

Lifelong Labour supporter and trades union man, Franco had found
the transition to tub-thumping Tory relatively painless. Especially
when the Tory party were footing the bill.

Being a union man had served Franco well on the trains; gave him
a day a week in the office in Brighton, feet up on the desk, planning
wildcat strikes over a cup of tea brought round on the trolley by some
other bugger for once.

Franco's conscience was clear. As a hotelier he couldn't afford the
luxury of political opinion. He was with whoever's name was written
at the top of the bill.

When Larry approached him with an idea, Franco had jumped at it. Helpfully suggesting that Margaret might want the whole of the top floor of Belle Hotel blocking out for her private purposes. Private purposes that saw Franco trousering thousands in room rates and hundreds more on top for the hot- and cold-running buffet that kept the Thatcher show on the road. The free market economy was born in Ship Street. Franco could have written a seminal book on the subject.

Maggie and Franco's careers were on the up in tandem. As Belle Hotel opened, the television critic Clive James wrote in the *Observer*, during the voting for the leadership, comparing her voice to a cat sliding down a blackboard.

Something would have to be done about it, pronto. A chance meeting with Laurence Olivier at Belle Hotel, after a particularly gruelling day at conference for Mrs T, resulted in Larry arranging lessons with the National Theatre's voice coach in the reassuringly expensive and discreet surroundings of Belle Hotel.

Thatcher succeeded in completely suppressing her Lincolnshire accent, except under extreme provocation from James Callaghan, and Franco managed to completely suppress his glee at the good fortune his crossing to the other side of the House had brought about.

Franco and Larry spent more time than they had planned in the company of Denis Thatcher and the able comfort of a gallon's worth of G&T. Franco even challenged Denis to a game of golf, which was played pie-eyed at stupid o'clock in the morning on the pitch and putt in Rottingdean, while Maggie worked on her speech in the comforts of the newly named Churchill Suite at Belle Hotel.

Franco enjoyed the most comfortable 'Winter of Discontent' in the land. One particularly stormy day, force 10s whipping in up Ship Street, Franco quipped that 'Labour Isn't Working' to Maggie as she perused a picture of a dole queue supplied by her advertising agency. Maggie thanked Franco for the tray of tea and freshly baked shortbread in her newly minted RP and then reached for her notebook.

Maggie fought on cutting income tax, reducing public spending, making it easier for people to buy their own homes and curbing the power of the unions.

'Quite right,' said Franco to Larry on election night, 'damn unions have become too powerful. You'd see a union here at Belle Hotel over my dead body.'

They raised a glass to Britain's first woman prime minister and sat watching the thinly coloured BBC coverage on the new box Franco'd bought for the bar. He noticed that every time he raised a toast to 'Maggie' his till rang loudly in response. Never was a political candidate more roundly toasted than Margaret Thatcher, the grocer's daughter from Grantham, was by Franco Sheridan the hotelier from Brighton.

Tick-tock, tick-tock. Time and tide can't beat the clock.

Callaghan's government lost the battle and the war. Maggie was sitting pretty in Number 10 soon after. Franco had been banking on her success. The seventies had been good to Franco and, with the dawning of a new decade, the self-made man's time was about to come.

1980s

Franco Says Relax!

Hookes Bank

Franco Sheridan
Belle Hotel
Ship Street
Brighton

15 September 1983

Dear Franco,
Confirming your repayment to L.O. of £100,000 as per your instruction. Please see below a current statement of your cash position and liquid assets. Thank you for your hospitality over the August Bank Holiday weekend. I have to tell you that I am still in recovery!

–£100,000 Funds transfer to L.O.
–£4,500 Love Machine Jacuzzi delivered and installed.
–£80,000 Herd of 80 Highland Cattle. Glenlow Estate.
–£12,000 Purchase of Jaguar XJS Limited Edition
+£950,000 Cash at bank.
+£250,000 Krug Champagne entire remaining '73 Vintage in bond at Tooley St Bonded Vintners

Here's to the next ten years!
Yours,
Paul Peters

*

Belle Hotel
Invoice
Date: 14 October
To: Number 10 Downing Street
Services: Emergency floor of rooms – 4am–6am, 12 October
Cost: £2,500 including complimentary tea, biscuits and brandy

The call came in soon after Franco heard the thud. Bomb. His old soldier's bones knew it the second it went off. Few seconds later it all fell into place. Right: action, Franco. He woke up Charlie and Janet then went downstairs to open up.

'Belle Hotel, Franco Sheridan speaking.'

Brighton Constabulary. Major incident at Brighton Grand. Probable fatalities. Many wounded. Mrs T at Brighton Police Station, requesting Franco's hospitality.

'Of course. Her rooms will be ready in twenty minutes.'

He'd have to take the current incumbent's bills off his fee, but this was an emergency. As the disgruntled former residents of Belle Hotel's fourth floor dissented into their dressing gowns, Franco sent Charlie round the bar sharpish with a tray of brandies and shortbread biscuits.

Janet had the warm sheets off and fresh ones on before you could say IRA. Not that Maggie would be sleeping.

Franco greeted her at the door. Shook her trembling hand and led her and Denis up to a place of relative safety.

They were gone two hours later. Composed and ready to face the world. The IRA claimed responsibility, saying 'Mrs Thatcher will now realise that Britain cannot occupy our country and torture our prisoners and shoot our people in their own streets and get away with it. Today we were unlucky, but remember we only have to be lucky once. You will have to be lucky always. Give Ireland peace and there will be no more war.'

Margaret Thatcher began the next session of the Conservative Party conference at 9.30am that morning, as scheduled. She said the bombing was, 'An attempt to cripple Her Majesty's democratically elected government. That is the scale of the outrage we have all shared, and the fact that we are gathered here now – shocked, but composed and determined – is a sign not only that this attack has failed, but that all attempts to destroy democracy by terrorism will fail.'

Franco watched Maggie's Jag rumble down Ship Street to take her to her speech, blues and twos wailing off every wall, refunded his disgruntled punters, went to his Remington and thumped out an invoice.

The Times

10 April 1984

Tragedy struck the great actor Lord Laurence Olivier last night at the Oscars. Lord Olivier was presenting the best picture award and appeared on stage looking somewhat confused. Instead of reading out the list of nominees before announcing the winner, as protocol demands, Lord Olivier simply walked onto the stage, opened the envelope and said one word, Amadeus. *The faux pas was greeted with huge gasps and then deadly silence. Fortunately for Lord Olivier and the Academy, this was indeed the winning picture. After some further confusion, not least from Lord Olivier, the* Amadeus *cast and crew took to the stage to receive their prematurely bestowed award.*

Larry's roller pulled up at Belle Hotel's entrance. The scent of beach and Brasso assaulted his senses, making him reel slightly as he grasped for the golden handle. He mouthed 'fuck off' for 'thank you' to his long-suffering chauffeur and stepped into the sanctuary.

Franco, a crisp apron splatter-proofing his houndstooth suit, was busy with the usual pre-lunch prep, bossing people about, battering his cod. He one-handed the copper bowl under the tap and with the other pumped a hearty shot of ale into the pale eggy gloop. He tunelessly whistled Sinatra as he went about his duties

"'Da, da, da, da, Chicago…" Morning, sweetheart.'

Janet groggily acknowledged Franco and fixed herself a coffee from the shuddering boiler.

Whisking as he walked, Franco shouldered the double swing door and side stepped into reception.

'Larry!'

He put the bowl down on top of the ledger – full occupancy tonight – lifted the hatch and strode over to the banquette to greet his old friend. Larry didn't get up. He just sat there, scrunched Savile Row suit over a leather buttoned beige cardigan. Franco noticed soup stains on the tie.

'The shame of it. The utter shame… utter…'

'Larry, relax.'

Franco noticed a PVC British Airways flight bag, its brash logo in marked contrast to the discreet hide banquette.

'Can I have a drink? What time is it?'

'Sherry o'clock. Come on in, I'll set your table for you. Can I put this anywhere?'

Larry kicked the bag in the general direction of reception.

'Fucking Yanks. Fucking movies. Thank God for fish and chips.'

Franco steered Larry by the elbow through the rose-stained glass divider and into the starched linen comfort of the restaurant. The five-year age gap and, no doubt, a gin-soaked night on the red eye, gave Larry the older part of the two men.

'Here you are, Larry, take a seat, I'll be back with your amontillado. No need for the menu, eh, shall I put something on ice?'

Larry beamed on cue and flicked open the copy of *The Times* Franco had picked up for him at reception. Reception. Franco ran back to rescue the bowl, setting it down on the long metal table in the kitchen before leather sole-ing off to the bar for Larry's livener, then, once he'd set the schooner and its fortifying contents in front of a visibly relaxing Larry, went to check the wine cellar.

'Krug forty-seven. The year of his knighthood. Should do the trick.'

It was early, just shy of noon. The first table was booked at one. Pandemonium after that, mind, but it gave him an hour with Larry before the first plates went out. Franco issued a couple of curt instructions to his sous chef and set off for an ice bucket. Fish and chips, he fancied that himself.

Tartare Sauce
4 pints mayonnaise
1 lb gherkins
1 lb capers
Bunch of parsley
Bunch of chives

Franco cut, chopped and mixed the tartare sauce, seasoned it with a snatch of S&P from the battered wooden pots by the hobs, wiped his hands on his apron and put his book back up on its shelf. He'd give Charlie a taste of tartare later, explain how the acid in the capers cut perfectly through the creamy emulsion.

The end-of-the-pier cod floated up in its batter life-jacket, Franco switched the oil down to standby, tonged the crisp fish onto a rack and shook out the chips. Then he fetched two oval plates from the warmer, wiped them with damp muslin and carefully arranged the Great British grub, loading the plates, along with a steaming bowl of mushy peas, onto a pock-marked platter. Fish knives and forks and ramekins of tartare sauce were waiting with Larry.

'Come and get me when you're ready.'

Franco nodded at his sous chef, lifted the tray up onto his shoulder and exited backwards into the hush of an almost empty restaurant.

The two men sat side by side and took their lunch. Opposite would have been too intimate, and besides, Olivier had already grabbed the banquette. They savoured the champagne. Caged memories rushed out with the release of the cork. Shakespeare on celluloid. The first self-directed, best actor Oscar.

'The damned Academy.'

Franco let it go. He topped Larry up and grated some black pepper onto his cod. Trembling fingers snatched the silver pot from his hand.

'The damned *Academy*.'

He wanted to talk about it. Hard to ignore, the *Times* picture of Larry's Oscars black-tied cock-up was face-up on the banquette between them.

'Have you seen this? Fuck. The shame.'

'Well, Larry I—'

Franco had read all about it over coffee at dawn. Poor Larry. He picked up *The Times* and pointed to the headline.

'Look, Larry, it was an easy mistake. We're getting on, you know. I forgot how to make tartare sauce just now.'

'Yes, but you didn't do it in front of a global audience of millions. The fucking shame of it. I'm a laughing stock.'

He mimed opening an envelope.

'*Amadeus*. Silly old fart. I am Archie Rice, the washed-up stage comedian. I am not Hamlet.'

'Oh, Larry, forget it,' Franco leaned across with the napkin-wrapped Krug and poured. 'It could have happened to anyone. Who did you go to the after-party with, may one enquire?'

'One may not enquire. Anyway, enough of my troubles. How is that grandson of yours?'

'Well, thank you. He's starting to help me in the kitchen, peeling your spuds and such like. I'm giving him little tastes of this and that, getting him to know his flavours, what good presentation looks like. Teaching him about the senses. The ones you need for our two professions, Larry.

Touch, taste, sound, smell, sight and the elusive sixth sense.'

'Common sense, Franco, common sense. Good, good. Ah, family.'

Again Franco knew what was coming.

'You've got to provide for them, Franco, old boy. Got to provide for them. Wild Geese, too.'

'It's not on the menu any more, Larry.'

'No, *Wild Geese II*, my new pay cheque. If any one of those fuckers mentions *Amadeus*, I'm walking off set.'

Larry pushed his plate away and wiped his face and necktie, mushy peas slimed over the in-flight soup stains. Franco noticed that two guests were standing by his reception desk.

'Excuse me. Can I get you any pudding? Coffee, cognac?'

22 June 1987

Charlie had been officially 'going out' with Lulu since Valentine's Day and had just spent the best part of half an hour stretched out on her single bed. Together they'd enjoyed the emptiness of the June-drowsy house, the thrill of an illicit fumble. Not bad to have got this far with a girl at just thirteen, shame his body was yet to catch up.

'Charlie, why won't you let me? Come on, I just let you.'

'No, Lu, I gotta go. Johnny's turning up soon and we've gotta pack our stuff before we go to the boat.'

He'd been good with his hands, gentle, once she'd shown him what to do and he'd stopped shaking. But when it came to her turn he'd pulled away, too embarrassed by the lack of any signs of maturity down there to let her in.

'There'll be none of this once we're onboard, Charlie. I'm sharing the captain's cabin with Dad. You'll be in the bunks with the crew.'

Lulu rolled over and hopped from the bed, her pants hanging from one foot. She smartly stepped the other leg back into her pants and pulled them up in one quick movement. Lulu smoothed her school skirt back down over her bottom and sat down next to Charlie.

'Do you mean what you say?'

'What, that I can undo a bra one-handed?'

'No, you spassie, that we'll run Belle Hotel together when we're older?'

'Course, who d'you thing I'm gonna run it with, Parvez bloody Moondi?'

'Charlie, say you love me. Before we go fishing. It'll be torture being there and not being able to kiss you.'

'Tell you what. I'll give you ten snogs now to keep you going while... shit, look at the time. Yakking on and I've got to get my rucksack.'

Charlie raced home, out across the Hove border and back into Brighton, punching the air as he ran at the sheer thrill of snogging Lulu, before spinning around the corner and into Ship Street and his home at the three-way crossroads. Belle Hotel.

'Shit.'

He'd never meant for him to actually come. It was Franco who'd suggested inviting Johnny. Janet had scowled and left the table. Charlie had shaken his head, thrilled at the idea, but never expecting Johnny to take him up on the offer. He'd rung him for a dare, never actually meant it. But Johnny jumped at it.

He'd barely seen his father in the eight years since he'd left Charlie's mum and Franco holding Belle Hotel. Only knew it was his brand-new Audi Quattro outside Belle Hotel because Father's secretary kept Mother updated on all extravagances.

'Oh. No.'

Charlie shook. Just been a dare, a stupid dare to make him feel guilty. Or so he told himself. He was looking forward to spending the weekend with Roger. Let the other boys have their boring dads, he'd have the carpet king and Lulu all to himself. The ache in his chest tightened once more.

'Shit.'

He saw his father's silhouette, narrow head haloed by smoke, at the restaurant window. He went in, through the recently Brassoed front door and turned right for the restaurant, where she'd no doubt sent him the moment he'd shown up. Janet would be in the bar, attached to the lager tap.

'Hello, Jonathon, Johnny. Dad.'

'Hello, Charlie.'

'Where's Mum?'

'Next door. She doesn't want to talk to me.'

'No?' Charlie looked at his father.

'And your grandad?'

'Gee gees.'

'Convenient, that.' Johnny looked at the floor.

'Shall we go then? I saw your new car. Stay here, I'll go get my stuff.'

Charlie could hear his mum sobbing from the bar. He slipped behind the reception desk and picked up the metal-framed rucksack, packed the night before.

'Cheerio, then. We're off.'

More sobs. Charlie shrugged. He didn't like to see her crying and was ashamed to be siding with his dad. What was he supposed to do?

The Quattro's boot was hastily opened to make way for Charlie's stuff. He had to admit, Jonathon had bought the kit.

'A new fishing rod. I want you to have it for your birthday. Sorry I missed it, I've been so busy with work lately.'

Busy bonking your boss, Charlie thought. The secretary kept his mother well up to date on that front, too. She made The Savoy sound like a hotbed of sex and scandal. All Charlie knew was that he'd liked the big copper pans he'd seen in the Savoy kitchens. Only thirteen years old and he was starting to find his way around a professional kitchen. And he was going out with a girl.

It felt good, being in the car with his dad. Driving down to the marina, free for the next few days to be… To be what? Father and son? Friends? Jonathon had made the first move on what Charlie should now call him when he'd written on Savoy headed paper to suggest that Daddy was too immature, Father too Catholic, what about Johnny? What about Johnny? Torn between a new life and a bitter ex-wife. He'd probably jumped at the chance to spend a few days with his boy, away at sea and free for a while from work and love. Now they were in the car, there was the problem of what to say. They passed The Grand without comment and said nothing of the Brighton Centre's windows glinting in the midday sun. Passed the Palace Pier without remarking on the ice-cream and helter-skelter years they had once enjoyed. Passed Larry's old house, black tiles hot and curtains drawn. Johnny turned on the cassette deck, Phil Collins. Charlie grimaced and Johnny turned it off. Silence reigned on Marine Parade.

'So, tell me about your girlfriend. What's she called?'

'Lulu, but I call her Lu. Do you remember her? When we were little before you… er, had to go. Well, before all that… Lulu used to come and play. Mum says we argued like cat and dog. Anyway. She's in my tutor group at school now. She's great fun and Roger, her dad, he's rad.'

'Rad? Oh, rad. Yes. I know Roger, of course, he laid our, your, carpets in Belle Hotel.'

'Yes, here we are. Park here. Look there's the boat.'

Twelve fathers and sons waited on the newly built Brighton Marina dockside for Roger Hardman's boat to dock. *Shagpile* bounced on its bright red fenders and everybody gasped. The boat was nothing short of a gin palace and Roger's treat to himself when Hardman Carpets made its first million. Lulu had begged him not to, but Roger insisted. Just the tonic I need after working wall to wall for a decade while single-handedly bringing you up, sweetheart. Franco egging Roger on, bored behind the Belle Hotel bar and daring Roger to get the biggest boat in the brochure. The fishing trip had been Franco's idea, too, but Franco had vowed never to go to sea in a small boat again after his somewhat choppy Channel crossings during the war.

Someone brought a camera, so the moment was not lost. The men gathered at the front looked a sturdy lot. Strong folk, good with their hands and their offspring all healthy boys ready for anything the weekend's deep-sea fishing could throw at them. Arms rested on shoulders in easy familial affection. A huddle of four hung back, disconnected, their unease about to be caught on camera. Johnny Sheridan, son of Belle Hotel Franco, and an unsmiling Charlie waited with Fizal Moondi, the Ship Street Newsagent and his son Parvez. Two boys, in different sets at school – chess for Parvez, chests for Charlie – were about to discover how much they had in common. Neither knew their fathers from a bar of soap. They were the final four to board the enormous boat as it rocked against the marina wall.

Lulu's dad came on deck, with Lulu slouching along behind him. She cringed under her fringe at the captain's uniform, the jokes, him. She wished that she'd let him get away with his 'men only' rule for the trip.

'Roger the cabin boy, at your service. All aboard, landlubbers, jump down!'

Even before they had left safe harbour, Parvez and Charlie were in troubled waters. The two fathers sat together staring into space at the back of the boat, while the sons made their own small talk on the seat opposite. Charlie would normally have sat with his mates from school: Bing, Dan and the rest. Centre of attention, leader of the chat. But they all seemed a bit different with their dads. So this was the way it was going to be.

Halfway to the first fishing site Jonathon the hotelier from Brighton and Fizal the shopkeeper from Bengal were stumped for conversation.

'Dad likes cricket.'

Thank you, Parvez. Two hours into this trip and Charlie was already tired of filling in for his dad.

Lulu took Johnny's offer of a lift back to Belle Hotel with Charlie. Roger would be fiddling about with his tackle for hours. The fishing trip had been a roaring success. They'd only caught enough for a couple of fish fingers, but Roger said that didn't matter. It was the being together that made the trip special. She'd even seen Charlie relax a bit with his dad as they sat looking, ever hopeful, with their rods out over the deep. Johnny had even tried to slip an arm over Charlie's shoulders on the voyage back to the marina. Charlie had shrugged him off a couple of times before Lulu had glared him into submission. They'd even grabbed a quick kiss on the 'Bridge', as Roger ridiculously called his steering wheel bit.

'What you two sniggering at?'

'Nothing, Dad, get back to your radar.'

And now the prospect of a couple of hours at Belle Hotel. Lulu felt fuzzy inside at the thought of it.

Franco welcomed them both in the lobby, only appearing when the growl of Johnny's Quattro had stopped echoing down Ship Street. The old man had a kiss for Lulu and punch on the arm for Charlie.

'The adventurers return. Now then, how about a spot of supper. Two courses, mind, and nothing toppy. Be my guests!'

Franco bowed and gestured them to leave their bags in the lobby. 'Walk this way.'

Then with his best Basil Fawlty, he led them into the empty Belle Hotel restaurant.

Charlie rolled his eyes at Lulu and passed her the menu. They'd better look sharp, the table would be booked solid from seven.

Lulu feasted her eyes on the menu. Delicious dishes swam before her eyes. Steak and prawn cocktail, she knew from the Berni Inn, but some of this stuff, scallops and venison, she'd never even heard of, let alone tasted. She was about to order what she wanted when Charlie got up and made off for the kitchen door.

'Charlie, don't you want to know what I want?'

'I was going to surprise you, Lu.'

'But what if I don't like it?'

'What's not to like about chicken liver parfait followed by fish pie?'

'I thought I might have the deep-fried Camembert and cranberry sauce to start and then the steak.'

Charlie came to sit back down, not opposite, as he had been, but next to her on the banquette. He pointed at the starters.

'That fried French cheese thing is horrible. Franco only put it on the menu because Delia did it. And steak… tut, tut. Too expensive for family. Trust me, Lu, you'll love the parfait and fish pie.'

She watched him karate kick the swing doors and heard him yell a couple of words to Franco over the din of the mixer. That was that, then. Overruled. Pâté and pie. And she didn't even like pâté. Charlie was just like her dad. Lulu wasn't sure about this boyfriend lark. Only done it because Susan James said she fancied Charlie. Lulu didn't want him, but she deffo didn't want him going out with anybody else. Lulu looked at the photos on the wall of the restaurant of them as kids and cringed. That bowl haircut. Who cut it? Franco? Awful. Typical of her dad to dump her at Belle Hotel while he was working. She remembered getting coins for keeping out of Franco and Janet's way. That Christmas shot, look at those awful jumpers, the day they first kissed. The last time they'd been able to fit into the cubbyhole behind reception. Lulu's mind wandered down the gallery of her childhood. Time passed. The mixer got switched off. Lulu could hear Franco murmuring at Charlie behind the kitchen door. Then Charlie reappeared from the kitchen, shoved by a starched white arm.

'Er, Franco says are you sure that's what you want?'

Charlie blushed as he carried out Franco's command. He'd torn a strip off Charlie for not letting the lass choose what she fancied. Lulu thought for a moment, then nodded her assent. He looked awkward enough having to come back and was red around the eyes, like he'd been crying.

They ate the two courses sharpish and pretty much in silence. It was the best food Lulu had ever tasted, including the time Roger had taken her to Dieppe in *Shagpile*. The heaviness of the pitted silver cutlery, stiff table linen and proper salt and pepper pots were the poshest things she'd ever eaten off. And then, the Wedgwood china plates, cold fluffy wedge of parfait under a butter top she'd had to crack with her knife before piling it into hot brioche that Charlie pulled from a napkin in a basket. This was rad. Lulu was in heaven. Just wait till she told Susan James.

Janet, Charlie's mum, came in with a Coke for each of them and said how lovely it was to see them at the table together when they used to crawl around its legs, and Franco came in in his chef's whites, fish pies on a polished silver platter and lifted the cloches with a 'ta-da' and no, she couldn't have ketchup with it, tut-tut, what did Lulu think this was, the bloody Wimpy, but Franco winked at her as he said it. And then the clock in the lobby chimed seven and Charlie said time to scarper and beep, beep, that was her dad outside in his Beemer and she'd better be going and another kiss, this one from Charlie at the door of Belle Hotel and Lulu knew that she was in love. S-W-A-L-K. In love with Belle Hotel. She would never forget that fish pie and parfait for as long as she lived.

Omelette Arnold Bennett

11 oz smoked finnan haddock fillets

8 eggs

2 oz butter

1 cup hollandaise sauce

1 cup béchamel sauce

3 tbsp double cream, lightly whipped

2 tbsp grated parmesan cheese

S&P

Franco sometimes made the weekly takings trip to Hookes in person. He had a facility at the local bank, but this gave him an excuse to cross his viaduct, get out of Brighton and away from Belle Hotel, for a few hours at least. Sherry with Paul Peters. Pop into the Guild for the industry gossip. Then Omelette Arnold Bennett at The Savoy. If he was lucky, Johnny would sit with him for a few minutes. The two men would trade takings and industry tittle-tattle and Franco could head back to Brighton feeling he'd done his duty for another week.

Things had been tense, at first. It had taken Johnny a while to talk to the old man. By the mid-eighties they had reached an understanding. Open-faced omelette, glass of Savoy red and Franco would stroll back down the Strand in time for the West End *Standard* and the one o'clock home.

He'd left that first visit with a recipe tucked into his wallet. It was a new one on Franco, and gave the stuttering men something to do.

'Dad, it's named after the writer, Arnold Bennett. He lived here at The Savoy while he researched *Imperial Palace*. He was so delighted with this omelette that he demanded that chefs made it for him wherever he travelled.'

'Yes, I met him. Great writer. Annoying man. Larry couldn't stand him either. We used to spit in his soup on the trains.'

Johnny, the successful front-of-house manager, had tried to tell his father how to cook an omelette.

'All right, son, just give me the basics. Omelette Arnold Bennett. I get it. Poach the fish, what if I can't get finnan? Yes, any haddock will do, they'll never know. Mix the sauces with the cream. Cover in the cheese, comforting combination fish and cheese, and grill it, ta, you got a light?'

The younger man pulled out a gold Dupont, probably a gift from that new girl of his, and flared up in his father's face. Franco strained back on the cigarette and blew a tube of blue to the chandelier.

'Righto, better be getting off. Anything you want me to pass on to Charlie? Champion. Ta, ta.'

Later that day, when Belle Hotel was quiet, Franco had hauled his Remington onto the reception desk.

He had pushed the half-moon glasses back up the slope of his nose, smiled at a passing guest, and pressed on.

The omelette went down a storm at Belle Hotel. In Franco's telling of it, Bennett over-wintered in room 14 and ate his saucy confection three times a day. The Yanks lapped it up. Larry laughed for Franco, and time and tide rolled by.

The Smithfield Knives
Receipt
Complimentary Engraving 'Born a Chef'
Paid £10 Cash
With Thanks

Charlie did well on his fourteenth birthday. Fishing rod in advance from his father, knives from Franco.

'Mind you give me a penny, Charley Farley. We don't want to sever our relationship.'

Charlie uncoiled the coarse fabric wrap and pulled out the longest knife. The steel blade glinted in the late afternoon sun.

'Wow. The Smithfield. Stainless, Sheffield. What does that mean, Grandad?'

'Best meat market, metal and city in the world, son. It's where the knives are from, the trinity that forged them. Don't forget it. I had to earn mine the hard way. Self-taught. British Rail, Fanny Craddock, Delia Smith. You, you're lucky. I'm going to get you professionally trained. And this. This is lesson one.'

Franco re-sheathed the knife, sat Charlie up on the gleaming table top and talked him, left to right, through the tools of his trade.

'Peeler, does what it says on the tin. Palette knife, spread, turn, lift. Veg knife, four-incher, chop, chop. Fork, lift and hold.' He pinged the prongs against the table side and pointed at the rest of the set in turn. 'Filleting knife, for fish: see, it bends. Boning knife, butchery, my boy. And this: your knife. The big one.'

He put down the fork and unsheathed the ten-inch blade from its pocket.

'This is your knife. Fuck the rest. Keep it as sharp as your first cut and never, ever raise it in anger. You with me? And remember, a good craftsman never blames his tools.'

Charlie watched, wide-eyed, as Franco slipped out the steel. It came with its own sharpener, and straight away Franco went to work on his knife.

'Always draw it away from you. Forty-five degrees, seven times on each side.'

Flash of steel, blade on grooved. Sound of swashbuckling. In a moment it was over. Franco handed Charlie back his knife. He took it into his hand with a mixture of fear and excitement. This was it. Charlie was entering the man's world of his father and grandfather. Part of him wanted to stay a little boy, put the knife down and go back to his toys. The other part of him glinted with excitement as he held the lethal potential that lay within his grip. His right arm trembled a little.

1 April 1988
6am

Tick-tock, tock-tick vegetable chopping going on both ends of the clock. Sacks of earth-clung matter come in the back and are brushed, peeled and cut to Franco's command. Julienne and baton. Cube and dice. Different permutations for different purposes. Franco's book ever present, Charlie getting the basics before he'll be let loose on its pages. In his first week, he'd taken the tip off a finger but Franco, always close by, grabbed the severed digit and dunked its bloody end in the pepper pot. Charlie felt a slight quiver in the old man's hand. First sign of age and a weakening of the iron constitution that the boy had ever noticed. Franco's gaze, however, was rock solid. He held Charlie under scrutiny for the longest time, as if looking for signs of fear in a fellow soldier. Charlie took Franco's look and gave it back. As good as he got. No way Charlie was going to be boo-hooing in front of Franco again.

'Now then, the first cut is the deepest. This'll sort you out. Natural antiseptic.'

The seasoned stump stopped bleeding immediately and a week later made a brief reappearance only when it flaked a piquant scab into some Jerusalem artichoke. A year of correct cutting and naming and Charlie was deemed to know his onions. Onions that were grown, along with all the other alliums, at Franco's allotment.

'That's yer leeks. Good for stocks and a greeny oniony taste in a stew. See that row there, Charley Farley, that's garlic. See the bulb poking up from the ground. I grew that from just one of last year's cloves. Magic, ain't it?'

Franco ruffled Charlie's hair and gazed out to sea. The Dieppe ferry was just pulling out of Newhaven. He'd take the boy over to Dieppe market one day soon. Get him up to speed with buying what's fresh from the market. Today's task was herbs and spices. Bit of time in the fresh air at the allotment, then back to the kitchen for a bit of spice school before service.

'I love it up here, Charlie, grow all sorts of stuff you can't get in Brighton. Let's have a look round the herb garden. Got a lot of these as seeds from my pals at the Guild. They can't believe I can grow them down here on the Sussex Riviera. Now pay attention, lad, and take a nibble of each leaf I pass yer.'

Charlie nodded and prepared to accept each offering as it came.

'Now herbs are different from vegetables in that they are used to provide flavour rather than substance. Apart from, say, flat leaf parsley in Middle Eastern cuisine. Ignore that, we'll cross that bridge when we get to it. So, where was I, herbs, right. Flavour rather than substance. Hey, Charlie! Got that? Good. Righto, let's start with something you'll know from Sunday lamb. Two herbs. See if you can name 'em, Charley Farley. There's a farthing, sorry, ten pence, in it if you can. Now close your eyes.'

Charlie could hear the snapping sounds of Franco gathering the two herbs for his first test. His nostrils flared to woody aromatic sweetness and bitter bright jag of torn leaf.

'That's easy, Grandad. Rosemary and mint. Rosemary for roasting the lamb, mint for the sauce.'

'Good lad. What goes with the mint to make it a sauce, then?'

'Vinegar.'

'What vinegar?'

'Erm, malt.'

'Yes. Good man. So now we'll move onto some trickier ones. I'm going to sing a few to give you a clue and you guess which one's which. Parsley, sage, rosemary and thyme. Keep yer eyes shut. You already know the rosemary, so that's a help. Do you remember the sage leaf from that pork casserole the other day? Come on, look sharp. We'll do the spices when we get back to the kitchen. Spices. Now they're harder to grow. Seed, fruit, root, bark. Thing is, I don't label the jars. No chef ever does. First thing you've got to know before you get let loose in a professional kitchen is your cinnamon from yer star anise.'

The feeling of pride at passing Franco's tests, first base camp on the long ascent to becoming a chef, made Charlie's heart sing. It even lifted the dull throb he often felt, sort of homesick but not really knowing why. Belle Hotel was Charlie's home, always had been. It was where he lived with his mum and grandad. But with his dad gone, Charlie's empty feeling was best filled with work. The years it'd take to be what it took to lift Franco's apron from the back of the kitchen door and stand tall at the pass as a chef, a man, was a trek Charlie and Franco felt worth taking. Not that it didn't hurt when the old man bawled him out. Charlie had to toughen up, Franco as much as said so, no more blubbing behind the kitchen door like the time he'd forgotten his manners with Lulu and the menu. Man-up, Franco had said. You may be Johnny's son, but you're my grandson and while I wear the apron around here you'll do things my way. That or you can sod off to London and go and live with him at The Savoy. Charlie went to correct his grandfather – he doesn't live at The Savoy, he lives at the Barbican – but Franco made to give him a clip round the ear, which soon shut cheeky Charlie up. Franco laid the hand that had been raised in anger on Charlie's broadening shoulders. He fixed Charlie with the steel gaze.

'Righto, lad, I'm sending you out to learn two trades. Fish and meat. You've been working like a dog for a reason. There is a plan behind all this, Charlie. When you're ready to cook, I'll be ready to tell you what the plan is. You'll come back to me ready to cook, and that's a promise.'

Charlie's fifteenth year flashed by in a scaly sea-stink of Saturdays. Apprenticed to N. Sinker, fish-face and -monger to Brighton's catering trade, Charlie raced late out of the twitten, his wrap of knives spearing the sharp south-westerly whipping in off the Channel.

Sinker, Nigel to his friends so Sinker to most, was the last in a long line of Brighton fishermen, the one who sold the boat and dragged the show a hundred yards inshore to a paint-faded arch under the prom.

Sinker still wore bright yellow boots and apron, shunning the white of his new trade in memory of his forebears. He rarely spoke, showed Charlie most of the moves in mime, and made the best fishcakes Charlie had ever tasted. Better than Franco's, and that was saying something. Summer had been pleasant enough, gazing out at the two-blue horizon, beheading and gutting cod by the boat-load.

Most of the stock now came from Newhaven. Sinker's boat was run aground with the rest of the fleet, props for posterity in Brighton's Fishing Museum. Winter was a fridge. Charlie could handle the heat, he positively thrived on it. But cold. Sinker's icy-mongers was where he learnt the meaning of cold. November was ocean-frozen crustacea, shells hard on wet, ribbed fingers.

Charlie looked out of the door of Sinker's arch, open to let in the light, and the icy sea fret. The sea was an ever-present sound against the shingle and a handy timer against each mackerel he had to trim. Each time a wave crashed on the shingle, Charlie had his timer. A wave a side and Charlie knew he'd be done to Sinker's satisfaction. The miserable monger worked deep in the rear of his cave, salty shanty laments for lost lovers and friends echoing against the dripping brick and filling Charlie with the old melancholy. Sinker had been chucked out of the Fishermen shanty singers because he couldn't bring himself to smile for the funny numbers. That grimace was putting the audience off, they'd said one night in the Belle Hotel bar, making the holidaymakers' kids cry, bad for tips, he'd have to go. Sinker had been seen that night, kicking the pier sign over in anger as he wove his way back to the hammock in his sail loft above the fish arch. Salty laments, sea frets and slithers of oily fish, fresh from the Channel. Lunch for the two-man crew whipped up on Sinker's trusty primus, finished off with a squeeze of lemon and served with crusty bread.

Sinker looked at Charlie, eyes pooling in the light of the puckering stove. He struck up a deep baritone hum. The fisherman's grace. The song of the dying seaman to his mates.

'Oh wrap me in my country's flag,
And lay me in the cold, blue sea
Let the roaring of the waves
My cold requiem be
And I shall sleep a pleasant sleep
While storms above their vigils keep.'

Amen to that, said Charlie, tucking in the moment the throaty drone had stopped. The feeling inside him as the translucent mackerel, oily, salty, warm and slippery, sailed its way down his throat on a boat of bread. So simple, but the balance Sinker intuitively struck between salt, fat, acid and heat, those exact moments on the stove, made the difference between a good mouthful of food and something sublime. Charlie did what Franco had told him to do. Watch, listen, taste. Take each morsel you are offered and make something more of yourself from it. That is the way you'll become a chef, my son. Fish, fresh from the sea. They warmed their hands a little on the last of the flame, each taking a tot of rum before going back to work, as the mid-afternoon darkness descended across the shuddering shingle of Albion Beach

Then suddenly it was spring. Sinker nodded at a well-trimmed mackerel, flung rib bones, fin and tail on to the pile of parts and let Charlie go.

'Says you'll make a bouillabaisse yet,' said Franco, with a wink, later that week. 'When you come back from your dad's we'll start you on flesh and bones. Butchery. Here, have a little nibble of this daube of beef. New dish, Provençal. French. See the way the meat is so soft you could cut it with a spoon. That's the effect of three things: time, heat and good butchery. And we know a good butcher, don't we son. I'll let Mr Brampton know you're on your way. Sharpen your knives, Charlie, this is where the fun really begins.'

Brampton's Butcher's of Kemp Town – purveyors of meat, offal and game for the Prince Regent, and boy could that old queen put back a brace or two – was little changed from its former self, as witnessed by the black-and-white photograph which hung proudly inside the door. John P. Brampton, the loud, meaty opposite of Sinker's fishy silence, made Charlie laugh while he learned. Brampton joked, burped and farted in between popping next door to his wife's cheese shop for a noggin' of Sussex Valley Blue. Brampton's was all smut, blood and muscle and heaving half-calf carcasses onto the Stilton-hued marble slab, watching where to plunge in the boning knife before tugging back with all his pre-pubescent might. Charlie liked working with meat, feeling his way with fingers and blade between the flesh, fat, bone and sinew. Learning to truss and dress, prepare the whole animal for use in his own kitchen. He felt competent and proud to be working in this way. Strong. It suited him, butchery. Charlie was there to learn how to prepare an animal as food. Brampton was sure of the need to know more.

'You are now a member of the carnal confederation of butchers. You are learning to work with meat like a butcher. You must now make love like a butcher. For the rest of the night you must enact the dark acts of carnality, a butcher's carnality. Got a girlfriend, Charlie? Yes. Go home and fuck the cream cheese out of her. Then rise in the hours before dawn smelling of carnality and unload the meat from the lorry like a butcher.'

Brampton thumped a shocked Charlie on the arm. He was still a virgin, but not about to tell that to the bawdy butcher. He ran home to tell Franco.

Franco didn't mind.

'Take no notice of him, he's all piss and wind.'

'But, Franco, he says—'

'Enough.'

Enough. Charlie had done enough of that particular ascent. He'd scaled the arts of fishmongery and being a butcher. All was going according to Franco's plan. His plan to win Belle Hotel a Michelin star and him a gold lapel pin from the Guild to stick in his best suit. Charlie felt proud to be doing well in his grandfather's education. So well that he'd been perhaps neglecting his school work.

'O levels,' Franco had nearly spat out his coffee, 'O levels? D'you think I got where I am because of O levels? Let me let you into a little secret, son.'

Franco took Charlie's chin in his cup-warmed hand.

'The thing we're working towards doesn't begin with an "O". Oh, no. The thing we're working towards begins with an "M". Sit, down, we've time before service. Janet, love, fetch me another coffee would you sweetheart and a Coke for the boy. Righto, before I let you loose on my book it's time to tell you about the masterplan.'

Brighton Secondary Modern
School Report
Pupil: Charlie Sheridan
Mock Exam Results:

English: GCSE Fail
Maths: GCSE Fail
Geography: GCSE Fail
History: GCSE Fail
R.E.: GCSE Fail
Home Economics: GCSE Level Grade A
Head Teacher's Comments:
Charlie is welcome to leave school now and return for his Home Economics GCSE Examination. I would like to say it has been a pleasure having Charlie at the school. I would like to say this, but I can't. We wish him well in his chosen career.
R.S. Caner, MA B.Ed

Eggs Benedict was the first recipe Franco ever taught Charlie. At sixteen, out of school uniform, and into a pair of the absent chef's trousers. They'd got sixty for brunch and double that for dinner. Franco was calm. High white hat, pencil in rim; pressed check slacks. He took the book down from its shelf above the hotplate and fixed his grandson with his gaze.

'Charlie. Are you ready?'

He nodded. Franco would never throw a pan at Charlie. Franco, who'd thrown that pan at Johnny. Franco who was standing there fathering Charlie, doing Johnny's job, when Johnny had not been up to the job in the first place. According to Franco. Charlie kept his gaze on his grandfather, pushing the memory of the day his father left from his mind. The feeling of loss inside him being slowly filled up by Franco's little tastes, flavours and notes on presentation. He was starting to love it, really love it, and want to be good. Good like Grandad.

'The cause of hollandaise sauce curdling is either because the butter has been added too quickly or because of excess heat, which will cause the albumen in the eggs to harden, shrink and separate from the liquid.'

The waiters hung back from the pass, they knew to let chef finish.

'If it does curdle, place a teaspoon of boiling water in a clean number two' – he swung down a copper-bottomed pan from behind Charlie – 'and G-R-A-D-U-A-L-L-Y whisk in the sauce. Got that?'

Franco had his back to the waiting staff. All chefs in his sightline were heads down and ready. Franco gave Charlie a wink and turned to face the hotplate.

'Shall we begin?'

You can't keep a sauce this unstable during service. Any chef worth his salt knows this. It has got to be stabilised with a quart of béchamel. Béchamel is another page out of Franco's book, another lesson for Charlie. Another part of the masterplan...

The Masterplan
1) *The Basics*
2) *Fish & Meat*
3) *Recipes from Franco's book*
4) *Catering College*
5) *Switzerland*
6) *London*
7) *Belle Hotel*
8) *Michelin star*
9) *Keep the bloody thing*
10) *Make your old man proud*

1 September 1991
9am

Tick-tock. Time for Brighton Catering College, two years of pressure-free training, with a sweet stint in Switzerland for afters.

The knife wrap, carrot-, cod- and kidney-spattered, was meant to live in Charlie's locker at college. It didn't stay put for long.

'Henry's gone sick. Bastard. Can you…?'

'Just an hour or so, come on, do your old man a favour, Belle Hotel needs you, just till we break the back of it… good lad. Have a taste of this, too. Pondicherry Poulet Rouge. New dish. Something special about it, Charlie Farley. Something unusual in Indian cuisine. Because of the French influence. Vinegar, lad, just a tablespoon for this whole vat. But can you taste the sour edge it gives the dish against that heat and spicy sweetness? Goodness gracious me, this curry ain't half brilliant, eh, Charlie? Got the recipe off Fizal at the newsagent's just now. He got it off his mother-in-law who'd been brought up in Pondicherry and had a French cook who'd adapted the curries to suit colonial palates.'

Aged seventeen, Charlie had his head in the cookbook canon and his hands in Franco's washing-up.

*

It didn't matter that he'd left school the proud holder of one GCSE in Home Ec. Franco had a masterplan and, now, Charlie did too. No amount of washing-up was going to put him off. He and Franco had their plan.

'The masterplan is this: Michelin star. If you don't know what it means to win one I'll tell you, Charlie Farley. The French did a guide for their motorists before the war. If a place had got a star, it was worth a detour. Now then, the Roux brothers in London have got them. You remember Albert and Michel and Albert's son, Michel Jr, don't you? Friends of mine from the Guild. Now then, the Rouxs have got stars, but they don't count because, well, they're frogs, aren't they. One of their own. But you, you are going to win Belle Hotel and Brighton a star. Give folks a reason to make a detour. I'll never win one now. Too bloody old and set in my ways. Self-taught, too, they don't like that. But you, you're young and talented and we've got a plan. Stick to it and, mark my words, we'll have a star over our door before I'm dead and buried.'

Charlie's heart swelled. Like the masterplan made him feel, for the first time since his dad had left, strong, no room for the dull ache. Each day that went by, little by little, his kitchen confidence growing. Like what Franco was saying might come true. Charlie would win a star.

Sweet seventeen, Charlie and Lulu, bedroom confident. Another drowsy June afternoon in a single bed. Charlie's room at Belle Hotel this time. Best chance of being left to their own devices. Miles Davis on. Little else. Three years older and, as of two minutes ago, wiser.

'Lu, that was mega. I feel. I dunno, just want to hold you. Love you, Lu.'

Lulu let him take her again in his arms.

'Charlie. I love you, too. I'm glad we waited. It just felt… right today. You sure it didn't split?'

'No, all good. Are you okay?'

'Yes, a little… but that was lovely. And to do it here. Just like we planned.'

Charlie stroked Lulu on the shoulder. He felt the anxiety lift. That was it. They'd done it. He was a man now. This wasn't part of Franco's masterplan, but it was part of his and Lu's special pact.

'So now what, Charlie Sheridan?'

'We live here at Belle Hotel together. You're front of house and I'm in the kitchen. Just like we used to play when we were kids.'

'I've got to go to uni first. Get a degree. I don't want to be just a hotel manager.'

'Ohh, get you.' Charlie slapped her bare bum. 'La-di-da.'

'Ow! That's not fair. We agreed it. Charlie. Do we need to go through it again?'

'Yes please, lover girl.'

'Stupid, I mean the pact.'

'Okay, Lu. Here we go… I'm going off to learn the craft in Europe and you, you're going to university.'

'And…'

'And we'll be faithful to one another. That's why we just… so that we can be together like this before we have to be apart.'

'Before that,' Lulu squeezed him tight, 'yes. I wonder what we'll be saying to one another after making love in, say, ten years' time?'

'Something like, did you remember to turn the lights off in the bar? Something romantic like that.'

Lulu shoved Charlie away and laughed. He tickled her and she laughed some more. Then he softened his touch, swirling his fingertips across her goose bumping flesh and slowly, tenderly, they began to make love for a second time.

Brighton Catering College
Professional Chef Diploma
Charlie Sheridan
DISTINCTION
Chef-Lecturer's Special Award for Progress

Last Formal Day at Catering College

'Students, you leave us with the technical skills and repertoire know-how.'

The chef-lecturer scanned the room. Charlie felt his gaze land and settle on him.

'Do you remember the day we made bouillabaisse? The aroma, the balance of flavour, size and variety of fish?'

Charlie could taste that rich fish dish, as if he'd just spooned it into his mouth.

'Remember me the next time you encounter this dish. What I taught you and what you will teach yourself the next time you taste it. The next time you prepare it.'

Charlie could feel the weight of the simmering joy as he spun his imaginary ladle around the giant pan, fishing for the perfect portion to pour into the warmed bowl.

'Know now that those of you who are serious about our profession will revise this dish, perfect it until it becomes your bouillabaisse. The one you want to be known for.'

Charlie Sheridan's bouillabaisse, thought Charlie, nice.

'And now, students, before we release you into the world of professional catering for your period of training, your *stage*, think on all of the wonderful dishes from the repertoire that we have prepared together here. Each of these dishes will be tasted, touched and refined by any of you who really want to elevate yourselves from mere cooks into, what, students?'

'CHEFS!'

March–September 1991

Tick-tock Swiss clock. Switzerland, Suisse, Sweige, or whatever the Italians and Krauts sprecht. Six months free from Belle Hotel. Basel Bahnhof Buffet. Finest railway station catering operation in all of Europe, so Franco said. Two enormous brasseries that fed folk onto their trains and a street-facing Michelin-starred restaurant, L'Escargot for Basel's best.

Charlie flew to Basel, Bale, Basle with two of the prettiest girls on his course. He'd beaten a scrawny chef named Graeme to get the place. Graeme had all the techniques, they'd said, but none of Charlie's basic gift for flavour. What luck, months and months of fun for the three of them, and the girls understood they might have to share him. Sassy, aspirational and way out of his league, they soon took up with the restaurant manager and sous chef, while Charlie got lumbered with Tom, a sardonic, second-generation Irish Manc from the hotel school in Shannon. Together they played merry hell in the kitchen that spilled out into the bars after hours. Goading the chef who was trying to mentor them and trying it on with the barmaids were all part of the learning experience, or so they told themselves.

Charlie sat at the back of the bier keller, waiting for Tom to finish the sack of potatoes he'd been given to turn as punishment. He'd bought the postcard at the Bahnhof cabin with the change from forty Marlborough Red. Now he sat chewing his pen in the wood-panelled heat of a mid-European summer night and wondered what to write.

Franco Sheridan, Belle Hotel, Brighton
Rösti
Potato
Onion
Garlic
Chives
Butter
Peel and grate the potato. Mix with chopped onion, garlic and chives. Fry off in butter until golden brown. Ciao, Charlie!

'Good idea,' Franco muttered to himself as he clasped the postcard into his book. 'Good idea, Charlie.'

Franco had taught Charlie about the joys of a crispy topping way back, how it added a delicious taste sensation to food. Every culture had their own version. For the Spanish, it was the socarrat crispy rice at the bottom of the paella pan. This'd be it for ze Swiss.

So, Belle Hotel became famous for its rösti. The bar did a roaring trade with eggs, cheese and bacon for brunch.

Roger and Lulu had one each the Saturday her A level results came out. It was meant to be a celebratory lunch in the restaurant, but the Ds dictated a downgrade to the rather more shabby surroundings of the Belle Hotel bar.

'Days like these I wish your mother was still with us. She'd know what to do.'

'Dad, you always say that. She'd not know what to do. One, because she's dead and, two, because nobody's died. I just flunked my exams.'

'And failed to get your university place. My God, what have I been working for all these years. What do you want to be, a bloody carpet fitter?'

'Well, it did you all right. But, no, I don't want to be a carpet fitter, like my knees too much for that. I want to go into catering.'

'You what and end up a, oh, thank you, Janet. They look lovely. How's Charlie getting on in, where was it, Switzerland, yes? Lulu's not heard from him since he left, have you, sweets?'

Janet gave as little away as she possibly could, never remembering whether Lu and Charlie were on or off at any given moment. They'd certainly had a loud send-off the night before he left. Janet'd slept with the pillow over her head. Though whether they were rowing or the other 'it' was hard to tell. She backed away from the awkward exchange and went back to her lager tap.

Once Roger had scoffed his rösti, he soon saw sense in the idea and, after the three of them had a quick chat with Franco at the kitchen door, Lulu's future was sealed with a sweaty handshake. Lulu grinned all the way down Ship Street.

'Don't think I have forgiven you for failing your exams. You'd better make this Belle Hotel thing work, or you can go back and re-take them. Okay?'

'Yes, Dad. Okay.' And she squeezed his hand.

Later, in her room, Lulu looked at the postcard from Charlie. Three words, typical. Loads of kisses, though, under 'Auf Wiedersehen, Pet', scrawled in Charlie's appalling handwriting. Charlie Sheridan. Why she'd put up with him for so long, Lulu did not know. Habit, she supposed, like sucking her thumb. She'd managed to kick that in the upper sixth. Maybe it was time to give Charlie the old heave-ho, too. In spite of all those promises, they'd agreed to be unofficially on an 'off' while Charlie was in Switzerland. This, technically, leaving them both free to date other people. Most of her friends were seeing guys at Sussex Uni, guys they'd picked up at the Arts Club on a Friday night. Maybe Lulu would give that a try? Not that she'd sleep with anyone willy-nilly. Charlie and her had taken until they were sixteen, and not all because of her. For all his showing off, Charlie could be quite the sensitive sort when they were alone together. Maybe he was just inexperienced? Maybe he'd come back from Switzerland having done so much shagging that he'd not want her any more? Well, sod him, Lulu was going to express herself, like Madonna sang. Isn't that what she was supposed to do at eighteen, rather than mooning around for her childhood sweetheart day in, day out?

Lulu thought about Belle Hotel. About her job. She loved the place. The way it smelt, the way it charmed, the way she felt at home. It was quick thinking of her dad to ask Franco there and then and she loved him for that. Great that Franco had gone for it, too. Imagine Charlie's face when he found out. No, don't imagine Charlie's stupid face. Lulu got off her bed, put the postcard in the wastepaper basket and went off to call her mate about going to Sussex Arts Club that Friday night.

*

In Switzerland, blissfully unaware that Lulu had got herself a job with Franco, Charlie was having his first experience of split shifts, the beginning of a lifetime of up at six, nap for a couple of hours in the afternoon and back twelve hours after he started. Bar by midnight, if he was lucky. Bed, sometimes, sometimes not. Best thing about this industrial-sized operation, thirty chefs on shift at any one time, was fresh whites before every service. Charlie met Tom by his locker and together they hatched a plan.

'Look, it's festival time. The kitchen is gonna be crazy. How bad do you think we'll have to piss them off before they kick us out?'

'I dunno, man' – his accent was Dublin via Didsbury – 'I'm up for the craic anyhow. Fair play to us if we pull it off.'

'Cool, what we gonna do then, Tom?'

'Shafheitel?'

'Shafheitel.'

Oldest chef in the kitchen and a rumoured Nazi sympathiser during the war, no mean feat in a neutral country, Shafheitel was as mad and as bad as they came. Raging at the *stagiaires*, students, *estudentes* all day long was, Shafheitel felt, his duty. Shafheitel was in charge of sauces and stews. A lowly position, yet one that suited his personality well.

'Yo, yo, *Stagiaires, alles gleich, gottverdammt, wo ist mein Salz?*'

Charlie and Tom took great pleasure in goading the beast of a man, moving small but important objects the moment he returned with a simmering pan. Jamming his mixer with spoons, that sort of thing. The low-level attrition that was hard to prove but built up a handy store of suppressed rage. Suppressed rage that was very ready to release when you needed it.

Tom winked at Charlie, in a watch-this kind of way. Shafheitel was lumbering out of the chiller with his plat-du-jour trolley loaded with shallow trays of indeterminate stew. So loaded was that trolley that the ageing chef was unable to see the *stagiaire*, student, *estudente* lock a wheel with a discreet tip of his toe. With all the grace of a holed liner, the trolley listed forward on its frozen wheel, losing just enough balance to slide out plat-du-jour all over the floor.

Shafheitel exploded, once he'd stopped trying to catch the chunks of mutton with his bare hands. Head chef only stepped in when Shafheitel started throwing portions, *portiones*, *portzion* at Tom and Charlie.

'*Genug, Koch, genug. Man muss nicht.*'

The rösti-flipping subordinates shuddered beneath their gravy stained whites. The war was won. What else could Chef do?

He took the two boys into his office, a raised glass box with a view of the pass, shut the door and pretended to read them the riot act. As with most cultured Swiss, his English was perfect.

'Right, you two idiots. You win. The first time, I accept was an accident. The second time, a coincidence. This third time, impossible to believe you have not just been goading my most loyal and longest-serving chef all along. That is not only cruel, it is bad for business. I cannot have you here during the festival. Ten days' paid leave. You tell no one. Not your fellow *stagiaires*, Herr Director, anyone within a hundred kilometres of this operation. No one. Do I make myself clear? Now get out. I don't want to see you two again until the festival is over. I'm letting you off lightly. Your actions were unacceptable in a professional kitchen. Even towards... him. Unacceptable and funny. So, go... go!'

The two friends ran shrieking through the locker room, swinging filthy whites into the laundry bin and pulling on jeans and tees that were barely cleaner. Charlie couldn't believe his luck. Ten fucking days. To do what? Luckily, Tom had a plan. And a guitar.

'Côte d'Azur, man. How many francs can you lay your hands on? I'll go get me axe. You wanna come back to the flat, or shall I grab your passport for you?'

Charlie and Tom went back to the accommodation they shared with the twenty other *stagiaires* employed by the Bahnhof. They banged the doors to their rooms and ran yodelling down the echoing concrete stairwell, setting off shouts and groans from their fellow chefs and waiters as they tried to catch up on their sleep between shifts.

They had francs, but not enough for the sleeper.

'Hitch, roite, it's easy, man, we do it all the time in Ireland.'

Pitch black, warm night, still giggling, half-pissed, holding up a ragged piece of cardboard.

'Lyon, it'll get us halfway there, I had a look on the map. Best chance of catching the Paris traffic if we break it there.'

A black Opal coupe pulled up.

'Fook, a Manta. Here we go, here we go, here we *go*.'

The car's driver wanted to get out of Switzerland quick, something about a bit of pharmaceutical business. Dutch, all the dodgy ones are, a cassette deck full of Dire Straits and a duty-free allowance worth of Marlborough, the three amigos sped across the border and on down, down into the hot Gallic night.

Tom sat up front and talked chord progressions with Wiki, 'call me Wiki, man.' Charlie shared the cramped back with Tom's guitar and the two sailors' hats they had bought at the station gift shop before setting off for the autostrassen and freedom. Ten days, Charlie could barely believe it. Best of all, nobody knew. Franco, his mum, Lulu, college, Belle Hotel… A recent reading of *On the Road*, the first and last novel of his teens, gave the Manta-fuelled flight south an added sense of adventure. Windows down, the smoke of their skunk coiled round the sounds of Dire Straits' "Romeo and Juliet" from the radio's tape deck.

At four the Manta pulled onto the hard shoulder, 160kph to 0, fast enough to jerk the sleeping beats awake. Wiki waved a friendship-braceleted arm and sped off.

'Fuck, what time is it?'

'Dunno, Oi left me watch in me locker.'

Tom picked up his guitar and strummed B7, Em, G.

Charlie watched his fingers morph the chords in awe, not just at the golden light striking taut silver wire but at the fact that he'd never, ever be able to do that. At that moment he was in love with Tom, in love with his talent, in love with making music. Together.

Tom put down the guitar and shivered.

'Fook, I wish I'd brought me jacket.'

Wiki had dropped them under a well-lit AIX-EN-PROVENCE sign. He was obviously less stoned than they were, what was it about Dutch skunk? Provence, Charlie recognised, even through the fug. He could conjure up a memory of that taste of Franco's daube of beef Provençal as though he had it in his mouth at that very moment. Charlie felt a tingle of joy at the knowledge that he had travelled through the night to the source of that joyous wine- and herb-infused cheap cut of beef cooked languidly. He was a taste tourist. Barrelling through the night towards the tastes of his past and possibly his future. What better way could a Michelin star wannabe get to what they were looking for?

'What do we do now, Tom?'

'You got that pen and board?'

'Yeah, in my back pocket.'

Tom jerked his thumb up at the sign.

'Breakfast in Aix, wherever the fuck that is.'

The first four wheels to pass stopped. A baker's truck, loaded with warm baguettes, its floury driver shifted his dog and, amid loud whines of protest they jumped in.

A smattering of kitchen French got them by, that and the word 'café'. The baker nodded in understanding and jerked a thumb back at his crusty cargo.

'Cool, he's gonna take us wherever that lot is going. Oi'll be hopin' for some jam and coffee to go with it. How much cash you got?'

'Fifty francs.'

'Well, Oi'm broke. That should get us breakfast. We'll have to sing for us supper. Oi hope the good folk of Aix loike Simon and Garfunkel.'

They drove down an elm-lined avenue and into town. It was still early, shutters were going up, birds were about the only ones going about their business. They jumped down at the baker's first stop. Only one of *Les Deux Garçons* appeared to be up and about, but the place looked open enough. Tom and Charlie helped the baker with his baskets, nearly half his load for this place, must be a busy joint. They had a face, hands and elbows wash at the stone and copper fountain in the middle of the boulevard and took a table for breakfast.

Warm bread, tart jam and robust coffee soon cleared their heads. The sun crept around the ancient Roman corner, spreading a buttery yellow light down the boulevard.

Their bill came to fifty francs exactly, with a tip for Garçon. They were now broke.

'Roite, let's fix our pitch.'

'You've done this before, haven't you.'

'Galway, Cork, Dundalk, and ooh, Lisdoonvarna.'

More chords, then a Christy Moore song that Charlie came to remember as the anthem of their ten days on the road.

Tom explained the drill. He'd play and sing – sounded good so far – Charlie was to join in on the hand claps and la, la, la's.

'But when Oi tip you the wink, take the hat round quick and I'll blast 'em with an encore.'

Nervous at first, but with his confidence building as the notes started to fill his seafarer's cap, Charlie was a falsetto franc extractor by lunchtime.

'… and you're a hootchi, cootchi woooomaaan, toooooo. Roite, how much we got?'

'Just over two hundred francs.'

'Jeez, Oi'm famished. Is that enough?'

*

Menu du Jour. Four courses. A simple slice of terrine de foie gras outlined with Madeira jelly. Daube of beef Provençal with the creamiest mashed potato Charlie had ever tasted. Tarte au citron, sugared zest over flaky pastry. Three cheeses – hard, blue, soft – with a couple of slices of clarty raisin bread. Heaven. So this was what Franco meant when he said brasserie. Charlie got it, now.

Tom polished off the last of the rosé and ordered a couple of balloons of brandy to go with their coffee.

'I dunno about you, but I'm whacked. Oi'm gonna find a shady spot for a little siesta.'

They slept under a cluster of trees by some empty petanque gravel until it was time to earn the beer they needed to get them through the night.

Dusk fell and with it came a promenade of shoulder-slung jumpers and well-cut slacks, couples out for dinner, *garçons* mobyletting in for a pastis and gangs of *hommes* and *filles* fresh from the *lycée*.

They were getting to know their act. Tom had ten songs, Charlie knew most of the choruses and did a little dance while he went round with his hat. Captive audiences sat at tables, sipping Evian as they dipped into monogrammed pockets.

When darkness fell, the festoon lighting flickered into life. Charlie felt like ringmaster at an exotic circus, with the diners as his audience and Tom as his lyrical lion. Food, wine, warmth, music… this was the life.

They slept in their empty ballpark and rose early for ablutions at the fountain, then breakfast with the boys. Day two of ten and Charlie had already let go of time. Hand to guitar string to cap to mouth. Rest and repeat.

They busked all the next morning, with less success than before but enough for two second-class train tickets to Marseille and a fetching bomber jacket for Tom, who had shivered in the small hours. The train journey was fast, less than half an hour, they slept all the way.

Coming out of Gare St-Charles, the familiar sound of seagulls reminded Charlie of Belle Hotel. Home and Mum and Franco. Home and Lulu. They'd argued on that last night and nearly wasted it. Clinging to one another in the final hours. Lulu. Charlie wondered what she'd be doing right now? He shook his head as if to forget, and pointed towards the dipping sun.

'The port must be this way. Come on, I'm starving.'

Tom, his low blood sugar making him snappy when woken, took a while to be coaxed down to the water and longer to get strumming. Charlie wanted two shifts out of them before bed, one for food and booze that night, the other to give them the morning off and a chance to sightsee before setting out for the next town.

A rough edged, salty crowd, the Marseillaise gave generously, albeit in smaller denominations than the Aixois. Charlie wowed the crowds with more of his mad dancing. Some of the fishermen joined in, until their drunken playfulness turned to aggression.

'Come on, Tom, I've had enough. Let's go eat.'

Bouillabaisse at L'Épuisette looked like the dish to die for here. Charlie having cooked it at college in his first term, the enthusiastic chef-lecturer talking saffron-infused aroma through glasses fogged with fish stock. And then that promise that they would find it again in their own way, as he'd said in his speech at the leaving do. That by tasting it again they may come to their own version of the dish. Charlie had imagined what that experience would be like. He'd hoped it would transcend what he'd tasted at college. And that it would be in France, naturally. But this was something else. Guillaume, the patron's son and chef apprentice, talked them through the dish. Charlie and Tom slurped the fish soup, cutting it with a pile of rouille and croutons. Next the five types of fish, fresh off the Vallon des Auffes boat, that had cooked in the soup.

'So, you son of chef too?'

'Yes, Guillaume.'

'You *comprends* what it like, *oui?*'

Charlie nodded and raised his glass of white to his Gallic double. No need for sleeping out under the stars that night with the risk of being woken by the fishermen, or worse, Guillaume wanted them to stay as his guests. Charlie, Tom and his guitar spent a peaceful night in bunks built into the eaves. Both beds had a tiny window so you could gaze out over the water. Charlie was woken briefly by the sound of the boat setting out, full moon over flaked blue, and again at dawn as the catch came in.

Morning meant pastries, a hot bath in a tiny French tub and Guillaume's top tip for buskers.

'Ed for ze Côte d'Azur.'

No charge for dinner. 'Maybe I come to ze Belle Hotel someday.'

This meant that they had enough left for first class to Cannes and a slap-up lunch on the train.

A postcard from Marseille
Bouillabaisse a L'Épuisette, is all about the saffron and the
rouille. Bouillabaisse without rouille is like Marseille without
sunshine. Or Charlie without any legover.
3 tbsp water
¾ cup course baguette breadcrumbs
3 garlic cloves
½ teaspoon coarse sea salt
½ teaspoon cayenne
3 tbsp extra-virgin olive oil (you can get it from the
cash'n'carry)
À bientôt!
Charlie
p.s. love to Mum

Franco read the postcard out to Janet and Lulu before service, omitting the legover bit in the interests of decency. Lulu was shaping up well under Franco's watchful gaze. This was what Franco had hoped for, all those years ago when he'd seen Charlie and Lulu playing chef and restaurant manager. Now that she was working for him, Franco was determined to show Lulu everything he knew about the art of hospitality. Nothing Lulu did, from silver service to the replacing of a dropped napkin, escaped Franco's gaze.

Lulu was under some other watchful gazes, Franco had noticed. Charlie could barely expect her to be a nun when he was away. All the staff were at it. What about that young chambermaid who conceived her first with his sous chef in the linen cupboard? And on a Saturday, changeover day, too, in the height of summer. Hats off to the buggers for finding the time.

Lulu feigned disinterest at Charlie's soup wisdom. Screw him, she was having a blast in Brighton. Sure, Franco was a bit of a taskmaster, but she was learning heaps. Certainly beat having a gap year, or whatever excuse for work experience Charlie was having gadding about in the sun. She'd got herself a good thing going with Massimo; well, if Franco was going to dangle delicious Italian waiters in front of her on a daily basis, what's a girl to do but take a bite? Janet had spotted something going on between Lulu and Massimo and tipped her the nod on the sly. What was good for the goose was good for the gander. And, anyway, she was in love with Belle Hotel, not Massimo, or Charlie, come to think of it. Lulu had fallen head over heels with Belle Hotel and at eighteen was sure she wanted to spend the rest of her working life within its four walls. She could see this better than Charlie could. His determination to follow Franco's masterplan was matched in intensity by her own plan to be the queen bee of Belle Hotel. Franco seemed to be helping her with this, too. Taking time to show her how to do a Dover Sole at the table the proper way.

'Watch me, Lu. Then you do it. Spoon and fork, the old-school way. Fish knife if you get in a spot of bother. Ask the punter to lend you theirs. Adds to the theatre of it. Now then. What say we share this delicious dish before they start pitching up for their dinner?'

Franco gave her the secret ingredient of the Belle Hotel Café de Paris sauce, so that she could whisper it to preferred guests and so build her own network of loyal customers. Lulu liked working for Franco, he was a class act. Which was more than she could say for her dad. Roger, for his part, came and spent his nouveau riches as often as Lulu would let him.

'Daaad, don't tuck your napkin in your shirt, it's naff. Here, let me lay it on your lap. There. Now you look proper.'

In Cannes, Charlie and Tom blearily busked the Croisette for the afternoon, vowing to stay sober until they had made their pay next time, then it was siesta on a couple of benches and more songs for supper before early to bed in a clearing on the road out of town.

The next morning, bust once more, they hitched to Monte Carlo, took up a winning spot outside the Casino, then blew the lot on blackjack and cocktails, in tuxedos borrowed from concierge. Broke again before sundown.

Tom wanted to busk by the boats, so they set up shop on the jetty with some of the biggest gin palaces Charlie had ever seen. Made Roger's boat look like a dinghy. They played for over an hour without a single donation, then as if by magic an Arabian princess descended from *Montélimar II* and dropped a thousand-franc note into their hat.

She stayed and chatted a while – Charlie guessed the three of them were all about the same age.

'I wish I had your freedom.' Princess gestured up at two black-clad bodyguards keeping them within gunshot.

'I wish I had your boat.'

Charlie thought for a moment that their Marseille luck would hold up on them, but the invitation to come aboard was withheld.

'My father is up there. If he even knew I was talking to you…'

With that, the princess salaamed and jetted back up the

gangplank. Charlie grinned, rubbed the big note between thumb and forefinger and set off for the bar.

They eked out their last desultory days, bust again, in mellow Menton. The honey-hued border town took them into its bosom, paying when they played and allowing them to slip unnoticed over the border into Italy for a bowl of pesto-flecked pasta when they'd had their fill of crêpes. On their last night – Tom had been keeping count – someone laid on a farewell fiesta. They sat hidden in their cliff-top cave and watched the firework frenzy colour the sky goodbye.

'Oi'm the happiest I've ever been. This is it, Charlie. Music is my ting. Fuck cooking. I'm gonna be a star. Next toime I come to the Côte d'Azur, it'll be on a fookin rock 'n' roll tour bus.'

'I believe you, Tom. I'll come and do the catering for your aftershow party. If you can afford me with my Michelin star by then.'

The Nice sleeper to Paris and a quick gig under the Tour d'Eiffel saw Tom and Charlie back at Basel Bahnhof Buffet in time for evening service, as agreed.

They changed out of road weary jeans and tees into starched chef's whites. Nothing, and everything, had changed. The trip took Charlie out of the closed world of catering and shook the straitjacket of meal service from him. He'd tasted freedom, loved it and yet knew his duty: his birthright was to continue on his quest.

Chef saw the two boys re-enter his domain. He pointed at Charlie and flicked the finger back towards his serious face.

'Welcome back, Herr Sheridan, I trust you enjoyed your vacation?'

The sun-tanned face and carefree grin answered him. Yes, *oui, ya*.

'So, it is time to take things seriously. Your friend, Tom, he will see out his time frying rösti. For you I have other plans. You are going to L'Escargot.'

Fucking hell, was this Franco's fiddling? The Michelin-starred, street-facing superstar of the operation. He'd seen a few of the chefs from L'Escargot in the locker room, they made Shafheitel look sane.

'L'Escargot. Yes, Chef. Thanks, *merci, greutzi*. Shit.'

Charlie served out his last four months in flame. He barely saw Tom, just a quick beer before a weary begging bed. Ten days of freedom from food, ten days. Then the focus.

The focus. All work and no play. Sleep, cook, drink, don't sleep, cook, cook, cook. Sleep, dream about cooking, wake, cook, cook, drink, cook…

The skills. The skills that Michelin-starred joint transmuted to Charlie daily. He'd seen nothing like it. Nothing to that interstellar standard. Sure, Franco knew his way around a lobster. He'd been self-taught by the best: Delia and Fanny. The sous chef Charlie was apprenticed to at L'Escargot spoke no English and Charlie had little French beyond *'oui*, Chef' and the most basic of culinary terms, but what passed from the six senses of that man was the magic that elevated Charlie from a cook to a chef.

Charlie watched sous chef handle the still-live lobster with such tenderness as he sacrificially lowered it into the simmering bouillon. He lowered the lid onto the top of the pot and then leant down so that his ear was close to the steam emitting from between the two.

'Pas de sel dans le bouillon. Seulement minéral végétal. Ècoute, Charlie, écoute.' Chef gently tugged Charlie towards the simmering pot. *'Pap, pap, pah.'*

He mouthed the sound of the lobster gently poaching in the liquor while tapping out the seconds with his clog.

Charlie watched, transfixed. He knew the bouillon came from the central kitchen. Charlie had made it himself enough times that summer, the giant pot needing a small step ladder to enable one to give it its hourly stir. L'Escargot got all its basic stocks and sauces sent down in the dumb waiter from the enormous central kitchen above. It was the alchemic things they did to those basic stocks and sauces that made them Michelin star. More often than not, it was a case of doing less than was done in the mass catering kitchen above. Add less, season less, listen to the food, smell it, taste frequently, make every cut of the knife matter.

Sous chef lifted the lobster out of its poaching liquor and shook it gently so that its exoskeleton gave off a staccato rattle. He then laid it so very gently upon the chopping board, lifted his largest knife away from the magnetic strip before him, crossed himself, then located that same pattern on the cusp of the lobster's carapace and drove the point home until it bit through shell on both sides before pulling it out, one swift sword in the stone motion, before plunging swiftly back in at an exact ninety-degree angle.

Charlie watched his mentor compete the rest of the task in silence. So different, so very different from the way that Sinker and Franco went about it. Something reverent and artistic in his touch compared to their workmanlike stabs. In moments, Chef had the tail meat out from both sides of the lengthways-split lobster. Next, he executed a flawless crack on the claw using the middle part of the knife's edge. Leaving the blade in the cut he twisted sharply in both directions, mimicking the sharp snapping sound with a snap of his lips. The shell around the claw meat snapped cleanly and he prised the flesh away in an undamaged single piece.

Not everything in the hot, cramped kitchen of L'Escargot came away undamaged. Charlie took his fair share of beatings from that sensitive sous chef. Little jabs with the tip of his knife when Charlie messed up on an order. The scorching flat of a palette knife across the back of the hand when he'd put his hands on the clean surface of the pass the moment after sous chef had mimed not to. Little acts of violence that, Charlie felt, helped embed the generations-old skills and long-held codes of a Michelin-starred kitchen brigade. Franco just threw pans. These guys took their violence as seriously as they took their food. Charlie loved every single fucking bit of it. The simmering anger that they barely kept a lid on. The way they urged one another on to greatness. The slap on the back when they got the plates out. The stab in the back when they fell short. It intoxicated Charlie like Wiki's skunk.

11 September 1992
4pm

Soon enough, summer ended and Charlie had to go back to England for a two-week stint at Le Gavroche, arranged by Franco as a little welcome-home surprise, no, don't bother to unpack, you're on the next Victoria train. Albert Roux's driver is picking you up and you're going to work under his son Michel Roux Jr. Good luck! Charlie stood in the lobby of Belle Hotel, shivering from the cold shoulder he'd just had from Lulu, shrugged his duffel bag back on and set off for Brighton Station, stopping at Brighton Ink to get 'Born a Chef' tattooed on his right bicep, just in case it was ever in doubt.

Lulu's cold shoulder was more of a frozen shoulder. She thought she'd seen a ghost. Him, standing there smoking, gaunt, with the bag she'd given him for Christmas slung over his shoulder. She'd been messing around with Massimo in the restaurant and wouldn't put it past him to follow her out into the lobby and smack her on the bum. Lulu had heard rumours about Charlie messing around in Switzerland. Belle Hotel gossip, Franco bragging in the kitchen. But she had her own guilty secrets, too. Just over there in the restaurant. She turned on the heels of her sensible work shoes and ran to hide by the bins until he'd gone.

Lulu felt miserable. Things were going so well at Belle Hotel. She was Chef de Rang, the term they used in the trade for the person who runs a whole section of the restaurant. Damn her childish attachment to Belle Hotel. Why hadn't she taken an apprenticeship at another hotel? Her father laid the carpets all over town. Stupid move. Lulu wanted to be at least five hundred yards away from Charlie right now, along the seafront, somewhere. If the Paddy's hadn't flattened the Grand, maybe she'd have been there right now, instead of cowering by the rubbish. What Lulu needed was some way of knowing what her future held, when she was so unsure herself. With no mum to talk to and a dad whose life advice came from the thought pieces in *Playboy*, Lulu knew she'd have to take matters into her own hands.

Tick, tock. Charlie hugging Janet by Franco's striking clock. Lulu straining to hear the clicking of the lock.

She begged the rest of the afternoon off. It was, after all, strictly speaking meant to be a split shift rather than a straight through shift. Franco said that the stupid rules didn't apply for family and, hell, she was almost family and, who else was going to polish the silver before evening service. He'd let her sit, mind. He wasn't a monster. What, love, an hour to yourself? I don't think so. Oh, er, women's problems. Well, ahem, you'd better go and sort it. Be back by five, mind.

Madame Eva had the door to her arch slightly open; hopefully the sign she wasn't with anyone. Lulu had passed her seafront arch many times on her way to meet Charlie after his Saturday job at Sinker the fishmonger. She knew from something her dad had once said that her mum had been a client of Madame Eva. Half the women in Brighton had crossed Madame Eva's palm with silver at one time or another to find out what their future held.

'Hello?'

'Enter.'

Lulu pushed at the bottom half of the stable door, it caught up with the top and together they swung inwards, flooding Madame Eva's boudoir with warm September light. The spiritualist raised her chiffon-wrapped head from the velvet.

'Hello, my dear. I've been expecting you. You're Mary Hardman's little girl, aren't you? So terribly sad what happened to your mother.

She came to see me not long before she'd conceived you. Wanting to know what the future held. I had a terrible vision. And I was right. But some things you mustn't tell. And I didn't. Sit, dear, sit. No need for that. This one's on me. For your dear mother's sake. There, there, dear. Dry your eyes. You're safe here. I told your mother that she'd have a beautiful baby girl and that one day that girl would come and see me. And, well, here we are. Close the door, dear. I need the dark and all its hidden wonders to tell your fortune. Now, what is it you want to know?'

Albert's driver, Marcel, did indeed pick Charlie up, in his 2CV from the taxi rank at Victoria. Any grandson of the friend and chef to Lord Olivier was a friend to Albert.

'Ello, you. Ow iz Chef Franco?'

Marcel used his *exceptionelle* command of English profanities as the little car zoomed around Hyde Park Corner. Marcel executed a cheeky bit of French driving to nip them into Park Lane, albeit on the wrong side of the road, and into Mayfair.

They pulled up outside the legend.

'Welcome to Le Gavroche. First restaurant to be awarded three Michelin stars in ze UK. Jointly owned by my boss Albert and his brother Michel wiv ze Waterside Inn. Zo zat is about to change. Splitting ze bizness along fraternal lines. Family bizness, eh, fucking hard work.'

Charlie knew all about it. Stuff of legend. Albert and Michel opening Le Gavroche together in Chelsea six years before Franco bought Belle Hotel, with ze 'elp of some old-school British aristo lolly. Then the torture of taking it in turns every week to run the kitchen and front of house. The odd cross word later, the brothers made the move to Mayfair at about the time Maggie made it to Downing Street, some said so she could just pop round in her slippers, but you know how people talk. Classic French food such as the noble

Soufflé Suissesse, Le Caneton Gavroche and Omelette Rothschild. Rothschild being the banker who was the patron of the first celebrity chef, Carême in the 1820s. By the end of the eighties, Albert and Michel held their three stars with pride, but they were not too proud to send Marcel in the 2CV on the Kent car plane to stock up on forbidden French fruits.

Marcel leant over to crank open Charlie's door, gave him half a second to get out and then sped off.

He looked up at the giant black door.

'Psst, oy, chef.'

Michel Roux Jr. Charlie would recognise those froggy eyes anywhere.

'Down here, mate. Kitchen entrance. Front door's for paying customers.'

Charlie had heard the rumours. Roux robots, they said. Nobody spoke. Apart from Albert. When he did finally return. Michel Jr had a touch of the Johnny about him when Franco was around. Thank God I'm not Franco's son, thought Charlie.

By the end of the first week, Charlie had learnt more about the repertoire than he'd learnt in the first two decades of his life. His job was to again feed the stockpots, giant cauldrons of brown, white and fish stock, and woe betide Charlie if the bouquet garni Michel Jr had made for the fish stock found its way into the brown. Franco had drilled Charlie in tastes, flavours and presentation; L'Escargot and his travels had done much to deepen this. Le Gavroche staffroom chat was abuzz with new smaller and lighter methods of presentation. A nouvelle cuisine, if you will. And Albert wouldn't. Michel Roux Jr would, at least his own lighter interpretation of the repertoire, if he could have a crack at it.

Michel Jr has just taken over the reins from his father, Albert, as head chef of Le Gavroche, something his father had been promising him for the last two years. While he had waited, Michel Jr was allowed the privilege of running the Roux outdoor catering empire in between shifts at Le Gavroche. That and running messages between his father in London and uncle at The Waterside in Bray.

Charlie made the tiny mistake of muttering to a fellow Roux robot that the kitchen regimen at Le Gavroche was a tad menacing, what with both Michel Jr and Albert prowling at the pass. His fellow chef kindly passed this information on to Albert, who took it upon himself to arrange a day for Charlie at an establishment on Wandsworth Common.

If Charlie had bothered to read anything other than *On the Road*, he'd have had a good idea what Marcel meant when he muttered the words 'Dante's *Inferno*' as he kicked Charlie out of the passenger door of the 2CV and sped off northbound on the wrong side of the road. Charlie just assumed it was the name of a good local pub that he could relax in during his breaks. He set off down the side alley of the restaurant guided by the sound of steel and screaming.

Charlie returned from Wandsworth scarred for life with his chef's whites in tatters, the initials MPW burned onto his back and a weeping young chef called Gordon in tow. Gordon begged for a job at Le Gavroche, saying Marco had sent him and that Albert would know what to do.

Albert knew what to do. This is what the Guild was for. Marco's food was incredible. The guy was a savage. Slept at the restaurant. Slept with the diners' wives at the restaurant. All this Albert knew. He'd trained Marco, after all. This is the way of the sacred code of cooking. The chef's cabal. The reason the Guild existed. To ensure that any punter with fifty quid in their pocket could be treated like a god. Albert picked up Charlie and Gordon and set them on the road to the stars.

For his last day, Michel Jr baked Charlie a cake. It was a thing of such exquisite beauty that Charlie took his slice outside by the bins and ate every mouthful very, very slowly, savouring every molecule. Almost as slowly as he'd savoured every mouthful of Lulu.

30 September 1992
3pm

Time to make a decision. To follow her destiny and, with Charlie heading back to Belle Hotel, end the holiday romance. Lulu dumped Massimo, begged the afternoon off again from Franco and was up on the train and waiting with two deckchairs in Hyde Park in time for Charlie's split-shift break. Madame Eva had told her two things about her future. That the initials B and… F—, no wait, H, would be important in her life and that she would marry a man who wore blue and white. That was it, all Madame Eva could tell her.

The sun was out and, even though it was late September there was warmth in the air, in the soil, in the still-green leaves on the centuries-old trees.

He smelt a bit sweaty and his hair was a bit long and greasy, but now she was looking at him properly for the first time in, what, six months, Lulu knew it was for keeps. Hadn't Madame Eva as much as told her so?

'So tell me again.'

'Well. The plan is simple. I'm coming back to Belle, taking over from Franco in the kitchen, and I'm going to win Brighton its first Michelin star.'

'No, the bit about me.'

'Oh, right. We're going to live together at Belle Hotel. And you are going to run the restaurant under Franco.'

'Charlie, I—'

'It's the only way we'll ever see each other. I'm working my fucking nuts off at Gavvers. Work, sleep, work, don't sleep.'

'You old romantic, you.'

'Knock it off, Lu. Are you in?'

'Charlie,' she straddled him on the deckchair, handy as the deckchair attendant came along and Charlie only had enough cash for one. 'Charlie Sheridan. I love you. And I want to be with you at Belle Hotel for ever. Do you remember that drawing we did as kids? The one Franco kept in his book? He showed it to me last week. It's you and me at Belle Hotel. We drew it and we knew it when we were little. It's meant to be, see. I'm sure of it, I went to see Madame... Charlie? Are you listening to me?'

Silence.

'Charlie?'

'What?'

'This is the bit where you go: "Lulu Hardman, I love you and I want to be with you at Belle Hotel for ever. Will you share my split-shift break from this day forward for ever and ever until in death do we part", or something equally romantic.'

'Sorry, Lu, I was just thinking about bouquet garni.'

She digged him in his bony ribs.

'Nah, Lu, only joking. I love you and want to be with you at Belle Hotel for ever. Will you share my split-shift break AND Michelin star from this day forward? Well, we'll have to wait a bit for the Michelin star. Earn it.'

Lu took the train back in time for evening service and Charlie followed the day after. Back down the tracks to Belle Hotel to take the reins from Franco.

He saw his mum and Lulu sitting together in the bar, waved, and made his way through to the kitchen. He'd chat to Mum properly later. And he'd only seen Lulu yesterday. He was excited to talk to Franco about his time in London. About the wonderful new methods of presentation he'd seen. Stuff that'd blow the old man's head off. New flavours, too. New world and old world working as one. Charlie couldn't wait to tell the old man about something big he'd heard about in Le Gavroche staffroom. A brand-new taste. One to add to the four that Franco had drilled into Charlie from knee height. Sweet, sour, bitter, salty and now... ta-dah!... umami! Savouriness. Recognised just a few years ago by some Hawaiian Symposium as an actual fifth fucking taste! All that time, the extra dimension Franco had been handing him on spoons and passing off as his own culinary genius was simply good old-fashioned chemistry! A long-lasting, tongue-coating, mouth-watering sensation that had been living on the skin of Franco's allotment alliums all along! Maybe Charlie should keep it to himself for a bit. Not come the big I am with Grandad.

Lulu nodded at Janet and they both waved as they saw Charlie walk past the door of the bar, heading straight for the kitchen. Janet took Lulu's hands in hers. Lulu could feel them tremble slightly, though the grip was firm.

'Are you sure you want this life, Lulu? I mean, it's not too late to change your mind. Retrain. I wish I had.'

Lulu made to speak. Then changed her mind. It was as if everything was so whisked up, like the very best hollandaise, that to try and pull them apart, Charlie, Belle Hotel, Lulu, would just cause everything to curdle. Whatever hardships it would bring, and there would be hardship, she could see it in Janet's face, this was the life she was choosing.

Charlie paused a moment and gazed in through the porthole to watch Franco at work. The ache in his chest rose and became a lump in his throat. Then Charlie swallowed deeply and it was gone.

Time to face the biggest target Franco had set. It wasn't going to be an easy target. After Mayfair, Charlie understood what people meant when they said Belle Hotel was a tad shabby. Still, it was the Sheridan family's shabby and people kept coming back, so they must be doing something right. He thought about his time in Switzerland, what it had taught him in terms of craft. In London, Charlie learnt about lustre, how equally important front of house was to what went on in the kitchen. To be complete, hit his target, Charlie needed Lulu. Couldn't do it without her. It.

'One Michelin star.'

Charlie'd muttered the mantra all the way back. Victoria–Haywards Heath–Brighton clickety-click, clackety-clack.

Franco was standing at the pass. The place in the kitchen where the chefs met the front-of-house staff and an exchange took place. He ticked off the last item on his list and looked up to take Charlie in. No smoke, no sunlight, but a touch of twinkling wetness hung about old blue eyes. Franco's masterplan was reaching its final ascent. The decade he'd waited, sweating it out when the talent had skipped a generation. He'd put it all on Charlie and had backed a winner. The kid would not let him down.

'All yours, Charley Farley. Now then, I'll go and put my suit on.'

Charlie watched his grandfather hang up his apron on the door and, with a second thought, take it down and hand it to him.

'Here, this'll see you through tonight's service. Barely a splash on the bugger.'

1990s

Rock 'n' Roll Star

Hookes Bank

Franco Sheridan
Belle Hotel
Ship Street
Brighton

15 September 1993

Dear Franco,
Twenty years, who'd have thought it? Congratulations!

This note confirms your wishes to transfer Belle Hotel to your grandson Charlie and daughter-in-law Janet in the event of your death. We understand that Johnny Sheridan will not be included in the transfer of assets, as per your instructions. We are in the process of drawing up a last will and testament and suggest we peruse it over lunch at The Savoy.

I look forward to the next twenty years!
Yours,
Paul Peters

A sunny Friday. Johnny and Charlie sat opposite one another in a dank Italian at the bottom of a Barbican Tower. Johnny wore his Jaeger blue suit, Charlie his double-breasted whites. They looked, to all the world, normal. Surrounding them were the washed-up remains of the eighties, sagging shoulder pads clutching orbs of pinot grigio for moral support.

They talked about work, their only common language.

'When are you going to the States?'

'As soon as my green card comes through.'

'Oh, what about the flat?'

'Sorry, Charlie, I'm letting it to a friend.'

A friend, what friend? He'd been staying with him on his day off for nearly six months and this was the closest they were ever going to get, thought Charlie. He'd let it to someone else. Git.

Charlie stared through the breadsticks at half of him. Drawn face and hang dog eyes. Different from Franco's. He looked at his wedding band, third marriage still looking solid according to the digit. The rings had got progressively thinner with each new wife, as if uncertainty dictated their width.

'How was the meeting, Charlie?'

'Good, they are probably going to have a buffet.'

They stared down at the cutlery – the shared language of catering covered years of absence. Charlie talked about peasant cooking, puy lentils, pigs' trotters. Maybe it was always like this with fathers. Charlie didn't know. Nor did Johnny.

The muzac changed, Jean-Michel Jarring, and Johnny picked up a fork, silver and pitted, each dent marking another passing. He looked at Charlie. They both knew that this cutlery was generations older than the restaurant.

Hand to mouth, bankrupt stock, family business on to family business.

This symbolised the fork that Charlie's grandfather first laid on the crisp clothed tables of Belle Hotel, his birthright. Theirs... and yet not, because Johnny was about to tell Charlie something important.

'Charlie, I—'

The blast shook the square mile to its granite foundations. Johnny dropped the fork and they left the dust-stormed basement gasping

100

for air. Someone had detonated something chunky inside the ring of steel.

They made their way slowly back to the flat, shaken, yet guessing that there would be no further attack. Police everywhere, stopping even those on foot.

Charlie's mobile rang, he hauled it from his bag. It was his mum.

'Are you okay? The 18.45 lot have told me about a bomb. Lulu and I are worried about you… He's okay, Lulu… no, costs a fortune on these things.'

He could picture his mother at the Belle Hotel bar, bulging apron against the zinc counter, swollen ankles in the pit dug over decades by her father-in-law's own feet. Lulu leaning on the bar top, itching for news. Something hissed in the background, perhaps the copper water boiler stoking itself behind the bar, or maybe it was just a bad line.

'You coming home tonight, or staying with him? Come home, Charlie love, they aren't going to bomb Brighton again, are they?'

His father swung open the fridge door and gestured to a row of Budweiser tins, alone there with an unopened pot of double cream.

'Ah, no thanks, Mum, I'll be okay here tonight.'

'Well don't forget that you promised to help with the christening, starts at noon. Franco's back's still bad, so we'll need you back in time to shift the tables.'

Charlie groaned goodbye and clicked the phone shut.

Janet dismissed Lulu with a wave. The girl needed to know her place in this family business. The girl was shaping up well under Janet's training. Everyone wanted to work at Belle Hotel. The money was good and the guests were all celebrities or wannabe celebrities who tipped well and were good to gawp at.

Janet set off upstairs to find her head housekeeper, Jean. She found her on her hands and knees on the third floor, going at the skirting board with a toothbrush.

'That's good, Jean. We're going to need three maids on shift tomorrow. And can you put an ad in the *Argus* for temporary cleaners. We're going to give this place a deep, deep clean. Front door to roof tiles. Lulu will be on hand to help, of course, she's family, but I'll need another four for, say a week, to work under your instruction. Charge me a couple of hours for sorting this out and take the money for the ad from the petty cash tin. You know where it is, just sign the chit.'

Quaglino's
St James's
London

Franco Sheridan
Belle Hotel
Brighton

My Dear Franco,
Well, we've both come a long way since I did Belle Hotel bar for you back in the day.

I've considered your request for an assistant restaurant manager position for Lulu Hardman, and can quite understand how she'd benefit from a few years in a big London restaurant. They don't come any bigger than Quag's, I've a team of twenty just taking reservations on the phones!

You may have heard of our head chef, exciting chap, Aussie, big on Pacific Rim food. Far cry from Brighton Beach, no? I must make it down for your fish and chips soon.

So, have Lulu contact me, and we're sure to find her something suitable.
Best Wishes,
Sir Terence Conran

14 February 1995
9.35am

Tick-tock, tick-tock, is that the sound of a second bomb going off?

'You're fucking what?'

'Going to work at Quaglino's.'

'Does Franco know about this?'

'He arranged it.'

'Fuck, fuck, fuck, fuck. We need you here. I need you.'

'You don't need me, Charlie. When's the last time we…? And as for Belle Hotel, I'm stifled here, Franco's never going to retire and Janet won't even let me answer the phone.'

'I'll get you a phone. Christ, is that what this is about?'

'It is not about a sodding phone. It is about me. And you and me. Charlie,' Lulu sat down on the banquette, air wheezed through ancient brass and leather, 'you had your travels, your London.'

'Lulu, it was two fucking weeks.'

'And a whole summer putting it about on the French Riviera. I gave you my life. You gave me herpes.'

'We've been over this before. I need you here. We are so close to winning that Michelin star. Please don't leave me, please. They might come and do an inspection at any time.'

'And I need to be anywhere but here. Christ, Charlie, I'm twenty-one, ancient. And the having a baby thing hasn't worked, isn't going to work, plus you can't keep your hands off the other waitresses for more than five seconds the minute my back is turned. What was the name of that posh student from Portobello? Lizzie, something? I know for a fact you shagged her in the boiler room. And don't go denying it. Brag about it to Claire and Emma, and everybody gets to hear about it, including me. Me, your so-called girlfriend. Remember our pledge? I thought Belle Hotel was all I needed, but it isn't. There's more to life than a silly drawing we did as kids. I have a career, too. I want to go to London and further it. It's not easy doing this. Don't you think

I haven't thought long and hard about this. All your jealousy over Massimo. And for a final time, for the record, it never happened again after I committed to you. You've just got over-tired, over-emotional and judged me by your own standards. You've said nothing romantic to me for years, nothing in bed that's remotely a turn on. In fact, the only thing you've said to me in bed in months is "Did you remember to turn the lights in the bar off?" Oh, Charlie… I just, feel… I feel stifled by you Sheridans. So I'm going, and this, us, is over.'

Lobster Belle Hotel

2 live lobsters

1/2 bottle white wine

2 shallots, finely chopped

1 tbsp black peppercorns

1 star anise

2 pints fish stock

1 tbsp Dijon mustard

Bunch flat parsley

1/2 pint hollandaise

Franco had never dared have lobster permanently on the à la carte menu. Too bloody pricey by half. Charlie was having lobster and that was the end of it. Or the beginning of it. He'd boiled the lobsters to death, whisked up a hollandaise and flashed the lot under the grill in the time it took the Gallagher brothers to belt out 'Rock N' Roll Star' on the kitchen radio. They had their own heathen chemistry. Charlie added a couple of strands of his own secret heathen chemistry to the Lobster Belle Hotel dish. A secret spice, something that he'd conjured up late one night working alone in the kitchen. Fizal Moondi had sorted him out, tapping up generations old contacts from way back along the Silk Road. Charlie checked that none of the other chefs had seen him add the secret spice and slipped the small, flat, gold

Persian-script-embossed box back into the inner flap of Franco's book.

Belle Hotel Restaurant was 'hot right now', as they said in *Time Out* and the *Standard*. Hot enough to warrant a visit from the Michelin man? Charlie wouldn't hold his breath. But he did a bit, when Franco swung in to tell him that a lone male diner on table three had requested an extra jug of hollandaise.

Charlie cooked and waited. Five years' hard graft. Half a decade of his life for an asterisk. And now Lulu was leaving him, just at the moment when he needed her most. What did she expect, that the star would come out of thin air? That nights off and trips to the cinema to watch rom-coms would get him, them, what they wanted? Maybe she didn't want it badly enough? Charlie banged his hand against Belle Hotel's front door and, as if by magic, an envelope franked 'Michelin' plopped onto the mat.

Michelin Guide
Notification of Michelin Star Award

Charlie Sheridan
Chef
Belle Hotel
Brighton

Dear Charlie,
We are delighted to inform you that Belle Hotel Restaurant has been awarded one Michelin star.

Your listing in the Michelin Guide will be complimentary. Our advertising team will be contacting you to talk you through our half- and full-page advertising opportunities that we have available on the South-East pages of the guide.

Congratulations and enjoy your celebration!
Yours,
The Michelin Guide

'Screw the advert. Let's get Bob.'

Franco brimmed over with pride at Charlie's achievement. Ready to throw money at the fact that they'd only bloody well gone and done it! Bob Carlos Clarke had made that lunatic Marco Pierre White famous in the eighties with his menacing monochromes, maybe Bob could be coaxed down to the seaside to do a 'Brighton Rock 'n' Roll Star Chef' shoot?

The press went crazy for Belle Hotel's news, and, before he knew it, Charlie was on the cover of the *Sunday Times Magazine*.

Charlie Sheridan, fag in mouth, Brighton beach, dirty whites, bloody shark slung over his shoulder. Rock-star stance, kitchen-greased curls, heat-chiselled jaw and simmering gaze. Charlie Sheridan. Not an ounce of fat on him. One hundred and sixty pounds of prime chef snarling down the barrel of the lens. Fuck you. Cook you. Looking like it was his God-given right. Tables laden with opportunity, just out of shot. Journalists, diners' wives and girlfriends, waitresses, wine reps, and, hell, even the environmental health officer come to swab sample his surfaces.

Girlfriend, nah. There was, but she left me. Just before all this happened. That'll teach her.

Charlie Sheridan, darling of the London weekend break set, hot fodder for the gossip mags, he who could do no wrong in the kitchen, could cook or seduce anything with a pulse to perfection. Taxis on the tip jar up to the Groucho straight after service, back in time for a bleary-eyed breakfast shift, smiling at the hazy memories of coke and copulation. Cook, fuck, flirt and fist-fights with those who tried to snap him at it. Unless it was Bob. Bob's monochromes developed the legend. Fixed him in time and place for ever.

Charlie felt he owed himself a celebration. A two-day bender. Franco had agreed that a grand as a bonus for getting the star sounded about right and Charlie was determined to burn through it before he went back to his hob. So he started his bender with cocktails on Belle Hotel for his brigade after service, continued it in the cab up to Soho with two of Belle Hotel's waitresses, girls that Lulu had recruited and trained personally. But not for the things they did in the back of that taxi. They had learned that stuff all by themselves.

Charlie signed the three of them into the Groucho Club with a flourish, even though he'd never paid a month's membership fees in his life. By 4am he'd worn them both out, in and out of the toilets to snort, blow or swallow whatever took their fancy. Charlie was champion of the world, unstoppable. He poured the waitresses into a cab, paid it a ton for the trip down to the coast, and went back inside to look for more sparring partners. Damien Hirst and Alex James took Charlie under their wings and before long Charlie was butt naked with the best of them, taking his turn at the billiards table.

He may have passed out for an hour or so around 6am, but awoke with a raging need for bloody Marys and Twiglets, which was handy, as the Groucho had both in plentiful supply.

Charlie felt the fire returning to his loins and was fortunate enough to get talking, then snogging, then shagging with a nice young lady from a good family gone bad.

At nine, Charlie staggered round to Bar Italia and got himself a triple espresso, eased down with a cheeky balloon of brandy, and got chatting to the owner about the Wurlitzer he'd sold to Franco back in the seventies.

Soho's notoriously liberal workers and residents did baulk slightly at the sight of a man in dirty chef's whites puking in the gutter at noon. The staff of a production company took bets on what restaurant they should avoid that lunchtime.

Drooling into the drain, Charlie felt his spirits start to rise. He wiped his mouth, chin and nose with his sleeve and thought about where to go for a spot of lunch.

He set off sideways for St James's, took a one-eyed bearing while hanging off Eros, and was soon falling down the famous Quaglino's stairway that led to the subterranean dining heaven.

Lulu, who had enjoyed a simple staff lunch of seared tuna and jasmine rice, and a harmless flirt with her head waiter, was busy putting the eighty-seat section of her quadrant of Quag's in order. She looked up on the sound of the thud and suffered an involuntary shudder. The only involuntary shudder she'd had on account of Charlie Sheridan for a good many years.

'Look what the cat dragged in.'

'Hello, Lu, hic, I got a Michelin star.'

'I know. Well done. You can't stay here. Hygiene hazard.'

Charlie slumped into the white leather banquette. Lulu cringed, he'd left a muddy streak in his wake. She looked around to see who'd noticed, Quag's was filling up, corks coming out of bottles, floured rolls and salted butter landing on crisp linen.

'Can I have a menu?'

'No. You can not.'

'Chef John said I can sit anywhere I like. Just seen him outside. So, Lu, let me have a menu, there's a love.'

Charlie tossed his five remaining fifties on to the table, leant his head back and closed his eyes.

'Charlie, you can't sleep here.'

'Not sleeping, Lu, resting eyes only. Menu.'

Charlie ordered a one hundred and fifty quid pot of Beluga caviar and a bottle of house champagne. He'd have a tenner left over for the train, though that thought even crossing Lulu's mind made her furious with herself.

She keyed in the order on Quaglino's electronic Remanco system, something of a step up from Belle Hotel's pad and pencil and peg method, and went to the loos to give herself a good talking to.

By the time she was back, Charlie was deep in conversation with Chef John. Her waiter had served the caviar perfectly, it rested on the mountain of ice with the lid presented resting on the lip of the plate, text facing the customer, just how she'd trained him. Except the customer, the yob, was scooping the fish eggs out with his fingers, twenty-quid fistfuls at a time, swigging champagne from the bottle and generally making an ass of himself.

'Ex-boyfriend. Ex.'

Lulu muttered this calming mantra for the rest of lunch service as Charlie held court with a succession of famous faces that had seen his mug on the front of that Sunday's paper and wanted to buy him a glass of champagne to both congratulate him in person and secure any future reservations they may wish to make at Belle Hotel.

Charlie lapped it up. For what to Lulu seemed like hours.

To add insult to injury, one fawning punter ordered Charlie a Quaglino's Seafood Platter. Restaurant rules were that the section manager had to personally take the one hundred and twenty quid platter to the table and talk the guest through the tools they'd need to crack it open. Charlie thanked Lulu for her help and then cracked a claw off the lobster, crunched the thing open with his bare hands, slathered down the pure white flesh and didn't touch another thing. She let a waiter clear the platter away. Rules or no rules, Lulu had Hardman pride to contend with, too. Charlie tipped the guy with his last tenner. Charlie leaned back, hands behind his head and smoked a fag.

Lulu amused herself with a daydream of picking up the unused lobster crackers, easing Charlie's sweaty ball sack out of the crusty fly of his chef's trousers and squeezing the wizened handful between the glinting teeth of the crackers. After a while, Lulu tired of that daydream and moved on to beating Charlie about the head with the sharp end of the crab mallet.

Eventually, as the last lunchtime guests were collecting their coats and Quaglino's was getting a fresh one of its own for evening service, Lulu led Charlie by the arm back up the stairway to heaven and blinking into the weak afternoon light.

'Well done, Charley Farley. Now fuck off back to Brighton and don't ever think of turning up at my place of work again drunk. In fact, don't ever turn up at my place of work sober, for that matter. Fat chance of that happening. If you do, I will never, ever speak to you again. And that would be too soon. Goodbye.'

'Lu?'

Her heart jumped a beat. An apology? A proposal of marriage? She'd refuse, naturally, but it'd be enormously pleasurable turning him down.

'Can I have that tenner back for the train?'

With a shove, Lulu propelled Charlie Victoria-wards. Let him solve that problem by himself.

'Oh, well done on the star, by the way,' she muttered after him. 'Try not to fuck it up.'

Too late now to tube it back to Tooting for her break, she'd have to grab forty winks in the staffroom before the evening shift began. Her section was turning tables two and a half times that night. She'd be hoping to meet two hundred people's high expectations head on. After a lunch shift of looking after Charlie, Lulu was knackered.

Chef John passed her in the corridor on the way to the staffroom.

'Nice guy, Charlie, you two an item?'

Lulu grimaced and stomped past him, finding a hard plastic seat right at the back of the staffroom to curl up on. Lulu had half an hour before she'd have to fix her hair and make-up and be back on show. This really hurt. She'd done what Franco had suggested, only to find herself out in the cold the moment they got what they had all been working for. Yes, Lulu had wanted London experience. Yes, she needed to get some space from Charlie. But, the Michelin star, right after she'd left. Cruel. They'd all earned that star together. She'd worked her butt off for Franco, putting in the same double shifts as Charlie. Often it'd be Lulu shaking Charlie awake at six, when he'd slept through the second alarm. It wasn't just their love life that suffered on four hours' sleep a night, it was everything else. The way they talked to each other. The way he held the plates for her to take, then snatched them away at the last moment. The way she'd slop sauce over his gleaming hot top at the pass, just to give him more to scrub off at midnight. It hadn't started that way, they'd been loved-up for the first few years. Learning to take Belle Hotel higher than she'd been before, grafting towards the accolade they all felt was within their reach. And then, just when she'd doubted them and left...

Lulu let out a long sigh. Quag's was wonderful. The hours, a mere eighty-hour week, considerably less than Franco had made them do. A day off a week, guaranteed, too. Not snatched away because Janet's varicose veins were playing up again. It was tough, starting again at the bottom, working her way up to being one of many restaurant section waiters in London's restaurants. Just as Lulu was at rock bottom, flaming Charlie hit the lofty top. Lulu felt dog-tired and now sick as one, to boot. Sick with jealousy that he'd taken the reward that was theirs to share. She'd split up with him the moment before he became attractive to other women. It'd take him a decade to work through all the slappers wanting a celeb chef notch on their bedpost. She didn't want him, no. Lulu ran her hands through her hair, must wash that when she got back to the flat tonight, but she damned well didn't want anyone else having him, either.

Time to go back out there. She'd wasted her entire break on Charlie. When would she ever learn?

Charlie reversed the charges to Belle Hotel and, a couple of whimpering sentences later, had Franco saying let me take care of it, wait under the station clock and one of my guys will find you. He travelled first class for free back to Belle Hotel, a fitting end to a memorable, or for Charlie, un-memorable, two-day bender.

Lulu spent her evening break pouring her heart out to Quaglino's fruit and veg man in the canteen. Gregg patted her on the shoulder.

'Never mind, darling. Plenty more Michelin-starred chefs in the sea. Ere, d'you fancy a night out with me? I know some clubs in Hackney that'll make yer hair curl. Mine, too, if I 'ad any.'

She worked until close, dashing for the Tube and repeating the fact that it was over with Charlie, over, over, over as she walked down the long flight of steps to the platform.

Lulu fell into sleep the moment she sat down on the last southbound train on the Northern Line. A fellow passenger shook her awake at Morden, where she swore and set off for the now familiar mini-cab office. If there were any cabs available, which it didn't look like there were, she'd be lucky to be in bed by two. Up at seven and back at Quag's by nine, this was the life her mother should have warned her about.

Belle Hotel Restaurant Receipt
13 October 1995

Starters
Sevruga Caviar 30g £30
York Ham £6.20
Mains
Poulet des Landes £40
(for two)
Buttered Carrots £3.75
Pudding
Crêpes Suzette £6.75
Wine
Glass of Chianti £5.50
Coffee
Double Espresso £2.50
Filter Coffee £2.50

TOTAL £97.20

Tip £2.80
Bill to Labour Party master account
Signed by: G. Brown

'I'm a lifelong Labour supporter. Was a union man on the trains before I opened Belle Hotel, used to drink with John Prescott at the union conferences back in the day. Boy, John could whack them back.'

'Still can, er, we're having trouble deciding. Can we have a word with the chef?'

'For you, Mr Blair, anything.'

'Call me Tony. Neil Kinnock told me about Belle Hotel. Said you gave him a dry pair of trousers when he fell into the sea. Thought it'd be good to get to know you. Never know when one might need a dry pair of trousers.'

'We.'

'Pardon, Gordon, *avez vous* gone French on us?'

'No, Tony, we. One implies that it will be you requiring the dry trousers. "We" suggests it could be one or both of us.'

Franco averted his eyes.

'Shall I fetch chef for you? I'm sure he'll be able to help.'

'Thank you, look, we've got to sort this out, Tony.'

'Oui, I mean yes Gordon, thank you, Franco. That would be a great help.'

Charlie needed no cue from Franco, he'd been watching the two politicians tussling with the menu through the kitchen portholes, pissing himself. He tapped Franco on the shoulder as they passed going through the swing doors.

Franco lit a fag, wafting the smoke half-heartedly away from the direction of the pass. Charlie rocked back on his clogs in front of Tony and Gordon, thumbs tucked in his apron strings.

'Good afternoon, my right honourable gentlemen. Now what appears to be the problem?'

'Hi, I'm Tony. And you must be, er, Charlie. Cherie and I saw you on *TFI Friday* – it's a television programme, Gordon – cooking that truffle omelette for Chris Evans. Looked fabulous.'

'Thanks, Tony. So…?'

'Well, Gordon and I want the same thing, but I suggested that I get what I want, and he settles for our second choice, then we swap halfway through. How does that sound?'

'Messy, to tell you the truth. How about Poulet des Landes, a truffled chook with dauphinoise potatoes. It's for two, so you get to share, and I'll make sure Franco carves you a breast, wing and drumstick each. That way all you'll have to fight about is the Parson's Nose.'

'You've got yourself a deal. Do you have any polenta to go with it?'

The two men sat at loggerheads over the roast. Then came time for debating the big issue of the day. Pudding. Tony ordered the crêpes, Gordon wanted humble pie, so sat fuming with a filter coffee for the rest of the lunch.

'Great actor, that Tony,' said Franco.

Janet watched them leave, then went back to her game of knucklebones. Having finally persuaded Franco to strip out the seventies-looking bar, so bad it wasn't even ironic, Janet was now running the pub she'd always dreamed of. Franco had given her half of what he'd chucked at Conran twenty years ago, but Janet had a whale of a time trawling the Shoreham shipyards for props, fittings and fixtures for her Ship Street themed pub. The wood-panelled bar and walls, when she'd stripped off the padded hessian, did half the job for her. She'd liberated the big brass bell from the *Athena B* when it had run aground a decade earlier and now hung it in pride of place at the end of the bar. Anytime she got a tip, Janet rung it. Ringing Janet's bell became something of a pastime for the locals from that day on. Janet had got herself a couple of shore-leave tattoos along the way and what with her dark hair, gold filling in her front tooth and hoop earrings, she was quite the pirate these days, with a crew of sea-dog punters that swigged from her jugs like they contained mother's milk. In fact, Janet felt so salty that she started singing the shanties she'd been humming while she worked. Add an admirer on the accordion and the Belle Pub soon had itself something of a reputation to rival Charlie's restaurant. A listing corsair to Charlie's tight ship.

Charlie may have run a tight ship, but he was getting a touch of the piratical about him, too, borrowing his mum's gold hoops, having his Michelin star tattooed between his thumb and forefinger and wearing the skull and crossbones scarf given to him by Keith Richards as his chef's neckerchief. Franco offered to get Charlie a parrot to complete the look and wondered if he, Tony and Gordon were the only folk in Ship Street still wearing a suit.

17 May 1997
Midday

Tick-tock, tock-tick. Labour won a landslide. Charlie held onto his Michelin star. Lulu moved in with Quaglino's head waiter. Johnny spilt soup on Bill Clinton, leaving a nasty stain, and was deported. Janet charmed Charlie's pot-wash boy up four flights to her bed. Franco had palpitations. A new dawn had broken, had it not?

INVITATION
A RECEPTION for MUSIC AND
ENTERTAINMENT BUSINESS SUPPORTERS
10 DOWNING STREET
FROM: TONY BLAIR PM
TO: CHARLIE SHERIDAN +1
DATE: 29 May 1997
TIME: 6.30pm–8.30pm
DRINKS & CANAPES
DRESS CODE: SMART CASUAL
NO DRUGS

Dear Charlie, Thanks for agreeing to cater this reception. Noel Gallagher and his wife are coming and I'm hoping that you'll be able to tear yourself away from the kitchen and keep him from trashing Downing Street. Do bring a guest, Cherie and I would love to meet her.

Tony

'A what?'

'A refrigerated van.'

'Who do you think you are, a fucking butcher?'

'I need one, Franco. With Number Ten and the Good Food Show coming up, there's no way I'll get the lobsters up there and keep them fresh.'

'Get them up there, they sell lobsters in London and Birmingham, don't they?'

'Yes, but not my lobsters. It is all about provenance, Franco. Like France. You can't have Lobster Belle Hotel with Brummie lobsters.'

'Look, I'll get onto Brampton and Sinker and see if we can borrow one of their vans.'

'No. I want a new refrigerated van. With Belle Hotel on the side. I notice that your new Jag has turned up. All I'm asking for is a van.'

'Bet it'll cost as much as the Jag, too.'

'No, we lease it.'

'What? Lease it? Over my dead body. Everything you see here, including the bloody Jag, is paid for. Leasing, my fucking God. Leasing.'

Charlie drove, squeezing his two best chefs, nicknamed Fish and Meat on account of their jobs, on to the two seats beside him. Charlie kept whacking Meat's knee with the gearstick, accidentally at first. Then on purpose.

The three chefs cheered as they whizzed, London-bound, past the welcome to Brighton posts.

The press, who'd been permanently camped outside Number 10 for over a month snapping the comings and goings, went into shutter overdrive as Charlie pulled up outside the famous black door and started to unload the stuff for the party. That'd shut Franco up about refrigerated van costs, the Belle Hotel van splashed all over the front pages.

They loaded in and soon had the bottles of Krug chilling in plastic boxes filled with ice and water. Tony's people had rung to make sure that Charlie took away all the bottles with him and always served with the labels covered by a napkin.

Charlie laid the cold canapé bases out on rows of plastic sheeting he'd brought and stapled to the trestle tables, also brought. He and Fish went down the line, scooping quenelles, drizzling sauces and popping garnishes on top. Down below, Meat fired up the ancient Downing Street ovens to warm through his stuff. All tricks learnt at the knee of Roux Outside Catering, since disbanded, and, already knackered with a night's work ahead of him, Charlie began to understand why.

Charlie went to brief the Downing Street waiting staff on the way he wanted things served and, on the way back bumped into Noel Gallagher.

'All right, man. What you doing here?'

'Cooking.'

'Cool.'

'What you doing here so early?'

'Tony and Cherie invited us up for a livener and a look round the flat. They've got an ironing board up there, for fucksake. Prime Minister and he's got an ironing board. Mad.'

At that moment, Meg came out of the toilet. The one that Charlie had been instructed not to use. On account of it being the Queen's privy, for the use of HRH only. Charlie thought he'd better appraise Noel of the fact.

'Oh, she wasn't taking a piss. Just doing a line. Charlie?'

Never one to turn down a toot, Charlie slipped in while Noel stood guard. Meg had wiped down Her Majesty's toilet seat as a courtesy to the next user and Charlie made sure that he did likewise.

'Madferrit,' he said, coining a popular phrase. Noel accepted the proffered twist and popped in after Charlie. Charlie went back to the kitchen to change into his clean chef's jacket and go and meet his plus one at the Downing Street gates.

He saw her coming before she saw him. She took his breath away. Lulu had thought long and hard when she'd got the invite from Charlie. She put the invite in the drawer of her bedside cabinet and then into the bin and back again. Five times. Bloody Charlie. She had a life, thank you very much. A great life. A life that involved fishing a rectangle of cardboard from tangles of hair, spent tissues, Tampax wrappers and laddered tights at 2am on a Saturday. Right, decision time, she thought, plucking a dried blob of bubble gum from the back of the invite and flicking it back into the bin. Obviously, she hated Charlie's guts, obviously, they would never, ever be an item again, and, obviously, she would not be turning this opportunity down. Her father would kill her.

Lulu took a pilgrimage to Joseph on the Fulham Road the Saturday before during her break. Previously the scene of the most successful purchase of Lulu's life to date, and sod it that it had cost her a week's wages, the black trouser suit that hugged her behind just so and bagged her the head waiter, not that he was that fickle, like Charlie, but he'd said she looked just, superb, and with his French accent, she just couldn't help folding it up carefully at the end of his bed that night after service and shagging the life out of him.

It was in the window when she'd bought the trouser suit. Women were stopping to look, causing a traffic jam on the pavement that rivalled the one on the road. Lulu chained her bike to the railings outside the shop, heart beating a little as much from what she was about to do, as from the uphill bit by Harrods.

Five hundred and fifty quid, for a piece of black-and-white material that was no bigger than a pillowcase. But what a pillowcase. Lulu tried it on and knew she'd be wearing it to Downing Street. She'd have to go into her overdraft – Roger had always believed in protecting her from his wealth, as he so eloquently put it – but what the hell. Lulu freewheeled through Knightsbridge with the Joseph bag flapping from her handlebars, feeling like she was in a French movie until her sunglasses flipped from her head and clattered into the gutter.

'My God. You look—'

'Hello, you. Don't touch me. You'll no doubt have greasy hands and this is dry-clean only, not to mention the fact I'm about to meet Tony Blair. Charlie, wheeeee. I am a bit excited.'

She leaned in to allow him to give her a peck on the cheek.

'Charlie, you're sniffing. Have you been at the marching powder? Godsake, Sheridan. You'll be arrested.'

'Honest, Lu, it was just a little toot, to be polite.'

'To who? Cherie? Oh, don't tell me. Are people already there? Come on. I don't want to be the last.'

Lulu wasn't the last. She wasn't even the last in that Joseph dress. Once her twin and her had got over the shame, they'd had quite a lot of fun swapping partners as the Blairs went round high five'ing everyone.

Tony had people eating out of his hands, especially when he took a spin round the room with a tray of angels on horseback. Lulu had to shield her eyes from the flashbulbs of the cameras when Tony stopped to chat to Noel. He was only there for about five seconds, but the press got their front page right there and then, bumping Charlie's van to the graveyard of page two.

'Oi, Charlie Sheridan. How are ya? All of them toimes we harmonised till dawn.'

'Fuckin' hell. Tom. Me ole buskin' mucker. What're you doing here?'

'Oi was in Westlife for a week. Boyzone for a day and after a little dust-up with Louis Walsh, I'm going solo. Here with me new manager, Simon Cowell. He's crap, but I'm gonna be the next Robbie Williams. Apparently.'

And later, when Meat and Fish were passing the gates back into Brighton, Charlie asked Lu up for a nightcap in his Johnny-provided suite at The Savoy.

'Forget it, Charlie Sheridan. You're lucky you got me back to The Savoy. You've a snowball in hell's chance of getting me up to your room.'

They'd rocked up at The American Bar on a high. A high that not even Johnny with his long face could dampen. Johnny was still sulking after having to beg for his job back at The Savoy after his ignominious return from the States.

Apart from a slap on the back, Charlie barely acknowledged his father, who nursed a still water while Charlie ranted on and on about himself, slinging back the old-fashioneds in a style he was accustomed to, knowing that it would all be comp'ed by Johnny in the morning.

On one of Charlie's over-long trips to the loo, Johnny leaned in and told Lulu a secret. The kind of secret that families like the Sheridans kept. He told Lulu quickly, glancing towards the door as he spoke, voice calm, resolute.

'Of course you know if you tell him it'll break him. All that "born a chef" stuff. And if Franco knows I've told you he'll disinherit me. Probably has already. But I can't keep it a secret any longer. All that shame. Had to tell someone. I hope it explains some of why Charlie is being such a dick. Secrets do that to a person. He knows something's wrong between Franco and me, even though he doesn't know what it is, and it disturbs him. Always has.'

Lulu nodded and touched Johnny on the arm. She felt a wave of sympathy for Johnny. For Charlie, too. If only she'd asked Madame Eva for a bit more information, she might not be sat here, suddenly feeling like giving Charlie a sympathy fuck. What other hotels or restaurants began with the initials BH? Maybe she should open one? Other men wore blue-and-white check trousers, too, not just chefs. Maybe she would buy Thierry a pair?

Johnny excused himself at midnight, giving Lulu a kiss goodbye and a squeeze on the arm for luck.

Charlie was back, oblivious and warming to his theme.

'That's enough of me talking about me. Why don't you talk about me for a bit.'

'Pig.'

'That it? Seriously, Lu, what a mega night. And having you there at my side, just made a mega night perfect.'

Charlie slipped a hand around the back of the sofa and pinged her bra strap.

'Get off, you old charmer. I'm taken. Thierry. Remember. T-H-I-E-R-R-Y. And even if I wasn't, you wouldn't stand a chance.'

The Thames-struck sun woke Lulu and she instinctively reached for her sore head. Then she noticed other sore areas and let out a long groan. Charlie, asleep naked on the rug at the foot of the bed, looked up and smiled.

'How the fuck did you do that?'

'What?'

'Get me up here and do what you did to me without—'

'The old Charlie charm, Lu.'

'You bast—'

'Though it might just have been the brandy, always got you going. You weren't half knocking them back after Johnny fucked off.'

Lu flopped back on what she noticed for the first time was a very comfortable bed.

'What the hell am I going to tell Thierry?'

'That he's chucked. That you're coming back to Belle Hotel with me. That we're going to live together happily ever after.'

'That I stayed out all night with my new Joseph dress twin and you went back to Brighton in the van. Honestly, Charlie, this is never happening again. Correction, this never happened.'

'Never happened,' said Charlie to his cock, flopping it from side to side on each syllable, 'any chance it could never happen again in a minute? You look gorge on that bed.'

Lulu didn't deign to reply, instead she toured the room, picking up her smalls from the lampshade, bra from the back of the sofa and dress from the pelmet of the curtains, how the hell did it get up there?

She locked herself in the bathroom and turned to face her disgrace. Ten minutes with the Savoy moisturiser and cotton balls and a quick slash of lippy and Lu looked lobby fresh. If it had been night-time. Instead, Lulu had to totter across a sunlit lobby looking every inch the hooker she felt.

Charlie waved goodbye to the slammed door, rolled over and went back to sleep.

When Lulu got back to the flat, Thierry had already left for work. A one-mark note was propped up on the bed:

?

Even with Thierry's limited English, he'd managed to communicate his feelings very clearly. It was over, Lulu knew it. Charlie had managed to ruin another good thing in her life. For what? There was no way she'd be going back to Belle Hotel. She had a good job and a good life with Thierry in London. *Had* a good life with Thierry in London. Working together was going to be awkward. Damn her vanity in accepting the invitation. Damn her for lending Johnny a sympathetic ear and then

Charlie other sympathetic orifices. The sex had been good, she had to admit, now she remembered it. But, oh, the shame. One Sheridan step forward, two steps back. She stuffed the dress in her dry-cleaning bag, binned the stretched knickers and went to take a very long shower.

Johnny stared at Charlie's cocktail bill and shook his head. The boy certainly didn't get it from him. How was it possible for two people to drink eight hundred and fifty pounds' worth of cocktails? Even with his staff discount, Johnny would be paying this off for months. Add to that the damage bill for the suite and Charlie's 'visit' had taken Johnny well and truly to the cleaners. All the staff were talking about Johnny's son, the rock 'n' roll chef. That accolade had done him no good; Johnny was ashamed of Charlie and wanted to disown him, for the time being. Johnny was glad to be out of the whole bloody thing; Franco had used him to get what he knew he couldn't get for himself. Family business brought nothing but trouble. Look at the spoiled brat Charlie had become. Johnny tutted. Maybe if he'd been a better father, been more involved. Fat chance of that with Franco ruling the roost. At least Johnny had shared the secret.

The ungrateful boy had not even popped his head in to say goodbye before he left. When Johnny was his age, he had responsibilities, a kid to bring up and Franco to gofer for. When was Charlie going to grow up? Johnny put the boy to the back of his mind and went back to the rooming list.

'Charlie.'

It was Franco, yelling from reception. Damn, Charlie thought he'd be able to creep by and get some more sleep in before service.

'Oh, hi Franco.'

'Charlie. The van.'

'What about the van?'

'You know what about the van. I've already hauled Fish and Meat over the coals, took me the threat of taking it out of their wages for them to confess.'

'Ah, that about the van.'

'They say you clipped the Downing Street gates on the way out.'

'Sort of. Yes.'

'The Downing Street gates?'

'I guess so, yes.'

'Did you stop?'

'No chance, I was pissed. We burned up Whitehall a bit and I swapped seats with Meat.'

'Oh, that is good news.'

'We'll never hear from them. Don't worry, Tony will sort it.'

Ministry of Defence
Whitehall Branch
London
7 July 1997
Bill for repairs to Downing Street Gates.
£4,350.00
Payment Terms 30 days

12 September 1998
1.30pm

Tick-tock, no time to stop.

Charlie executed a near perfect handbrake turn on the seafront.

'Now leg it down to Sinker's and get the lobsters. And do it quick, we're running late.'

Fish and Meat piled out of the van and set off at a trot for the fishmonger's. They had to be at the NEC in Birmingham for a four o'clock show and the sun was already past the yard arm.

Gary Rhodes' ever-so-nice assistant had telephoned Charlie the night before, just to check.

'Just to check if you need anything else? We're rather excited to be having you on the Good Food Show. It is a super turnout for day one and our Supertheatre will be rammed as always. Bring along any music you'd like to play.'

Which gave Charlie an idea.

Franco had been checking his watch from seven and was up to boiling point by the time they'd finally loaded the van. He flipped his lid when Charlie set off down Ship Street, screeched to a halt and reversed back to ask for directions.

Franco jangled the coins in his pocket, rocked back on his heels and spat forth the travel orders.

'M23, M25, M40. Now go, or there'll be no food show, good or bad.'

He tutted them into the distance and then welcomed young Dawn from the allotments who had a lovely box of veg for him to serve with that day's lunch.

By the time they'd been on the M1 for over an hour it was too late to turn back, so Charlie had to hazard a guess as to when they'd reached about the middle of the country and turn left. As the van veered off the motorway exit, a suspicious swing, scrape, thud noise emitted from the back of the van. A noise that continued with mildly alarming regularity every time the van took a turn.

They'd found the NEC all right, with twenty minutes to spare, no problem. Problem was in the back of the van. Or wasn't.

'Fuck.'

'Oh, no.'

'Where's it all gone?'

The *Edgbaston Echo* would be reporting a plague of lobsters the next day. Charlie had a problem, one that standing there bickering wouldn't sort.

'I told you the handle was fucked, you knackered it on Downing Street's gates.'

'Shut it, Fish. We need a plan. And I think one may just have landed.'

Charlie pointed at the newly opened Birmingham Aquarium opposite them in the car park.

'No.'

'Yes. You're in charge of fish, Fish. We'll see you at the Supertheatre in ten minutes. With lobsters, or something that looks like lobsters. Meat and me have got to go get our make-up done.'

The Gary Rhodes girl was waiting at the loading bay with a clipboard and a frown.

'Cutting it a bit fine, aren't you? Where's your stuff?'

'We're getting the lobsters locally, I believe in provenance. And, I wonder if we can beg a few basics from Gary?'

Charlie waited in the wings, whisk in one hand, knife glinting in the other, grinning at Meat, who'd filled a box of the basics under the beady eyes of old Gary the hedgehog himself.

Charlie had handed the sound guy the copy of his song, told him the cue, 'die, you bastard', told him to crank it up to 11 and gone back to wait in the wings. He took a peek around the edge of black.

'Bloody hell.'

A carpet of grey hair met his gaze, stretching all the way back to the Sabatier stand. Charlie hoped they'd like the show. Where the bloody hell was Fish? Talk about cutting it fine.

'And now, lllladies and gentlemen. Please give it up for Britain's youngest Michelin-starred chef, Chaaaarlieeee Ssssssssheridaaaan.'

Charlie stepped, blinking, into the light. This was a new one on him. The TV studio had nothing on this, anyway, Chris Evans had made sure he was well oiled up in the green room beforehand. This, this was 4pm of a wet Wednesday in a big barn in Birmingham and a sea of serious faces hanging on his every word. Except he hadn't said one yet.

A quite uncomfortable few moments elapsed, folk shifting in their seats, clipboard flapping from the back, then Meat was pushed onto the stage by Gary, forcefully enough that he bumped into Britain's youngest Michelin-starred chef, spurring Charlie into life.

'Mother's cunt.'

The Good Food Show had invested in the very best lapel radio mikes and speaker technology that money could hire. Charlie's lapel mike had been clipped onto the flap of his chef's whites by the sound guy while he was busy talking him through the cue. The mikes were able to pick up and amplify the lightest of voices. Even phrases muttered under one's breath would carry at full volume throughout the Supertheatre.

Charlie started to speak, if only to cover the gasps, the clipboard at the back now covered the face of its owner.

'Good afternoon, Good Food Show Supertheatre fans. I'm Charlie Sheridan and I'm going to demonstrate Lobster Belle Hotel for you today. The most important ingredient of this dish is…'

At that moment Fish appeared, arms dripping water all over the stage, holding a beast from the deep in all its gog-eyed spiky-shelled gory glory.

'… not a lobster.'

That was not a lobster, not even related, bar both being from the sea. Charlie glared at Fish and snatched the snappy fucker off him.

'What we have here, food lovers, is… a rock 'n' roll lobster.'

Charlie strolled to the footlights, hoping he'd got away with this made-up name, turned to eyeball the beast – what was it? a grouper of some sort – and paused.

The sound of bodies squeaking on plastic seats filled the air. And still Charlie paused. Pinter would have been proud.

'Right, it's time for you to die, you bastard.'

'Rock N' Roll Star' kicked in on cue at gig-level sound, people held their ears, but didn't take their eyes off Charlie.

He threw the creature in the air, it spun twice under the glare of the spotlights, water arcing out into the crowd, and came down to land on the point of Charlie's twelve-inch knife.

At the moment Liam started to sing, the dead bastard was slung into the rolling, boiling pot on the hob. Fish and Meat stood at the side of the stage, no more use than standard lamps. Charlie shooed them off with a flick of his wrist and turned to the audience.

'Right. Hollandaise sauce. Sure you all know how to make this one, right? Well watch me whack one off in under a minute.'

Charlie whisked fast under the tilted mirrors of the Supertheatre, he had five minutes dead, the length of the song, to pull this off.

'Hollandaise… done. Now the white wine reduction. Shallots, sweated down backstage just now, bit of a cheat that, but hey, this is theatre, right? Fish stock, a good slug, star anise, tablespoon of mustard. Er, where's the bloody mustard? Found you. Flat parsley, chop, chop, then. Where are we, now? The bridge of the song. Time to fish our rock 'n' roll lobster out and slice the bastard in half. Fuck, that's hot. Need asbestos fingers for this job, now I gotta scoop out the guts, fling it in the white wine sauce for about…'

Charlie looked at his watch as the song ticked irrevocably away.

'… anyone know a good curry house around here? We're gonna be starving after this gig.'

Laughter from the audience.

'I'm going to pull these two halves out of the sauce, lay them on this platter, this platter was from the *Brighton Belle* and presented to my grandfather, Franco, when they retired the train and he opened Belle Hotel. Do look us up when next you are down in Brighton. I'll give any Good Food Show goers a free glass of bubbly when you dine. So… thirty seconds to go, it is just rock 'n' roll, Liam, just rock 'n' roll. I'm going to ladle hollandaise onto this beautiful seafood and flash it under the grill.'

Charlie turned. No grill. A heartbeat.

'I'm going to blast it with this blowtorch that my assistant Meat is going to bring me NOW… thank you, Meat. Just fire this up. Luckily, I

128

am a smoker, as our friend Mr Lobster will be in a second… *Et voilà!*'

The song ended, Charlie strolled to the front of the stage with the Lobster Belle Hotel, cue loud applause.

Charlie stepped off the stage, barging his way past a young chef named Jamie Oliver, up for the day to assist Ruthie Rogers and Rose Gray from the River Café, and made straight for the large bin by the fire exit. He slung the contents of the poisonous platter straight in and set off for the pub without so much as a backwards glance.

The audience enjoyed the River Café demonstration enormously. They commented on their feedback forms that they had especially liked that cheeky chappie assistant they had with them, Jamie. More of him, please. As for the previous show… 5/10. Interesting, but the language, and too loud for a cookery demonstration, what did that chef think this was, a pop concert?

Eight pints and one amazing Shimla Pink curry later, Charlie took the executive decision that they'd be better off sleeping in the van than risking the journey back to Brighton. As a concession to comfort, they turned off the refrigeration unit and rolled up their aprons to use as pillows.

'Night, Meat; night, Fish. What a fucking day.'

The journey back to Brighton was uneventful. Bar the fact that Charlie had run out of cash and done a runner from the petrol station in Shirley. Fear of the West Midlands Constabulary chasing them down the M40 certainly got them back to Belle Hotel in record time. Franco was waiting at the back door, looking at his watch.

'Hello, Charley Farley, how'd it go?'

'Great. Sure they'll have me back. I was mega, wasn't I guys?'

Fish and Meat nodded in accord.

'Good. Journey OK? M23, M25, M40? What time did you make?'

'Ah, good time, especially on the way back.'

'Do you want a hand unloading the stuff? I'll go get Janet.'

'No, Franco, you're all right.'

Charlie waited until Franco had gone back inside to unload the lonely platter from the back of the van. His body shook and it wasn't just the hangover. He could not stop, had to get back to his stoves. Keep his star and reputation intact. Had the Good Food Show helped? Charlie thought not. But they all did it. All the big-name chefs. He'd got to bloody keep up, or he'd lose it. All it took was a fuck-up. One wrong plate to the wrong diner and disaster. Just when you thought you'd got it all... another envelope through the door and you've got nothing. Fucked it up for everyone. Not Lulu, though, she'd bailed on him for good. Not returning his calls. So what if it was four in the morning? Again. Charlie wanted to talk. Someone to talk to who understood. He tightened his grip on the platter and walked unsteadily back into the kitchen of Belle Hotel and another eighteen-hour shift.

Lulu sat alone in Quaglino's staff canteen.

'G'day.'

She smiled at the Aussie head chef, until he opened his mouth again.

'Charlie.'

'Charlie, what?'

'Charlie put on quite a performance at the Good Food Show.'

'Oh, really? Do I look like I care?'

'C'mon Lu. Must be a bit bloody galling knowing he's poncing about on stage and you're stuck running a section of Quag's, looking at my sweaty crew every day.'

Lulu covered her ears with her hands.

'Nah, nah, nah. Not listening.'

'Well, you'll want to bloody listen to this. I've come to tell you you've been promoted. Deputy Restaurant Manager. We know

Charlie didn't win that thing on his own. You need to get some of the kudos for what you did. And now you do. Congratulations, Deputy Restaurant Manager. If you accept, I'll let the Guild know and they, no doubt, will let Charlie's grandfather, wotsit, Franco, know. Won't that feel good? There you go, mate. Now get back to fucking work and wipe that fucking smile off your face. This is the most fashionable restaurant in London Town, we don't smile, girl, we pose. Now go give it your swinging London pose. You are running the centre of the universe here, baby. Yeah!'

10 November 1999
1pm
Franco's clock struck one and the kitchen carried on at full tilt. Shepherd's pie on the menu and four slaves manning the flames.

'Table six, two shep, one poulet, one fish, side of bubble and side of greens. Away.'

'Yes, Chef.'

'Yes, Chef.'

Charlie stared at his commis. The boy kept his head down, working.

'Yes what, Worm?'

'Yes, Chef.'

Amid the whirr of eight other orders, table nine began to take shape. Great British menu, with a twist. Omelette Arnold Bennett, Leek and Truffle Flan, Chicken Liver Parfait, Cut York Ham. Mains to die for and a Lobster Belle Hotel special that some said earned Charlie Sheridan his star. The papers buzzed with the story of a boy sent off to the great restaurants of Europe to learn his trade; stock, season and soufflé, school of Escoffier, of Robuchon and Carême. The prodigal grandson come back with a head full of flavour and a hunger to turn Belle Hotel Restaurant into the South Coast's Savoy Grill. Move over, Franco, hang up your apron and manage out front for me. Watch out, you Roux Brothers, the Sheridans are stalking your stars. Gastronomy-on-sea. So much hope, sweat, heat and ambition. Surviving on a diet of freeze-dried caffeine, fags and licked sauce spoons, Britain's hottest kitchen fired on anger and gas.

Front of house, Franco directed his sommelier back to the table. More wine, more water? Magazine lunch, on expenses. Profit and chat. Profitable chat.

'So I said to her. This is soo swinging, soo now. We've just got to get a model, hair and make-up down to The Belle and do a cover.'

Hair and Make-up were nodding for England. Model stared at a soup stain on her low-slung jeans. Magazine flicked on.

'Just purrfect for us right now. Soo fucking purrfect. We'll have another bottle and some still. And some sparkling. You all right, darling?'

Model nodded – they weren't paying her enough for this job and she was missing her new man. Hair popped to the gents for a line. Make-up powdered her nose.

'So I said to these people. We are chic. I expect the best. Move me now. I can't work here.'

Franco smiled across the humming room, slipped a finger inside his starched shirt collar and pulled. Magazine said something funny. Model and Make-up cracked up. Franco swung back into the kitchen and squared up to his grandson.

'How are we doing with table six? I want them ate-up and out of here before my Rotarians come through.'

'Table six, shift it up. Out on special.'

'Yes, Chef.'

'Yes, Chef.'

Silence.

'Worm?'

Meat and Fish moved table six to the top. The poulet was pulled from the back of the oven and flashed under the grill for a couple of minutes. Meat, a big-boned fellow, grabbed two Shepherds from the walk-in and threw the whole order on a tray, then back into the oven. Top shelf, five minutes max.

'Five minutes,' muttered to Fish. 'Five minutes, Chef.'

Worm, or Anthony Clarke, as he became known, did nothing. No greens, no bubble, not a squeak out of this two-week-old kitchen baby. Great placement, his lecturers had said to the angelic-looking seventeen-year-old. More like six months in the flames of hell. He tried running through the side orders in his head. Nothing. What didn't help was having to deal with the steady stream of desserts. Pastry had called in sick and Chef thought Worm could handle it. Baptism of fire and all that.

Fish flicked back a scaly lank of hair and floured his flounder. Tapping out time on his hob-nailed clogs, he gave Meat just under two minutes, and the flat flesh thirty seconds on each side. Splash of Noilly Prat and a glance over at Worm, and he was ready, he'd plated and sauced his dish and placed it next to Meat's three offerings in front of chef.

Crack. Charlie slapped the palette knife flat on the counter.

'Where the fuck are the sides?'

Worm turned in time to see the plates smashing into the bin.

'I-CANNOT-HAVE-HOT-FOOD-WAITING.'

Meat and Fish snuck a glance at each other, both turned to Worm. Shoulders up by ears, his back braced against all this anger, he gripped a treacle tart for dear life. Meat and Fish grimaced. They knew what was coming next. Nobody spoke. Nobody ever spoke in Charlie's kitchen. Simmer, sizzle, time, flip… yes. But never, ever, speak.

'Chef, I was j-just too busy with the pudding.'

'Too busy with the pudding,' mocked Charlie, affecting a limp wrist and a simper. 'How d'you think I fucking managed back in the day? Marco Pierre White would have shoved a red-hot poker up your useless fucking arse by now. Fuck me, what do I have to cunting well do to get anything done around here?'

Front of house, Magazine consulted her Cartier.

'Come on, I want the set-up done by three. Fucking amateurs…'

She clicked, actually clicked, her fingers at Franco. A flicker of irritation showed on the face of the silver fox. He shot his cuffs, nodded and cut back into the kitchen. Into mayhem.

Charlie only meant to touch him with it, but something about Worm's young haunch flesh made it stick. Branded, they said. Charlie didn't know about branding, but he did feel a little sick as he peeled the smouldering palette knife away from fuckwit's flesh. The Worm turned and screamed. And screamed. Conversation in the restaurant stopped. Even Magazine. For a moment, the finely tuned world of Belle Hotel stopped. Then Fish slopped a bucket of ice and water down Worm's trousers and normal service began again.

Table six got their mains. Worm left the catering profession, scarred for life. Nothing much happened for a month.

HM Courts Service

Summons
Offence: GBH
Court Date: 10 December 1999

Charlie hated the cop shop. He'd been there a few times and it never got any better. The arrest for GBH on Worm came as a bit of a shock. He'd been out the back of the kitchen having a fag on some beer crates when two of the plod entered the alley. Wasn't long since he'd nicked the petrol in Shirley and, for a moment, Charlie wondered if it was the Brummie cops come to get him. But, no, this was closer to home. Worm, Anthony Clarke, had suffered third-degree burns, apparently, so the charge was raised from ABH to GBH. And GBH was a serious crime, sir.

What constituted third-degree burns, Charlie wanted to know?

Blisters? They made you cry? Come off it. What went on in the Belle Hotel kitchen was no worse than any of what went on in kitchens up and down the land. In fact, what went on in other kitchens was a lot worse. Just ask his chefs. What happened to Worm, all right, Anthony Clarke, was just the usual initiation stuff. It was worse in my grandfather's day. Even ten years ago. Look at the scars I got from my time in Marco Pierre White's kitchen. This, charge, it's just health and safety gone mad. Fucking mad. What, yeah, I'll watch my language when you lot use your time catching proper crooks instead of wasting your time with cooks. This bollocks was hitting him at the wrong fucking time. Everything he'd worked for depended on him being there every moment of every day and if he wasn't there he had to be keeping his name in lights somewhere else. This was not the way Charlie wanted his name in lights. No thank you very fucking much, Mr PC Plod.

The handcuffs had been a bit unnecessary, as had the photographer from the *Argus* they had tipped off to wait at the bottom of the alley. The fingerprinting and paperwork was a waste of Charlie's time, he had a hundred-plus for dinner to get ready for, couldn't they skip some of this. He did it, all right, he did it. So shoot him.

Belle Hotel Millennium Night Menu
Scallops Sheridan
Baron of Beef
Trifle
Cheese Soufflé
Wines: Krug & Gigondas

Millennium night, and Belle Hotel was set to party like it's 1999. Charlie had a kitchen full of triple-time cooks, a fridge full of over-priced food and a hundred highly expectant mouths to feed. At the same time.

Sure, he'd done banquets before, bigger than this, but never out of Belle Hotel's kitchen. Franco was feeling it too, Charlie could tell. He'd never wanted to open on Millennium anyway.

'Come on, Charley Farley, it's not like we need the loot. How about it, lad? You, me, your mother and a few close friends. Well, yours, hardly any of mine are left.'

Charlie had had his way. It had hurt too much to have his name missing from the gossip in the press. Thousand pounds and ticket this, champagne-drought that. After the branding story went national Charlie needed all the good press he could get, so Franco let him do it, on the understanding that he didn't have to pretend he was enjoying himself.

'Not for one bloody minute, lad.'

Janet had her hands full too, with four tables set up in the bar, rounds of ten for prominent Hove types, and her running the unlimited boozing opportunities listed on the side of Franco's menu. She too had taken a vow of sourness.

'Fuck 'em,' said Charlie as he helped Fish prep another platter of scallops, flash-fried in a pinch of chilli and onto the waiting shells ten at a time. The trainee stood by with a bucket of crushed peas, to scoop in each before Charlie shot each shell with a drizzle of sauce he'd bottled earlier. He loved it. Five hundred quid a ticket and they could have filled the place twice over. Silly money. Three-star food prices. Well, he'd just have to give it to them. Belle Hotel three star, that was.

Michelin were already expressing doubts about re-listing. There'd been mutters about lack of development. Scared of the backlash about bullying, more like. Lack of development. What did those fuckers want, blood? Charlie had grafted his arse off for that star. Taken Franco's classic dishes and elevated them. Added the fifth taste, umami, to everything he could fucking think of to make it happen. Wrung every last ounce out of his five senses to make each dish the best, the very best version of itself it could be. Touch, taste, sound, smell, sight…

he'd smashed everything he had at it. And then the sixth sense, the one that Franco had always hinted at. The one Charlie had to discover for himself. Well, Charlie knew what that sixth sense was now. No need to tell Franco like it was some part of the damn masterplan. Charlie had worked it out for himself. The sixth sense Charlie needed was his own bloody genius. Born a chef. Grafted like a chef. Earned his star like a chef. All on his own God-given genius, talent, time and dedication. If you wanted a taste of genius, book ahead. Bold complementary combinations of strong flavours, vividly coloured, confidently plated, served with panache, everybody on board, working to the beat of Charlie's drum, and damn well meaning it. Charlie and Lulu, getting good at it together and then falling the fuck apart in a fist fight of sexual jealousy and fatigue. Bone-tired, bitter, broken. She'd left him for what? Some trendy restaurant in London. Fickle fucking fashion foodie gastrodrome thing instead of being here at Belle Hotel where she belonged. The place they'd grown up and made their pact. No wonder Charlie had lost his temper. Lulu's fault.

Krug in buckets, not a napkin in sight, just look at the label and enjoy. Staff at the ready to pop on signal. Franco loved his pops. Thought the silent fart the French favoured too stupid for words.

'It's a celebration, let them have it!'

Franco stood on a chair as usual for the briefing, leaning down for a moment to steady himself on the its back before standing to his full seven foot and continuing.

'We've got plated scallop starters, watch those shells, they tend to slip about a bit. Give 'em a second show of bread. We've got a lot of booze to mop up and it's free pour. I don't want my cellar drinking dry. Baron of beef for mains. We're having the bugger piped in on the crêpes wagon. Charlie'll come in – Janet can you make sure he's got a clean jacket? – and carve. Queue up, three plates a person. You all know how to do three, right, and then go back into the kitchen for your spuds, sauce and veg. We're going to use the three-foot platters' – groans all round – 'and I want you to find room for the sauce boat too. It's a truffle and red wine jus. Not gravy. Got that, Glen?' Laughter. 'Belle Hotel Trifle for afters and then at eleven thirty we'll serve the savoury. Cheese soufflé. Charlie wants you to serve it fast. Too slow and you lose the effect. Got that? Now we'll have a little chat about the wines and a little taste of the red. Remember, the champagne they don't touch is ours at midnight. Good luck and remember, it goes down well at the Belle!'

Franco stepped down from the chair – he'd done jumping in the eighties – and set off to check on things with Charlie. Seven thirty start time and guests were already waiting in the lobby. Fools. Go home and come back when we're ready. Charlie and Franco had their customary bicker about music. Brel, Beatles, Blur... and the stage was set. Lights across the ground floor were all either low or off. Six-hour night lights flickered from frosted holders on every available surface. The whole of Belle Hotel swayed along with Brel.

Charlie stepped out for a fag and a breather. The traffic in Ship Street was already choking up the seafront, brake lights red against the roaring sea. Punters in outfits they'd been wearing in their heads for months, off to the most over-promised night out in a thousand years.

Eleven thirty and the soufflés were going out. So were the night lights, but everyone was past caring. Charlie was proud. Even Franco was smiling. He leaned across the heat of the pass and squeezed his boy on the shoulder.

'Well done, lad.'

'Well done yourself, old man.'

Glen brought the two of them a glass of champagne and they allowed themselves a moment of celebration.

Janet was wrestling with the rusty tops of the last few bottles of port. Shit, she'd cut her finger. No time to do anything about it now, just wrap it in this wet napkin. Ruby red was oozing through damp white. Table four asked for sambucas. What, now? They couldn't be serious. Better fetch Franco. Where was he? Let him sort them out. Flaming sambucas, typical of those Robinsons. Bastards.

Charlie was knocking them back at the porthole, his work was done. At a quarter to two thousand, his grandfather entered the dining room with a platter of blue flame. Charlie watched in horror as the old man slipped, no, crumbled, and the burning mess raged down his hand-cut suit. At first there was laughter. Nervous, of course, but laughter, none the less. Then some bright spark chucked an ice bucket of water at Charlie's fallen hero. The lumpen liquid stopped the flame and Franco's heart.

Everybody agreed it was nobody's fault. They managed to move him to the lobby. Janet wailing, Charlie pumped Franco's wet front. The ambulance took forever, a barrage of pissed, suicidal Whitehawkers taking precedence over this four score and ten survivor. Except he didn't.

Flashing blue faded away to red at the end of Ship Street and Charlie's grandfather's clock struck Franco Sheridan out.

2000s

0% Interest

Hookes Bank

Charlie Sheridan
Belle Hotel
Ship Street
Brighton

5 January 2000

Dear Charlie,
It is with a heavy heart that I write with deepest sympathy for the loss of your grandfather, Franco. Franco was a valued client of the bank since he opened Belle Hotel in 1973. I am honoured to have called Franco a friend. I've written to your mother separately with my condolences and the information I am about to give you.
Franco is [rest of letter burnt]

Charlie backed the Jag out of the garage. He'd not checked the insurance, but assumed Franco had him as a named driver. Not that Franco had ever let Charlie drive the new Jag. One look at the van put paid to that.

'Mum, get a move on,' he yelled from the wound-down window, 'it's almost ten.'

Janet came out of the pub door, shoulder to toe in black and a peacock-blue turban on her nut. Johnny had done his when he heard the contents of Franco's will and declined the invitation to come and mourn the old man's passing.

141

Charlie had been out the day before, to Badger menswear in North Laine, place where Franco was getting his John Smedley sweaters right up until his timely demise, and bought himself a Paul Smith peacoat, midnight blue with a scarlet lining. He wore the coat over his chef's whites in his own sartorial gesture to the old man.

He'd liberated the Hookes Belle Hotel chequebook from the inside flap of Franco's book and had already been on something of a spree. Franco would be turning in his grave, if he was in it; it being the Millennium meant that Franco had to wait on the slab for ten days longer than normal. Ten days, ten cheque stubs, that would have told quite a story, had Charlie bothered to fill them in. Peacoat, Porsche, powerboat, Pussy Parlour, Pioneer Hi-Fi, powder for marching, Portobello restaurant lease, page tribute to Franco in *Caterer* magazine, Paul Peters lunch and a parrot.

Charlie lost the parrot on the train home after the Paul Peters lunch, which, in his defence, came after he'd consumed all the marching powder and signed a ten-year lease on a Portobello restaurant, and before he spent the rest of the night gazing into space at Pussy Parlour.

Lulu stood next to Roger at the caterers' graveyard behind the station as he wept buckets onto Franco's coffin.

'Franco made me the man I am, Lu. The man I am.'

Charlie quit trying to get Lulu's attention after his mother had hissed at him to stop winking. Janet then joined Roger in slinging salt water into Franco's hole.

'Lu,' Charlie caught her arm, just as she was attempting a French exit.

'Sorry, Charlie, I can't stay any longer. Sorry for your loss.'

'My loss, your loss, too, Lulu, remember?'

'I'm sad, Charlie, I really am. But Franco wasn't my grandfather. In fact, you know. You've been acting like such a dick for years. It's very hard to love you. You're forceful, like Franco, but you… lack his… resolve. I'm worried you're going to fuck things up, Charlie Sheridan. With Franco gone.'

'What can I say, I'm a chip off the old block. If you hadn't abandoned me, chucked the towel in in the final round, none of this would have happened. I'm losing my birthright, Lulu, the one I got from Franco that skipped Johnny. Born a chef.'

'Born a twat, more like.'

'And you, what are you? A coward. Couldn't handle it, ran off to London leaving me and Franco in the shit.'

Lulu rolled her eyes and did the yak, yak, yak thing with her hand.

'Don't give me that, Lu. In fact, you know what? I'll tell you something. Franco wouldn't be in the ground if you'd stuck around. He was picking up your work that night. The work you should have been there doing. Your selfishness killed my grandfather.'

'My selfishness, *mine*. That really takes the biscuit. Okay, Sheridan, you asked for it. Both barrels, here, today. I don't fucking care any more. You want to know why Johnny isn't here?'

Charlie glared back at Lulu. 'Money. As per. Franco wrote him out of the will. Quite right. Another Belle Hotel deserter.'

'No, Charlie. Not money. Blood.'

'Eh?'

Lulu is hissing now, pulling Charlie close to her by the lapels of his peacoat. Just low enough for those pricked-up ears to miss it. 'Johnny isn't Franco's son. He told me that night at The Savoy.'

'What?'

'Yes, not his son. So that means… you, you "born a chef" bighead… aren't.'

'No, Lu. I don't believe you. It's not true. You're messing with my head. Lulu. Don't say this. I can't—'

Charlie left the graveside and went to sit in the Jag. Guests pretended to ignore him repeatedly smashing his hands down on the steering wheel. An act that only came to a stop when the airbag went off in his tear-stained face.

Brampton and his wife rode silently in the back of the Jag back to Belle Hotel. The buffet did Franco Sheridan justice.

Lulu caught the next train back to London after the burial. She couldn't face going back to Belle Hotel and felt terrible about the whole Franco, Johnny and Charlie thing. She'd ignored his call at midnight on Millennium night and only checked the message the morning after. It was Charlie's fault, she told herself, but the bastard had managed to make her feel guilty. And now, acting the fool at Franco's funeral to get her attention. That was taking it too far, even by Charlie's standards. But pushing her to the point of vengeful spite? That was quite a thing to do at a family funeral. Good work, Charlie. Lulu shook with anger. The worst thing was, betraying Johnny's secret hadn't made her feel any better and she wondered if it would have any positive effect on Charlie's unreasonable behaviour. Things were manic busy for her at work. Two weeks until The Wolseley opened and they had so much to do. Lulu knew that they'd get it all done, she'd done a stint for Jeremy and Chris at The Ivy after leaving Quag's. It was just too hard seeing Thierry on a daily basis. After The Ivy, Lulu had become a bit of an opening queen, moving from one grand new restaurant opening to the next. And in Blair's booming London there was no shortage of grand restaurant openings. The Wolseley was the jewel in the crown and she was proud to be offered assistant restaurant manager under the wonderful Byron who'd been with her at The Ivy. Sure, they were putting in eighteen-hour days, she never saw the new flat she'd bought in Brixton, but this place was going to be the talk of the town.

That is why, the invitation, when it came a week later from Charlie, was so supremely irritating to Lulu. Irritating, wasteful and disrespectful. Typical Charlie.

'Charlie, can I take five days off to go on Concorde to Barbados? I mean, don't you have any brains? One, I wouldn't go with you. Two, even if I did want to go with you, and Sandy Lane would be nice, what if I had the most important week of my career happening next week? Do you think I'll drop everything just because you flash Franco's cash? Not impressed. If I wanted to go to Barbados, I'd ask my dad. Goodbye, Charlie. Have a nice time on your own. Saddo.'

'But, Lu—'

She'd gone, slung the phone back in her bag and turned back to the wiener schnitzel tasting. A far more productive use of her time.

Charlie was asked to leave Sandy Lane on the second day of his flying visit. Two newlywed couples had complained to the general manager about his drunkenness. Not having anything other than Franco's chequebook with him, Charlie spent the final three nights of his solo honeymoon sleeping on the beach.

By the time he'd kicked his British Airways bag in the general direction of Belle Hotel's reception, over twenty thousand pounds' worth of new kitchen equipment had been delivered, including a state-of-the-art convection oven that was too tall for Charlie's greasy ceiling. After five seconds' thought, Charlie ripped out another cheque for as many grand to get the floor lowered by one of Roger Hardman's men.

'Convection cooking,' Charlie muttered to himself as he watched the guy hacking away at the floorboards, 'that'll get me my second star.'

Charlie looked up at the heavens, remembering what Franco had said over that glass of bubbly on Millennium night.

'Two stars, Charlie Farley, that's what that Roux lad's got. We're going to add getting a second star to the masterplan. You and me, kiddo, against the world. We can do this. Knuckle down and let's shoot for the stars.'

Michelin Guide
Letter of Commiseration

Charlie Sheridan
Belle Hotel
Brighton

1 April 2003

Dear Charlie,
We are sorry to inform that you have been de-listed from the Michelin Guide. Feel free to contact us if you would like to receive some feedback and pointers to set you back on track.

In the meantime, we'd still like to talk to you about advertising in the guide. One of our sales team will be in touch in the next few days.
Yours sincerely,
The Michelin Guide

Charlie snarled like the Pavlov's dog he'd become and stuck the fatal blow in the back of Franco's book. Drips of sweat ran down his back. This was serious. Really serious. Word had got out. The *Argus*, the Guild, Charlie knew how those bastards talked and now this, de-listing from Michelin. De-listing spelled death for most restaurants. Just when Charlie had big expansion plans. Fuck them. What did they know. Which of them had ever slaved over a hot stove for twenty hours straight. Damn, he should have done a Marco and given his star back before they took it away. Bastards.

*

Hookes Bank

Charlie Sheridan
Janet Sheridan
Belle Hotel
Brighton

13 October 2004

Dear Charlie and Janet,
This letter is to inform you that you are about to enter an overdraft position at the bank. As this is the first occasion in thirty years that the account has been in this position, I ask that you contact me at your earliest convenience to talk about an overdraft arrangement and covenants against Belle Hotel and its assets.
Yours,
Paul Peters

'Anything interesting in the post, Charlie?'

'Usual junk, Mum. How about a cuppa? I'm parched here.'

The Argus, March 2005
ROGER HARDMAN RETIRES

Local boy made good, Roger Hardman, has sold his carpet business for £5 million. Roger started out selling faux wool carpets door-to-door in the 1970s and has bought his business back from the receivers and built it back up again twice in the intervening years. Roger spent the first day of his retirement on his boat Shagpile II *in Brighton Marina with a glass of bubbly and the company of Tina Jacker, 23, a former model from Worthing. Hardman said of his bounty: 'I intend doing good works with this money. I have a comfortable enough lifestyle, as you can see, and my daughter Lulu is making her own way in the world without my help. So it is time to give something back.'*

Roger is reported to be looking into becoming the sponsor of the new academy school being formed out of the failed former Brighton Secondary Modern. He has also received in excess of 3,000 applications for funding from Brighton fringe arts collectives.

Charlie walked down to the marina. Thought the Porsche might give off the wrong message. He could see what he was looking for from the top of the cliff.

'Helloooo. Anyone about?'

'Charlie.'

'Hello, Roger. May I come aboard?'

'Sure, wait a sec, I'll go and put some things on.'

Charlie waited, feet up on deck as a weak English sun hazed off oily waters.

'So, to what do I owe the pleasure of this visit? Don't try twisting my arm to help you get back with Lulu, you know what happened last time.'

'Nothing like that, Roger. Actually, it's about business.'

'Business. You. Business. Well, that is a turn up.'

Roger reached for the bottle of health tonic chilling in the ice bucket on the low table.

'Yeah. I'm wondering if you'd like to invest.'

'Invest. Invest in what, Charlie?'

'Me.'

'Ah. It's like that, is it?'

Roger stood and paced across to the railings at the side of his boat. He tutted. 'Look at this, some spoilt bastard has bought a powerboat, left the cover off and now the rain has got in and it's sinking. I mean, who the hell would do something as stupid as that?'

'Beats me, Roger.'

'Lottery winner, probably. They have no respect for property. I've laid carpets for a few of 'em. Ghastly silk things at a grand a square foot. No style, some people. So, investing in you? How?'

'Well. And you're the first to hear this... I've bought a ten-year lease on this amazing restaurant in Portobello.'

'Italy?'

'No, London. Well, strictly speaking it's North Kensington, but you can walk there from Portobello. Amazing place, huge.'

'I think I know it. Didn't Worrall Thompson have it, then it went bust? Been Brasserie this, that and the other for years.'

'Yeah, well now it's gonna be Portobello Belle.'

'Is this what you're asking me to invest in?'

'No. All I'm asking for is working capital. I've already fitted out London, she's due to open once I get a licence. This is working capital for the mother ship, Belle Brighton, I'm taking about.'

'I don't know, Charlie. I've made a lot of charitable commitments lately.'

Charlie came a step closer to Roger.

'All I'm asking for is working capital to help me expand, you know, like Franco did for you back in the day. I can pay you back in instalments, if you like.'

Roger looked back down at the sinking ship and shook his head.

'This is against my better judgement, and I'll be sending Lulu in to keep an eye on my investment, right.'

'Great.'

'An eye.'

'Yeah.'

'Stay there, I'll go and get my chequebook. I take it this is urgent.'

'Yeah. Thanks.'

'You'll need to provide me with a full receipt. For contracting services, or something like that.'

'Bring me a pencil and paper, I'll write you one out now.'

'On Belle Hotel headed paper, with an official company number and VAT registration number. You do know what those look like, don't you?'

Lulu paid two visits to Belle Hotel to look in on her father's investment. As he'd made her promise to. There was no need to visit the London premises. Everyone in the restaurant trade knew that place was condemned and needed at least half a million chucking in before it could be re-opened. Also, the Royal Borough of Kensington & Chelsea turned down Charlie's application for a liquor licence. Something to do with a criminal record. So, for the ten years until his break clause, Charlie had secured himself a very draughty pied-à-terre near the Shepherd's Bush roundabout.

Her second visit, unannounced, confirmed her worst fears. Charlie, she was informed, was entertaining half the cast of *Riverdance* in room 20 while ten or so unsmiling diners waited impatiently for a lunch being reheated in the microwave by an equally unsmiling teenage waitress.

Charlie Sheridan
Belle Hotel
Brighton

March 2006

Dear Charlie,
Well, a year has passed since you extorted the £100,000 from my father. It is only due to his affection for Franco and Belle Hotel that you haven't heard from his solicitors.

I thought I should let you know that, after over a decade in London, I'm ready to come home. As luck would have it, I've been offered food and beverage manager at Hotel Epicure on Ship Street. I'll be working with their executive chef, Graeme. Remember him? The guy you beat to go to Switzerland. How

*times change, eh? The money isn't quite London rates and it'll
be strange being so close to you, but I'm sure we'll get used to it.*

*Charlie, you being you means I'm sure you'll take this news
badly and assume that I'm doing this to get back at you in some
way. Just like you did at Franco's funeral. I'd have been happier
at The Grand, or somewhere cool like Pelirocco, or Blanche
House, but this is the job that came up. If it helps you, imagine
that I'm having to take the job because you blew the hundred K
that was going to be mine from Roger to set up my own business.*

In fact, imagine what you like.

Lulu

*P.S. The Guild awarded me 'Young Restaurant Manager of the
Year' at last night's awards. Nobody mentioned you.*

Charlie did indeed take the news badly, and assumed that she was
doing it to get back at him. All lies, just like that bullshit about Franco
not being his grandfather. He'd opened the letter, scan read it, shoved
it in Franco's book and then fumed for days. But then other problems
took over. The 0% interest credit-card deals he'd been enjoying for the
last few years, slam £20K on MBNA for six months, when that expired
roll it over to Santander, had ended. Something had happened to
rattle the banks. Something they weren't saying and it can't have all
been Charlie Sheridan racking up eighty-eight G on plastic that made
them baulk, though if everyone was at it, reasoned Charlie, that's a lot
of unsecured mullah sloshing about.

Good Friday 2006
Midday

Tick-tock, everyone's spending on the knock.

With a full restaurant for Easter Sunday and no way of paying
Brampton's Christmas bill, let alone finding the lolly for lamb

he wanted up front, drastic action would need to be taken.

'Right, fellas, you've got to get entrepreneurial. You've seen *The Apprentice*, think like Sir Alan. Fish, I need six hundred oysters. Meat, six sheep.'

'But, what if?'

'No use bleating to me. Fish, there's a perfectly good powerboat sitting in Brighton Marina. All you need to do is get the thing going again, buy a fishing rod, net, whatever and bingo, let the oyster catching begin. Meat, I'm gonna throw you a lifeline. I'll lend you the Jag. But if I even get a whiff of sheep shit when you bring it back, you're sacked. Those bastards at Hotel Epicure are fully booked the whole weekend. Lulu and Graeme. Grey ham, more like. Right. Let's go to work.'

Charlie turned up the volume on his Pioneer Hi-Fi and went back to chopping mint. Oasis blared from the one remaining speaker that had not fallen into the deep fat fryer. He'd given himself the hardest task. The mint had been growing under a patch of nettles in the caterer's graveyard and Charlie had had a nasty couple of stings getting the green stuff out.

He sat with his back to Franco's grave with the mint across his lap, scratching his hands.

'Franco, old man. Grandad. If you can hear me, I'm sorry; I've really fucked things up. I'm not as strong as you. Know what, I've not even got the cash for mint sodding sauce. I'll be nicking vinegar from the chip shop on the way back. Do you remember how we used to do Easter? Back in the good old days? You out front, me out back. Christ, I miss you, Franco. And I'm letting everyone down. I just, just can't stop myself. I know, I know… stop yer blubbering, pull yourself together, we Sheridans don't cry. I'm screwing up, Grandad, and I get so, so, angry. Keep thinking I'm gonna lash out and won't be able to stop myself. Do some real harm. We just… find it so hard without you. And now Lulu's stuck the knife in. Trying to say you're not my grandad. She's gone to work with the enemy, too. Are you listening, Franco? I love you, you old bastard. There, I've said it. Right, back to work. Lunch isn't going to cook itself.'

Easter Sunday 2006
4am

Tick-tock, Franco's clock chiming loud enough to wake the dead.

Bong. Charlie rose again and raised the Jolly Roger his mother had given him as a present up the flagpole of Belle Hotel. Franco's Union Jack, though tattered, would wash and be cut up for cleaning rags. Made do and mend. The old man would have been proud.

Bong. Meat got off on the sheep-rustling charge. Pleading coercion and Charlie paid the fine, eventually.

Bong. They butchered and cooked so much sheep that weekend that Belle Hotel's drains clogged up with fat and biblical amounts of dirty water rose up from the basement and sloshed over diners' ankles as they sank their teeth into the South Downs stolen property.

Bong. Fish was less successful. He managed to start the powerboat, borrow an oyster catcher, and soon was hauling in masses of the molluscs off the sewage outflow pipe half a mile out from Rottingdean beach. Not that Fish knew that he was bobbing above the shit pipe. He thought he'd just got lucky. Wrong.

Brighton Council Environmental Health Department

1 May 2006

Dear Mr Sheridan,

We write with reference to the recent norovirus outbreak at Belle Hotel. We have received complaints from 167 diners at your restaurant and have taken ten stool samples, including your own. Unfortunately, your stool sample turned out to be 100 per cent Nutella when we'd had it analysed in the lab, so it will not count as part of the sample.

You will be sent details of the fine imposed and we advise you not to speak to the press about this matter until the case

is settled. The articles in the Argus *and national press have no
doubt had a negative impact upon your business and we advise
that you keep silent until the matter is settled.*

Yours,

Mr Spores

Ms Messer

Brighton Council Health Officers

*

HM Courts Service

Summons

Offence: GBH

*You have been summoned on the charge of GBH for the second
time. It is alleged by witnesses that you stabbed Ian Hunter, aka
Fish, in the left buttock with the tip of your ten-inch knife on
16 April 2006 in the kitchen of Belle Hotel. Although Mr Hunter
is keen not to press charges, Brighton Council wishes to prosecute
you under the Crimes and Misdemeanours Act of 1973.*

Court Date: 5 January 2007

*

Hookes Bank

Charlie Sheridan

Belle Hotel

Ship Street

Brighton

5 January 2007

Dear Charlie,

*I know you have a lot on your plate right now, what with the
court appearance and a number of reputation management
issues relating to Belle Hotel.*

This letter is an informal warning that you cannot keep extending your overdraft ad infinitum. There is a tipping point about to hit you at which the estimated sale of Belle Hotel, all its assets and business goodwill will be less than the figure that you are currently overdrawn.

If I were a less optimistic man, I'd also factor in a reduction in business goodwill of 50 per cent due to your mis-management of the business for the last seven years.

I have spoken to Janet informally about this matter and she will receive a copy of this letter. Do not destroy this warning, file it in your grandfather's book and think on it.
Best Wishes,
Paul Peters

The movie at the Odeon was good, hard men and soft women, just what Charlie needed to take his mind off things. While the good guys won, Charlie's mind wandered back up the twitten and he started counting containers in the walk-in. Béarnaise sauce, okay. Chopped shallots should get him through. Oh hell, did he do enough crème caramel? Shepherd's pie special today, thirty portions. Might get Janet to put it on the board in the pub tonight. Nice of Lulu to invite him over for supper with the competition. Totally unexpected. Hope Graeme, that arse of an exec chef isn't there. Must fix a time to see his father.

Charlie had been so wrapped up with his own demise that Johnny seemed dead already. Last time he'd swung by to see him at The Savoy en route from Hookes, when was that, dead already dad's final words had haunted Charlie. It'd taken him until Haywards Heath to latch on to what his father may, or may not, have been saying.

'Sorry, Charlie, I can't help you on this one. Bit stretched myself until the court settlement with Doreen is finalised.'

'But I just need you to countersign it. Come on. It's not much to ask. This is Belle Hotel we're talking about.'

Johnny looked up. Charlie looked away. The lobby of The Savoy ebbed and flowed around them.

'There's a rumour we're shutting down.'

'What, The Savoy... never.'

'No, restoration. The cracks are beginning to show.'

'Tell me about it. And anyway, you'll be okay, you've been here so long you're part of the furniture. Get a payoff, won't you?'

'Charlie, I've got something important to tell you.'

'What, look I'd better—'

Ashen-faced, Johnny opened his mouth to speak. Almost as hard talking to the boy as it was to Franco. He had to tell him, especially now that Franco was dead. Then, on cue, the fire alarm spontaneously erupted and the contents of the mahogany-clad lobby scattered.

'Saved by the Belle Hotel.'

Johnny forced a smile at the old Franco joke hanging on Charlie's lips and the two men parted. Strangers.

HM Courts Service

Court Order
Charlie Sheridan
Sentence: Eight weeks anger management
Weekly two-hour session
Completed to the satisfaction of the therapist

The judge leaned into the microphone. The jaded hack from the *Argus* licked his pencil. Charlie crossed his fingers.

'While I accept that your caution in, let me see, December 1999 for branding Anthony Clarke acknowledged your age, position, good character, the nature of kitchen labour and the pressures of work, I cannot accept that now, six years on from that offence, you are still using cruelty as a tool in the workplace.'

'He slipped, your honour, said as much—'

'Silence. All rise. I am sentencing you to an eight-week anger management course, to be completed within eighteen months of today's date.'

Mondays had to be the day and he'd dragged it out for as long as was humanly possible. As ever, Charlie was running late.

'Fuck, late. Sorry, fuck.'

Up past Churchill Shopping Centre, Winnie would be proud. Franco and Larry used to bang on about it often enough over a tot of Hine Family Reserve.

'A goddamn concrete carbuncle, just like the National. Cheers, Franco. Down-the-hatch. Churchill loved *That Hamilton Woman*, y'know. Always said it was his favourite picture. Goddamn carbuncle.'

Larry, Winnie and Franco were already dust when they had knocked down the concrete and replaced the rubble with a covered mall. What did Brighton want with a covered mall? No time to ponder, and on his final warning from Ernest, the very lenient therapist, Charlie surged past the ten o'clock shoppers, froggered through the buses and up into Queens Square.

Five-foot-flung flights and the celebrity-chef with a reputation burst into the cushion-strewn room.

'Hey, Charlie, man, here you are. Perfect timing, we were just getting started. Parvez is about to tell us what's on his mind and we are going to listen with open hearts and offer nothing other than positive affirmation.'

Yuk, thought Charlie, grimacing into a positive affirmation like his career depended on it. Which it did. Week seven, shame to blow it now after wasting two hours of his only day off since what had seemed like summer. Back then, stuttering introductions had been made. No need for second names, especially in Charlie's case, when the *Argus* and ten members of the national press, thanks to the snapper behind the wheely bin, had immortalised his name in their pages:

BRIT-FOOD SENSATION SERVES UP HUMBLE PIE

Bastards, it was years since he'd been on *TFI Friday* and taught Chris Evans how to flip that five hundred quid truffle omelette. The rest of his group had seemed a placid lot. Until they told their stories. Anger, rage, shame, frustration. And that was just week one. Ernest would peer through his round glasses, rub a hemp-soaped hand along the weft of his corduroyed thighs and sigh in deep understanding. What about Charlie? Did he want to share anything with the group? No, he did not. How much, or how little did one have to say to get through this? Nodding, Ernest gave little away.

Charlie's breathing slowed down to something near normal. Now he wanted a fag.

'So, as we achieved last week, feel free to enter the sacred space, with Parvez's verbal consent, and hold him. So: are we ready?'

Charlie gazed out over Parvez's greasy head to the glittering sea beyond. Freedom. There had been six inmates at the start of the programme, quickly going down to five when the lone single-parent female claimed discrimination. Shame, it would have been nice to hear what she was here for. The rest of them seemed like a nice enough lot. To Charlie the kitchen knife criminal, anyhow. There was Brian, a Leo Sayer look-alike divorce lawyer who had lost it when his wife had committed adultery with one of his clients.

'I even liked the guy. We were in the Haywards Heath Male Voice Choir together.'

Ian, an overweight, overwrought bankrupt was doing his eight weeks for slapping his business partner in the face with the pair of the hair straightening tongs he'd forgotten to patent. Charlie had nodded his understanding in week three, silently hoping for Ian that the things had been plugged in.

Now it was Parvez's turn to speak. Again. As far as Charlie could make out, Parvez had taken most of the airtime to date. Not that he, or Clive the easy-going yob puncher, seemed to mind. Neither Parvez nor Charlie had acknowledged that they'd once been friends at school and the co-owners of absent dads on that long-ago fishing trip.

Parvez was handed the programme as a step back to seeing his kids. Happy almost arranged marriage to unarranged affair with the Saturday girl had sparked his angry behaviour. So he said. Charlie groaned quietly as Parvez started up. Ernest, taking this as a sign of mutual understanding, gestured him to join Parvez in the circle.

'No, Ernest, sorry, I was just yawning. Late night, understaffed and all that.'

'Okay, well, what do the rest of the group feel? Are we happy to carry on after that interruption, or does anyone have anything they would like to express in non-violent form to Charlie?'

Silence. Ian shifted his buttocks across the cushions he'd hogged and farted. Charlie sniggered.

'Remember, folks: excessive anger, negative results. Learn to recognise the signs and symptoms of A-N-G-E-R and learn techniques to control it. Anger often results in criminal charges. Let's remember why we are all here, guys. Our behaviour has been deemed unacceptable in society and we are using this programme to get to the root of the problem, working together to share solutions that help all parties involved. I can only teach the negative aspects of anger, when it is warranted and how it should be displayed. Sometimes the cause of anger is deeply rooted in the subconscious. Isn't it, Charlie… Charlie?'

Charlie slid his watch hand into his pocket. Good, half an hour gone already. Instant coffee, jammy dodgers and diatribe. Three more of these and he'd be free. Whitehawk Hill, salt breeze on his shoulders.

'Let's all link hands and OM, for a few moments before Parvez offers us his thoughts and feelings this morning.'

The five angry men and their mentor kneeled in a loose circle and hummed to the rafters covered in seagull shit. Ten more minutes zinged by. Parvez, once again, took centre stage.

'It's like, oh, man, I dunno, just fucked, innit? She's sayin' that I gotta get out of me own house an all that shit and I don't wanna lose me kids and me house and, fuck her, man, is like she is killin' me slowly for what I done.'

'Calm, Parvez. Remember calm, you are among friends here.' Silence. 'Now, tell us again from the beginning and we'll try to make sense of your situation. Slowly, Parvez. Anger uses language to fan the flames. Relax, relax. Tell us in your own time. Feel free to ask any of us for…'

'Yeah, okay, man. It's just, y'know, I is not from this culture. Yet I is. Grew up in a Bengali strict family, arranged marriages for me brothers and sisters. Me father wanted me to be a doctor but I don't get the grades. Brighton Secondary Modern, innit. Birmingham Poly for pharmacy and I meets a pretty girl, right religion, so I marries her. Third year and I is a taken man. I'm tellin' ya that was a big mistake. Paying for that now big time. Fifteen years later, man, and we're doing good. Big pharmacy in Crawley, kids in private school, Boxster for me, four-by-four for her. Happy. 'Cept that aint enough for me. I gotta make mistakes. Make up for lost time. Fuck around.'

Come on, thought Charlie, we've heard it all before. Get to the juicy bit.

'At first it's no problem, just chicks on me hockey weekends. Then I gets the hots for the Saturday girl, innit. Me missus hires her, daughter of a neighbour. Eighteen, squeaky clean, 'cept she ain't. I can't keep me hands off her. In the stockroom, under the stairs, in the four-by-four, even gives me a blow job in the Boxster parked outside the house one Sunday night.'

Heads are shaking, more in curiosity than contempt.

'Then what happened with your infidelity, Parvez? Go on, unlock your anger.'

'Then I gets 'er pregnant. No problems I say, take three of these. But she tells her mum. Who tells my missus. Who kicks me out of the house.'

'Hardly surprising.'

'Thank you, Charlie, for your contribution, though I doubt if that takes us any further in our understanding of Parvez's situation.'

'Then she lets me back, but she's gone and got help. Y'know, counselling like, and suddenly I'm the bad guy. Treats me like shit in me own home. Won't cook for me after a hard day working for me family. Won't let me take the boys out on me own, makes me sleep in the spare room. Won't let me touch her. Six months of this and I've had it. Snapped. When me mum and dad was over from Brighton and all that. Threw the book at her didn't I. *Marriage After Infidelity*, or some crap like that. Now I'm barred from going near the house. And the Boxster. And the four-by-four. And me boys. And I have to pay for it all.'

'Yes, ultimately we all have to pay for the negative aspects of anger.'

'No, I have to *pay* for it all, innit. The house, the cars, the flat over the shop for me. Fucked. And she never did a day's work of her own.'

'Thank you, Parvez. It is time to move on.'

'But I can't even get a girlfriend now, not living broke in that grotty flat.'

'No, Parvez, I mean, please move out of the circle. It is time for another member of the group to be heard. Charlie.'

'No, you're okay there, Ern, let Parv have his say. Do you think he brought any of this on himself?'

'Charlie, the circle. Now, please. We will summarise and support once all have given to the group.'

Charlie shuffled onto Parvez's spot, winking at the angry adulterer as he went back to bite his mucky fingers against the woodchip.

'So, Charlie, let's try to go deeper than we went before. If you remember last time, the group felt that your reasoning was a little skewed, and that you were particularly confrontational with Brian. Brian, do you want to bring any negative feelings into the group as a result of Charlie's actions?'

The unseen clock tower chimed eleven. Halfway through. Good.

'Okay, we'll take that as a cue to move on. Charlie, I want to ask you about the red rage you mentioned to us last time.'

'What about it, Ern?'

'The uncontrollable urge to lash out that you felt those two times.'

'It was only once. He slipped the second time, remember?'

'I have to deal with the facts as they have been judged by society.'

'Fucking judged. Bollocks. Even Fish said he sli—'

'No aggressive language in here, Charlie, this is a safe space. Let's go back to those uncontrollable urges.'

'Let's not, can we? There's not much to say. It's hot. I'm working hard. Some fuckwit lets me down and I give them a slap. Bad boy, shouldn't have done it. Sorry.'

'The group knows that the first incident was a premeditated branding using a red-hot palette knife. Can you talk us through this?'

'Well, you hold the tip of said utensil under a flame for a few seconds and hey presto, lethal weapon.'

'The feelings, Charlie, the feelings. Anger, red rage.'

'What do you want me to say, Ern? Shit happens, this is a kitchen. On my first day in Switzerland they stood me on top of the hob and made me stand there until the soles of my shoes burnt through. Blisters for a week. Just a laugh, you know? Kitchen initiation. That wimp should never have been in my kitchen. I get burns worse than that most days. Branding? Pathetic. It was just a bit of kitchen banter, anyone worth his salt knows that.'

'Charlie, I need you to recognise the negative aspects of your anger in order that you complete the course.'

Five minutes is a long time to be looking at expectant faces.

'OK, Ern. I was working myself into the ground, six days a week, eighteen hours a day. I was obsessed with work and achieving recognition. Pushing myself to the limit all the time had a detrimental effect, and not being a great communicator, I took my anger out on others. For what? Something marginally overcooked or mis-seasoned? It all seems a bit silly now, but I thought I was infallible. I have learned. I have moved on.'

'Good, Charlie, good.'

Charlie uncrossed his legs and fingers to make way for Clive. Thank God that was over. Now he could get back to the good stuff. Anything to avoid having to talk about his feelings, his problems with anger management. Things had got worse since Franco died and Lulu stuck the knife in at the funeral. Now, to add to it all, Charlie didn't know for certain who he was. He didn't know if he was born a chef, the one certainty he'd based his life upon. The reason he followed Franco's masterplan.

Clive sat down awkwardly in the middle of the room, not knowing where to put his boot-shod feet.

'Well, I've not said much yet. And I guess now we've all heard from Charlie, I'm the only one left. I'm a bit shy, you see. You probably guessed as much. That's why it surprised me when I clumped that lad. Not that he hadn't provoked me, like, it's just that I've never done anything like that before.'

'Go on, Clive. The group is with you. Aren't we?'

Five heads bobbed in rapt anticipation.

'I'm shy, see. When I met Julie, she was me first serious girlfriend, if you know what I mean. I married late, mid-thirties, like, and Julie was a lot younger than me. Full of life she was then, like. The first five years were great. Then we got new jobs with our employer and relocated here. Great for both of us, by the sea for me, near the shows for her. Then she got ill, see. Kidneys. And everything changed. I guess I became her carer, like.'

Ernest waited, with nothing from the handbook to say. Clive continued.

'Ten years without having sex or a holiday. It can get to you, like. And Julie's moods. Then remission. The chance of normal life. Just

163

before that lad, we were hoping to take a week in Spain, like. She collapsed at the airport. Had to be taken to Horley Hospital for three nights. Spent the cancellation money on medical bills. So I gets her home and settled in her room downstairs when I hears a ring at the door. Knock down, ginger, I think they call it. But this lad has smeared dog dirt on the knocker. I lose it. I just lose it. Chase him into the cul-de-sac and smash the living crap out of him, like.'

Silence once more. Then a slow, steady handclap of support.

'Hold on a second, folks. We need to, er, help Clive with these negative feelings of anger. To prepare him.'

Two large tears swelled and broke down the shattered man's features. No group hug was going to put this right.

The fluorescent tube that bathed the room in blue light buzzed once and died. Ernest looked up and raised his hand from the cord in defeat.

'Enough for today, let's end on an OM.'

Lulu looked up and there he was. Graeme with a cup of coffee from the staff espresso machine. Lulu hated that coffee, hated its portion-controlled button-pressing mentality. Her formative coffee years had been Belle Hotel's dented silver pots and a generous shot of Franco's hand roasted blend. She did her best to smile.

'Thank you. This'll help. Head office want us to drive GP up to sixty-five per cent. I can't see how it can be done.'

Graeme took the chance to pull up his lumbar support chair. He smelled shower fresh, Lulu noticed, as if he'd taken the time to wash off the worst of the kitchen before coming to see her. He bared his upper teeth as he concentrated on the lines of numbers. A not altogether unattractive look, that at least brought a smile to Lulu's face. Lulu thought about Charlie, how he always looked at numbers sideways, or the wrong way up. Anything to avoid the facts.

'Mmh. Maybe. Well, I can switch to frozen New Zealand lamb,

if you sack the sommelier. Make the waiters promote the wine. Put them on commission for the high margin stuff?'

Lulu saw the sense in this. With her head. Her heart sank a little more into the grey carpet-tiled floor.

'Of course, we could put this back in the laptop safe and make love on the desk.' Graeme bared his teeth again and produced the office door key from his pocket. 'Would you like me to lock us in, so nobody can disturb us?'

Lulu wavered. If she did this, would that be it? Lulu and Graeme an item. No chance of ever getting back with Charlie. Not that that is what she wanted. No way. Graeme was a nice guy; Charlie a shit. Maybe he was the best option for her? Her dad seemed to think so. Why was it always the bad boys that did it for her? What was wrong with having a bit of head as well as heart? But the offering to lock the door thing... creepy.

It was the kind of commitment that was tempting, but permanent. Like Graeme's offer to help her buy Belle Hotel from the bank. She'd gone as far as to have her dad approach Paul Peters and pool her savings with Graeme's super-savers account, the one he'd had since he was a child, the one he got the free ruler and calculator for opening. As Graeme, her father and Paul Peters were quick to tell her, if she did this, ditching any chance of Charlie permanently, she'd be getting a hell of a good deal and her freedom, to boot.

'I'm sorry, Graeme, I can't do this. It's my time of the month.'

Graeme flinched slightly. A second or so later, he'd regained his executive head chef composure.

'Well, we could always...'

What was he suggesting? Whatever it was there wouldn't be much in it for Lulu. Graeme drove a hard bargain, like her dad. His savings were a bit higher than hers and it meant that she'd be the junior partner in buying Belle Hotel from the bank. Her dad, as a matter of principle, would not help. And as a matter of fact, could not help.

The capital he'd made from selling the carpet business was invested to the last penny in Hardman Academy and an obscure Icelandic bank. God forbid that Roger would trust the tax man to invest in schools anonymously on his behalf.

The time of the month thing was a lie. The handy fib had bought Lulu a bit of time. Graeme had a good heart and she very much wanted Belle Hotel, always had done, but she and Charlie, bloody Charlie, were unfinished business. He was showing annoying signs that he cared. That he might be committed to turning Belle Hotel around, rather than driving her into the ground. Lulu felt so very guilty about what she'd told Charlie at Franco's funeral. It was spiteful and a betrayal of Johnny's trust. No wonder Charlie was going off the rails. At least he was trying to get himself back together. The anger management classes were a start, anyway.

'Can we… I'm sorry, I need some air. I'm getting a bit of a headache.'

Lulu clicked the spreadsheet shut and set off to stare at the sea.

Tick-tock tick-tock every hour, more on the clock.

Charlie breathed in the fresh air, sunlight and freezing cold. Freedom. Whitehawk Hill. Left-bank Brighton at its bohemian best. He pulled the lapels of his peacoat tighter around his throat, tossed his cigarette into the bushes strewn with rubbish and climbed higher. Not long after noon and they were just arriving. The Food Collective had sprung out of a draconian decision taken by the council to pass on unkempt allotments to the eager influx from London, each desperate to have their little slice of the Downs for frisée and dinner-party chat.

'All right, darling?' It was Dawn, Franco's veg supplier since he'd quit tilling his allotment. 'Hard frost's going to hit us, you want some spuds?'

'No thanks, love, I'm up here looking for beets. Got an idea.'

'Okay, see you in a bit. I'll shout you when I've made a brew.'

Dawn's shed, an old railway carriage, had to be the best on

Whitehawk Hill. Some said she lived in it, but Charlie had been to her flat on the council estate that had robbed the hill of its hawks. She was a decade older than Charlie and, at forty-six, still sexy as fuck. Charlie thought she might, if he asked her, then he remembered the hordes of kids that buzzed about her come summer. None of them his, but this was not the time to be entering into a love-child lawsuit. Mother nature's emissary on earth, Charlie knew that Dawn eschewed all contraception. It messed with her germination.

He tramped down the frost-tinged planking, low-lying sun still not touching ground level yet, and soon saw Franco's allotment.

Franco had had the allotment since the fifties. He loved his shed and his spade, his only hobby, apart from the gee-gees. Charlie was less enthusiastic, but he'd kept the allotment on. The shed, roof worn and floor wonky, was his thinking space away from Belle Hotel. There was an old army camp bed in the corner and a potting table and stool under the cobwebbed windows that looked out to sea. Strewn across the table were not the usual seeds, pots and plant tags, but rough sketches of plates. Plates that bore pictures of food. Dishes half created, a visual map of flavours to come. Charlie pulled out the stool, lit up a fag and turned over a roughly sketched soufflé to settle over its blank side. He picked up a stub of pencil that had rolled to the far end of the table and snuck it behind his ear. The pot-bellied stove gaped open. A fire would be nice, but Charlie had cooking on his mind. The venison on his menu had been bothering him. Not the cut, braise or presentation, but the sauce. Too heavy, too alcoholic. He needed something as bold, but fresh. It was on the final OM at anger management that it had come to him. Beetroot. Took an act of God not blurting it out. What would Ernest have said? A healthy release of anger, root vegetable as expletive, we dig that.

Beetroot: bright red, bold enough for the gamey flesh and yet fresh enough to cut the mustard when it came to flavour. Charlie drew his dual lobes of venison, sitting atop some sort of ring-cut gratin. Sketching out the presentation of the dish before plating it, as Franco had taught him to do all those years ago.

'Layered beetroot and potato. Garlic, thyme and cream. Prepped first thing, then left on top of the grill for flash service.'

Everyone talked to themselves at their allotments. It was eccentric behaviour that came with a royal seal of approval. Charlie sketched in the sauce, stub of HB at forty-five degrees for effect, then with its newly sharpened tip drew three dark orbs.

'Baby beets to finish it off. Nice dish. Venison fillet with beetroot purée and gratin.'

Charlie pushed the paper to one side. A facsimile sketch was etched inside his skull. Coming to the allotment calmed Charlie like nothing else apart from cooking. He pulled across the butt-filled Belle Hotel ashtray to concentrate on his fag. Franco had brought that BH-embossed trophy up from the restaurant back in the days when people thought that nicking silver was just not done. Now they were down from a rack-full to about three or four and Charlie had no intention of replacing them. Neither did he have any intention of bringing this one back down. Charlie looked at the low bed and considered, for the first time, the reality of living here. But what would become of Mum? A kettle-shriek from Dawn's carriage roused him from going bust and beetroots. Tea.

It was nice and warm at Dawn's. Her stove was full of wood and flaming. I could be happy here, he thought. Just Dawn and me. She bent down to stoke the fire and he took a gulp of the tattooed cleft of her bum. He sipped the tea, three fly-flecked sugars, and weeded out the idea. Dawn was way beyond him and then his reputation would be mud up here, too. Too much talk of his bad behaviour went down in the chalky soil to make Dawn think twice about fucking Charlie, who now took a different tack.

'You growing any beets at the moment? I've got a crop ready to pull out, but I want some tiddlers. Got an idea for a dish.'

They went out along the wicker fencing to the cold frames and Dawn drew a handful of ink-veined leaves from their frost-free bed. Gathering allotment-grown veg for Belle Hotel as she had been doing since she was but a girl.

'Perfect, just what I wanted. Thanks. Righto, I've got lots to do, thanks for the tea, Dawny. See you soon.'

He kissed her on wind-burned cheeks and went back to his shed. He shut up sharpish and set off down Franco's track to Belle Hotel.

Charlie came in the front entrance, too much chance of meeting a supplier out back, and sniffed for a sense of service. The restaurant was empty, most Monday specials were back at their desks by three, though the place reeked of their consumption. Beef on the bone. Lamb shank. Truffle oil and mustard. The faint taint of cognac rang Charlie's till and taste buds. That party of accountants must have had some big numbers to celebrate. Claire and Emma had left the place pretty tidy, totalled to Charlie's eyes but good enough for any tiptoe punters peering in about dinner. He could hear laughter from the bar. Another bawdy cackle from Janet. How could she do it? Same bleary faces, same jaded jokes, day in, day out. All for what? Charlie knew the answer. For family. For love. For want of anything better to do. He left the bag of beets on table nine and swung through to rob the till to pay Sinker and Brampton when they came banging.

'Hi, Mum, it'll be ready 'bout four.'

Family tradition. Their Monday, Sunday roast. Regular as clockwork when Franco was alive. Three pm, rib of beef and goblet of Gigondas. Janet tutted her tardy son back to the kitchen. She was hungry, knew she shouldn't do it and, sod it, grabbed another fist of nuts from the greasy bucket under the bar.

'Half for you, Jan, darling?'

'Don't mind if I do, Rory, love.'

Hazards of the job, those handfuls of halves and peanuts – they were hell on the waistline. Janet banged the now empty till shut with her beer gut and gulped her lager/nut starter.

The phone rang as Charlie passed reception. Damn, why did it always do that? He leaned over the desk and picked it up.

'Hi, Charlie, Chris Evans here. How you doing? Good. Me too. Listen I'm holding a corn on the cob. Yep. What's best? Oh, should I pan fry it then?'

Cookery demonstration over, Charlie slung the phone back over the counter and carried on towards lunch.

'Hi, Fish.'

The tiles gleamed white, the grouting a grotty brown. Fish was just mopping himself out of the back door.

'Oh, all right, boss. All done, thirty for lunch, all on set menu though, tight-arsed bastards. Apart from one. Artist fella. David Wiggly or summat. Drew a lobster on a menu. I've stuck it on the wall by the fryers. Wanted something called a Dave Salad. Sounded like cold egg and chips to me, so I did that and charged him twenty quid. I'll see you later, hey?'

Charlie made a show of walking carefully across the mopped floor. He dropped it the moment Fish had swung out of the back door. The heavy steel slab was about to slam shut when four blood and sausage fingers appeared halfway up.

'Hello, Charlie boy. I've come for my money. Three weeks, I'm 'fraid. Hard cheese on you if you've not got it.'

Charlie had just enough to see Brampton off the premises and back to Mrs B for a noggin of brie. He was about to slither over and slide the lock when four fishy fingers slipped around and stopped him. Sinker, come for his cash. People were so predictable when it came to getting paid.

'Sorry about this, Nigel, I'm clean out of cash, it'll have to be a cheque.'

The fishmonger stood there, looking down at his yellow wellies, and emitted a salty sigh at the unfairness of life. His last Belle Hotel cheque had bounced three times. Still, a cheque in the hand, better than a slap in the face with a wet fish. Unless of course you were Sinker. Charlie had been bouncing cheques on Sinker for the best part of a decade. This gave Sinker nothing much to smile about, which in a way suited him. Belle Hotel was broke and all of Brighton knew it. More fool you if you left the place with one of Charlie's rubber cheques.

Charlie reappeared brandishing the chequebook and a bag of beetroots. He handed Sinker the cheque, Sinker slipped back to the sea, and Charlie tipped earthy beets onto stainless steel. The pitter of grit resounded to the bass thud of the beetroot. Charlie slid the baby beets to one side, scissor-cut the tops off the big ones, double jacketed them in foil and slung them in the ever-ready oven, then trimmed, peeled and boiled his baby beets in a two-inch copper bottom and rag-dried the prep table before setting up the mandolin.

The angled slicer, with its knuckle-shredding blade, gleamed as it had the day that Franco brought it back from Catering Supply Co.

'Righto, that's her set up. Now hand me a spud, Charlie Farley.'

Charlie had watched in amazement as with a quick flick of his cuff-rolled wrists his grandfather dispatched the starchy orb above into see-through slithers below.

Now he watched his hand, and remembered following Franco's. This time it would be half spud, half beetroot layered with cream, garlic and thyme, just as he'd decided up on Whitehawk Hill. This was his craft, what he did for family, for love, for want of anything better to do. As he went through the motions, aping Franco, Charlie had a Damascene moment. Maybe he wasn't a genius after all? Maybe he was just a cook with a raging ego, eh, Ernest?

He finished the top of the gratin with a light grate of Emmenthal, slung the grater into the sink for Fish to do later, and popped the tray into the oven under his beetroots. The foil-wrapped chunkies were beginning to sizzle, red-hot juice dripping down silver sides. Charlie liked the idea of root juice dripping on to the gratin below. Meat was always roasted this way once, why not veg? He pictured the drizzle of dark red infusing with the garlic-lashed cream below, could taste the flavours. Not a turn was wasted. He reached up for a circular cutter from the tub above the oven and placed it on the table ready for when the gratin slid bubbling from the depths.

The cooking calmed him further. Belle Hotel might be going bust, but as long as Charlie had blades, flame and bubbling pans, he'd be happy. His world may be collapsing, but at least his soufflés weren't.

He moved his baby beets off the flame, fished the garnish out of its juice and blanched them under the cold tap. These too he turned out onto the table next to the cutter. Glancing up his eye caught the lobbo drawing on the menu that Fish had stuck up. Nice work. Funny. Shaking its claw at the punters. Damn you all! David, eh? Wasn't there an artist who stayed in the seventies called David, too? Did that painting of Franco, Janet and the cat. Maybe he'd copy that lobster onto the menu in future. Be good that. Then Charlie forgot all about the lobster and remembered the slosh of port Franco always gave his venison sauce and set off for the bar with a plastic jug.

At reception, the phone rang yet again. On his way past the bar, Charlie picked it up.

'Belle Hotel?'

'Charlie, it's me.'

'Who?'

'Lulu, that's who. Not a good time to be forgetting the sound of my voice when I'm about to put a business opportunity into your ungrateful lap. Don't forget, you're invited to late supper at mine on Saturday. Though I don't know why I bother.'

'Oh, Lu. Sorry, I'm cooking. Fine-tuning. Beetroot.'

'Oh, okay. Well I thought you'd like to know that—'

'Lu, can this wait? I'm cooking.'

'What is this? Pass up on a business opportunity day?'

'Okay, Lu, thanks. Look, I gotta go.'

'Thanks, Charlie Sheridan. Is that it? Don't you want to know what the opportunity is? Or are you happy to drift into bankruptcy? I'm helping you here, against my better judgement, Charlie.'

'Okay, thanks. Tell you what, send me a note. See you, later. Lu? Are you there?'

She'd slammed her end down.

Lulu looked up from her open-plan desk in the cool interior of Hotel Epicure's lobby. She sighed and rapped her thoroughly buffed nails on the empty surface. Two guests walked in. Armani jeans, watch and wallet. Lulu's sigh eased into a sunny beam as the highlighted heads flashed past. She dropped the smile and went back to worrying. Buying Belle Hotel with Graeme wasn't only a back-up plan. It was THE plan. Only Charlie could fuck things up enough to mean she'd be using it. It was Charlie that had given her this dilemma. Charlie, Charlie, Charlie. Sadly, Lu knew Charlie. Paul Peters had warned her dad that Charlie and Janet were hanging on by a thread. One last missed payment away from repossession. What she and Graeme were doing was a sensible way to save Belle Hotel from a chain like Hotel Epicure. Where the GP mattered more than the guests. Lulu could barely remember what it was like to work with Charlie. Apart from the memory that nobody had made her so furious since and nobody had worked as well with her as a team since, too. Charlie had lot of growing up to do and an on-time payment to make to ensure Lulu didn't have to press the Graeme option. But, oh, the absolute anguish of having to give up on Charlie if she did have to do this. Graeme and Lulu being business partners was getting more and more likely. The idea of them being an item was getting more likely too. He fit Madame Eva's 'man in blue and white' premonition. Another bloody chef in blue-and-white check trousers. Graeme's would be clean and pressed, whereas Charlie's... God, it didn't bear thinking about. Although Lulu had come to rather like being single. Men weren't as satisfying as work.

Tock-tick, tick-tock, Charlie passing Franco's clock as he tossed his jug up into the air dotted with dust, and caught it by the handle as it span back down to the threadbare carpet.

'*Send me a note.*'

Thinking of Lulu angry made him feel horny and a little bit sorry that he hadn't tried it on with Dawn up on the hill earlier.

He saw his mother through the bottom of her half-empty glass as he side-slid past her to get to the port rack.

'You nearly ready? I'm half starving here.'

'Four. Just like I said.'

With Janet breathing down his neck, he'd have to cheat the beetroots. Charlie pulled them from the oven, tore the foil off with his heat-hardened fingers and gave them five minutes each in the microwave to soften the flesh, but not lose the flavour. He rubbed the skins off all four and chopped them all finely with his eight-inch Sheffield Stainless. The blood of the beetroot stained the blade in ways he'd rather not remember. Took a double dousing under the spray and draw across the front of his chef's jacket to erase the memory.

Charlie took chunks and board over to the cooling copper-bottomed pan, tipped the steaming flesh into scarlet water and followed it with the jug of port. Twenty minutes on the fast back burner and he'd be ready with his hand blender – Franco would have loved that contraption – to turn it into purée.

Tick-tock, drip-drop. As Charlie puréed, a drop of toilet water plopped on Janet's head. She looked up and groaned.

'Bugger, that's room three again.'

The dark circle on the ceiling was growing ever wider. She flicked the latch on the bar door – if anyone was desperate they could come in through the front – and went off for her tools. The damp bag of wrenches, wire and putty were Franco's answer to everything wet.

'We don't need a plumber, I'll go get me bag.'

This, bravely said, when torrents of water were flowing down the main stairway, out across Ship Street and on to a churning sea. Once Franco had popped his stop-cock, it was pretty clear to Janet that she'd be looking after the twenty showerheads, one hundred and sixteen taps and four urinals – just one more thing on her ever-lengthening list of duties. Charlie had food and she had just about everything else. Still, Janet, mustn't grumble. Mustn't grumble, mustn't grumble. Must run, instead, like hell up the first flight of steps with her rusty answers to whatever dripping disaster awaited in room 3. Whatever it was, there would be no paying for a plumber. Not thrifty pride, like Franco, a very real and very frightening lack of money to pay for anything that went wrong. Sod it, thought Janet fumbling with the pass key, that room had had a new carpet last month. One of Roger's remnant specials, pay when you can. Don't want that up again. Quick.

Charlie rooted around in the back of the walk-in for the last of the venison. There it was, behind the bucket of stock that Fish must have made earlier. Good lad. Charlie picked up the shrink-wrapped loins and trotted back to his bench.

Tick-tock, drip-drop. Things were not looking good up in room 3. Once Janet had finally got her pass key to work the crime scene hit her full on. Whoever was staying in this room had blocked the toilet with a turd the size of a baby's arm. Then the recently relieved guest had taken the decision to abandon the rising waters and scarper.

'Shit.'

Precisely. Janet had two choices. She waded through the brown-flecked water and grabbed the plunger from Franco's sack as she went. One swift plunge and the rubber dome ploughed on and through the poo like a hot knife through butter. Sadly, Janet followed through, ending up elbow deep in muddy waters.

She pulled the plunger back, registering the suckering sound and the scent of shit on the air, and gagged. Seeing the excreta-splattered arm of her best white shirt up so close to her face turned the gag into a chunder. Janet sent forth a plume of fizzy peanut arcing onto the already untidy mess of the cramped bathroom.

Not good. It was not good. She sat on the bed and wept.

Charlie removed the gratin from the oven, crisp brown on umbered red, and quickly cut four perfect circles from its farthest edge. Two of each circle went onto the pre-warmed plates. This was good, he was feeling it, coming back. The focus. No need to look at the sketch, he knew what he wanted to do with this dish. In flow, spinning from hob to plate, carefully constructing, creating, inventing, drawing on Franco and his other culinary fathers to realise something new.

Upstairs, Janet snapped out of it, cleared up the crime scene and went upstairs to change her shirt.

He'd sealed the venison five minutes earlier with a flash in the pan and stuck it into the oven for a sizzle to pink. Holding the red-hot handle with a double folded cloth, careful not to burn himself unnecessarily, he forked the four fillets onto a gratin apiece. Pan with its precious juices back on the hob, ladle of stock from the stock bucket and over to the baby beets just as it comes to the boil. But, wait. The beets were too big. Charlie pulled focus in his mind's eye and could see the beets upstaging the meat. Chop, chop from the eight-incher, more stain removal needed, and the quarters took their rightful space in the bubbling pan. Fresh ladle at grab height and a quick dip in the blood-warm beetroot purée. Charlie circled the meat with a wide ring of purée then brought the saucepan and its contents over for the final touch.

The splashes of thin sauce bled to the edge of the purée, halted as Charlie had guessed by the viscous ring. Venison fillet with beetroot purée and gratin.

The dish was very Joel Robuchon. Charlie had been there on one of his solo trips eating his way through Franco's legacy. Robuchon was a crazy place but the cooking had been amazing, as had the loyalty of the brigade. Same number of chefs as customers, sixty in all. Bit like Belle Hotel these days. Robuchon still had his star, bastard. Charlie lost his by accident, on purpose. And when he did, he lost everything. But they couldn't take his cooking away from him. They couldn't do that. He'd meant what he said at anger management. He had learnt. He did want to control his anger. For the sake of his cooking, if nothing else.

The plates were already at table two, so they could watch reception, when Janet entered. She didn't mention what happened upstairs, nothing worth telling, really. Just another shitty day at Belle Hotel for Janet Sheridan, née Gay. If she'd never married Johnny, Janet would have never got stuck at Belle Hotel. Lulu had made a lucky escape.

Just as her buttocks touched the banquette the phone went.

'I'll get it,' she wearily murmured to Charlie, 'it'll be a weekend break.'

Charlie watched her through the divider and knew from her shoulders it was him. She held the phone up for Charlie to see and mouthed 'H-I-M.' Johnny, John, Dad.

One shake from Charlie and Johnny was gone. Janet could bear to be civil, but she wanted to keep it as short as she could.

'Righto, I'll tell him. Bye, then.'

She shuffled back, rolled her eyes at her son, ruffled his already ruffled head and picked up a pitted fork. If they talked about it they would end up rowing and Janet didn't want that on her two hours off. Charlie was volatile around anything to do with Johnny. He blamed her, in some ways, for Johnny's departure, more than Franco. If only he knew.

There was an empty chair at the table. Franco's. But he was with them now, filling their heads in the silence: a bit of chat about Larry, pulling Charlie's leg about the busty blonde in room 14. Rolling his Gs on his Gigondas, half an ear on the racing running on the radio to an empty kitchen. Family. Fresh linen. Flowers and all that. Belle Hotel. If we can't enjoy it ourselves, then who can?

Charlie moved his plate to cover the worst of the earlier stains from a fixed-price diner. Janet took her first bite and, for a moment, forgot. She forgot they were up to their necks in it – work, shit, debt. Tick-tock, tick-tock, Belle Hotel on the knock. Forgot she had lied to her ex-husband and neglected to tell her son. For one delicious moment, Janet forgot everything except flavour. Christ, this was good. Maybe his best. She knew better than to ask him, Charlie hated commenting on his own cooking, so they ate the dish in silence. Janet slurped the glass of house, Gigondas no more, she'd brought through for them and then, in a habit that annoyed the hell out of Charlie, slurped some of his.

He fought the urge to stab her in the neck with his fork, although the handle found itself wedged in Charlie's palm, tines braced towards his mother's fleshy folds. In a moment, the urge abated. He returned to fork, plate, mouth duty and mother and son munched on in silence until a pair of yellow heads bobbed up at the window. A moment later they were leaning their high-waisted jeans against the reception desk.

'I'll go.'

She said it as a matter of fact more than in any kind of protest. Janet: going, going, gone… Two for dinner, yes I think we can fit you in. Seven o'clock? Hell, the place would be empty then. No, but I can get you a table at eight. OK, good, do you have a contact number? Yes, I know it. See you later, then.

A bellow of blue announced that Charlie was ready for coffee. Janet set off for the bar to get his triple shot and a camomile for her still delicate system. Her hand shook as she held the little jug of milk under the steam wand. Janet dreaded the conversation that was to come, the red demand burned a hole in her back pocket. Still, as Franco said, Monday was always the day for talking business. Too busy doing business the rest of the week for all that.

She came back in and fell in love with him all over again. He had his feet up on the banquette, fag jutting out of one of the three remaining ashtrays and he pushed the end of his lunch around his plate. Tinkering, fine-tuning, in search of perfection.

Now or never, now or never…

'Now then, Charlie, what about this?'

She passed him the Hookes bank statement, which he duly opened and read. Upside down. Charlie nodded and passed the creased piece of paper back.

'Charlie, what are we going to do? I can't pay the staff. We can't pay the overdraft fees. God alone knows what we're going to do next month for stock.'

'Oh, *stock*. It's OK, Ma, Fish made a load this morning.'

'Don't be flip, I want to know what we're going to do.'

Charlie swung round, feet flat on the floor, fork in the palm of his hand.

'I'll go and see Peters. Friday.'

'Friday may be too late. You have a look at the bookings, they're down on last month. Restaurant too. It's my guys in the bar that keep us in bog roll.'

'We could let Fish go. I'll run the kitchen by myself.'

'Don't be foolish, lad. What would your grandfather say to all that? Now then, I don't know what's to become of us.'

'You, Ma. You don't know what's to become of you.'

She looked up from her aproned lap – at least he'd stopped her crying.

'What do you mean, me?'

'Well, I can get a job and a bed anywhere, but you… This is your home. I'm supposed to leave home, but you…'

'Charlie, we may have to sell, you know.'

'Fuck's sake, mother, we can't sell. Wouldn't even cover the overdraft, let alone the other debts.'

'I know, I know.'

'We're fucking wedged in tight, turning spuds, pulling pints until we go bust or die.'

'I hate it, hate it… but what can we do?'

'I've told you. I'll go see Peters, extend the overdraft. Fix it.'

'Franco, what would Franco say?'

'He didn't have to compete with Hotel Epicure or easyJet.'

'Franco would've known what to do.'

'Don't tell me, I'm just like my father.'

'Now, I didn't say that. Talk to him, Charlie. Spare me having to do that again.'

'Maybe I will. Listen Mum, Lulu's sending me a note with a business opportunity. Could be big. I need a break, Ma. I know I've messed things up. It's just so hard without Franco.'

Janet waited, slipped her hand onto her son's knee under the table and gave it a little squeeze.

'We'll see. I just want—'

The phone rang again in reception. Too drained to give a damn, Janet rose to get it.

Charlie looked down at his chef's jacket. The bright red slashes had faded and would come out in the wash. Another thing on Janet's list. He lay back on the green leather of the banquette. Home. In less than a minute Charlie was sound asleep.

'Yes, we could fit you in a sea-view room. It has got a little supplement. What? OK, no supplement. And a Z-Bed. Yes, I'll just need to take your credit-card details to secure the reservation. Why? Well, it's to secure the reservation. Hello? Hello?' Gone.

Janet looked up into a pair of beady eyes, which met hers over the reception desk.

'I'd like the keys to room three, please.'

MEMO FROM: HOTEL EPICURE
FROM: LULU HARDMAN
RE: STAG & HEN PARTIES IN 2008
DEAR CHARLIE, GRAEME, OUR EXECUTIVE HEAD
CHEF AND I HAVE DECIDED TO DECLINE STAG
AND HEN PARTY BUSINESS AS IT DOESN'T FIT WITH
OUR GUEST PROFILE CRITERIA. WE WONDERED
IF YOU WOULD LIKE TO TAKE ALL OUR FUTURE
BOOKINGS? IT IS DECENT BUSINESS, AND AS AN
INDEPENDENT HOTEL, YOU AREN'T RESTRICTED
BY HEAD OFFICE GUEST PROFILE CRITERIA.
BEST WISHES,
LULU

The Stags and Hens Express departed London Victoria at 6.06pm every Friday. Normal commuters knew to avoid it. They either quit the capital early or hung back in bars awaiting its passing. Girls in gangs of six, always six, sat blocking the aisle with their Asti Spumante smiles and blow-job bobs. The guys, lucky seven for some reason, hogged half a carriage, feet up, cans cracked; aggression at the ready. Here they go, here they go, here they *go*. L-plates and love handles for the hens. Handcuffs and charlie for the stags. And the T-shirts. The fucking T-shirts.

Lisa's Last Cluck.

Boys, too cool to wear such stuff, made do with a limited range of pressed dress shirts by Ben Sherman, Ted Baker and, for the flash Harry of the outfit, a bloke called Paul Smith. Who are you, Paul Smith, who are you?

Charlie swore he'd stop taking stag and hen parties long ago. Then he lowered his standards and just swore.

'Fuckers. I want them out of here by eight, we've got residents and locals to feed from then.'

He could see the fluffy devils' horns and bobbing stars reeling in the street through Belle Epoque glass that might once upon a time have afforded a view of a gentleman's top hat or a lady's parasol. Now Charlie had to make do with joke shop tat and a tall bloke with kids' TV hair. Wait, a stag. Oh no, they've hooked up.

It was his worst fear. Charlie knew the score, he'd even been on a few of these with the staff over the years. Pub, curry and club Friday night, make your presence felt. Saturday morning heave down a fry-up then off to the pier for a few hours of salt air and funfair. He could picture the stags and hens making their way down opposite sides of the boardwalk, the hens breaking heels on the gaps in the planking, stags breaking wind, spanking and guffawing. Then they'd meet at the end of the pier, all at sea, together at last, six women, seven men. Always an odd one out.

'All right?'

'Yeah, you all right?'

'Yeah, where you from?'

The karaoke bar opened at eleven and in poured the newly formed crowd, 'Wonderwall' and 'Like a Virgin' going down like thirteen pints of lager twice. And the smell. Opium, cocaine and copping off. What, already? It's not even noon. Only a snog, nothing to write home about. 'Cept you can't write, hah, hah. Off the pier and land leg it to the nearest pub for peanuts with your double digit and vision pints of lager. Then Gina, the posh spice of the Hen camp would check out her Gucci.

'Oh my God, it's six o'clock. Come on, girls, Belle Hotel.'

They'd been bumped from Hotel Epicure.

'Ain't that the place where the chef's got a right temper? I read about 'im in *Heat*. Burnt a bloke a few years back. Now there's this stabbing scandal.'

The stags thought they'd come too. Well, it was less of a think than a leer in the general direction of the hens. They staggered up Ship Street, stopping to let Gina puke, and Ocean's Thirteen washed up outside Belle Hotel, where the chef's got a temper.

'Out by eight, Mum. Especially if there are blokes with them. Cash only, too. In advance.'

'Charlie…'

'I'm not having another walk-out.'

Janet looked at her son and pursed her lips slightly – not enough to be saying no, but enough to mean OK, but you do it.

'OK, I'll do it.'

She smiled and touched him on the arm. Charlie turned and went back to the kitchen.

'Hello, Mr Brampton, Belle Hotel here. Sorry to bother you at six on a Saturday, but I need seven chunks of venison. Last-minute stag and hen party, if I let them order à la carte they'll dent a big hole in my stock. Can you help?'

'For you, Master Sheridan, anything. For cash. We're still humping carcasses over here. I'll pop over in five with one of them, should see seven blokes all right. What about the birds? Any Edams worth looking at?'

Charlie rang off and smiled at Fish, his loyal number two through thick, thin and stabbing. It wasn't a stabbing as such, just a bit of blade in the buttock. Charlie and Fish swore blind it was just a slippery patch between them. The bloody council, prosecuting him for something that Fish was ready to let go.

'Okay, Fish, we'll whack this table out, then you can go. Early night, mate.'

'Thanks, Chef.'

Charlie knew where the stags and hens were heading. He'd been there too. Adonis at the Babylon Lounge for the hens and Brighton Babes at Planet Club for the stags. Two hours of striptease from the opposite sex then they'd be thrust together at the Babylon Lounge for a school disco until bedtime. Two hundred drunken animals making out it was their last night of freedom. Charlie had thirteen of them out front, baying for his blood.

'Chef, chef, chef…'

Franco would have known how to handle them. Even his meek father knew how to handle undesirables at The Savoy. But Charlie just couldn't do that front-of-house stuff. That was Lulu's thing and she'd deserted him years ago. Left him for dead. How to handle them? Like a chef.

A bang on the back door. It was Brampton, bloated and bloodied from his day at the slab.

'Here you go, Charlie, well-hung venison for your stags. Can I take a peek at those hens now?'

'Here, come on, John, let's go say hello.'

Janet had sat the rowdy crowd at their table and shot off to the pub to fetch the thirteen shouted pints. Half lager, half soda water. Good for us and good for them.

The kitchen nightmare rose from the depths and appeared at the head of the hens and stags.

'Chef, chef… fuckin' hell.'

Silence.

Charlie bared his chopper, eight inches of Made in Sheffield, and flashed a steely grin. Behind him stood a bloodied apparition, gazing out vein-eyed, chest height at one half of the table.

'Now then, I'm Charlie Sheridan. Welcome to Belle Hotel. We want to cook for you, don't we, Mr Brampton.'

'Yes, Chef.'

'But we won't take any of your bullshit, will we?'

'No, Chef.'

Charlie held the blade up, chandelier glint on ground edge, meaning eat then leave.

Fish was seasoning the venison loins, Franco's book down from the shelf, as Charlie came back in.

Loin of Venison with Sweet Peppercorn Sauce

1 Saddle of Venison (prep into 6 loins)

S&P

Olive oil

3 tbsp spiced cranberries

3 oz mixed wild mushrooms

1 large celeriac (julienne)

2 oz butter

¼ pint double cream

6 shallots, sliced

1 tbsp crushed white & black peppercorns

2 tbsp red wine vinegar

½ pint red (Rhône!)

1 glass port

1 pint game stock

'Thanks, John. See you later, pay you sooner. Fish, I'll do that. Can you get me six chicken breasts? That bunch of hens won't do venison.'

Brampton's face lit up at the mention of breasts; he left Belle Hotel deeply aroused, hard cheese on his missus.

Janet dispensed the thin lager and went to check the menu with Charlie. The hens and stags clucked and rutted for their supper.

Without looking round, Charlie clocked the sound of chopping. Good on Fish.

Sat by the spiced cranberry jar was julienne of celeriac. Good to go. Charlie fired up the hotplate big enough for all six at a sizzle and waited for the red glow at its iron edges. Fish had already sent the prawn cocktails with Janet, no need to check these days. Charlie flash-seared the meat, pink flesh frazzled to dark brown, game scent in his sinus from the fast-rendered fat.

'Fish, you do the chicken… Kievs, I think. I'm going to do that beetroot thing with the venison that I did at the weekend.'

'Yes, Chef.'

Charlie knew Fish would do the starch and veg for thirteen, he could smell a two-inch dauphinoise somewhere at the back of the oven. Potato, Emmenthal, garlic. Veg would be green and orange to complement both flesh and fowl. Now then, the new sauce from the beetroot. Charlie added a couple of pencilled notes alongside Franco's wobbly typing. No point in wasting paper, Charlie knew what the adaptations meant. Good enough for him, who else was going to read it? Apart from Fish and he didn't count.

The bones and sinew from Fish's preparation of Brampton's saddle was bubbling away furiously at the back of the hob. Charlie skimmed the pot and placed the loins onto a metal tray, ready for finishing in the oven. He span around the kitchen diving into drawers and shelves, ducked into the bar for bottle and glass; slung a bent copper bottom onto the blue flame. The stags and hens had finished their starters and were tucking into a bottle of house each, kerching, as they waited for their mains. The sauce Marie Rose seemed to have had a calming effect upon them. Amazing what a bit of ketchup, mayo and Worcestershire can do.

Franco helped Charlie with his cooking. His instruction coming back to Charlie every time he had an old recipe down from the book. The dance of adaptation, the codifying and refining, altering and reinventing.

'Now then, Charlie Farley, you want to caramelise those shallots. That's it, the sticky glaze before it gets burnt. Flick in yer sauces and spices. Heat down, don't want to burn it. Next the vinegar. Always vinegar for that sour snap. Now boil. Like hell. Add your booze, oh right you're doing that, nice, I never thought of that and reduce by half. Stock and do it again, by half. OK, now sieve it. Here, take this chinoise, best for itty-bitty sauces, and pass it into a clean pan.'

Charlie passed his sauce and slung the itty-bitty utensils into the sink for Fish to wash later.

Seven o'clock and the two restaurant girls came on shift. Claire and Emma, mid-thirties, broad-hipped, survivors of that unforgettable night at the Groucho, and simply indispensable. Claire had sworn off men in favour of women. She claimed that the Groucho night made her mind up. The two loyal restaurant staff soon took the unlucky thirteen firmly in hand.

'Don't fancy yours much.'

'Are you finished with that, or do you want to lick the plate too?'

'Ooh, saucy.'

All that stag and hen banter was making Charlie horny. He sat back in the cubbyhole behind reception and waited for the chick he'd checked in earlier to come looking for him. Sure enough, back she came: Daisy, the boho from Soho with blue eyes and a thing for big-headed chefs with hot tempers. She was happy to take the Belle Hotel tour, it didn't last long. Charlie knew what she was after, a trophy to take up to her mate sharing the room with her, so he kissed her in the kitchen and asked her for a quickie in the boiler room. Something to take his mind off Lulu's sympathy fuck of a note. Charlie flicked her G-string into the air, his usual party trick, Daisy laughed and left it wherever it had landed.

By the time tock-tock had sounded the eight bells the stags and hens had paid and gone. Charlie fingered the seven hundred and fifty quid, cash if you please, and smiled. He sniffed his fingers, both his favourite smells, passed a tatty twenty to Fish, put half a monkey in the tin to pay Sinker and Brampton come Monday, popped a ton in his pocket, and took the rest through to the bar.

'Here you go, Mum. Nearly four hundred quid for you. Not bad for an early evening's work.'

Janet took the notes from her son and popped them in the back slot of Franco's ancient till.

'Righto, our evening trade will be dribbling in soon, I'd better go and wash up a couple of plates.'

Charlie felt fine for the first time in months. The hundred quid was burning a hole in his pocket, he'd need that for later in case they went to Sussex Arts Club, and thanks to the fact that the stags and hens didn't want the shellfish, something to do with a story they'd heard about Belle Hotel and mass food poisoning, Charlie now had a large bag of clams to take over to Lulu's for supper.

The two hours of service dragged. Even the fruity banter of Emma and Claire did little to pass the time. Three twos and a four – it was hardly the stuff of Belle Hotel Saturday nights past.

He slipped out of the now grotty whites, chucking the jacket on the floor for Janet to pick up and wash in the morning. A couple of trays' prep for breakfast, sausages, mushrooms Belle Hotel and bacon left on the trolley just inside the walk-in door, and Charlie was ready for whatever the night could throw at him. He could knock out the full English with his eyes closed, which is what he hoped they would be. Charlie grabbed his peacoat, felt for his fags and transferred the roll of twenties from his chef checks to his jeans.

'Righto, bye, Ma.'

'You not having a quick one with us before you go?'

'No thanks.' Charlie nodded at the barflies. 'I'm off to cook these clams at Lulu's.'

Janet raised an eyebrow to her regulars. Lulu.

He swung the briny net onto his back, shouldering them for the two-mile trot to Lulu's new houseboat in Shoreham.

The seafront was blissfully stag and hen free, most of them would be moistening nylon at their respective strip shows by now. Ten pm, strip show o'clock. A few taxis shuttled not-much-to-say couples back to their babysitters, a pink stretch limo rolled past. Charlie flicked the bird at its mooning inhabitants, grinned, shot across both lanes and down the ramp to the boardwalk.

The unseen sea thundered at the shingle giving a backbeat to the hi-tempo house that smoked out of the doors of the clubs as he strode past. Charlie nodded at most of the door staff. Most of those shaved, scarred heads had given Belle Hotel service in one way or another.

'All right Charlie? How's tricks?'

'Not so bad, Eddie.'

'Whatcha got there?'

'Clams, I just been doing a spot of fishin'.'

'Yeah, fuck off, we seeing you later?'

'Dunno, Lu and her crowd from the Hotel Epicure said something about the Arts Club.'

'Oh, yeah, well take it easy.'

A high five to Eddie and he continued on his way, a blue cloud of Marlborough cutting the salt lit air.

Charlie crossed into Shoreham, shipbuilding coast, and cut back across the traffic into Surrey Boatyard. He hoped she was home alone. He buzzed the entry box.

'Hello, stranger, come aboard.'

Charlie shunted the steel door to the boatyard with his shoulder and stepped out onto the jetty.

Lulu shouted at him to come aboard. The lights were low and he could see her outline through the glass screen to her bedroom. Some minutes later she came through to greet him.

She looked beautiful. Dark hair up, wool dress slung on after a recent shower… no, he couldn't go there. Again.

'Hi, Lu. Is he coming?'

'Who he?'

'The stocktaker.'

'If you are referring to Graeme my colleague, yes, he is coming. Just finishing up at the hotel. We did over two hundred covers tonight.'

'Stocktaking.'

'What was that?'

'Er, clams. I brought you clams. You got any white wine? And anything better than this?'

He grimaced at the Dido muzaking away in the background. Probably the Hotel Epicure influence.

'Listen, Charlie Sheridan, cut the crap. I'm pleased to see you, really I am, but this was Graeme's idea so *be nice.*'

Charlie chucked the clam bag in the sink and looked in the steel fridge for a drink.

'Champagne OK?'

'Hey, mister, we're not celebrating, remember?'

'Lu, I need to ask you for something before they get here.'

'No, Charlie. Whatever it is, no. Sex. Sex and money. Sex and money and somewhere to stay. No. We were over a long time ago. This is, this is… work stuff. Call it industrial relations, if you like.'

'You got any chilli?'

'Oh, er, yes I think so. Bottom of… there.'

Lu put on the Miles Davis CD they had both loved as teenagers. She stood behind him in the spotlit kitchen and watched him work.

'How were the hen party?'

'Yes, thank you very much for the sympathy fuck.'

'Well, I thought you'd need the business and they are not really our type of cus—'

'Yeah, OK, I geddit, thanks. Spent over a grand, as it happens, where there's muck there's brass. Vongole OK?'

'Yummy. Graeme's bringing over bruschetta and a lemon tart for afters. We're sitting you next to Cindy, she's new and up for a bit of rough.'

'Oh, thanks a bunch.'

Voices could be heard on the gangplank. Lulu stepped away from Charlie, leaning awkwardly against the butcher's block her father had bought her as a birthday present, shipped in from Sicily, no expense spared, as usual. She stole a last solitary look at Charlie, resisted the urge to run her fingers through that nest of hair, missing the stink of kitchen fat and fags she knew would linger on her fingertips for the rest of the night.

Graeme and the others came aboard. Graeme kissed Lulu a little too slowly to Charlie's eye. Then, when he'd finally taken his hands off her, he squared up to Charlie.

'Hellooo, Chef, what's for supper?'

'Spag Vog, Chef. How's it going? You finished your spreadsheets for the night?'

'Fuck off, Charlie.'

'And—'

'You two, cut it. Charlie, Cindy. Cindy, Charlie. Tanzie and Tom, you know Charlie, the beast from Belle, yes?'

The caterers filled Lulu's houseboat with chatter while Charlie clattered about comfortably in the kitchen. Graeme came in for a while and sat on the butcher's block. If Charlie didn't hate what Graeme stood for, corporate catering, they could have been friends. They had worked very well together in the kitchen at catering college before Charlie beat Graeme to the stage in Switzerland.

'I'm just going to soften this garlic. Then, hey, pass me the wine.' He sloshed it in, watched it flame up. 'Make yerself useful and chop some parsley.' Charlie pulled the green sprig from his back pocket and tossed it across to Graeme. 'Suppose you've never seen it done this way, I expect you just cut the bag once you've boiled it.'

'Up yours, bankrupt boy. Hey, are the rumours true?'

'Nice bruschetta, by the way and no, they are not. Who says, anyway?'

'Just a few of the suppliers, y'know, I don't like to listen to tittle-tattle, but when they are affecting my margins…'

'How can my not paying for potatoes possibly hurt your calculations?'

'Drop it, you two,' interrupted Lu. 'When do you want that crusty bread?'

''Bout now would be good. Has that oven gone off?'

Charlie span round, grabbed Graeme by the parsley and clattered it into the vongole with a ratchet of his huge wooden spoon.

'Nice utensil, this. Must nick it. Righto, grub's up.'

The six of them ate with the ease of odd-hour workers with Dido, reinstated, as background. Through the putter of hot candles, Lulu glared at Charlie, warning him not to complain. The tart went down nicely with a bottle of Muscat de Beaumes de Venise that had passed its last hours in the bottom of Lu's freezer. A line or two later and the friends were ready for Sussex Arts Club.

The white Georgian building leaned as unsteadily as its punters into the narrow confines of Ship Street. Charlie's party jumped the queue, thanks to Deano, and slumped in the huge leather sofa that faced the street. Charlie sat too close for comfort to Lulu, longing to reach out and hold her. Graeme took an age at the bar.

'Probably checking up on their weights and measures.'

'Ha, ha, Mr One-joke. What you going to do, Charlie?'

'Get a couple of shandies down me and dance till they put the house lights on.'

'No, with Belle Hotel.'

'Same as ever. Keep buggering on, as Franco used to say.'

'Yes, but you're not Franco. My dad—'

'Oh, here we go.'

'Well, my father happens to have created a lot of wealth in his time. Some of which he wasted on you.'

'He told you to say that, did he? Come on, Lulu, love, he was a carpet fitter. Hardly the restaurant business.'

'Yes, but he knows how to make the most of what you've got. He says you should—'

'What, you've been talking to him about me?'

'No, he talked to me after a Hookes luncheon he—'

'Fucking Peters, he doesn't know when to keep his mouth shut.'

The piano man struck up a Billy Joel classic.

'Graeme'll love this, where are our fucking lagers?'

'They care about you, Charlie, your talent. Belle Hotel. Your mother.'

'Enough, Lu, I don't want to talk about it. You, caring about me. That's a laugh. I suppose that bullshit you told me at Franco's funeral was caring, too?'

'No, Charlie. That was cruel and, I don't know, I'm sorry. Have you spoken to Johnny about it?'

'Nah, too busy.'

'Hopeless. You Sheridans are hopeless. I give up.

'I'm going to see what Graeme's up to.'

Two hours later the exes were back together on the sofa. Graeme had gone home, early start in the morning, the other couple and Charlie's love disinterest, Cindy, were dancing to Human League in the back room. Pissed enough to slur the words and blur the distance between them, the conversation kicked off once more. Charlie burped loudly and a cloud of clam, wine and garlic wafted seductively in the general direction of Lulu.

'Revolting. You really are the end, you know that. Okay, I'm going to say my piece for one final time, and fuck you.'

'Thank you. Fuck you. I wish.'

'Shut it. Just hear me out, come here, I don't want to have to shout. I've got another business opportunity for you. The Belle Hotel Cookbook. How about it? Judith Langdon, at Haddon. The cookbook supremo. Remember, the publisher that did The Ivy cookbook? I've contacted her and she's interested. She's interested in a meet. It'd be good for business, good for your personal brand as a chef. Don't shake your head. All the chefs do a cookbook now. All the ones I've worked with. It's good for business, keeps a bit of extra cash coming in and codifies your life's work. It'll help you move on from the Michelin star and the anger reputation and all that. What do you say? Recipes and revelations. Bring some of Franco's book to life. Come on, Charlie, go and see her at least. It could be your last chance.'

She let go of his hand. Graeme was a much more sensible choice than Charlie. Sensible, but... She leaned forward on the sofa and kissed him. She'd tasted his food and it had made her mouth water. Now she wanted to taste him. He tasted good.

'Say you'll do this, Charlie.'

'I'll say anything, if you'll do that again.'

Then they were in a cab and all over one another like teenagers. Then on the houseboat, Lulu stripped and Charlie watched and then they made love for the first time in a very, very long time.

Six thirty am and half past the hour bong from Franco's clock. Janet banged on Charlie's door.

'Come on, Charlie, love. Time to cook.'

He lay there for a few minutes more, letting his brain ease into his eye sockets. He'd only got back from Lulu's houseboat an hour or so earlier. He'd taken his time, strolling along the seafront, watching the sun come up, scarcely believing his luck. Smiling, crying a little bit, then checking that no one was about, punching the air. He had won Lulu back at last. Charlie forced himself up and rummaged around in the pile of clothes in the corner for his chef's whites. Down all four flights at a pace, ignoring fluff, litter, and came barging into the dark kitchen – fuck, he hadn't locked it – and lit the stove and his fag in the flick of a match.

'Morning, Emma, you get it last night, love? You got a glint in your eye.'

'You get hit, Charlie? You got what looks like bruises under yours.'

'Nah, just the usual. Too much ale and not enough kip. How many we got in for breakfast?'

''Bout twenty. They'll be down pretty early, some sort of private tour around the Royal Pavilion before it opens.'

'Ta, you wanna fix me a coffee? and I'll pay yer with a nice bacon butty.'

'You're on.'

Trays from the walk-in – thank God he'd prepped them the night before – on the hob for a flash browning then into the oven for twenty minutes and… hold. Belle Hotel Breakfast. From butt-kicking Michelin star to button mushrooms. What the fuck happened? Anger, that's what happened. Anger that he'd have to learn to manage if he had half a chance of keeping Belle Hotel, Lulu and getting his Michelin star back. He'd got it all, then nearly lost the lot. This, this cookbook and Lulu and him back together, it was a sign. A sign that things were about to get a whole lot better. He'd been in the shit and now he would come out smelling of roses.

Charlie leaned back against the range and let the hot metal warm his bony behind.

'The Belle Hotel Cookbook.'

He leaned across the pass and took down Franco's old leather binder. He uttered the title once more, book in hand, then held it up to the light. Could he do it? Should he do it? What other choice did he have? Good for business, Lu had said. That beat tossing twenty fried eggs. Whatever they paid as an advance, it'd be more than the hundred he'd siphoned from the stags and hens and sunk down his throat at the Arts Club. He was broke. They were broke. Monday tomorrow and the people who made Belle Hotel tick-tock would be turning up for their lolly. Lolly that Charlie had borrowed and spent a dozen times over. What was the word for it? The word was insolvent: bust, tits up. Belle Hotel was bankrupt. It was only Charlie's cooking of the books that was propping it up.

Charlie flicked through Franco's book. Its faded, stained pages taught him how to cook. Every secret of how to run a successful hotel. Could he share it? Should he? What the hell would he have to say about the… incidents? Anger management class again tomorrow, at least the idea would give him something to talk about.

Janet came through the kitchen doors and caught him. He shot his mother the look. What are we going to do, Mummy, what are we going to do? She came over to her son, took the book from his hands and placed it back on its shelf above the pass. Then she held onto him for dear life.

Charlie stood on platform six at London Bridge, waiting. Sure enough, the shiny Charing Cross train slid in. Moments before, the ageing Thameslink shuddered off towards the river and its northwards haul to Bedford.

Flat broke, the Ks had been reeling around his brain all morning. Ten K for the over-overdraft, six for staff, five worth of bookings…

Franco had rarely banked less than ten K. Today, Charlie had about a fiver in coins in his back pocket. It had been touch and go if the ticket office would take his Visa.

'Fucking hell.'

Charlie pulled into Charing Cross on the back foot, two-fingered his way across the Strand – *bastard* bus drivers – and entered the cool plate glass lobby of Hookes Bank.

'I'm sorry, Charlie, I really am. Franco would have wanted me to help you. But we are owned by GBS now. Corporate rules, I'm afraid. You can't overdraw any more. I've got Belle Hotel secured as a guarantee up to the roof tiles for you. Can't do any more.'

Paul Peters shifted in his stuffed leather seat and gazed out of the window for want of something to do. It was awkward, really, especially as he'd been down at the Belle Hotel himself the week before, with one of his assistants, for an away day.

'*Having it* away day,' Janet had whispered to Charlie as Peters took his pinstripe, Viagra and mistress up to room 14. What did she see in him? Maybe a comb-over was the Essex in-thing. It kept Janet smirking for the rest of the morning. Dirty old bastard, he had to be in his seventies, looked ancient when Janet first met him over three decades ago.

'No dice, Charlie, old boy. Good luck at the publishers. Push them for every penny you can get.'

Peters walked his oldest client's heir back down the corridor of Hookes framed greats and into the lift. Charlie glanced back at his banker, grinned, winked and ran his trembling fingers through that thatch of hair. Peters blocked the lift door with his brogue.

'Here, have a bite at your dad's place on me. I'd join you, Charlie, it's just that I'm having a one-to-one with Janine at midday. New GBS policy, quality time with your subordinates.'

Peters gave him a wink back with the fifty and the great glass elevator slid shut. Charlie gazed at his reflection. Back in the lobby the door opened and Janine switched her choice of lifts, unnerved by the sight of lift number one's inhabitant banging his head on the smoked glass.

Charlie made it as far as the Euston Road, yards from the door of Haddon publishing, but the pub next door looked *so* inviting and the fifty quid was burning a hole in his pocket and he didn't know if he could write this bloody book anyway. He didn't know who he was. Was he even born a chef? So he fucked the thing off and drank ten pints to celebrate.

A voicemail on his phone, when he woke up in the train carriage at Brighton Station.

'Charlie, I really need to come down and see you. Can you square this with your mother and let me know when suits? I can be with you any time in the next month. No later. Let me know. All the best, er, Dad.'

Johnny, John, Dad. He'd been avoiding his calls for months but there was no avoiding this. Something about the urgency and fact that Johnny seemed to have no work commitments for the next month hinted at something serious. What now? Another business venture gone wrong? The truth about the Lulu bullshit story? Whatever it was, Charlie doubted if the Savoy Group's new owners would tolerate the kind of nonsense they had in the old days. He sighed and texted an answer back.

'How about Monday?'

There'd just be the weekend to get through and he wouldn't tell Janet. No point getting her worked up. What to cook? Simple. Lobster Belle Hotel, Johnny's favourite dish. Charlie called Sinker and promised to pay on delivery. Johnny could join them for Belle Hotel family lunch. Some family. Charlie sighed, shrugged to the empty lobby, sat back in the cubbyhole behind reception and waited for the chick he'd checked in earlier to come back looking for what she'd heavily hinted she was after. Brown-eyed this time, the last one, Daisy was it, had blue eyes.

Tick-tock, tock-tick, one last outing for Charlie's dick. But brown-eyes came and Charlie turned away. It was time to commit to Lulu, if she promised to swear off Graeme and the next foreign friggin' waiter that took her fancy. They were back on for good, Charlie hoped. If he'd made it back into her bed, maybe he could get her back to Belle Hotel and everything would be okay? Together they could turn it around, win back the star, get the bank off their backs. Franco's clock struck two and Charlie swore to lay off the Daisys and Maisys and commit to what he'd wanted all along: Charlie and Lulu at Belle Hotel.

*

The weekend came and went. Janet took badly to the news of her ex-husband's day trip. By mid-morning, Charlie noticed she'd tied back her hair and wasn't wearing her apron.

'I'm shutting the pub. We're always quiet on a Monday anyway and I don't want to be running back and forth when he's here.'

Charlie frowned. Shutting the pub? Didn't they need every penny? He shook his head and went back to his *mise en place*. Twenty in for lunch, Fish could do that with his eyes shut. Sinker and Brampton were early with their deliveries and paid directly from the pub till. He put the cold, dozy lobsters in the walk-in, mentally reserving the largest two for the family – *family*, what did that mean? – and went back to butchering his fillets. He could have let Brampton do it, but since he'd had the training it was hard to let go. Anyhow, it gave him an enormous sense of satisfaction. He flipped the long shank of red meat onto the counter and slipped a slim plastic chopping board under one end. Then he sharpened his eight-inch knife, like Franco had showed him back at the start, and slipped the steel back in its wrap. Charlie deftly cut eight-ounce portions of fillet and piled them up in an ice-cream container ready for service. This, with a pepper sauce, was on the fixed-price menu. Fish would get through the eight, no trouble, more if the table of six were all men.

Lunch found Charlie back at the Odeon watching sci-fi. He couldn't focus on the movie, but was finding it hard to admit to himself that he felt nervous. Janet was up in her flat watching her chat show. She felt it too, but for different reasons.

At half-past two Charlie pushed his way into the kitchen – why did Fish always leave the veg boxes there? – talked numbers with his loyal sous and set about making Lobster Belle Hotel.

He fetched the sleepy Scottish sea creatures and sat them on the counter next to Franco's book. He needed a piss. On his way to the toilets he spotted John, Johnny, Dad's narrow head though the stained-glass window. In the early afternoon light, Charlie saw his hair had lost its darkness and was almost pure white against the precision cut glass. He was early. Damn. Charlie back-tracked to the kitchen contemplated relieving himself in the hand basin that health and safety had insisted he install three years earlier. At least it'd be getting some use.

One of the lobsters had made a break for it and was halfway across the table to freedom via Ship Street. Oh no you don't, Jimmy. Come here. Time to put on the lobster pan. Charlie hauled the high-sided pot from under the counter, filled it with bouillon and whacked it on the back burner to boil. In his escape attempt, Jimmy the lobster had floored Franco's book. Charlie picked it up and glanced at the recipe, for old time's sake more than anything. He knew Lobster Belle Hotel like he knew the back of his hand. From Franco's hand to the sous chef at L'Escargot, to Le Gavroche and finally Charlie's own lobster dish. The summation of all those skills and mentors. The one that had earnt him his star.

Charlie gathered his ingredients on the counter – say hello, boys! – and knew without looking that his bouillon had come to a rolling simmer. Jimmy first, for the attempted escape, then Dozy. In you go. Charlie had plunged so many lobsters he hardly heard their screams. He'd stopped knifing their brains out after the bad Good Food Show in the nineties. Out came the eight-inch knife and a large pair of tongs from the rail above his head. He knocked up sauces in the time it took his lobsters to die and cook.

Charlie cut the heat, fished them out of the bouillon, shook each over the sink and set them down on the chopping board. He crossed himself, then brought his blade down lengthways through Jimmy with a satisfying crack. He took out his stomach sac and cut and rapped both knuckles then removed the tail meat that smelt so good, and cut it into medallions which he sat in Jimmy's empty shell before applying both sauces.

Dozy next, and Charlie flung a packet of wild rice into the re-ignited bouillon on the hob. Steam a bit of sprouting he'd picked at the allotment first thing, and Bob's yer uncle. Right. Time to face Johnny.

'Hello, Johnny, how are you?' Charlie stretched out his unwashed hand.

'Not good, Charlie. I'm about to die.'

Was he serious? 'Not before lunch, I hope. Come through and have a glass of champagne. I'll let Mum know you're here.'

Janet came down and popped the bubbly. Charlie flash-grilled his Lobster Belle Hotel and served it with the dome of wild rice. While they ate, Johnny told them what he'd come to tell them. He was serious about going to meet his maker. The big C. Advanced stages. Time to put his house in order. So here goes. His secret.

Johnny handed Charlie a gossamer thin piece of paper.

'Here, you'd better put this in Franco's book, where it belongs.' Janet made to stop Johnny. But he raised his hand.

BIRTH CERTIFICATE
BRIGHTON REGISTRY OFFICE
NAME: Jonathan Sheridan
MOTHER'S NAME: Vera Sheridan
FATHER'S NAME: Nathan Barrow
DATE OF BIRTH: 19 March 1944

'I'm seventeen and about to go to Switzerland, you know Franco sent me there too as well as setting up The Grand bellboy thing. I ask Mum, your gran, for my birth certificate. Got to go to the post office and get myself a passport. Franco is on the trains and mum is busy with her sewing. So she hands me the lost and found paper. This is 1961, so not much to look at in the queue, and eventually I am bored enough to look at my birth certificate. I look at Mum; name, date of birth, occupation. What is a milliner when it's at home? I look at Dad. And it's not Franco. Nathan Barrow, born in the nineteenth century, pawnbroker. I know what one of those is. Franco is not my dad. My dad is called Nathan and my mother never told me.'

Charlie looked at his mother. This was too much to take in, in one lunchtime. Too much, perhaps, in one lifetime. What Lulu had said was true. Janet shook her head; she never knew. Never knew, Johnny. What chance did they have? Johnny looked at the linen, Nathan's white hair there for all to see. Then he looked up, Nathan's brown eyes glazed with salt water.

'I wasn't his son. Made in the war while the cat was away. Then suddenly it's VE Day and Franco's back from the war. Peace reigns. A time to forgive and forget. Foster the boy in a spirit of reconciliation. But he never could reconcile himself to what she did. Never could forgive her. Then the hotel. Making of Franco, breaking of me. Good man, your grandfather. We became friends, you know, towards the end. Used to visit me on his trips to London. Good man. Tough luck.'

Johnny looked down once more.

'So now you know.'

Janet shook her head once more. The phone rang, and was ignored. Silence.

The three of them remained at the table. It was the end of a good meal. Though Johnny had barely had a bite. Lobster eating implements lay scattered among the empty claws and shells. An upturned bottle of champagne sat in a frosted bucket. Just three people, seated together, after lunch. Janet wiped her eyes on a napkin and left the room. Charlie put his arm awkwardly round the shoulder of his father. A couple of tears fell on the flimsy piece of paper.

Janet returned with three coffees. Charlie got up and made his way over to the trolley of liqueurs. He poured three balloons of cognac, then removed and clipped a broad gauge cigar from a walnut box with a red collar, Partigas Series D. Johnny drew a flash of gold from his suit pocket. Blue flame toasted the cigar end and a wisp of smoke crept up to the ceiling. The lighter was returned to its hiding place and the clipped top of the Cuban cigar drew properly. Its charred end glowed deep red and smoke engulfed the little scene.

'I'm sorry. I should have told you about Franco not being my father. It's just that, after the war, secrets were easier to keep. And once they'd been kept they became harder to tell. I did tell Lulu, years ago, but I knew she'd keep my secret. So, this is it. I'm riddled with tumours. Pancreas, spine, lungs,' Johnny saluted them with his cigar, 'and I want out. I've come home to ask you to help me die.'

Charlie and Janet said nothing. Charlie's face drained of colour, Janet's went bright red. Both stared at Johnny, neither daring to catch the other's eye.

'One of the Arab doctors who stays at The Savoy, a regular guest, got me the cyanide.'

Johnny reached into his breast pocket and fished out a tiny, snaplock plastic packet. The transparent square contained an innocuous-looking pill.

'Cyanide. Death. Turns out Dr Ahmed lost his wife to cancer a couple of years ago, so he's more than happy to help me on this occasion. This is a relic from the Cold War. Brutal, swift, effective. Nought to death in ten seconds on an empty stomach. Plus, he owes me for turning a blind eye to the comings and goings to his suite in the small hours all these years. Will you help me? All I need is your blessing and a room key. We didn't have this conversation. Help me. I have nobody else.'

Johnny took himself off to the loo. Even the near-dead need to relieve themselves. Janet let out her longest sigh.

'Well, that explains a lot. Poor Johnny. Why didn't he tell me?'

'What are we going to do, Mum?'

'Help him. If we don't he'll only do it anyway. I'd rather he rest easy than go to his grave angry at us too.'

'Do you think he ever told Franco?'

203

'No. Some things are better left unsaid.'

'Like, hello Dad, I know I'm not your son. Fuck, I'd rather know. It messes with your head, not knowing who you are. Franco should have told him when he was a little boy. Which room are you going to give him?'

'Yours, that way we can cause as little disruption as possible.'

'Oh, thanks a bunch. Dead dad in my bed. That's just what I nee—'

Johnny came back, picked up his smoke and pulled. For a man about to end it all, the ash on his last cigar stayed remarkably still.

'Johnny, Dad, are you sure about this?'

'More sure than I've ever been about anything ever before. I want to be put out of my misery. I'm sorry I've been such a fucking useless father. You got any more brandy?'

The three of them sat there for what to Charlie seemed like a lifetime. Finally, Claire and Emma turned up to set the restaurant for dinner. Forty booked with a likely same again as walk-ins. There was a medical conference in town. Business as usual for Belle Hotel, no point in committing commercial suicide, too. They stood in the lobby to say their goodbyes.

'Well, Dad.'

Charlie welled up. The tight feeling in his chest was back. Suddenly it was the day Johnny left again. Franco standing there holding both Charlie and Janet, saying there there, we Sheridans don't cry. Charlie looked from his mother to his father. Both his parents were crying silently, tears pouring down their cheeks.

Janet handed Johnny his key.

'Top floor, end of the corridor. Room twenty. It's Charlie's room now.'

'Yes, I know.'

Johnny turned at the first landing and raised his hand in a stiff wave. Charlie and Janet, aware of the staff present, tried to casually wave back.

'He's just going for a nap, Charlie love, remember that. Oh Johnny, what a way to go.'

They set off to their respective places of work. Janet turned at the door to the bar. She hesitated.

'Charlie, come in to see me once you've set up. There's something important I need to tell you.'

What now? Charlie thought.

Johnny walked slowly to his fate. His back and lungs ached and he'd passed blood into the urinal earlier. Better to end it this way than a slow, painful death somewhere lonely. Lonely. It felt good to have told them both his secret. Not Franco's son. It was out now. Johnny was ready to meet his maker. About fucking time. Nathan Barrow, you've got some explaining to do. Johnny paused on the second landing and gazed out to sea through the rubber plants and rose-tinted widow. He had never loved this place like the rest of them. Give him the severe art deco of The Savoy over this Belle Epoque nonsense any day. Any day. Funny, really, what he was about to do made that into rather an odd expression. That one hollandaise sauce had changed the course of Johnny's life and he was grateful to Franco for forcing freedom upon him. Up in the corridor in the eaves, Johnny unlocked the door marked twenty. Jesus, was this how the boy lived? He felt as if he barely knew him. As if he wasn't his. The shock of finding out that Franco wasn't his father had made it hard to be a father to Charlie.

Johnny sat on the edge of the unmade single bed and opened the plastic packet.

The new council-funded trainee was shaping up well. Charlie liked the way he handled food, there was a lightness to his touch that signalled a born chef. All Charlie had to do was hold his temper. The anger management classes were helping. He remembered to breathe when he felt himself losing it and found taming the rage brought better results than succumbing to it. Whatever. Charlie knew that if it happened again there'd be no Fish to cover for him. It'd be chokey, for sure. The thought of prison food alone was enough to keep him in check. Now, he found himself wondering what the anger management group would make of the afternoon's surprises. He also wondered if his father was dead yet and did his damnedest to keep his emotions in check. When Franco had passed, life drained of all flavour, but with Johnny gone Charlie wouldn't have much to miss. Or would he? What did he have now that he knew for sure that Franco wasn't blood. He watched the lad batoning carrots. This. He had this.

'Good job, son. Keep the knife straight. That's it, then you can chop 'em all at once.'

Janet polished her glasses. A crack, and a second pint halved in her hands. Hardly surprising, her ex-husband was four floors up and rising. She polished, poured, drained and waited. This was it. For sure. He'd be gone now. It was quick, cyanide, wasn't it? She'd seen enough films, and didn't Hitler go that way? Janet fed a fiver in pound coins in to the jukebox and filled the empty bar with Sinatra. Her hand went unconsciously for the nuts and she found herself humming along.

'She gets too hungry for dinner at eight…'

Hell, she'd have to tell Charlie. Too late for secrets now, look what keeping secrets did to Johnny. And anyway, it didn't matter any more now that Johnny was almost certainly dead. Janet poured herself half a lager, sploshing a shot of lemonade onto its head. All that champagne and brandy had given her a thirst. She downed the fizz in three mouthfuls, wiped her sleeve across her lips, reached behind the boiler for her own secret piece of paper and waited for her son.

A party of gynaecologists pitched up for supper. With startling ease, Claire and Emma sold them the Chateaubriand concept: amazing what can be done with a bit of peer pressure and a NHS Hospital Trust Amex card.

'It's for moments like this that we pay our taxes.'

'You don't pay any, Charlie.'

'Shut it, Fish, get back to the Béarnaise.'

He popped through to see his mum to put her off telling him her news, gazing up as he crossed the landing, half expecting to see Johnny's ghost appear. There she was, feet in Franco's pit, leaning on the zinc, finishing her crossword.

'"Da, da, da, da, Chicago…" Hello, love.'

'Hi, look, can this wait, I've got three threes coming in ten minutes.'

'No, it can't, Charlie. This has waited long enough and with him gone I want to tell you the truth about your father. Come with me.'

She led Charlie by the hand to the boiler room. He felt a bit awkward going in there with his mother. The Soho Boho had flicked off her G-string somewhere near the fuse box. Charlie knew what was coming next.

'This is where you were conceived. Your father and I made love standing up. Quietly in the dark.

'Thanks, Mum, I've always wondered.'

The sarcasm didn't put Janet off her stride. Today was a day of revelations and she was about to top Johnny in the paternity stakes.

'I know your birth certificate in Franco's book says you're Johnny's son. You know I conceived you at the opening party for Belle Hotel. Well your father, Johnny, was sulking in the kitchen when it happened. He'd accused me of flirting with Roger Hardman, Lulu's dad. As if. Well, I was working hard and when the offer came, I took it.'

Charlie stared wide eyes at his mother. The cogs turning fast.

'Charlie, you're not Johnny's son. You're—'

'No, mum. NO, NO, NO. You didn't? Not him. How could you? Do you know what you've done? You've fucked up my life.'

Then he was gone. He knew what she'd done. Betrayed Johnny with Roger. Betrayed Charlie. Worse still, made it impossible for he and Lulu to ever get back together. He'd always, on some level, known it. That was why it was all so fucking weird between them. What was the word, incense, something like that. Damn his education. Fucking *Deliverance*, banjo playing whackjobbery. That's what it was. Charlie ran back to his kitchen to bury himself in work. Janet gazed at the slammed door and let herself remember.

The opening party, 1973. Their first big function and things were going swimmingly. Janet had been at the sherry and her surly man-child of a husband was sulking through the washing-up. He came into the boiler room just as she stacked the last crate.

'Here you are. I've been looking all over.'

Janet stumbled slightly as she made to leave. He reached out to catch her arm. She looked at him, face tilted inches away from his. Lip to lip. What happened next was as natural as the birds and the bees, as natural as an Axminster carpet. With a flash of an expectant smile he gently shut the door and turned off the light. Before she knew what was happening, she was committing adultery. Delicious adultery in the boiler room. A couple of minutes later the lights were back on and he was pressing his finger to his lips. 'Never again,' was silently sworn between them and up she went, with a little bit of him still inside her.

That little bit became bigger and soon she was starting to show. Janet made a point of making up, and making love, with Johnny as soon as she suspected, but she knew. She knew her baby was his. And she knew it was wrong. Even though it never happened again. She'd known it was wrong all these years.

Why hadn't she told Charlie sooner? This anger at untold secrets may have saved them all a lot of pain. For Franco and Johnny, it was too late, Franco was pushing up daisies behind the station, and Johnny would soon be joining him. But at least Charlie knew that Johnny wasn't his father. She'd let out her secret. Janet sank to her knees and sobbed. Sobbed for her younger self. For her son. She went to blow her nose on the green lace handkerchief that lay at her knees... but it wasn't a handkerchief, it was a pair of knickers. How the hell did they get there?

Charlie sent Fish home and cooked the hell out of himself with his apprentice. By himself. That meant something more than it had ever done before. He was Roger's son. Lulu was his what, half-sister. Christ, that was deep shit. Deep, deep shit. Why had Janet never told him, warned him off? What if...? Didn't bear thinking about. And the Johnny news that kicked the whole thing off. Johnny was nothing to him; water to blood. Dead upstairs on his single bed. And not Franco's son. No wonder Franco had been a bastard to him. Charlie looked up from the flames and saw a ghost at the porthole. Johnny, back from the dead. He shook his head and went back to the reduction.

'See how it has halved. Now then, we're going to deglaze it with a knob of butter. A KNOB OF BUTTER, NOW.'

The apprentice did not flinch, he simply span round and in a flash was back with the fat.

Tick-tock, tick-tock, death is a comin' and he won't knock.

Janet was well into her fourth lager when she saw him. Not that she could be sure. All that booze and emotion, things were getting a bit blurred. She shook her head... but, no, he was definitely standing there.

'I choked, and now I've lost it.'

'You... what?'

'The pill, it stuck in my throat. I choked it up and I've just spent the last hour on my hands and knees looking for it. I need your help.'

Janet looked at her hapless ex, remembered the recently released secret and was already on her way up the stairs.

'Donald, mind the bar for me, I've just got to find something for... this guest.'

Johnny followed a swaying Janet to the top of Belle Hotel. It took her ten minutes to find it, it had flown out of Johnny's mouth and taken an odd trajectory under the bed. After shaking out every last dirty T-shirt of Charlie's, she'd eventually resorted to fumbling about under the bed.

'What's this?'

She pulled out Charlie's secret tin and with the lame excuse of searching, opened its hinged lid. Inside, sitting on top, was a blurred photograph dated 1987 in red dots: Charlie, in his fishing gear, beaming out beside Johnny and the other dads.

'Fishing trip. The happiest weekend of my life.'

'Oh, spare me the melodrama, John.'

Janet made one last desperate sweep under the bed. Her wedding finger touched something hard and wet.

'Here it is.'

She handed him his exit and went to the bathroom to wash her hands and get him a glass of water. She didn't want him to have to go through failure a second time. Johnny was shaking silently. She handed him the glass, kissed him on the head and beat a hasty retreat. Halfway along the narrow corridor she stopped. No, that was wrong. Johnny had been a man she had loved. He had no one else. He was here at Belle Hotel, he wanted to be here. She owed him better. Where was the dignity, her decency?

She tapped on the door.

'You still there?'

Silence. Then a muffled whimper. He couldn't do it alone. After some fiddling Janet let herself in with the tricky pass key. Sure enough, Johnny was face down, fist clenched, on the bed. She sat down beside him.

'John. I know we've not... well, been there for each other since... since you left. But I want you to know that I am here for you now. Please sit up and look at me.'

The condemned man raised his trembling, white head and fixed Janet with that stare. Not Franco's, that much she knew. Whose? His mother's? Nathan Barrow's? Janet reached across and took his unclenched hand. She knew full well what the other fist was hiding. They were sitting together, closer than they had been for decades. Janet had to look away.

Minutes passed. Somewhere on the floor under a pile of Charlie's kitchen-stained clothes a clock radio hissed white noise. Come on, Johnny. Do it. Now.

Janet's gaze took her out of the Velux window – dirty, needed a clean, she noticed – and out to lead-lined clouds scudding across the seafront on their way to the English Channel. She spied a boat, sails flapping black, riding the horizon en route to safe harbour. Still Johnny sat there, his hand limp but alive in her salty grip.

She remembered their wedding day. Before any of this. Belle Hotel. Just a couple of fellow workers from the Grand, bell-hop and chambermaid, happy with their simple lives, love and work. Cream nylon two-piece for Johnny, white polyester for her. The sparks flew as they hungrily made love in the bridal suite, courtesy of the manager, who needed it back by midday for paying punters due to pitch up at two.

This. This family business… they hadn't stood a chance. The boat sailed out of frame and Janet was about to say something, but she felt Johnny move slightly. Nothing more than a flinch, but it was a flutter in the right direction.

A tap dripped in the dimly lit bathroom. Had she left it on or did it need fixing? Janet pictured Franco's bag, his tools. The ones he'd never handed on to his son. Still she could not look. Christ, this room was grotty. At least she had some pictures up in her space next door, *Chatsworth in Winter* and a couple of framed Schweppes posters given her by the rep in the seventies.

She felt him flick his other wrist towards his mouth and heard the crunch of the pill as it connected with his molars. She did not look. She felt his grip tighten. He was hanging on for dear life. Then, in a moment that had felt like a lifetime, it was over. The hand stayed in shape but seemed to lose its substance. Death came. Johnny was gone.

She stayed with his slackening body for another half hour. Closed his still, brown eyes and moved him out of his slump and onto the pillow. Time to leave the scene of the crime, the pub was probably in disarray below. What was the law's position on assisted suicide? Maybe it would be better that she'd missed the grand finale, came down after helping him to find his... key. Key, that was it. Janet stood and looked out to sea. The boat was now lowering its sails, lifeless sheet dropping to the cold deck, turning stern and throttling into still water.

She'd loved him, once. This still hurt. But she was glad it was over. Relief swept through her like morning lager. Thank God Charlie didn't see him after, after what she'd just told him. She could hear Franco's voice in her ears. 'No, not the window, yer daft 'apeth. Pull yourself together, what's done is done. You did what was best. Now go down and face Charlie. Make things right with him.' Like you did, Franco? Not always that easy, though, is it, love?

Janet took one last look at Johnny, clicked off the hissing clock and left her ex-husband to rest in peace.

Brighton Constabulary handled them well. The chief of police was an old friend of Franco's and, although he could have ordered a full investigation, he managed to wave the thing through.

'He was just having a nap. Believe me, this has been a shock to all of us.'

The body went down the fire exit, minimum fuss for Belle Hotel's guests, as ever, and things carried on much as before.

They buried Johnny next to Franco in the caterers' graveyard and walked down together for the wake. Not much of a do, Charlie had laid on cold lobster in honour, the wake was made up mainly of Belle Hotel staff and friends. Lulu wanted to be there, but was badly sick that morning and had to call Charlie to say she'd not be able to make it. By about four the party was over and Johnny's two friends from The Savoy, the night manager and a doorman, made their way up to the station to be back in time for their shift.

Best thing to come out of this latest revelation was, as predicted, the looks on the faces of his anger management cohorts. Shaken heads and mutters of 'well, that explains it' reverberated around the woodchip walls. At anger management, Charlie told Ernest he was still confused by the whole experience but yes, he did feel a lot of his negative anger ebbing away as he, yes, came to terms with the lies and half-truths of his life. Ernest nodded and lifted his notepad from twitching corduroy. He made a line of notes and appeared to be ticking something. Charlie clenched his fists in delight. He'd got through anger management with a cast-iron excuse.

Ernest did say one wise thing. As Charlie was about to leave the sacred space for ever, Ernest nodded sagely and said,

'You can't un-tell the fact that the previous generations haven't. And you do have a chance to put things right with the living.'

Getting through anger management was one thing. Getting through the twin catastrophes of looming bankruptcy and discovering that the woman he'd loved all his life was, in fact, his sister was a personal crisis that matched the global one in its awfulness. Charlie had felt the credit crunch coming since Franco died. Hell, he'd played his part in causing it. No wonder he could sense the size of it. When it came, on the day he stood to lose the two loves of his life, it surprised even Charlie. Charlie wasn't the only one in for surprises on that dark October the thirteenth day in 2008.

Chat Magazine
MY STEAMY NIGHT WITH CELEBRITY CHEF
By Daisy Swallows

Graeme took great pleasure in plonking the article face up on Lulu's normally paper-free desk. She'd just finished a call with Judith Langdon at Haddon, who wanted to know why Charlie hadn't shown up for the meeting the other day. Great news, on top of the conformation from Paul Peters, via Roger, that Charlie had defaulted and needed to find ten grand by lunchtime or bye bye Belle Hotel. Graeme waited until she'd glanced at the headline before intoning in his nasal twang.

'Says that he bonked her a month ago. How long since he stayed over on your boat, that weekend, wasn't it? You've barely seen him since. Been busy, has he? I'd say so.'

Lulu felt sick. Not just sick in a tabloid sex revelation sort of way, but in a morning sort of way. And when she felt it in a morning sickness sort of way, she meant that she was going to be sick. Right now.

Lulu barged past Graeme, hand to mouth, frozen parbaked croissant and staff coffee machine spew spuming from between her fingers. She made it to the ladies loo by the time the motherlode came.

Then, crying and puke-spattered, she staggered down Ship Street and into Moondi's newsagent. Screw what Fizal would say. Yes, he did have one back there somewhere. A little dusty, perhaps, but very good value at £9.99. Lulu had left her bag at Hotel Epicure, Charlie would be paying for this. Oh, yes, Charlie would be paying for this. And could she use the loo, please?

The Moondi News loo was as revolting as Lu imagined it would be in the three steps it took her to slip past Fizal and into his own private homage to a Bengal shitter. Once Lulu had emptied her stomach for a third time she was ready to pee on the stick. Sure enough, a thin blue line told Lulu that feelings were not the only things growing inside her that morning.

Lulu gasped and put the tester down on the loo seat. She flushed and then pulled the handle of the toilet. My God, this was a shock. And Charlie, stupid bloody Charlie, had only been sticking it in some tart behind her back. Again.

Lulu's head spun. She needed to see him. To tell him. Then maybe, just maybe, this would make sense to the two of them.

Lulu blew her nose and pushed through the bead curtain to re-enter Moondi News. Graeme was standing in the middle of the shop flicking through a martial arts magazine.

'There you are. I wondered—'

'Not now, Graeme. Not now. Can't you see that—'

Lulu barged past him and out into the cool air of Ship Street. She needed to see Charlie.

Couple of bangs on the kitchen door got a response.

'Charlie's not here.'

'Charlie, it's Lulu. I know it's you. Stop doing that stupid voice and let me in. I need to talk to you.'

Charlie looked at Lulu in the dimly lit kitchen. A few greasy pans were all that remained of breakfast. A breakfast that Janet had cooked while Charlie looked at Franco's book.

'Charlie, I've seen the thing in that magazine.'

'What thing?'

'You and that, girl, Daisy something. And after we... Charlie, how could you?'

Charlie's eyes widened. Silence, bar the distant ticking of Franco's clock.

'Well, we weren't. And I thought you were, y'know, with Graeme. And I, hang on, let me get the time frame straight, I get so tired and confused, Lu. It was before, wasn't it. Christ, I just don't know what to

215

say, Lulu, anyway I know some stuff that makes it very difficult. That, er, means we can't be together. I'm sorry, but—'

'Charlie, shut up. I'm pregnant and the baby is yours.'

'What? Are you sure?'

'I did the test just now.'

'No, I mean, it can't be mine. Mustn't be. You sure it isn't Graeme's?'

'Charlie, you are digging yourself deeper in your hole. You sure you don't want to rephrase this before I cry? And for your information I haven't slept with Graeme. Yet. Some of us are able to restrain ourselves when we've just made love to the person we've always loved. Oh, my, this is all happening so quick. But I just think, maybe, you know. Maybe this is a sign.'

Charlie stood and backed away from Lulu. A sheen of sweat broke out across his face.

'Oh my God. Fucking hell. Pregnant. With my child. No. We can't. Get rid of it. Lu, JUST DO IT.'

Lulu was shaking her head, letting the tears fall onto the dirty lino.

'I thought you'd be shocked. I hoped it'd be pleasantly shocked. At least a bit. I am. I mean, shocked, but excited. Charlie, why are you being such a bastard?'

Charlie manhandled Lulu back towards the kitchen door, opening it with his left hand and pushing her through the open hole right into the arms of a bailiff with a raised knocking fist and an envelope in the other. Behind the bailiff stood a photographer and the slapper with the blue eyes, Daisy Swallows, that was it, Lulu recognised her stupid face from the magazine article. Christ, they were queueing up. Lulu fled down Belle Hotel's back passage, slipping as she sobbed on eight years of accumulated grease.

*

Hookes Bank
NOTICE OF INTENDED REPOSSESSION

Charlie Sheridan
Belle Hotel
Ship Street
Brighton

12 October 2008
Delivered by Bailiff
9am

Dear Charlie,
If we have not heard from you by noon tomorrow then we will have no option other than to use our bailiff team to repossess Belle Hotel. We require £10,000 in cash paying to Paul Peters by noon tomorrow, or we will repossess the hotel immediately. Please ensure that you respond to this letter as a matter of absolute urgency [rest of letter burnt]

Tick-tock,
    tick, tick,
    tock, tock,
    crunch.

Tick-Tock

14 October 2008
Day One: –£5,000

Lulu woke up on her houseboat and crept from the bedroom so as not to wake him. She made herself a coffee on the stove and sat at the big window looking out onto the mudflats.

She wondered what surprises today would be offering. Take a lot to top yesterday. Betrayal, pregnancy, a bare-knuckle fight at Belle Hotel. Charlie's credit had well and truly crunched. She checked her phone. One voicemail from her dad. Nothing from Charlie. Bastard.

Lulu put the phone on speaker to hear what her dad wanted.

First the sound of sobbing, then a heavily drawn breath.

'Lulabell. It's Dad. I've lost everything. All my carpet cash. The Iceland bank I had it all in. Gone. Nothing left. And Tina's left me.'

More sobbing. Lulu shook her head.

'Poor Roger.'

Graeme, wearing Lulu's satin robe and looking as bed-ugly as Lulu could ever have imagined.

'Oh, he'll get over it. When he says he's lost everything, he means his liquid assets. And his silicone ones. Don't worry about Roger. Do worry about my half of the cash he was putting up against this.'

Lulu patted the bulkhead of her houseboat. Her life's savings and now the only asset she had in the world. Apart from the little bit of Charlie growing inside her.

She looked at Graeme.

'Thank you. And thank you for being there last night and not trying anything. I'll always remember that.'

'That's okay, Lulu. Seems I'm always destined to get bested by Charlie. What do you want to do about Belle Hotel?'

'Let me think about it. My mind's all over the place. Charlie's got five days to pay the other five grand and you can bet your bottom dollar he'll take it to the wire again. Then there'll be another five grand five days later, until he gets the debt down. He'll never do that on his own.'

Graeme went to get his clothes from where he'd optimistically stowed them in Lulu's locker.

'Bye then, Lulu. Shall I tell them you're, er, unwell, at work.'

Lulu nodded and welled up. She kissed her hand and pressed it gently over the executive head chef embroidery covering Graeme's heart.

Then, when he was gone, Lulu went back to bed to decide what to do with the rest of her life.

Charlie slept well, considering the broken wrist, bankruptcy, impending fatherhood and incest. Rebinding Franco's book had calmed him. As he worked his way back to the present from 1973, he started to see a pattern emerging.

'Oh my God.'

Franco. Built Belle Hotel up from nothing. All there to see in bills, recipes and receipts. Even the Dulux paint colour cards for the two-tone effect in the lobby. When had Charlie last painted the lobby? Franco's book had the answer: 1999, the year the old man died. Then a steady decline that, if he'd only bothered to reflect, to look back in Franco's book, would have saved Charlie a boat load of bother.

This sudden self-awareness, and perhaps a bit of the anger management course rubbing off, calmed Charlie the morning of 14 October 2008, the first of his five days to save Belle Hotel from bankruptcy. That and the couple of blue V, Valiums Janet had palmed him when she'd helped him up to room 20.

Charlie roused himself from bed, slipped into his bloody chef's jacket and took Franco's book back down to its rightful place on the shelf above the pass. He wanted to be a better man, or at least get back to the guy he'd been at catering college. In love with food, in love with Lulu, in love with Belle Hotel. But it was all so complicated. Now what?

The bunch of carrots, still muddy from the allotment, caught his eye. As good a place to start as any. Charlie scrubbed them in the sink, topped and tailed them and cut them into batons for later. He flipped a Marlboro out of the crumpled packet in his chef's trouser pocket, last one left, and leaned in to light it from the gas. No gas. Bugger, time to make a list. Charlie brought Franco's book down again, grabbed a pencil from the pot by the hob and wrote on the back of the letter from Hookes that had just been delivered by courier.

Hookes Bank
SENT BY COURIER
FIVE DAYS REPRIEVE

Charlie Sheridan
Belle Hotel
Ship Street
Brighton

14 October 2008

Dear Charlie,
Further to our 'meeting' at Belle Hotel yesterday, I hereby give you final notice that you have five days to produce the balance £5000 needed to be able to service your overdraft and additional loans.
Yours,
Paul Peters

*

1. Fags
2. Get Lulu to abort
3. Pay the gas bill
4. Cook the carrots
5. Haddon and The Belle Hotel Cookbook
6. Get £5,000 and keep Belle Hotel
7. Be a better son
8. Give Fish a day off
9. Make peace with Roger
10. Get Michelin star back

Lulu pushed gently on the door to Belle Hotel's pub. Through the crack she could see Janet polishing the taps and no sign of Charlie. Good.

'Hello, love. You come to make up with Charlie. No good you two squabbling over Belle Hotel.'

Janet looked up when she got no reply and clocked Lulu standing there with tears running down her cheeks. She put down the tin of Brasso, went round the bar and took Lulu in her arms.

'There, there, love. Whatever it is, we'll be able to fix it.'

Lulu blurted it out.

Janet froze.

'Charlie's, you say? And he said what?'

'Get rid of it. Horrible, Jan, it was horrible.'

'But, I don't understand. Getting back with you was all he's ever wanted. So that you could run Belle Hotel together. Charlie needs someone to kick him up the bum. Not me, I'm too soft. Someone's got to run the place. Someone with Franco's rod of iron. It's funny, but the two of you work so well together, you're like brother and sis—' Janet gripped Lulu's arms, 'Oh my God. The stupid sod thinks he's Roger's son. Charlie…'

Janet dashed from the pub and into the hotel.

*

Charlie was standing at his cold hob, unlit fag in mouth, looking at his list. Janet came in through the portholes to put Charlie right.

'You idiot. You're such a hothead. Why didn't you let me finish? The bloody birth certificate can say what it likes. A mother knows the truth. Think you're Roger's son, do you? Grant me some taste. Get Franco's book down. I only had to change one word. Did it last night.'

Janet turned on her heel and went off to get Lulu.

Charlie flicked through Franco's book. This was getting to be a habit. He put the fag behind his ear for later and stuck his tongue out of the corner of his mouth until he found what he was looking for.

BIRTH CERTIFICATE
BRIGHTON REGISTRY OFFICE
NAME: Charlie Sheridan
MOTHER'S NAME: Janet Sheridan
FATHER'S NAME: Franco Sheridan
DATE OF BIRTH: 22 September 1973

Charlie was still standing there, tongue lolling from his mouth when Janet frog-marched Lulu into the kitchen. It was like she'd been when they were kids. It was like she'd been hiding in the pub for two decades buried under lager, peanuts and shame and, now, with her guilty secret out she could be back in her power. Take her rightful place at the head the family. Karma.

'Now, Charlie. What have you got to say to Lulu?'

'Er, Lu, I'm really fucking sorry. I got it wrong. Thought you were… never mind. I'll tell you later. It's just, I thought we couldn't be together and now I know I'm Franco's son and not… it just makes sense. I feel, I dunno, whole. And this, with you having our baby. I was wrong yesterday. Got it all wrong. You'll see. I love you, Lu. Want to do this together. Can we?'

Stunned by this new man Charlie, Lulu simply nodded her head. Then shook her head. Then laughed a bit. Then cried a bit.

Janet left them to it. Somebody'd banged for her from the pub.

'So, now what, Lu?'

Charlie, turned his attention back to his list.

'Don't think this is it, Charlie. You've got a lot of making up to do. The money, the relationships. OUR relationship. I can't trust you, yet, Charlie. But I'm willing to try to trust you. OK?'

'OK, Lu.'

He's beaming. Gold-ringed ear to ear.

'Let's see how these five days go. I've still got to decide what to do with Belle Hotel. If you fuck it up, it'll be down to me and Graeme to save it from the vultures. I've got to protect our child, Charlie. And you, from this mess you've put yourself in. Maybe knowing the truth about Franco will help. He always felt more like a father to you than a grandfather. And now we know he is. Was. Oh, I don't know, Charlie. Let's take this a day at a time.'

Charlie nodded furiously, did a little dance and then remembered something pressing.

'Can you pay the gas bill for me? If I don't stump up three hundred quid, they won't turn us back on in time for lunch.'

Charlie went back to work, smarting from the slap, relieved that the gas would be back on soon. His head was spinning with the paternity news. He'd got number three on his list sorted, and number two, getting Lulu back, rather than convincing her to have an abortion, was well under way. Charlie high-fived his reversal of fortune and then grimaced at the pain in his wrist. He needed to get that fixed, another thing on the list.

Charlie popped into Ship Street Newsagent's and blagged a pack of fags off Fizal Moondi for an update on Parvez's mental health.

Charlie stood in the lobby with his back to the rest of Belle Hotel and sparked up. Janet, four floors up, deaf to what happened below. Unless anyone rang her bell.

Charlie sniffed to clear his nose. A month of paternity shocks was turning him into a wreck. He backed to the entrance from where he could see most of the ground floor. He could hear his grandfather-father bragging.

'A beautiful bit of Brighton Belle Epoque.'

His spattered kitchen clogs were on the welcome mat. He looked down and saw BELLE HOTEL, a sight that still caught him out. Beauty, innovation, peace. Wood, stained glass, sunshine. The rose window beamed onto the floor in front of the reception desk. When Charlie was a boy he thought he could catch it, put the dusty shaft and red projected stem in his bag and take it off to school.

From the door he could see both sides of the business, the bar arching away to his left. Stools, legs up on tables, waiting for Janet's pre-lunch sweep before the first pint was poured. Sussex ale, Rhône wine and Scotch whisky. Franco had stocked what he drank and drank what he stocked. If you didn't like it, he'd say, take *it* to The Cricketers. Franco's pictures nicked from the train and Larry's review from Kenneth Tynan still had pride of place on the shelf behind the bar, along with all the nautical knick-knacks that Janet had added along the way.

Charlie turned right and took in his life. The Belle Hotel Restaurant. Brighton's only Michelin-starred restaurant. OK, so it was only one star and he only held it for a few years. But, he held it. He could hold it again, taste it. Couldn't he?

Charlie took a seat on the green leather banquette. Beeswax creaked up to his nostrils as he leant back as far as the panel behind it could take. His eyes were closed, no need to look in the dining room, Charlie knew it like the back of his hand. Twelve tables; three twos, four threes, four fours and a twelve. Forty covers à la carte, sixty set menu. Tonight they'd be lucky to serve ten. Double that and they broke even. Full house and they pay the potato man. Let alone getting the five K for Hookes.

He'd written a list. Ten steps back to success. Five days to do it in and he'd already ticked three things off it. Probably. Time to go to work. Charlie slipped behind the bar, turned down the copper boiler a notch en route, and out of the side door that clicked him into the twitten.

Lulu sat in bed on her houseboat. She felt completely alone at sea. Charlie's behaviour had been terrible. Cruel. Heartless. What was wrong with him? Maybe he was a psychopath, as Graeme regularly suggested. Graeme had a book on the subject and was always happy to profile Charlie's antics against its 'Are you a psycho?' checklist. She'd done sobbing for now and was due at work for the late shift. Whatever Charlie had been wrongly thinking about her and the baby had now changed. That was good. He was the father of her child, after all. But he was still Charlie. That was bad. He was going to have to do a hell of a lot of proving himself over the next five days to win her back.

Eleven thirty going on twelve. Belle Hotel silent without Franco's clock. Charlie had gone out. Janet sensed it and, for the first time in weeks, felt calm. Her boy who refused to grow up. Belle Hotel. All she'd ever known, all her adult life. The two men in her life, both pushing up daisies in the caterers' graveyard on the hill behind the station. Brighton. The town of cooks and crooks. Not much of a choice when it came to love interest. Sure, she had her diversions, the salty shanty singers, hell, she'd even shagged Sinker one dark and stormy night, but they weren't love. Just a bit of comfort to pass the time between services.

Janet wondered for the umpteenth time that decade, what would become of her if Charlie lost the hotel? Who'd say, eh, Janet love, how about that cuppa? How about that pint? How about that bedknob, broomstick, butter knife and beer mat? Daily life as a hotel wife. Thirty years of struggle and strife… for what?

Janet shifted in her little worn chair and tutted the chat show shut. 'Half an hour of morning telly.'

As if saying it out loud made her daily play sound better. Janet ate, slept and rested Belle Hotel. Always had done, always would. Unless…

She put the copy of the Hookes letter that Paul Peters had sent her back in her pocket and went to see her chambermaid.

'That the lot, Jean?'

'Yes thank you Mrs S. You doing the third?'

'What? Oh, I guess so. Thank you, Jean. See you tomorrow.'

'Can I have that advance we was talking about?'

'Oh, yes. No. I'll have it. Tomorrow.'

Janet felt the sweat. That prickle of money worries that struck with almost every new conversation she had. My God, she wished Franco were still alive. He'd never have let things get this bad. Still, at least the secrets were all out now. Maybe things would get better now because of that.

She wandered down to the ground floor, picking up fluff and litter as she went. She had about half an hour to opening. What's left for the specials? Janet worked the pub lunch shift, swinging between the kitchen and the pumps. It has been like this since Charlie lost it. Hard to hold onto a mother's love when it meant you had to do their share of the work too.

That fight yesterday. Awful. A new low point. Good that she'd forced them to make up today.

She unlocked the kitchen, pulled the keys from the bulge in her apron and slopped in. At least he'd left it clean. Now she glanced in the walk-in and checked up on the specials. That was it, shepherd's pie. Janet had made them herself at two o'clock on Sunday morning. She'd pulled down Franco's cookbook and measured out the ingredients with scientific precision. Not much of a cook, herself, but Janet placed herself in Franco's hands.

Shepherd's Pie

(Makes 20)

5 lbs lean minced lamb

3 small onions, finely chopped

½ pint olive oil, not extra virgin

½ pint water

2 pints lamb stock

4 large carrots, peeled and finely diced

Bunch of thyme, leaves only and finely chopped

Salt and freshly ground black pepper

HP sauce

Worcestershire sauce

3 lbs Desiree potatoes (red skins)

'Heat a large roasting tray on top of the hob. That's it, Janet, one of those. Now sweat down the finely chopped onion in the olive oil. See, now make sure it don't stick. Add the lamb and fry for a few minutes. Now then, break up any big lumps. Add the water and bung the tray in a gas seven oven. You want yer fat to render out, Janet, love. Cook it until it's golden brown. That's it. Now bung it in that big sieve, here we are, I'll pass it to yer. Drain off all that grease. No, not down the sink, we don't want another bloody block. Bung it back in the tray and cover with the stock.'

It was two thirty in the morning, yet working to his recipe revived her. Thank God Charlie had made a tank of stock. She yanked a couple of ice-cream tubs full of stock from the back of the freezer and lumped the frozen broth into the mince. Ten minutes on the hob should sort that lot out.

'Slowly bring the whole lot to the boil and add yer diced carrots. See how much easier it is to blanch them before. Now we'll add our seasoning, love. It's all according to taste. Mine. I'll throw in the thyme and sauces, you salt 'n' pepper for me. Righto. That should be it. Here, have a lick.'

She pulled the warm spoon from between her lips, savouring the flavour just as she'd done decades before. Janet would never be a chef, but she could cook. Franco had made sure of that. The clock crept up to three. If she finished much later she would be too tired for the dawn start. She piped the last of the mashed potato onto the trays of pie dishes.

'That's it, a large star nozzle. I always keep them up here so they don't get lost. Now fridge 'em on the racks at the back and blast 'em for fifteen minutes at full heat when you need them. If your meat was fresh when you cooked it, a batch of shepherd's pie should last you a week.'

She stood on the bar and chalked 'Shep…' – now how did you spell it? Got her every time and she hated the way some of her educated punters sneered over their literary lunches at her elementary spelling. Charlie was no better. Herd, that's it. They herd their flock. Fuckers. She chalked it up and jumped down as a crusty face appeared at the door.

'Won't be a mo, Jack.'

Another lunchtime service at the Belle Hotel Pub had begun. Lunchtime service twelve thousand and two, but who was counting. Janet stepped to the door and pulled back the frosted glass to let Jack in.

Jack was half her age, but he'd seen her right for years. Why Charlie hadn't found out was beyond her. Too wrapped up in his fallen Michelin star, she supposed. Janet's talent for nurturing the talents of Belle Hotel's many pot washers was the stuff of legend. Legend for everyone in the pub, bar Charlie. Jack had been under her wing for, what, a good five years or so. Not that long after Franco died, anyway.

'Hi, I got you something.'

He held out his oily hand and turned it over to reveal that day's pharmaceutical treat. A blue V. Nice one, especially as she'd given her last two 10mg Valium to Charlie the day before. She assumed he'd wolfed them both, he'd certainly been banging about less before he went out. Jack had tried them both on the other blue V, too. It'd certainly turned him into Captain Endurance. Janet had enjoyed herself, too. The tiny rhomboid pill had taken thirty years off her.

An hour later and the specials were going well. Luckily the gas had come on just before service, so Charlie must have done something right that morning. Eight specials so far out of the raging oven and putting in the ninth.

'Ouch.'

She'd burnt her arm. Cook's curse. An angry bar of flesh raised above her watch line. Check any chef, if they are working, the hot flecks of contact were their stripes of honour. Charlie barely noticed his. But Janet's always hurt.

A few hours later, hard to tell without Franco's clock, Charlie returned refreshed from The Cricketers. He'd spent the fifty he'd slipped back into his pocket when he'd paid Paul Peters yesterday. Charlie was back at the Belle with a cast on his wrist, the pain in his heart from all the stress with Lulu dulled by the pints, to find the pub in enemy hands.

'Hey, Jack. Where's Janet?'

'Upstairs having a disco nap, she was feeling a bit dizzy.'

Charlie gazed around the bar, one literary lunch coming to a close and two of the Brighton barflies left at the counter, swaying by their beer bellies against the pumps. Charlie hated Janet letting the locals mind the bar for her, but it beat paying one extra. What the hell was Janet doing having a nap? There was work to be done.

Someone had left the lights blazing in the kitchen. No doubt the stoves were raging at full blast in sympathy. Charlie promptly forgot his mother and swung through to his life's work.

The stoves were on and, worse still, someone had left one of the oven doors open.

'Fuckin' hell, Lulu's only just paid for that.'

Day Two: –£5,000

Charlie took the train directly to St Pancras and then walked along the Euston Road. He stopped at the newsagent's where banging bhangra and the heady scent of nag champa assaulted his senses as he split a tenner into twenty Marlborough red, a can of Coke and some shrapnel. He set off down the Euston Road looking for somewhere to sit outside and smoke, and lighted upon a Caffè Nero with outdoor seats that were chock-a-block with smokers from the offices above.

Charlie made an effort to tune out the chattering around him. He looked down at the first thousand words Lulu had typed out for him weeks earlier before his aborted trip. Charlie avoided looking in the direction of the pub.

He reread the text. Not bad, you had to start somewhere. Charlie had always enjoyed telling stories at school, not as much as home ec, mind, but he had the same way with words that he had with food. Problem was his terrible spelling. And grammar. And command of the English language. But Haddon didn't need to know about that yet. The stuff Lulu had hacked out for him read well. Light yet bold. The Kipper Wars. Hardly Elizabeth David, but they had to start somewhere. He stubbed out fag number four and went up for another espresso shot.

Charlie felt jittery and it wasn't just the coffee. He'd come so close to losing the two loves of his life that it scared him even to think about it. And now, every step he took could end up losing them both, just like that. This trip was one of many that he was going to have to take to prove his love, prove that he had changed once and for all and for the better. Prove that he was going to stay that way, not stray off on any wayward paths of old. Stay on the route to redemption lit by the small gleam of self-knowledge he'd recently discovered.

He pitched up at Haddon's offices ten minutes early and took the chance to catch up on the competition. Charlie sat under the jaunty 'H' and flicked through the latest offerings from Haddon Cookery. He held up the new Gordon, *The Ultimate Cookery Course*. Charlie read the message from Mr Shouty-Sweary on the back. 'I want to teach you how to cook good food at home. By stripping away all the hard graft and complexity, anyone can produce mouth-watering recipes. Put simply, I'm going to show you how to cook yourself into a better cook'. Back to basics from Gordon. Very, very nice. Ramsay, now there was a man with a business to behold and a rep as rocky as Charlie's. He was a lot richer, though. Charlie remembered the day that a guy called Gordon had traipsed after him from Wandsworth to Le Gavroche, and allowed himself a little smile. Also in front of him was a copy of the catering college legend *Practical Cookery*. Franco had been a tad jealous of the book when Charlie had brought it home that first day after college, mumbling something about all Charlie needing to know being in Franco's book. Charlie noticed that Michel Roux Jr had given a puff for the new version of the book 'The ultimate must-have buy for all young cooks and chefs alike'. Charlie couldn't have got his qualification without it, whatever Franco said, and, having screwed up his school education, that qualification mattered to Charlie. It was his badge of honour. Charlie picked up a copy of one of his favourite cookbooks from the display table. *The Ivy* by A.A. Gill. This beautiful book had inspired Charlie to add much more to his menu from the East and not to be afraid of delivering top-flight comfort food. He also loved the way that the book was written, not just the writing, but the structure. Gill had used a day-in-the-life format, starting at stupid o'clock and finishing not soon before to give a real taste of what life at that London icon was like. Charlie gave a small sigh, shame that Portobello Belle hadn't worked out. Shame that Charlie had to work out how to keep paying for it until the break clause kicked in. Maybe he'd give London another go sometime in the future, he could but hope.

'Mr Sheridan? I'm Hope.'

Yes, you are, smiled the broke chef, and he followed her legs all the way to the elevator before reminding himself that new Charlie didn't do that kind of thing any more.

'Have you been here before?'

'No.'

'Well, Judith's office is here, on the fourth floor. I'm her assistant. Can I get you anything? Judith is having a macchiato and a glass of iced water.'

The elevator opened onto a cool marble lobby with glass wall views out over the Euston Road.

'Phew.'

'Yes, it is rather. This way, please.'

Hope swiped them through ebony inlaid doors and into the editor's suite. Serious glasses peered out from every cubicle. Pressed checked shirts and clean Levis laughed and leaned back as they swapped endings with Chloé tweed and buffed pumps.

They passed an open door, Charlie looked in.

'The slush pile,' said Hope. 'Who'd want to write fiction?'

Hope hovered at the door while Charlie took in the towers of typing, all those tales and dreams. Hope switched off the light and shut the door.

'Someone has obviously been in there. Strange… anyway, this way please, Mr Sheridan.'

'Charlie.'

'Yes, Charlie.'

Judith Langdon's office was one of four that took in the building's Soho view. One for each of the four best sellers, he guessed. He could see the horror king's editor, stacks of classics up the walls, at his desk hunched over a chunk of newly handed-over manuscript. The other two, judging by their wall decorations, looked like romance and crime. Running along the entire inner wall was a shelf of framed black-and-white photographs of Haddon authors, past and present. Charlie spotted Hugh Fearnley-Whittingstall grinning across at his editor, Delia beamed out at her public, and some serious tweed and dandruff spoke for the older generation.

'When do I get one of these?'

'Er… some time yet. I'll see if Judith is ready for you.'

A tap at the door and the cookbook legend looked up from her Delia Smith cake.

'Ah, the elusive Charlie, do come in, I was just examining these handsome photographs by dear, dear Jason Lowe. Do you know him? He simply turns the page into a plate.'

Judith raised a recently threaded eyebrow.

'I suppose you know all about me and, more importantly, our list. I'll give you the potted "me" history anyway, so we get off on the right foot, as it were. Thank you, Hope, that'll be all… yes, I'll have my elevenses now. Good gosh, is that the time? Look, Charlie, it's quite simple, I need people who can hold a saucepan in one hand and a pen in the other. Are you one of those people, Charlie? I can work wonders with a good manuscript, but you've got to give me the words first.

'Penny Lee, now, you remember Pen? She always said it's not the nit-picking or the pedantic doggedness that makes Judith Langdon the best cookery editor and one of the best publishers in town. It's both those formidable things together. Now when I started here I was on poetry and classics. But Tony said to me, "You're a girl. Can you cook?" I said no but I still got the job. I was the only female member of our embryonic cookery list, you see. Anyway, we got to work on Cordon Bleu. The authors and I laboured through it for three to four months. When we started I couldn't even jolly an egg. At the end of it we had an excellent book and I had learned to cook.'

Hope came in with the coffee. Charlie took slow sips, it gave him something to do.

'Dear Pen was outraged at our first meeting together. Over a hundred and fifty queries on her first draft. As for you, Mr Sheridan, the Michelin star debacle should sell it, but can you deliver in print as well as on the plate?'

Charlie pushed his thousand words across to Judith. She read, nodded, stirred her short coffee with an initialled silver spoon and let out a rasping laugh.

'Fantastic… I think this can work. But can you keep it up? I'll need twenty times this at least. And what about the food? What are you going to give us that we can actually cook?'

'Well, I want to take Franco's old recipes and show how I brought them up to date.'

'Hmm, been done. What else?'

'I want to bring my grandfather's recipe book to life. It's the story of Belle Hotel.'

'Good. Warts and all? Including the attack?'

'Yes, including… that.'

'Good again, Charlie. Would you like to join me on my balcony for a cig?'

She hopped up, cranked open the metal framed window and climbed up on the table to gain access to the ledge.

'Shoo, go away. Bloody pigeons. Hop up. If you dangle your legs over here most of the smoke blows away.'

Charlie took the proffered Dunhill and let her light it for him with a pearl-handled pistol. They exhaled and took in the view. The BT Tower stood proud over the sordid goings on of Soho.

'I suppose you'd like to know what I can offer you.'

'Well, yes… Do we have a deal?'

'We certainly do, Mr Sheridan. But I'll tell you now, you'll bloody well earn it. I let Penny off lightly.'

'How long?'

'Twenty thousand good, clean, words and I expect nothing less than twenty times the quality of what you've just submitted. We'll discuss the deal after I've talked to my colleagues but it'll be a third on signature, a third on delivery of a mouth-watering manuscript and a third on publication.'

'Can you put that in writing?'

'Can you?'

Back at Belle Hotel that afternoon Charlie was suffering from writer's block. The more Charlie thought about it, the less he knew what he wanted to write. Judith Langdon would be as good as her word: 'Third on signature', he could invoice the money today, he'd learned how to knock one up in double quick time. That'd mean two and a half grand in their account by Friday – halfway to the Hookes' target, as long as they didn't blow it on anything else. But newly commissioned author of the Brit-food cookbook sensation was yet to put pen to paper. Or even nail-stubbed digit to Remington. Weak autumn sunshine flowed up Ship Street, filling the lobby with pale light. Charlie sat at the reception desk, Franco's ancient typewriter at his fingertips, attention wholly distracted by Franco's book at its side. Charlie had no fucking idea whatsoever of what to write next. He'd given it his all, well, Lulu had, with that opener to get the deal. A whole day had nearly passed and he'd not heard a peep out of her. He needed her to write this bloody thing for him, if they found out that he could barely write his name, wouldn't they cancel the contract? Oh well, maybe re-type what Lu had written, just to get him started.

He thumped 'M' for my on the Remington. Nothing, the ink was dry. Eight years in the salty air had parched the ribbon. Stupid, romantic notion. He yanked the M-embossed sheet from the Remington's grip, flipped its card and leather lid and put the ancient writing machine back in its place. It'd have to be the WP. Now then, how did you get that working?

*

Lulu had been absenting herself, but she had been busy on Belle Hotel's behalf. She made a couple of calls to contacts from her London years and put the gossip machine into overdrive. The *Evening Standard* picked up on the story of the seaside chef with issues and a cookbook deal. They called to ask if they could send their reviewer down, pronto. Chit chat about Charlie echoed around Town.

'Back in fashion, a cookbook with some confessions? Juicy! So now, we must go again, oh you've never been to Belle Hotel, darling you must.'

Lunch gossip in Soho sent signals down the tracks. Victoria–Haywards Heath–Brighton. The phone was ringing off the hook. Dinner for two, yes Victoria, and… do you have a room?

The phone rang again, Charlie nodded at Janet who was passing reception.

'You can answer the phone while you write, Shakespeare. Don't get carried away, we're not out of trouble yet.'

Janet flicked the duster at her son. He looked just like his father, sitting behind that desk. Just like him.

'You look just like your father, sat there.'

Charlie grinned, came out from behind reception and did Franco doing his silly 'walk this way' walk from way back when.

Day Three: –£5,000

Charlie knew what he wanted to write about after the Kipper Wars. Eggs Benedict. Top of the breakfast menu at Belle Hotel and, if he was going to be honest – and he was going to be honest – a dish with some meaning for Franco, Johnny and him. He typed the ingredients from memory, telling himself he'd check with Franco's version later, and leapt into the anecdote of the slung pan and Johnny's departure.

Twenty thousand words, Judith had said. That, and pictures, would fill the two hundred and fifty pages she'd said they had to fill. There had been something of a disagreement between them over pictures, but it seemed like Charlie was going to get his way.

'Hand drawn, like those great cookbooks. Elizabeth David and Simon Hopkinson.'

'You don't need to tell me, darling, I published them both. Okey dokey, I'll tell you what we'll do. I'll send Kerry down for a day to take a look. Kerry Matheson. The best food illustrator in the business. She'll know what to do. Front cover a line drawing of Belle Hotel and maybe some chef's knives or cloches for the cover, but we'll have eight full-page colour photos. No discussion.'

Charlie finished thumping in the recipe and was stumped. What to write next?

'Penny for them?' It was Lulu.

'Oh, Lu, well I was just thinking about Franco. And Eggs Benedict. Well actually I was just thinking about Baron of Beef. To tell you the truth, I was wondering where the crêpes Suzette trolley had got to.'

'Under the champagne rack in the cellar.'

'How the fuck d'you know that?'

'I put it there, remember? How's the book going?'

Charlie showed Lulu his flickering cursor.

'That it? Typical, Charlie, I can see I'm gonna have to help you. As usual. Here, shift up.'

Lulu lifted the lid of the reception desk and climbed in. She'd not been this close to him since the night on her houseboat. Apart from the fight, but Lulu was trying to block that out. Charlie did his best to disguise his pleasure. It was just her smell, the hint of lavender in her hair and the jut of her breasts against the black cotton top.

Two Soho Bohos wafted through the lobby. The blonde winked at Charlie, who pretended not to notice.

'Can you ever stop it?'

'What, Lu?'

'The tarts.'

'Yes, I can stop. If you—'

'I haven't decided yet.'

'Oh.'

'What we need is some sort of order.'

'Lu?'

'A recipe and an anecdote, that sort of thing. Like we did for the first thousand. We can write them as separate Word documents. Here, I'll put them in this BHC Folder.'

'What's BHC?'

'Belle Hotel Cookbook, dummy.'

Charlie leaned in slightly in this token of affection. Lulu elbowed the token back.

'Oi, not while we're working.'

'You're working for me.'

Lulu glared. Charlie broke out into a broad smile.

'Old Charlie, just teasing. Why don't we write the book together and it can say *The Belle Hotel Cookbook* by Charlie Sheridan, with Lulu Hardman.'

'With?' Lulu raised an eyebrow.

'And.'

She typed on, neat French polish on grimy English keyboard.

'Okay, crêpes Suzette. Even I know that one. The day Franco set the place alight.'

'He swore blind I'd over-boozed the sauce.'

'That's the kind of thing. You got the recipe handy?'

'Here, where it should be. Like you, Lu. I'm sorry I was a dick about you being pregnant. It's just I was scared and I got some stuff mixed up that meant… well, just know I got some stuff mixed up.'

'I know. Now shut up and let me type.'

One hour later, another thousand-word section of *The Belle Hotel Cookbook* had been put to bed and a closer working relationship established between Charlie and Lulu, who now fully understood why Franco and Charlie had been so tight. This news, like her pregnancy, would take some time to soak in. Back to work. What else was there?

First, he read out the recipe.

Crêpes Suzette
1 tbsp caster sugar
For the sauce:
Juice & zest of 4 oranges
Rind & juice of 1 lemon
1 tbsp caster sugar
Slug brandy
Knob butter (unsalted) for frying
Grand Marnier for flaming

Charlie talked her through some amendments he'd made to Franco's original recipe, such as burning off some of the alcohol in the brandy, and together they embellished the tale of the flaming chandelier.

'Say there were five fire engines. They always call out three, you want to pile it on a bit. And say it was 1997, it'll remind everyone of when we were swinging. Oh yes, and singe his eyebrows. That's always good for a laugh.'

Lulu pinged the document shut and stretched back.

'Two down, eighteen to go. If we keep up this work rate, you'll be done by Christmas.'

Charlie asked Lulu to come to the family lunch on Monday. Now that Lu was in the Sheridan family way it seemed the right thing to do.

'I'll think about it, Charlie. Shall we do another one?'

'You bet. I'll talk you through shepherd's pie. Can't have *The Belle Hotel Cookbook* without that.'

Lulu kissed him on the cheek.

You can't un-tell the fact that the previous generation chose not to tell. Lulu typed while Charlie tried to describe it, something about a family business and the family bond. You are working together and you are family. Family is work and work is family. Family business is the business of Belle Hotel and the business of family. That was the complicated bit. The bit that was harder to bind into Franco's book.

Lulu wanted to stick with her idea of twenty recipes and they made their way, that day, through two further dishes, keeping Franco's book close to their sides. They talked about the recipes, they talked about the past and Lu noticed the painting. She'd looked at it on credit-crunch day, but barely taken it in.

The painting of Franco and Janet and a cat, hung out of the way over the key rack. Lulu remembered it from her years as a waitress at Belle Hotel, but she'd taken no notice of it then. Now, with her London years under her soon-to-be expanding belt, she knew instantly that it was a Hockney. David Hockney. Sure of it.

'If that is a one hundred per cent bona fide Hockney, Charlie, that'll be the overdraft taken care of.'

They went to ask Janet and, she confirmed that yes an artist friend had settled his account with a canvas. Janet remembered the sitting, now you came to mention it. Late afternoon in the bar. Her at the pumps and Franco posed on the zinc surface. Charlie and Lulu driving her nuts. The cat? Maybe he'd painted it in on a whim. Artists.

Hookes Bank
TWO-DAY WARNING
Charlie Sheridan
Belle Hotel
Ship Street
Brighton
16 October 2008

Dear Charlie,

Confirming a credit into your account within the ten-day period set by the bank in lieu of calling in all overdrafts and loans against Belle Hotel and repossession. I hereby confirm:

+£2,500 Haddon Publishing

I have moved this money into the bank's client account and await the payment of a further £2,500 within two days. Otherwise we will revert to a repossession scenario.

Yours,

Paul Peters

Day Four: –£2,500

'I do like my authors to snarl.'

Judith, down with the lovely Hope and the photographer, though it had taken Judith's iron will to get Charlie to pose with his stainless steel.

'That's it, tiger. Now give me that glare again for the camera.'

That this was the blade that Fish, er, slipped onto was not lost on Judith. It would not be lost on readers either.

'That's it, now I want that on the cover.'

'But, Judith, I thought we'd agreed to have a Belle Hotel sketch.'

'Precisely. That can go on the back. This'll scare the hell out of those other pansies up there, with you on the shelf. Maybe even give Gordon Ramsay a little run for his money.'

Judith looked at some new recipes, artfully ignoring the fact that it was Lulu who printed them off, and talked her through them. Charlie had obviously found his ghost in the form of this capable woman.

'By whatever means necessary,' she'd whispered to Hope as she bore Judith's handbag to the powder room.

Charlie served them coq au vin and regaled the table with the tale of Franco and the French wine merchant.

'That's going in. Make a note, Hope, I want to see coq and that anecdote in the first half.'

Judith and her entourage took tuk-tuks up to the station and were back in London in time for cocktails.

Lulu kissed Charlie on the cheek.

'I tell you what, that coq looked fantastic, why don't you come over to the houseboat later. We can cook it together.'

Great idea. What time could he get away? Nine at the latest. Full again tonight, word was getting around.

Charlie was running late. He was also running.

'Hi, Eddie, how's it going? What? Chicken.'

He cut across the late evening traffic and jogged the two miles to Shoreham, past the elegantly wasted remains of the West Pier. Seagulls swooped, the chicken bits bounced about and all was well with the world. He wrist still hurt a bit, but you can't have everything.

Her houseboat felt good. Dimmed halogen, lapping water.

'So, Charlie 1, Graeme 0.'

'Stop it, Charlie. Graeme was a good guy. It was just—'

'Couldn't cook?'

Charlie recited the coq au vin ingredients to Lulu as he tipped out his pockets. She typed into her laptop. Out came the Le Creuset from the bottom of the sack.

'Used to have ten of these. Now we're down to this. I'll have to buy some new stock if coq is going back on the menu. Not cheap, mind you, they're are a hundred quid a throw.'

Lulu looked at the cast-iron orange pot. Burnt flecks of Judith Langdon's lunch darkened the lid.

'OK, I'll tell you what we've got. Copied verbatim from Franco. Don't mess with a classic, he always said. But then, that's why he never got a Michelin star.'

Lulu looked at this savage in her kitchen. She loved him. She always had done. Like Cathy loved Heathcliff. Their love had that touch of the gothic that Lulu had so loved in her A level English Lit. Writing the *Belle Hotel Cookbook* was a real way for Lulu to flex muscles she'd not used since school. She could write well, they'd always said that. Writing Charlie's story deepened her love. It was her story, too, after all. She wanted his child, the decision hadn't been that hard, once she'd got over the shock of his Jekyll and Hyde moment. Lulu was knocking thirty-five, this could be her last chance. And she wanted him again, physically. He'd changed, softened since the breakdown, and that made him attractive to her. Old Charlie attractive. Miles Davis on in the background, little else on in the foreground attractive. But first he'd have to feed her.

'A large chicken, jointed into six, see, I did it earlier. An onion. A carrot. Fist full of pancetta, bacon just won't cut it. Knob of butter. Two onions. Two sticks of celery. Four cloves of garlic. Some flour, you got any? Good. Bottle of red wine. French. We don't want to upset that merchant again. I guessed you'd have some. Good again. Bunch of thyme. T-H-Y-M-E. Some bay leaves. Half a pound of button mushrooms. Half a pound of shallots.'

Lulu nodded, she'd got all that.

'OK, now I'll do the Delia.'

He placed the heavy pot on the hob, lit the gas with his red plastic lighter and chucked in the chicken.

'Here goes. Carrot, onion and garlic.'

Lulu fetched two bottles of wine. One for them, one for the pot.

'Pancetta in now, that's it, let it stick. We want that goo for the flavour. Now the mushrooms and shallots. And the celery, oh and cognac. You got? VSOP, super.'

Charlie stood over the pan, stirring it continuously with his wooden spoon. Time passed, nothing was said. Lulu finished her take on the Franco anecdote, took a sip of her claret and waited.

'Good, now we can add the wine, put the lid on, lower the heat and give it forty minutes. What we going to do?'

He looked at her, bedroom eyes over a pot of food.

'You are a naughty boy, Charlie Sheridan.'

He picked her up and plonked her on the butcher's block, Brampton style. Lu was still wearing her pencil skirt from work. As they kissed she found that it rode up quite easily. Her head span with the sensation of sex and simmering chicken. He'd somehow found his way back inside her. And it felt fantastic.

Charlie was over and out with plenty of time to make and cook the noodles and open another bottle of claret. They sat at her glass-topped table to eat. How could he make something so simple taste so good? Same ingredients. Different hands. Totally new sensation.

He stayed the night and didn't think he was making a habit of this, as Lu reminded him in plain English. Her body language told him something different. They kissed, hugged, tasted the flavours of Charlie's food on one another, and made love once more.

Day Five: −£2,500

As soon as the sun was over Whitehawk Hill, Charlie bounced back along the front, dirty Le Creuset in his sack. Lulu flopped back in bed and considered her options. This wasn't just love, it was business. She'd be stupid to confuse the two. Anyway, with Roger Hardman for a father she was never short of a second opinion on the subject. If she was serious about him and, let's face it, she'd loved him since she was eleven, and she was going to have his child, then they would have to do it properly. Day Five and Charlie still had to find the other half of the money. He needed to do this himself to prove his seriousness to her. Was she really ready to commit? She needed a sign, something more than Charlie staggering on for another five days. Lulu turned Franco's book over absent-mindedly in her hands. Charlie had let her borrow it to search for new recipe ideas for *The Belle Hotel*

Cookbook. She started again at the beginning and soon came to the crayon drawing she and Charlie had done as kids of the two of them at Belle Hotel. She smiled and turned the crinkling paper over. It was then she saw what was written on the back, in block capitals by Franco's hand.

LULU, DO NOT LET CHARLIE THROW THIS AWAY

She thought about Franco's command from beyond the grave. Bit forceful for a kid's picture. Then the penny dropped. The 'THIS' was not about the picture. It was about the thing in the picture. Lulu, do not let Charlie throw Belle Hotel away. Franco knew Belle Hotel needed the two of them. More than that it needed someone with Franco's rod of iron to run the place and keep Charlie on track. Keep Charlie on track so that he could do what he did best. Cook food that made mouths water. And if she was going to do this, Lulu needed her name above the door. She didn't need to buy Charlie, she needed to own him. And on that satisfying revelation, Lulu shut Franco's book and fell back asleep.

Lulu's alarm beeped eight. Charlie was running up Ship Street and Lulu decided to take the day off work for the first time in her life. She'd probably be chucking the job at Hotel Epicure soon and then the work would really start. Lulu called Graeme to let him know and then asked if he'd do himself and Charlie a favour.

Charlie was late for breakfast, but he didn't care. Janet tutted as he entered, flung her apron at him and left him with a trough of sizzling sausages. He couldn't see her face, he knew she was smiling.

*

Evening Standard
BRIGHTON ROCKS AGAIN!
By Fay Mentor

Now that summer's finally here it seemed a good idea to head for the seaside – a good excuse to show off our British coastline to Mimi Marriot, my old friend and former food critic of the New York Times.

We took a bracing stroll along the prom before slipping up Ship Street, past the ghastly Octopus restaurant at Hotel Epicure (scene, as readers will know, of the most revolting risotto I have ever tasted) and in through the famous stained-glass art deco door marked Belle Hotel.

Invigorated by deep breaths of briny air, laced with the fumes of the passing cars of holiday-makers and day-trippers, we dived straight into a perfectly chilled bottle of Krug and a platter of oysters so fresh you'd have to dive down yourself for better as we perused the menu. Mimi was keen to try our heritage dish, and one of Belle Hotel's specialities, bubble and squeak. I was intrigued to see how the place had fared since my last visit, when Franco Sheridan, with his famous clientele of actors, was still owner, maître d' and celebrity character of the Old School, who had perfected the art not only of great food but of unrivalled customer service.

His grandson Charlie Sheridan has taken over the family business and was even awarded a Michelin star in 1997 – this must be the most discreet Michelin-starred restaurant in the country! Though as celebrity chefs go Charlie seems to be a bit of a recluse, I can assure you, Charlie Sheridan's food is breathtakingly good. He understands, psychs out and goads ingredients in a manner that has never been bettered outside the M25. Not one for trios of cubes or cylinders, eschewing the dribbles-of-sauce school of cooking, he has carried on the tradition of Belle Hotel with good, traditional British dishes with a twist – the combination that won him his star. A fallen star, alas, but once a star nevertheless. Our simple slices of terrine de foie gras outlined with Madeira jelly was a dream, and typical of what he does superbly. Mimi's verdict on her omelette fines herbes (Charlie perfected his omelette technique in Paris) was 'light, luscious and redolent with the scent of new-mown herbs'. Charlie has clearly done little to upset the local devotees. Classic dishes introduced by Franco have survived and even been bettered. My scallops with pea purée were light as the briny air. For her main course, Mimi bravely tackled a British classic, commenting that her fish and chips with a Harvey's Best batter would for her become the taste of the English seaside: classic, memorable and fresh as the cloudless sky. My coq au vin came in its own oven pot and was, from the first lift of the lid onwards, the best interpretation of this Gallic classic, in fragrance, presentation and taste, I've tasted this side of La Manche.

One thing I love about the Belle Hotel, and the reason I've always wanted to come back, is its eclectic mix of seediness and sophistication, but the food is sophistication itself. Crêpes Suzette flamed by as we talked, a fabulously tempting spectacle, but eventually we went our own ways. My trifle was unctuous perfection; Mimi said the tarte tatin turned her taste buds upside down.

The menu itself, laid out Escoffier-style, is Franco's invention, a throw-back to his days as head steward on the Brighton Belle *train, where in his youth he plied the silver service platter back and forth to the capital eight times a day. It taught him speed of delivery, and Charlie continues the tradition of presenting dishes speedily and with panache. If you haven't got all afternoon to enjoy the fading glory of the*

Belle Hotel you can be in and out within the hour: a boon for the hotel's theatre clientele, who regularly enjoy the full six-course menu, including savoury. Our Welsh rarebit came with a glass of superbly selected Château d'Yquem, a favourite of the establishment that rose from the Belle Hotel cellar chilled to perfection.

We left the place in love with Brighton and all things Belle Hotel. Our train seemed somewhat sterile after the Pullman époque grandeur of Brighton's much loved foodie treasure. I came back to London with only one pang of regret: throughout the nineties it was the presence of Franco, always immaculate, ever charming, that set the seal on the dining experience. But front of house now sparkles with two Brighton Belles, *and with Claire and Emma in the chorus and Charlie in the kitchen, Belle Hotel has successfully walked the tightrope of keeping up traditions while moving with the times. She's had her ups and downs; these have been well documented in less savoury publications than our own. The food, to my mind has remained top notch. The chef has got his fingers burned, but always put up great food. He now needs to keep a lid on his temper. Front of house... Belle Hotel needs a new maître d'. The grapevine tells me Charlie's in the running to regain his star. Watch this space.*

Charlie was reading the review and whooping and slapping Fish on the back with the rolled-up *Standard* when Graeme came knocking.

Charlie flung open the door. The review had rendered him fearless.

'Executive chef, to what do we owe this honour?'

'Cut it out, Sheridan. I come in peace.'

Graeme made the Mr Spock sign and Charlie gave it back.

'Come in, mate. Let's smoke the peace pipe, eh?'

'Sorry about your nose. Is it broken?'

'Nah, just a bit bent. Good thing you're a better cook than you are a black belt.'

'Coming from you, I'll take that as a compliment. In fact, that's what I've come to talk to you about.'

'You'd better come in. We'll sit in the restaurant. Talk this through over a coffee. Fish, mate, go get Janet to fix us a coffee.'

Ten minutes later, once they'd shared a strong coffee from Franco's pitted silver pot, Graeme made Charlie an offer.

'I've got a bit of money saved up, you need that. You've got something I need. Maybe we can help one another, rather than always competing. Charlie, I'll pay you two thousand five hundred quid today if you agree to teach me to cook the way that Franco taught you.'

Charlie nodded and lit up a fag.

'We don't tell anyone, Charlie. Not a soul. Agreed?'

Agreed. And sealed with a handshake. Lessons to begin on receipt of the cash in Belle Hotel's Hookes account. Same amount every month for six months, if the first month worked out.

Charlie smiled and waved Graeme back down Ship Street and muttered 'Fuck me,' under his breath.

2008–10

The Belle Hotel Cookbook

Brighton Museum's Curator and Keeper of Fine Art was absolutely delighted to receive Lulu's telephone call. Delighted, but not in the least surprised. Roger Hardman had told him to ring fence 500K and hold his balcony space for an undiscovered Hockney.

The deal was not yet done. Janet was yet to acquiesce. Janet was yet to agree to anything. But they knew it was just a matter of time.

'Come on, Charley Farley, let's set up the laptop on table two. Bring Franco's book, will you? We're going to need some inspiration.'

Charlie's very much alive ghost-writer was getting to the end of her tether. Last words, puddings, and her lover was proving worse than useless. Never really his thing, the sweet stuff, he usually left it to Fish to deal with food from the main course forwards.

Charlie reappeared with the book and a pot of camomile to soothe Lulu's stomach. She was feeling proper queasy at the moment and needed something to fortify her for the confections to come.

'So, let me see, Charlie. At the end, you say… what's this, dates on the back?'

Lulu flicked over a yellowing lemon meringue tart page and pointed at Franco's spidery hand.

'June 1989. Yes, our home ec. GCSE.'

'You lent me an egg.'

'You flicked butter at me behind the examiner's back.'

She turned the frail pages and read out dishes and dates.

'Pondichery poulet rouge. Twelfth of August 1998. So you mean to say he was still feeding you these, then?'

'I guess so. You're the first to notice. Good dish, that chicken curry, it's the fusion of French and spices that make it work. That wasn't the first version. He developed it over decades. Gave me a lecture once about vinegar and that being the froggy bit. Think he got the original recipe from… Fizal Moondi, I think, who had some relative who was brought up there.'

'Jesus, he never stopped training you, did he. Talk about dedication.'

'Well, it paid off. For a bit. Come on, Lu, I've got lots to do.'

'Just pick your top few, hit me with the anecdotes and you can get back to your kitchen.'

Tarte Tatin

8 Cox's orange pippin apples

1 fresh vanilla pod

7 oz caster sugar

5 oz unsalted butter

10 oz puff pastry

1 egg & tbsp double cream for wash

5 fl oz crème fraîche

Butterscotch sauce

5 oz butter

5 oz caster sugar

5 oz golden syrup

3 oz whipping cream

'Franco said tarte tatin was first created by accident in Lamotte-Beuvron, France in 1889. B-E-U-V. He told this tale a thousand times. The hotel was run by two sisters, Stephanie and Caroline Tatin. Stephanie Tatin, who did most of the cooking, was overworked that day, nothing new there. She started to make traditional apple pie but left the apples cooking in butter and sugar too long. Smelling the burning, she tried to rescue the dish by putting the pastry base on top of the pan of apples, quickly finishing the cooking by putting the whole pan in the oven. She turned out the tart upside down, and was surprised how much the hotel guests appreciated the dessert. Restaurateur Louis Vaudable tasted the tart on a trip to the Sologne region and made the dessert a permanent fixture on the menu at his restaurant, Maxim's de Paris. *Et voilà*. Franco would lift the cloche and tell them they served tatin on the trains because it tasted good even if you'd dropped it.'

Something about the sticky pudding and the swaying of the carriage sent Lulu off to puke.

'Right, I got most of that.'

She was back. Charlie was halfway through a fag. The supposedly banned fug was making her gag. Not long now. They pressed on.

'I've had a look and think we should do treacle tart and chocolate torte. You can copy them both verbatim, but I want to make a tweak to crème anglaise. Franco's custard came up like concrete, mine has less yolk and more cream. Mind you, I never got the hang of Ile Flottante.'

'Isle what?'

'Precisely. Weird how some stuff drops from the repertoire. We used to do a bomb on them in the seventies, right up there with crêpes Suzette.'

With that, Charlie slipped back to his savouries. Sixty in for lunch and only him and Fish on shift. Things were going in the right direction, Lulu knew that. Charlie was behaving himself, acting like he meant it. Belle Hotel owed so much money that it was a full-time job just paying back the debt. But it was being paid off! She sighed a sweet sigh of satisfaction, and looked up at the ceiling.

A flake of fading paint fluttered down from the cornicing as a couple of dirty weekenders shunted around the bed on the first floor. Making love or babies, she wondered. Or both? Lulu patted her stomach with her left hand and typed with the other. What was

Madame Tatin's name? She couldn't read her notes. Not to worry, Judith Langdon would pick it up in the edit.

Back to Hotel Epicure to make its shareholders some more money.

'Dad, I'm through doing this for other people.'

'That's my girl.'

'Are you sure, Dad?'

'Go for it. I didn't get where I am today without taking a few risks. It's only a boat and I only helped you with that first London flat deposit. This is Belle Hotel we are talking about. I'd have helped, but Hardman Academy and that bastard bank in Iceland have wiped me out. *Shagpile II* is on the market, but nobody wants a gin palace in a recession.'

Roger Hardman was entertaining a party of eight journalists for Saturday lunch. As sponsor and namesake of Hardman Academy, Roger was deep into the promotional activities for his new-found passion. Defending his decision keep an ancient Mr Caner on as the new principal of the Academy had been very unpopular. Especially with Charlie. Roger grimaced at the line of questioning taken by the *Guardian* and dashed down his duck terrine in between answers. He'd rather have been at Belle Hotel, as would most of his guests, but they'd endure the portion-controlled cuisine out of family loyalty to Lulu because she worked there.

'Marry him, Lulabell and put my taste buds out of their misery.'

Busy Brighton weekend, deep in conference season. Day-trippers, locals and delegates, demanding to be bedded, fed and watered. Both hotels were fully booked and bouncing late arrivals up and down Ship Street. Charlie cooked through the new menu. The cut coriander for turbot took him back to poulet rouge with Lulu and his last session on the book. Once it was done, then would she move in? He was staying at hers most nights, trotting along the wave-swept front after service, happy. Happy as Larry. But that was not saying much.

Monday morning he called her.

'Come for lunch, Lu. Mum wants to see you and I'm cooking curry.'

Lulu's stomach lurched at the thought of the creamy spices. She'd be better by three, she told herself, and readily agreed to the thinly veiled summit. Today is the day. She decided to take the morning off again. Sod them. Three years of covering her staff for their duvet days and she was feeling sick anyway. Sick as a pig and she was beginning to show. Time to do a deal with the Sheridans, for the sake of the Sheridan inside her.

Lulu lay in deliciously until noon, took a long shower in her soon-to-be-forgone houseboat and set her face for family business.

It was a windy day, gusts darting across the border between Shoreham and Brighton. Lulu decided to enter Belle Hotel by the pub, Janet's territory, and had her trajectory momentarily diverted by the door-barging departure of a lank-haired punter. He'd have to be barred, for a start.

'Hello, Janet, how was the lunch trade?'

She was swaying slightly, but seemed happy enough. It'd take more than topping her ex-husband to throw this bird off her perch.

'Hello, Lu, love. Curry for us, eh? Can I get you a drink? Lager or summat?'

'No, just a water with a slice of lime, thanks.'

Janet fixed the smeared glass of tap with a dash of disdain. She topped it with a half-melted cube of ice and a slice of limp lemon from the plastic pack, topped up her own lager, filled a metal bowl with nuts and zipped round the zinc to join Lu on the stools.

'Cheers, love. Here's to us.'

Janet knew what was coming. She was going. Of that much she was certain. The when and how would be hammered out next door, but for now raised receptacles spoke of conquest and defeat. The taking of places. But Lulu had a plan.

First they must eat. Table two, as always, view of reception and kitchen. Things were getting better, Claire now stayed on most afternoons to cover the phones and reception and Charlie had given his new assistant a sack of Sussex spuds to turn before service. And the food.

'This is just… delicious.'

'Thanks, Lu.'

'My God, Charlie, we haven't had this for years. One of Franco's, your dad's, favourites. Poulet rouge. Anyone want another lager?'

Lulu gave Charlie the look. He made himself scarce and she braced herself for Janet's return.

'Janet, I want to come here and live with him. I want my name above the door. It's time.'

'Good for you, love. It's about time, too.'

'I want to sort this out today and move in tomorrow.'

'Bloody hell. You don't hang around.'

'Yes, well, no time like the present.'

Move in here? thought Janet, spice-tainted brain chugging things over, what about me?

'I've been thinking about you. About you and me. What we'll do.'

'Me too, love.'

'Well, I wondered if—'

Charlie's quizzical face appeared at the porthole. No, she frowned, not yet.

'I wondered if you'd consider retiring. Taking my houseboat. It's only down the road, you know. Charlie told me about you wanting to go up north, but I thought a couple of miles west might do for starters.'

Janet looked at this proud alpha female and knew. She was going, and the best thing to do was to go with good grace. Nice solution too, the houseboat. Probably her father's idea. Sharp bastard, that Roger Hardman. Still, it'd give her a good send-off. But what about the pub?

'What about the pub? I could—'

'No, Janet. If we do this I am going to make some changes. I'm calling the pub Franco's. It'll be a gastro pub with his classic dishes from the cookbook.'

'Oh, I see.'

'Charlie and I… We're going to go for Michelin stars again in the restaurant. New food. Flavours. New ideas. It's what Charlie, his cooking, needs. I know you don't want to hold him back. We've made a three-year plan.'

'Three-year plan, I see. Well good luck to you both – and the baby. Eeh, I'm looking forward to being a granny!'

Janet hugged Lulu into her sturdy frame, holding them both tight in the embrace of the banquette.

'Shall we tell Charlie what's been agreed?'

'Sure, sweetheart. Franco's, eh? Good idea. Are we keeping shepherd's pie?'

'Yes. And we're going to do oysters, too.'

'Not Rottingdean oysters, I hope?'

'Newhaven.'

'No fancy sauces, mind. Franco liked his plain.'

'No fancy sauces. I'll leave that up to Charlie. Oh, here he is. You're back.'

'Hello, Mum, Lu. Everything okay?'

'Everything's just fine, Charlie, love. I'll leave you two on your own for a while. I'm knackered.'

Lulu quit Hotel Epicure that afternoon and took a whole two days off before taking on Belle Hotel. Janet's possessions filled a Brighton cab and she was surprised how at home she felt on her houseboat.

Lulu was on her hands and knees in her new two-room apartment at the top of Belle Hotel, scrubbing the lime-stained loo for all she was worth, when a gentleman came calling four floors below.

'Er, good morning.'

Charlie, ever the model of great customer service, failed to look up. He was engrossed in the final lines of Lulu's opus. His cookbook. Let the punter wait.

'Is the owner here?'

Charlie looked up this time. What now? Tax inspector? VAT man? Health and Safety? Brighton CID? He took in the tweed-and-bow-tie confection standing in his lobby. The Fine Art Curator.

Jeremy Beaker rocked back on his brogues, enjoying the handmade creak of last-cobbled leather on threadbare carpet. He already knew what he was looking at. Sausage fat pomade in that shock of tousled hair, spattered white jacket gaping open at the neck. The hum of nicotine and Nescafé hanging in the air. The Brighton Rock 'n' Roll chef.

'I am the owner. Well, in a manner of speaking. Are you looking for Lulu? She's upstairs.'

'Jeremy Beaker, Brighton Museum Keeper of Fine Art. Where is it?'

'What, Mr Beaker?'

'Come, come. Don't tease. I have it on good authority that you are hoarding a Hockney somewhere on the premises.'

'Ah, the Hockney.'

Beaker rocked back with another satisfying creak and ran a pinkie-ringed finger through what was left of a foppish fringe.

'Yes, *the* Hockney. Come along, Mr Sheridan, you are a tease. Where is it? I operate on a slim purchase grant, but if this is what I think it is I'll have a stab at it. Imagine. An undiscovered Hockney hanging on my temporary exhibition wall? Come, come, I've mentally cleared the gay, lesbian, bisexual, transgender community collage in anticipation.'

'Okay, just hang on a mo, I've got to finish this.'

Charlie took his time over the last line. Was his cookbook not art, too? Eventually he was happy with the phrase, as he hoped Judith Langdon would be. Done. He pinged it shut and emailed the twenty-thousand-word manuscript off, care of Hope at Haddon Towers.

'Right, thanks for waiting. It's in here. Come on in.'

The Fine Art Curator braced his senses. Sure enough, his delicate synapses flared up at the first sniff of fried food and dust mites. It'd take an evening of vapours to rid his senses of the smell, not to mention the dry-cleaning of his Cordings of Piccadilly suit. He was in the middle of damning the dirty kitchen worker when he saw it.

'You beauty.'

'Any good?'

'You *beauty*. Mind if I…?'

Charlie shrugged. Janet was gone and this guy had his chequebook poking out of his checked pocket.

'Just what I was hoping for. No. Better. Not Hockney, of course. Good, that would be beyond me anyway. More of a Hackney, if you know what I mean. This is a David London, similar style but more naturalistic. When?'

Beaker lifted the rectangle respectfully off its nail and tilted Charlie's parents into the pale light drifting in off the water.

'Beautiful. And kept out of direct sun. No bleaching. Mint. Let's look at your behind.'

He turned the picture over and voiced a thirty-year-old dedication.

'Franco, Janet and The Belle Hotel Mouse Catcher. Happy times.'

'Well, well. Mr Beaker, I presume?' It was Lulu.

'Yes, how do you do? We were just admiring this wonderful inscription. I have to tell you both that I am terrifically excited. Gosh, the buzz of anticipation was palpable among our many museum staff as I left my study this morning. Not a Hockney, of course. But still of enormous sentimental value to Brighton. Wonderful. I say, I think this calls for a drink.'

Lu set up a table for the three of them in Franco's – the new sign was already up on the Ship Street facing wall – and sent Charlie down below for a bottle of vintage Krug. Usually unmoved by either fine art or wine, Charlie sifted through the dust-shrouded bottles for a '76.

Lulu turned to Emma. 'Thank you, Emma. And we'll have some still water. Can you come back and pour in about twenty minutes? It should be suitably chilled by then.'

The silver ice bucket gleamed on the thick-linen-laid table. Franco turned over in his grave and slept soundly. A firm hand was front of house again.

'Now then, Mr Beaker. While we wait for our champagne, shall we talk turkey? What's it worth?'

Jeremy Beaker had removed his jacket and carefully laid it down on the battle-weary seat at his side. Damp patches were clearly visible under his arms and it was clear he'd neglected to iron his sleeves. So, the offer.

'Mint condition. Mounting a historical piece like this in my temporary space. Bringing such a piece into the National collection. Priceless.'

'Yes. Thanks, Charlie. Can we—'

Charlie, open-mouthed at Lulu's ordering him about, placed the elevenses, a silver salver of small parmesan puffs and egg mayonnaise tartine, onto the table beside Franco, Janet and the cat. He pulled up a chair from the adjacent table, got on it backwards and flared up a fag with a flash of gold. Emma appeared from behind the bar with a soon to be defunct BH ashtray. Good, thought Lulu, they were getting the hang of it. If Beaker was as good as his tailor, they'd have the money to hang on a few weeks longer.

The curator's hand made for the platter, long fingernails darting between warm pastry and chilled toast. His brain settled on the former and the flaky cheese sensation crumbled to his touch. He managed to shovel half of the horn into his mouth and spent the money shot sweeping greasy pieces onto the floor.

'Not Hockney money, but I think you're going to like it.'

In Charlie's telling of it, the art ponce got out his chequebook there and then. Brampton and Sinker loved it. Both asked for their month-long accounts to be settled in the same breath. In truth, it took a little longer for the triple-signed cheque for five grand for and on behalf of Brighton and Hove Council to come through. Not the extra couple of noughts they were hoping for, but better than a poke in the eye from an angry lobster.

Lulu used Jeremy Beaker's receipt towards another five days at Hookes. When the money came, it came as a temporary relief. Like somebody putting their finger back in the dyke. Lulu finally understood what it meant to be running your own business.

'That's my girl.'

'But Dad, this'll just cover five days. The quarterly VAT payment is due next Monday and it's the biggest one, too.'

'That's business. There's no business like business,' laughed Roger Hardman at his badly sung pun. He glanced at his arm where his Rolex used to be. 'Gotta go, Lulabell. How's my granddaughter cooking?'

'Good, I'm eating enough for two. Anyway, who says it's a girl? We haven't had the scan yet.'

He was gone, up on deck to join the boys for drinks and to check on his frozen funds in Iceland. Business. Roger read the global markets in his *Times* newspaper and tutted that things had got this bad. He'd worked hard for his millions and had the carpet burns to prove it. Then some banker in an ivory tower had gambled it away again. Bastards.

Lulu patted her stomach and placed the trimphone back in its cradle – she'd get round to refurbing their flat once she'd done the bedrooms – and went back to the laundry brochures. Down below in a gleaming kitchen Charlie piped truffled potato onto a buttered baking tray.

A knock at the kitchen door, just as he'd put the baking tray into the oven. Charlie opened it wide. He was starting to feel less anxious about visitors to the kitchen door now he had Lulu fighting his corner.

'Tom. Man, how are you?'

'Oi roite, taxi driver said this was the place to find yer. How long's it been man?'

'Tony Blair's party at Downing Street. What, a decade. Come in. Let's have a jar. Come in, man, come in.'

Charlie and Tom sat at the bar, the hotelier and the entertainer. A next-generation Franco and Larry.

'Summer season on Worthing Pier. I'm just in off the cruise ships. Having a month off. Say, can you do me a room at Belle Hotel, mates rates, mind.'

'Sure, no problem. Ah… wait. I'd better run it by Lulu. She sort of runs the place now. Well, the hotel side, anyway.'

'Lulu, that's a blast from the past. How lovely yous two are still together. Childhood sweethearts. Love's young dream.'

'Not exactly, mate. More like *War and Peace*. I'll tell you about it sometime. But we're happy now and about to have a baby and that's great.'

'Grand that it's worked out for yous. You'll see that my solo career didn't come to much. I had a falling out with Simon Cowell and he dropped me after my first single flopped. But you know, singing at sea has its upsides. It's good to see the world, and hell, it's better than being stuck in a kitchen. No offence, brother.'

'None taken, Tom. None taken.'

Lulu had been surprised how much she'd felt from her growing child. From the moment she'd seen the thin blue line she seemed to be having a sixth-sense conversation with the human being growing within.

Things were being created up the track in London, too. Judith Langdon was hard at work on the edit of Charlie's first draft, blinds drawn on the BT Tower and Soho, head down at laser-printed paper. Swift incisions of blue pencil were picked up by Hope, who turned potatos into potatoes at the flick of a French-polished finger. Judith liked the mix of food and fable. The folklorish feel of the piece was working as she'd hoped it would. It just needed a little more shaping around the dishes, this after all was what people would be wanting for their twenty-pound investment. Twenty pounds, she sighed, most of them would buy it for £9.99 at Tesco. Dear Lord, what was happening to the publishing profession? Allowing ourselves to be commodified like eggs.

Judith liked the recipes, too, she'd tried them at home on her Aga. Talking of eggs, there was a little too much of them in the manuscript. That'd have to go, forthwith. But Judith liked the anecdotes. Hope knocked lightly and swapped a double macchiato for the coq-au-vin (corr. coq au vin) chapter.

Lulu's egg was growing, too. She was putting on weight and finding it harder to nip up to the flat for the odd curtain swatch than she used to. Charlie had been too busy to go with her to the scan, but he'd cried when she'd shown him the photo so that sort of made up for it.

'Beautiful. Can I put this up?'

So baby Blue spent the next six months pinned up above the deep fat fryer, her thumbsucking profile gently yellowing like chips.

Things were cooking for Belle Hotel. The bedrooms were set for a refurb, Paul Peters and Hookes Bank not withstanding. Franco's was doing a bomb. Most of Janet's barflies had decamped to The Duke of Wellington, her new local. Suddenly a whole slice of Brighton and London life was flowing through the pub's newly painted doors. Hotel

Epicure's customers, smiled Lulu, as she took in tables of pressed hair and creased slacks.

Charlie added two new characters to his brigade. He had a new, leaner, Meat and – something unheard of in Franco's day – Salad. Yes, a whole human being dedicated to vegetables. Charlie had found his handshake a little limp, but he'd come highly recommended from The Savoy, via Johnny's old mate the night-shift manager. Salad had something of a thing for allotments and Charlie gladly handed over his spade. The ruddy-cheeked fellow was to be found up on Whitehawk Hill most afternoons tilling the soil between shifts. There were rumours he was doing Dawn, too, an arrangement that suited Charlie only too well, though he sometimes missed those chilly afternoons up there in the warm embrace of her railway carriage. It put Dawn out of temptation's way and that was a good thing. Hey, ho. He'd made his bed and he'd have to lie in it – though with Lulu growing as she was, Charlie increasingly found himself being shoved onto the floor to make room for Mummy and bump.

The Belle Hotel Cookbook was typeset, sent to proofreading and thence to repro. Judith demanded a signed copy of the proofs from Charlie, added her own mark to the sheets, and filed the shiny block in the cabinet by Hope's pumps.

Lulu entered her third trimester and her belly button popped out like it had when she was a kid. Keying of corrections took place on the page proofs, which was now actually a book, no longer a manuscript, and Lulu set about finding a spot to give birth to baby Blue.

After her lone trips to the clinic, there was no way she was going to have the baby away from Belle Hotel. The big question was; where would a birthing pool fit?

At London Bridge, Charlie helped Lulu down from the ageing Thameslink. Minutes later they boarded the shiny *Bombadier* for the short shunt to Charing Cross.

London somehow felt safer with her and his unborn baby. And with Johnny gone, going down the Strand seemed less loaded too. They hobbled across the compacted traffic and into the brightly lit lobby of Hookes.

Paul Peters came down ten minutes later, apologising: there had been a misunderstanding at last night's staff party and he'd just been debriefing the staff member involved. Lulu found it hard to look at Peters, though the Homer Simpson tie fetchingly set against a monogrammed shirt did rather draw the eye.

Peters led the couple into the lift, all backslaps and bonhomie for Charlie, portly courtesy for Lulu, and whisked the heirs of his favourite client up to his oak-lined office. Generations of venerable bankers, none in anything remotely resembling a novelty tie, glared down at Lulu from their gilt frames. A woman. Running a business. Pah.

Pah, indeed. Lulu handed Paul Peters the 'second for and on behalf of Haddon Publishing' cheque. She held her end for a moment longer than Peters was expecting. He tugged the cheque free.

'Good show! I say, this calls for a sherry.'

Peters decanted the golden fluid into three small glasses. They duly chinked, chin-chinned and downed their liquid elevenses. Peters had already enjoyed a nip of Scotch for nineses, to ward of the rumours that were creeping under his door.

'So, tell me about your plans.' He looked at Charlie.

'We're going for a new golden age at Belle Hotel.' It was Lulu, self-appointed spokesperson, who spoke, 'and Charlie is going to win back his star.'

'Sss…'

'Pardon, Charlie? Are you all right? Another amontillado, perhaps?'

'What he's hissing about, Paul, is the fact that this time he wants to make his Michelin plural. Stars.'

'Ah, I see. Well, jolly good luck to you both. I was wondering about popping down for a shopping trip tomorrow and thought I might add an overnight.'

'Of course, you are most welcome. We're almost full but I can accommodate you in room twenty, on friends and family rates.'

Charlie hissed once more. Peters paying for his stay, unheard of. The banker fumbled behind his double Windsor.

'Put it this way,' Lu took the velvet gloves off, 'you think about dropping your extortionate twenty per cent unsecured lending rate and I'll think about throwing in a treat tray.'

They crossed London in a taxi soon after that.

'I can't believe you said that to Paul Peters. He was one of Franco's oldest associates.'

'Yes, and he's been stiffing you ever since Franco died. Screw him. It's time somebody stood up to him. Don't worry, Charlie, he'll bounce back. I might even comp his room for him if he makes it down. So, here we are. How are you feeling?'

If he was honest, Charlie was quite nervous. This was after all publishing, making public your food and soul. Lulu felt it, too. She'd dragged the bulk of it kicking and screaming out of him. Let him have his day, take the credit.

Hope came rushing in and was all over Charlie. She offered Lulu a Tiffany-ringed hand.

'Do come through, we're all terribly excited to be showing it to you. Judith has already taken it up to the MD and they think we might be onto a winner. But I didn't tell you.'

Lulu waddled, aware of her saggy behind, after the ra-ra skirted pertness skipping along ahead of them. She watched Charlie's gaze, but... nothing. He seemed more intent on a locked door up ahead.

'Lu, that's where they keep all the unpublished fiction. Slush pile, they call it. You should see inside.'

Judith was on the telephone when they arrived at her glass panel. The window was open behind her, she'd obviously been up having a gasp when the dratted thing had rung.

She pointed across them. They looked. The Haddon Author hall of fame had a new face. Charlie's: a crop of the shot taken for the book jacket. He'd arrived, nuzzling between Clarissa Dickson Wright and Peter Gordon.

'Come, come,' the sound of clapping emitted from Judith's room. She had finished her telephone conversation.

'That was Marcus Jones, our sales director. Good news, the Waterstones team have bagged you a window in every store and a dedicated table at each of their bigger branches. I can smell success. Sit, please sit. Hope, we'll have that little bottle of pop now, please. Lulu, darling, you are blooming. When is baby cooked?'

The half bottle of champagne went off with a muted pop and the three of them toasted the book, Charlie hugging his copy.

'*The Belle Hotel Cookbook*!'

The glass of champagne went down like nectar and in a jiffy Charlie and Lulu were toasted, trundled out into the lift and Judith had turned to her next project.

'Christ, that woman works it.'

Charlie nodded at Lulu and nuzzled her a little closer. The pressing down of baby and the dropping of the lift made her want to pee.

'I gotta go, what time is it? Oh, let's get a cab straight to Gavvers. We don't want to keep the publicist waiting.'

'The publicist. Who said anything about a publicist? I thought he was a friend of yours.'

'Yes, a friend of mine whose job is to generate and manage publicity for a public figure, for a work such as a book. The Haddon publicity team are brilliant, but we need to invest in Charlie Sheridan, the celeb chef brand.'

'For fuck's sake, Lu, I could do without that kind of gastroporn.'

'Come on, grumpy. His name is William. Will. And he's very shrewd and good at his job. Kept the Hotel Epicure story sizzling in the press long after its sell-by date.'

The cab took them to Mayfair and a waiting Will the publicist.

'Charmed, I'm sure. Lulu has told me lots about you, but I know I'll read more. Is that it?'

Charlie handed Will *The Belle Hotel Cookbook*. He weighed the tome in both hands.

'Nice, manages to look both now and then. I like it.'

He gave it back. Charlie knew he'd read it looking for sizzle. This was a guy who thrived on gossip, anecdote and chat. He'd be hungry for more than the book could offer. Scandalous Hors D'Oeuvre to the £19.99 main menu.

'I'm famished. Shall we eat?'

Will led the three of them down into Le Gavroche restaurant. It looked as beautiful as it did when he did those two weeks, what, nearly twenty years ago. Charlie had a *salut* to do.

'If you'd both excuse me for a mo, I need to go say hi to Michel Roux Jr. We spent some time together once. I want to go ask him what you have to do to get two stars these days. Back in a mo.'

The French waiter ushered Will and Lulu to their table. Will had fancied his chances with Lulu late one night at Hotel Epicure. Frankly, if she hadn't been so knackered at the time, she might have given him a crack.

Michel Roux Jr looked pleased to see Charlie, but busy. Thumbs up, rolling of those eyes and a nod in the direction of the Remanco spewing lunch requests by the dozen. Charlie nodded back, no need to break his focus. Catch you later, *ami*, keep on cooking. Charlie was nearly knocked over by a chef racing towards the pass with a pot of Bouillabaisse. It was Guillaume, son of L'Épuisette in Marseille. So this is where he's working. Quick *bonjours* and that promise of the visit to Belle Hotel for lunch on Charlie gets renewed. Chef Michel jerked his head to get Guillaume back to his station and Charlie ducked back into the restaurant.

He arrived back at the table in time to see the publicist push the à la carte under his Burberry overcoat and pay deep attention to the set-lunch card. Cheapskate. So that was the way it was going to be. Charlie hoped his fees reflected this fiscal prudence, too.

The set lunch looked good. Charlie and Lulu had soufflé Suisse to start and sea bream for mains. The publicist looked through his rimless glasses and plumped for terrine of pork and foie gras to start and slowly braised pork cheeks for the trot on. He ordered a bottle of Châteauneuf du Pape, the cheapest of the three, Charlie noticed, perfectly matched to his lunch, the swine, and hopeless with both their choices. Charlie hoped he'd be as single-minded when it came to promoting the book. He looked down at *The Belle Hotel Cookbook*. Beautiful. Hard embossed back under glossy cover. Scarlet ribbon bookmark dangling down from a hundred, his favourite page. Lobster Belle Hotel.

'So what is our angle?'

'Pardon?'

'Our angle. Help me here, Lulu, I've got to have a bit of new news to set the press wagging when we launch the book. What you got?'

Charlie looked at Lulu. No, not that.

Their starters arrived, they took their time to appreciate the dishes. It gave Charlie time to think. He liked Michel Roux Jr's cooking. And so did the Michelin inspectors, obviously. It had been a bit of a blow to go from three stars to two, not long after Michel Roux Jr took over from his father, but he'd soon adjusted to the idea and made the point that it suited his lighter interpretations of his father and uncle's classic French dishes.

'OK, Will. William. I'll tell you what I'm thinking. English food. No, Sussex food. Food that knows where it's come from, with a clear idea where it's going, food that showcases the fabulous, often forgotten fact that we can grow and rear almost everything in this county.'

'Yeees, good for *Observer Food*. What about the *heat, Hello!* and *OK!* factor?'

'Well, he has just discovered—'

'*No*, Lu. I will not be used in this way. Ouch. I mean. Sorry, Lu, please finish what you were going to say. It's fine. I'm sorry I snapped.'

Charlie managed his anger, the kick in the shin from Lulu acting as a remarkably efficient prompt. London's chattering classes paused for what seemed like an awfully long time.

'If you'd let me finish, Mr Hothead… Will, Charlie is tipped to be getting his Michelin star back next year. How about that?'

'Good… enough,' the publicist conceded, 'I'm going to get you a paid gig that will do wonders for publicity. STOXO.' Will thrummed his fingers on the thick linen tablecloth and dared Charlie to turn this down while he waited for his pig cheeks. They were lunched, closed, coated and booted onto a wind-whipped Park Lane before the hour of two.

M&C SAATCHI

CONTRACT

TALENT: CHARLIE SHERIDAN

CLIENT: STOXO STOCK CUBES FOR THE FOOD CHANNEL

AD CAMPAIGN: BELLE HOTEL TASTES BETTER WITH STOXO

AD DURATION: 30 SECONDS

SCRIPT: 'Remember how good homemade gravy used to taste? We do here at Belle Hotel. With real meat juices slowly simmered for that delicious home-cooked taste. Well, gravy tastes better with STOXO. I'm Charlie Sheridan, so take my word for it.'

FEE: £4,000 buy out

＊

Charlie had enjoyed his day at Shepperton Studios. The car turned up at 6am, as scheduled, he had a nice kip in the back. Then a little flirt with the make-up girl, nothing too heavy, he was a taken man now. She'd fucked up his barnet, good and proper back-combing it so he looked like that prat Russell Brand. And then they brought out the STOXO chef's jacket and checked trousers. Red and black, Charlie looked like a giant STOXO cube. Thank God this was only going out on the Food Channel. Nobody watched the Food Channel, right? Four grand for a day's work, silly money. If only Franco could see him now. Charlie texted Lulu all morning from his dressing room.

Hi Lu, I'm in my dressing room now.

Still in my dressing room.

About to leave my dressing room and go on set.

Wish me luck, break a leg or something.

Oh, btw, we need to give Brampton £1800 by midday

'Mr Sheridan, if we can have you on set now.'

'Oh, okay. Are we done here, darling?'

Charlie allowed himself a small peck on the cheek for the make-up girl, this was show business, and let himself be led across the dark sound stage to the ring of lighting holding a kitchen set. Made that Gary Rhodes Supertheatre from the Good Food Exhibition in the nineties look posh. As soon as Charlie stepped onto the platform the cupboards wobbled. The pans looked like they'd come from Argos and none of the hobs worked.

'None of the hobs work.'

'Er, we'll put that in after, Jerry can we put that in after? Yes, good. Right-oh, er, Mr Sheridan, shall we have a go at a take?'

'Charlie, call me Charlie. Can I have a drink please?'

'Of course, what would you like, we'll send a runner.'

'Oh, I don't mind. Lager, brandy, whatever. Something to, y'know calm me down.'

Charlie stared out into darkness. One of the silhouettes spoke.

'Charlie, hi, I'm Doug Duboeuf, brand manager STOXO Europe. Hi.'

'Er, hi, Doug.'

'Just before you give us your performance I wanted to let you know that we've invested in a creative treatment that will build to an advert to communicate the strong taste and flavour credentials of the STOXO cube. I don't know if you are aware of this, Charlie, but the stock-cube sector is currently worth over £129 million, er, Charlie, and is in strong growth at five point one per cent. Isn't that amazing? We're confident that our innovative advert will bring double-digit growth to the stock-cube market, as consumer interest in stock cubes that offer strong taste credentials remains strong.'

'Right… good. My drink, thanks. Port. Yum. Thank you.'

'Okay, Charlie. This is your director, Yan, speaking. Now, I've worked with the best of you guys: Jamie, Delia, Ainsley. Let's see what you've got. How do you like to do these gigs? Wanna run a few off and we'll just keep the camera rolling, or do you want me to action and cut each take you do?'

Charlie could feel his breakfast sink rapidly into his bowels. He put the port down.

'Er, can I take a quick look at the script again, please.'

By 5pm the agency account director had calmed Doug Dubeouf down sufficiently to allow Charlie off set. He'd forced Yan to assure him that Charlie delivering his speech in three-word bursts that had to be read out to him before each take, with a new camera angle in between each burst, would give the STOXO ad a fresh, jump-cut feel that would very much appeal to the younger demographic that STOXO were seeking to attract. It made Franco's 'Goes down well at the Belle' seem like a monologue.

What hadn't helped, Charlie reflected the next day, was that he'd had a word with himself, as Lulu had told him to do when he started being a dick. That meant putting the bottle of port back under the non-working sink and getting on with the job in hand. Charlie did his best with the nerves. Franco had been wooden, Charlie was concrete, but it was getting increasingly difficult to concentrate, what with the heat, the lights, the bad-tempered clients and Yan's bad attitude.

Still, the journey back in the car had been good. Charlie had slept the whole way, arriving back at Belle Hotel refreshed for evening service. His fingers stunk of those revolting stock cubes for days.

His loyal staff had insisted on a 'premiere' in 'Franco's' and pissed themselves laughing at Charlie's wooden performance until he threw his clog at the telly, thus robbing them of the last ten seconds of the advert. The bit that Charlie had to confess, once he'd calmed down later, was probably the best bit. It was the bit where Charlie had to stay schtum and stir looking moody, 'like you want to stab somebody', Yan had helpfully offered Charlie as motivation. That was the bit, Charlie told the whole of Franco's, where I got to show my 'Born a Chef' tattoo. 'Born a Cock' quipped Lulu, not for the first time, and the whole bar fell about.

M&C Saatchi quibbled the bill, saying that STOXO had demanded money off from them. Still, two grand was better than a poke in the eye with a blunt stick, or some revolting plastic-tasting dehydrated stock substitute in your gravy. To add insult to injury, Will had sent Charlie for 'media training' after receiving feedback from the ad agency. Cost Charlie a bloody grand to have some bald, enthusiastic twat named Richard who'd once been on daytime TV make him read nursery rhymes to camera in a simulated live studio environment.

Spring sprung and summer sang. For the first time in years, by the first week in July Charlie had something serious to bank. Paul Peters seemed unaffected by Lulu's attack. More chipper than anything. Charlie downed his sherry and mumbled something about getting off, he needed to get back down the track pronto. At seven that evening, Brighton's B-list would be gathering for the launch of *The Belle Hotel Cookbook* to the world's press.

Charlie was fairly unimpressed by the whole circus, but had promised Lulu that he'd go along with it for the sake of the business. Anyway, Judith Langdon had prised a grand out of Haddon for the bash and, as he'd just banked it, Charlie thought he'd better go back and make it look worth it.

Will the publicist promised great things from the Metrop, a star turn from Damien Black, his TV mind-tricking client. Charlie was more excited about the news that Bing, from the fishing trip, and now Brighton's Rat Pack impersonator, would be bringing the bones of his band and digging up the Ol' Blue Eyes show he'd wowed Franco with back in '99.

Charlie sat feet up on the train and thought about the function. He was the happiest he'd felt in years. Since the day he'd won the Michelin star. Only happier, probably, because this happiness included Lulu in his life. Charlie realised he was happier with Lulu and without a star than he'd been the other way round. Both would be great, obviously, and a wonderful gift, but he'd keep what he had over what he had lost any day. He'd ordered the stuff for all twenty signature dishes from the book and was ticking each from a hastily scribbled list:

Kippers
Eggs B
Scallops Sheridan
Omelette AB
B Baisse
C-au-V
Lobster BH
Venison/Beetroot
F & Chips
Spaghetti V
Shep P
Rösti (Salmon)
Baron of B
Bubble & Sq
Tarte Tatin
Trifle
Choc T
Apple C
Ch Souff
Welsh Rbit

What to do about presentation? The recently reupholstered train flew across Franco's viaduct. He'd serve it on the pages of the book. Yes, but how? On the silver platters with... glass on top. Glass balanced on, yes, the pages underneath. It would take all his author's copies, but what the hell,

Cab from the station, and Charlie flew in the back door, measured a platter with Franco's old tape and made a call to Sussex Glaziers for forty shatterproof ovals... pronto.

Fish was already hunched over his puddings, getting most of them prepped and into the walk-in so that the two of them could double hand the mains and starters as Salad worked on the sides.

The restaurant was shut for lunch and Lulu passed most of the morning checking the newly bedded rooms for peeling paper and unsavoury stains on the floor. Moving around was proving difficult, it took her a good twenty minutes to puff her way up to bed. She was weeks off her due date, but no one had told baby Blue that.

'Thanks, Jean. We're putting Judith Langdon in here. Thought she'd like the jacuzzi. Have you dealt with that limescale yet?'

Lulu glanced out of the freshly cleaned window and spied the summer sun. She felt the glow of Belle Hotel's coloured glass windows illuminating the pavement below.

Charlie was on the phone to Sinker. The lobsters were crap. What was he going to do about it? Fobbing him off with crayfish today of all days.

'Come on, you fish-faced fuck. Get your finger out and get me some proper-sized lobster or I'll be throwing your scaly ass in the pot when you get here.'

He threw the phone back on its receiver and laughed with Fish. That felt good. Kitchen/supplier etiquette was always paramount. Charlie was a changed man. But not that changed.

Seven o'clock and the place was buzzing. Will, the publicist, had secured a film crew from Living TV and they were interviewing Dame Maud Stephens in the lobby. Lulu had already moved her out of the camera line of the toilets and into view of the oak and lead-glass divide.

'I was choked when I read *The Belle Hotel Cookbook* – so many memories. I knew Franco, and Larry, of course – spent many hours on the *Brighton Belle* talking, eating, drinking and learning lines, and quite a few here at the hotel, too.'

The ground floor was filling up. Guests poured down from their bedrooms: Faye Mentor and Mimi, Judith Langdon and Hope. Parvez chatted up Claire. Damien Black descended the outside of the building but the film crew, too busy with the Dame, missed it and he had to do the stunt over again. Charlie popped out of the kitchen to a smatter of applause – not yet folks, later – and spotted a sea of London A-list and the odd Brighton B-lister he knew and liked. Hey, Fatboy, how's it going? He was pleased to see the crowd from the allotment talking to Peter André, and went over to hug his mum. Janet, newly slimmed down, was with Jack, who had washed his hair. Lulu had told Charlie that afternoon about the two of them being an item and now he was over the shock, Charlie, with some surprise, discovered that he felt kind of pleased.

Lulu waded through the crowd, hair and face dripping water.

'The tap in the bar has just exploded.'

Janet laughed and fetched Franco's bag.

'Now then, love, isn't it time you sorted yourself out with a plumber? I don't think you can afford my rates.'

Bing swang from the chandelier and crooned Sinatra from the Sands, food flowed by on funky book-framed trays and Belle Hotel was the happiest she'd felt since Franco passed away. Tom arrived in a cab from Worthing, the senior citizens show came down early, and treated the crowd to a brace of Irish boyband numbers.

At nine the double bass was silenced with the clanging of ladle on pot and a bloodied Brampton crashed through the porthole doors.

'Ladies and gentlemen. It gives me great pleasure to introduce you to Charlie Sheridan. Your chef, author and host.'

Charlie entered to riotous applause, mostly from Will the publicist, to say a few words about food, Franco and his book. As Will had told him that he would.

Charlie stood in the middle of the room and took in the faces looking at him. No words came. It didn't matter. They smiled at him anyway. Charlie looked up at the ceiling of Belle Hotel, down at the floor of Belle Hotel and gave a glance around each of the four walls.

In spite of his absolute self-destructive best efforts, the love of his life was still standing. And despite his other best efforts the other, most important love of his life was standing beside him. They'd done their growing up at Belle Hotel. Well, Lulu had. And now, finally, Charlie had grown up, too. He looked at Lulu, tears brimming over. Instead of giving the speech he'd prepared, Charlie simply went down on one knee.

'Will you marry me?'

Then Sinker staggered in with Franco's clock on his shoulder. He and Brampton had had a whip-round and got the clock out of hock. Couldn't have the *Belle Hotel Cookbook* launch without the old tick-tock back in its rightful place. Tom did a couple of their old busking numbers and Charlie joined in with the hand claps and la, la, la's.

They partied until Dawn spewed on the carpet and Lulu flung the lights on.

The London A-List and press caught the last train, the Brighton B-Listers poured out to waiting cabs and Judith Langdon et al rolled up to bed. As Franco's clock bonged midnight, Lulu flopped next to Charlie on the banquette and her waters broke.

5 July 2009
Baby Blue Brunch!
Eggs Benedict
Kippers
Lemon meringue pie
Krug & Coffee

Charlie took the menu through to the restaurant and asked Emma, laying up the tables, for ten more.

'And wake up Bing, this calls for Sinatra.'

Charlie slipped down to the cellar for a bottle of Franco's finest.

Autumn was in the air as Granny and Blue moved eastwards along the seafront. Janet had taken her for the morning, to give Mummy a break. To let her take care of business, more like. Janet pushed the buggy, a present from the Bramptons, and hummed a little tune.

'The wheels on the bus go round and round.'

All day long. She'd be happy to have her all day long, but Blue needed to be back to Mummy by twelve for her feed. Two hours, just time for Janet to do what she needed to do.

She'd checked with Jeremy Beaker first thing. Nice man. Old school, bit like Franco. Janet had enjoyed talking to him at the book launch. Amazing how much the man knew about their painting. Now *Franco, Janet and the Mouse Catcher* was hanging in Brighton Museum and she hoped she and Blue would be the first to see it. Blue went off to sleep and Janet cut back across the traffic through the Lanes and into Pavilion Gardens.

Charlie was in the kitchen working on a new dish. He had some fantastic fresh turbot flat on the deck and was looking at a crate of earthy veg Salad had brought down from the allotment. Charlie had always had a thing for tarragon and fish. Time to try it out. But he'd need to flash in some lardons to support the flavour of the turbot.

Lulu was outside, supervising the painting of her name over Charlie's, which had in turn been painted over Franco's

Lulu Sheridan: Licensed to Sell Intoxicating Liquor

The Belle Hotel Cookbook was now in its second printing. Everyone at Haddon was delighted. It stayed two weeks at the top of non-fiction hardbacks thanks, in part, to Will the publicist's leaking of the magician and the miracle birth story to the red tops. Lulu smiled at the memory. Charlie was talking about writing a memoir, the full story of Belle Hotel. Lulu knew who'd be writing the bloody thing. As much as she protested, Lulu rather liked the idea.

*

Janet pushed Blue into the museum lift and caught sight of her ancient features in the mirror. Not so bad, for a granny. She loved her new life, its new purpose, and had no intention of moving up north. She was delighted with her houseboat and thought it ample compensation for her lifetime's labours. That, and the monthly allowance Charlie and Lulu paid her tax free, for 'plumbing services'. She spent most of it on Bluebell, anyway, apart from the odd night at the pub with Jack and the barfly crowd when the drinks were, as ever, on Janet.

She thought Lulu was making a good go of it at Belle Hotel. Not that she approved of everything, mind, the new flowers were a bit way out for Janet, but a lot of the girl's gumption reminded her of Franco. Can-do attitude, they called it in her paper. It seemed to be working for Charlie. Faye Mentor had been back and was full of praise for the front-of-house staff. The Michelin inspectors were due again this winter and Janet hoped they'd take to Charlie's new Sussex fad.

She'd joined them for the occasional family Monday lunch and, as far as her peanut pitted taste buds could tell, the food was fantastic. Charlie had been on telly recently advertising his stock cubes and for the *Great British Menu*. Sussex were beating the crap out of the Northerners, which cheered Charlie greatly. Not that Charlie fancied any of that TV celeb chef crap. But it was good for business, as Lulu said. Will the publicist was cooking up something new to do with reality TV and magic, but Charlie said he'd wait and see. And anyway, he'd do none of it until he got his star back.

'Here we are.'

The lift shuddered to a halt on the museum's second floor, the doors parted and Janet backed out. She had a moment's panic as they threatened to cut baby Blue in two, but then a sensor called them off at the last moment.

Janet turned and pushed Blue out onto the balcony.

There it was.

Baby Blue let out a gurgle of joy. Janet cooed in delight. Blue had probably just filled her nappy, but it's the thought that counts. Janet looked up, through brimming eyes, at the spot-lit watercolour.

'Look, Blue. That's your grandad. Franco. And that's me. And that's a little kitty cat. Meow. Do you see? Your grandfather fought in the kipper wars. They changed our fortunes for ever.'

Janet stood a while longer under her younger self, then turned the buggy back towards Belle Hotel.

Acknowledgements

Thanks to Mel Melvin for her love, support and ideas. Nick Sayers for years of advice and guidance. David Shrigley for the snappy cover. All at Unbound: Scott Pack, John Mitchinson, DeAndra Lupu, Jimmy Leach, Georgia Odd and Julian Mash.

The epigraph of this book is from Brillat-Savarin, *The Philosopher in the Kitchen*, a book I read at catering college and did a show about with a pillow stuffed up my shirt. We were lucky to have Albert Roux as our visiting professor.

I am grateful to my Creative Writing MA tutors at Sussex: Dr Sue Roe and Irving Weinman. Also to you, dear *Belle Hotel* reader, your table awaits…

A Note on the Author

Craig Melvin holds an MA in Creative Writing from Sussex University and is a restaurant consultant in London and Brighton. He was mentored by Albert Roux at catering college and has worked in the restaurant and hotel business ever since. He also runs www.lunarlemonproductions.com with his wife Mel.

craig@lunarlemonproductions.com
Twitter: @ccmelvin
Instagram: @melvincraig
Facebook: Craig Melvin Brighton

Unbound
Liberating ideas

Unbound is the world's first crowdfunding publisher, established in 2011.

We believe that wonderful things can happen when you clear a path for people who share a passion. That's why we've built a platform that brings together readers and authors to crowdfund books they believe in – and give fresh ideas that don't fit the traditional mould the chance they deserve.

This book is in your hands because readers made it possible. Everyone who pledged their support is listed below. Join them by visiting unbound.com and supporting a book today.

Harry Ackland

Imogen Ackland

Louisa Ackland

Tim Aldiss

Igor Andronov

Jonny Anstead

Llia Apostolou

Michele Attias

Lee Baker

Marian Baldwin

pauline barlow

Tim Barton

Adam Bates

Ramesh Bhayani

Richard Bingham

Carol Birch

Matthew Birkett

Vanessa Blackledge

Pete Blunt

Jehane Boden Spiers

Suzy Bolt

James Boyce

Stephanie Bretherton

Linda Bulloch

Simon Chapman

Andrea Childs

Anthony C Clarke

David Michael Clarke

Brian Clivaz

Martin Cole

Regina Connell

Jenny Crabbe

John Crawford
Daisy Cresswell
Tom Cutts-Watson
Hugh Daly
Nick Davey
E R Andrew Davis
Greg Day
Samuel Day
Miranda Dickinson
Graham Edgson
Al Elliott
Danielle Ellis
Lizzie Enfield
Tomas Eriksson
Sally Fincher
Claire Ford
Giovanna Forte
David Melvin &
    Connie Gartner
Nigel Gilderson
Meg Gordon Sussman
Dominic Green
Geoff Griffiths
Lucy Hainsworth
Araminta Hall
Louise Hamilton
Alex Hayward
Steve Higgins
Peter James
Jindra Jehu
Neil Jones
Vincent Kamp

Stella Kane
Simon Keating
Dan Kieran
Steve Kircher
Cicely Knowles
Hannah Knowles
Blake Lavak
Annabel Lawrence
Rod Lee
Sally Lefley
Max Levy
Paul Levy
Angela Lord
Karl Ludvigsen
Daniel Lynch
Alice Magand
Emily Magee
Elliott Mannis
Christopher McCarthy
Craig McPhedran
David Melvin
Mel Melvin
Steven Melvin
John Mitchinson
Graham Mulvein
Simon Newell
David Nicholls
Susanne Niemann
Peter Nunn
J. O
Scott Pack
Hugo Perks

Belinda Peters

Justin Pollard

Steven Pratt

David Prew

Lianne Raizman

Gordon Ramsay

Sarah Rayner

Alison Robbins

Sue Roe

Jane Rushworth

Niki Savage

Cathy Scannell

Dick Selwood

Clive Sheridan

Sarah Sheridan

David Shrigley

Adam Signy

Milly Sinclair

Nicola Smith

Steve Smith

Stuart Smith

Ben Stackhouse

Jane Stackhouse

Dan Storey

Kathryn Stubley

Jonty Summers

Leanne Targett-Parker

Maisie Taylor

Adam Tinworth

Elaine Vincent

Sally Wainman

Johnny Webb

Catherine Williamson

Peter Wiltshire

Pete Wingfield

R Wingfield

Elaine Wyse

Georgina Yates

Lisa Young